THE RAGING DRAGON

<u>Review Slip</u>
Will to Conquer Series – Book 2
The Raging Dragon
by Len Lamensdorf
376 pages 5 ½" x 8 ½"
Ages 12 and up – ISBN: 0-9669741-7-4
LCCN: 2001117313; CIP Data in book
$22.95 dust-jacketed hardcover
Publication date: September 21, 2002
For additional information or to arrange an
interview with the author
please contact Erica Kauls -- 800-929-2906
E-mail seapress@aol.com; Fax: 805-963-8188

Please send copies of any review or mention to
SeaScape Press, Ltd.
1010 Roble Lane, Santa Barbara, CA 93103
Book 1, **The Crouching Dragon**
Book 2, **The Raging Dragon**
Book3, **The Flying Dragon** (2003)
are available at bookstores nationwide, online
booksellers and the publisher

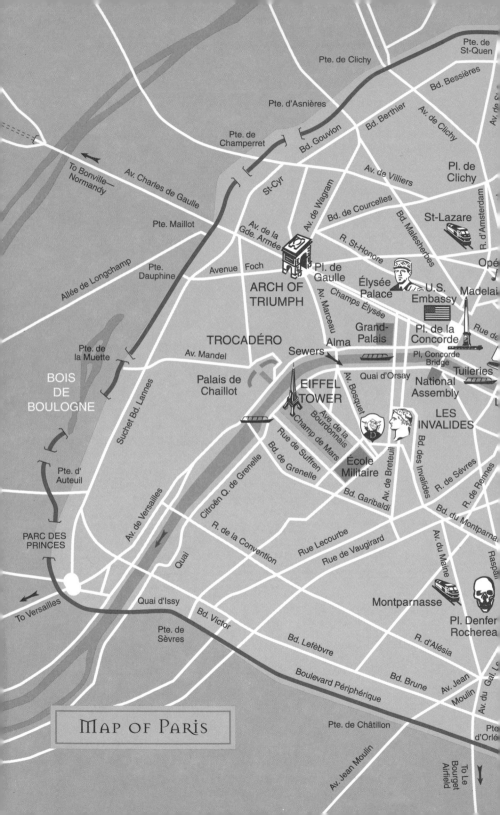

MAP OF PARIS

WILL TO CONQUER SERIES · BOOK TWO

THE
RAGING
DRAGON

A NOVEL BY

LEN LAMENSDORF

SeaScape Press ®

SeaScape Press®, Ltd., 1010 Roble Lane
Santa Barbara, CA 93103

First printing 2002

10 9 8 7 6 5 4 3 2 1

Manufactured in the United States of America

Cover illustrations by Uhl Studios
Cover and interior design by Lightbourne
Interior illustrations and maps by Bob Swingle

Publisher's Cataloging-in-Publication
(Provided by Quality Books, Inc.)

Lamensdorf, Leonard.
    The raging dragon / by Len Lamensdorf ; cover
illustrations by Uhl Studios ; cover and interior design
by Lightbourne ; interior and maps by Bob Swingle.
    p. cm. -- (Will to conquer ; bk. 2)
    SUMMARY: French teens defend Dragon castle, search
Paris catacombs, and use judo and aircraft flying skills to
save Presidents Kennedy and de Gaulle from murderous
conspiracies during the Algerian Crisis.
    LCCN: 2001117313
    ISBN: 0-9669741-7-4

    1. Castles--France--Juvenile fiction. 2. France--
Juvenile fiction. 3. Gaulle, Charles de, 1890-1970--
Juvenile fiction. 4. Kennedy, John F. (John Fitzgerald),
1917-1963--Juvenile fiction. [1. Castles--Fiction.
2. Adventure and adventurers--Fiction. 3. France--Fiction.
4. Gaulle, Charles de, 1890-1970--Fiction. 5. Kennedy, John F.
(John Fitzgerald), 1917-1963--Fiction. 6. Conspiracies--Fiction.]
I. Title. II. Series: Lamensdorf, Leonard. Will to conquer series.

PZ7.L175Ra 2002   [Fic]
                                QB102-701335

FICTION DISCLAIMER: Although some real people appear in their natural
settings, and some actual events, dates and speeches are included, this is a
work of fiction and presented solely as entertainment.

For Erica,
who not only made this series possible,
she also made it necessary.

━━━━━ ✦ ━━━━━

With special thanks to Fred Kenyon,
who helped teach Willi and Louise how to fly.

MAPS AND DIAGRAMS

Full Color Maps

Paris Street Map . . . . Front End Papers
Paris Metro Map . . . . Back End Papers

Interior Illustrations

William and William viii
DragonSlayers 17
Bonville. 26
Flying Dragon 41
Europe and Africa 69
Le Dragon Enragé. 113
Plane Diagram 123
Roxanne 135
Place de la Concorde 275
Château of Versailles, *Gardens* 337
Château of Versailles, *Ground Floor* . . . 342
Château of Versailles, *First Floor* 343

CONTENTS

1. The Crouching Dragon Roars Again. 1
2. Damage Control. 21
3. Town Meeting 27
4. Unsolved Mysteries 38
5. The Art of Self-Defense. 43
6. Framed 52
7. Strange Encounters. 57
8. Honors for Us. 73
9. Press and President. 88
10. Sorbonne 99
11. Desert Fox 121
12. Roxanne. 134
13. Solo. 154
14. The Riot in the Rue St. Michel 165
15. Kill All the Books 174
16. I Love Paris 192
17. Deeper and Deeper. 214
18. The New Resistance 230
19. The Coup. 253
20. Flight Plan 263
21. The Broadcast. 283
22. Casualties 294
23. After the Insurrection 309
24. Formalities. 324
25. Reflections 334
26. In Concert 359
27. Ambassadors 364

   Historical Timeline 374

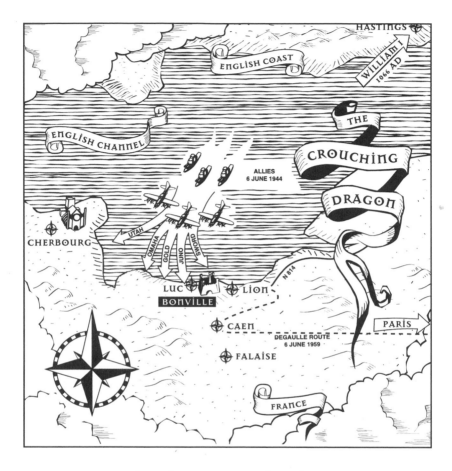

WILLIAM & WILLIAM

THE CROUCHING DRAGON ROARS AGAIN

My dog, Chien, woke me up. Chien, who had been allowed to stay in the house overnight since our great triumph at the Crouching Dragon, was usually very quiet, but that night he was yapping loudly and climbing all over me. When I first found Chien abandoned by the side of the road, he was a scroungy pile of gray and brown spots, but as he grew up his coat turned into a lustrous reddish-brown, and although I never learned his breed, he became rangy, alert and powerful. I came awake reluctantly, knowing something must be wrong, or Chien wouldn't make such a fuss.

"What's up?" I asked, sitting upright and trying to shake the sleep out of my eyes.

Chien was pulling at my shirt, which was a risky move. He had climbed up the sloping steps—more like a ladder—that led to my loft under the eaves, and if he pulled too hard we'd both tumble to the floor.

"Hey," I said, "don't tear my shirt."

Before I clambered down, I grabbed my handie-talkie radio—the one Roger had given me. It squawked and I thought I heard the word, "Help!"

I pushed the button and asked, "Is that you, Roger?"

No answer.

Ever since Roger had given handie-talkies to me and Louise, I had kept mine close to me. It was bulky, almost half a meter long and weighing over two kilos—nearly five pounds—and required my full grip to hold it. The pull-out antenna was even longer.

I didn't take it to school, but I sometimes carried it in Paul's truck (when he let me drive it), or when Louise and I were going somewhere and had the desire to communicate at a distance.

I felt important having a portable radio, especially in a town where very few people even owned a telephone. Roger had acquired the radios in 1943, during World War II, when he had been in the French Resistance, working with United States intelligence to sabotage the Nazis. The newer ones were much smaller, and the batteries easier to keep charged, but the old ones were still useful.

At that moment, both my mother, Helene, and my step-father, Paul, hurried out of their bedroom, still in their bedclothes. My mother was so pretty that even with her blonde hair loose and uncombed, she still looked great.

Paul was wearing long-legged, shapeless bottoms and no shirt over his muscular (hairy) chest and arms. He was shoving his thick black hair back from his forehead and squinting. I had never thought of the possibility that Paul might not have perfect eyesight. He had always seemed to be the ultimate physical specimen (although not always the ultimate mental one), and now that he had stopped getting drunk, he had turned into a pretty decent, all-around guy, but still the strongest man in town. Eyeglasses?

"Did you look at the Crouching Dragon?" Mother asked. She was pulling back the curtains, but I legged into my pants and ran outside, barefoot, still trying to raise Roger on my handie-talkie.

The sky was clear except for a few, low scudding clouds, and the breeze from the English Channel was strong over the Normandy coast, whipping the willow trees low and flailing the wheat, so that it seemed like every living thing was pointing up the hillside to the ominous looking castle, the Crouching Dragon. Suddenly, there was a sharp, growling sound.

"The dragon is roaring again!" I said.

The great, leering dragon was shooting flames from its huge jaws and its angry eyes flashed red and yellow, while smoke billowed from its nostrils. A powerful gust of wind made it seem like a blast from the dragon was bending the trees and brush.

The dragon hadn't roared or flamed since we had made our deal with President de Gaulle. As long as I could remember, everyone in our small town, Bonville, had been in awe of the castle, with its tower shaped like a huge, angry reptile that looked like it was going to leap down from its perch and devour our little town.

That was before Louise and I and the other kids had discovered Roger in the castle and learned its secrets. For months, our little army growing almost daily, we entered secretly at night, without our parents knowing. We discovered medieval swords and shields and other treasures. Step by step, we created a fantasy kingdom all our own, with Roger as king, and Louise and I as princess and prince.

On the very night of our coronation, with almost every kid in town inside the walls, our parents, the police and the school principal had appeared outside the walls, led by the mayor, Antoine Bersault. The adults wanted us to come out, but we didn't want to give up the little kingdom we had so painstakingly built. The mayor and others wanted to turn the Crouching Dragon into a tourist trap. We were outraged because we knew that Bersault was a crook who had stolen cattle from local farmers. In a daring midnight raid, Louise, Roger, Andre and I, dressed in medieval armor, including helmets, had freed the cattle, but the people had refused to believe that rich, powerful Antoine Bersault was a smuggler.

The siege of the castle ended on the 6th of June, 1959, when Louise and I intercepted our president, Charles de Gaulle, on his way to the commemoration of the fifteenth anniversary of the Allied landings on the Normandy beaches below our town.

The president was greatly impressed with our work and with Roger, who had not only fought in the Resistance, but had been a professor at University of Paris. The deal I made was that Roger would give the castle to the people of France and the government would waive the taxes. The Crouching Dragon would be further restored and opened to the public, but only for a nominal fee, and the restoration would be dignified and not designed to exploit visitors. The president would have Roger reappointed to his old post at the university. Mayor Bersault's crimes were revealed and he was sent to prison.

Thus, all had been quiet at the Crouching Dragon for a long time until the dragon began roaring again.

"Look!" I said. "There are some huge, dark shapes in front of the castle! I think the main gate is open!"

Chien was pulling my leg, trying to drag me towards the Crouching Dragon.

"Maybe you should alert the gendarmes," mother said to Paul.

He nodded, shouldered into his shirt, jammed his bare feet into some shoes and headed for the *mairie*, our tiny town hall.

Chien was now pushing me from behind. He was the one who had discovered the cattle smugglers and battled them fiercely and bravely.

"Okay," I said and headed for the pasture, clipping my handie-talkie into the shoulder sling that Mother had made for me.

"Wait for Paul!" Mother said, but I wasn't listening.

As I ran barefoot over the pebbly ground, Rapide, our only horse, was loping over to me, eyes fiery, nostrils flaring.

"You, too?!" I said. The night we secretly investigated Bersault's ranch, Rapide had been the one who had sorted though hundreds of animals and found our cow, Leonore, snoring contentedly in the pasture.

I scooped Chien up with one arm and, grabbing Rapide's mane, leaped up on his bare back. He neighed happily and started towards the castle. I had forgotten to open the gate, but that didn't stop him.

"Hold on!" I yelled to Chien, as Rapide gathered himself and soared over the fence. I was accustomed to riding the big guy bareback and I managed to hang on. I set Chien ahead of me and hunched low as we thundered over the rocks and through the briar, riding uphill. Rapide had been a champion thoroughbred, but he had cracked a bone in a major race. His owner hadn't put him down, and Paul bought him for nearly nothing. His brilliant black coat was flecked with gray and the once bright diamond between his eyes was fuzzy, but he was still remarkably strong and fast.

"Willi?" A familiar voice crackled over the handie-talkie.

"That you, Louise?" I called. "I'm on the way to the Crouching Dragon."

"Me, too," she said.

Flames poured from the jagged mouth of the dragon and smoke rose around its head. Once again, the deep-throated roar came thundering down the hillside, and even though I thought I knew all about the dragon, I flinched.

As we galloped closer, I saw that the shapes in front of the walls were three trucks, all with their tailgates down and crews of men carrying heavy loads up the ramps: furniture, paintings, medieval weapons.

I kneed Rapide to a rearing halt.

"Are you from the government?" I yelled to two bulky

men carrying a rolled up tapestry.

They both laughed and continued loading the tapestry.

"You can't steal that tapestry!" I yelled (I had the button down on my handie-talkie and I was broadcasting to anyone who was on the same frequency). "Everything in the castle belongs to the people of France."

One guy, a burly blonde with longish hair and a beefy belly that spilled over his pants, said, "I'm one of the people. I'm taking my share now." They both laughed as they started down the ramp.

"Get out of here, kid," the other man said, "before we tie you up and throw you in the truck."

I kicked Rapide and we raced along the outside of the castle walls. It was a strange scene: all those hefty men lugging treasures from the Crouching Dragon, while the dragon roared in anger above them.

Chien slithered out of my arms and leaped to the ground. He was racing alongside, barking as loudly as he could.

I kept yelling "Stop!" and everybody ignored me, except for one guy with a thick metal chain who swung it at me. I ducked, but it hit Rapide on the rump, scoring a deep cut. Rapide roared a protest; I was furious, but Rapide didn't miss a step.

"The gendarmes are on the way!" I yelled. "You won't get away with this!"

Another man tried to whack Rapide with a large piece of wood, but I kneed my horse and we sideswiped him and knocked him down before he struck a blow.

"Get that kid!" somebody yelled. I wheeled Rapide around and saw a short, skinny man in a dark shirt and pants aim a gun at me.

"Don't shoot him!" somebody called. "You'll bring out the whole town!"

The guy didn't shoot, but I could tell he wanted to.

Below us, I began to hear the sound of hoofbeats. I turned to see many of my friends on horseback—Louise, André, Maurice, Jules, Odile, and even Denise. Almost fifteen years after the war, few people in our area had tractors, and they still used horses to plow and to pull wagons.

The farm boys, Leon and Charles, were carrying a pitchfork and a shovel. Louise, riding up on her horse, Dumas, was brandishing a thick-handled hoe.

"They've got weapons!" the little guy with the gun said, and he raised his arm, aiming straight at Louise.

Rapide seemed to respond even before I moved a muscle. We virtually leaped at the gunman and Rapide, head low, hit the guy's arm with his muzzle. The gun went flying and the guy screamed and grabbed his arm, probably broken. I reached out to try and grab the gun while it was still sailing through the air. But I was falling off Rapide; I kept falling and lunging and caught the gun just before it hit the ground—and then I did, too, right on the seat of my pants. It was a pretty good catch, but my bottom was very sore. Rapide stopped almost instantly and trotted back to me. I got up, slowly. I had never held a gun before in my life.

"He's got a gun!" the brawny blonde with the floppy belly yelled.

I took one frowning look at the gun and flung it as far as I could down the hillside. It soared high and landed in the upper branches of a beech tree. I leaped back on Rapide and headed toward the gate.

Lights had been turning on all over Bonville. I saw Father Thomas's ancient black Citroen bumping up the hill. Next came Paul in his truck, and a number of local men running or on horseback. One farmer was riding a small tractor—one of the few in the district.

The thieves stopped loading the trucks, and the two armies met on the plain in front of the castle walls. Louise's father, Desmond Donnet, the new mayor, was wrestling with the blonde guy, who was twice his size. Paul was bashing a couple of thieves' heads together. I had always known that some day his tremendous strength would come in handy.

The farm boys were wielding their tools, and the men they attacked were fighting back with chains, wrenches and crowbars. So far no one had fired a shot.

Louise spotted another guy with a gun, and she used her hoe to sweep it out of his hands. Then she wheeled her horse around and trampled the weapon into the dirt.

There was a crackling sound on my handie-talkie.

"Roger!" I yelled, and kneed Rapide across the dry moat under the stone arch into the ward of the castle. Goods were strewn around—paintings piled haphazardly, furniture leaning on furniture, a great mound of shields and spears. And a fearsome steel army—the thieves had stood the ancient suits of armor against a wall and for a split second, with the changing light from the dragon washing over them, they looked like living people.

As we raced toward the keep, a man carrying a huge, metal crowbar headed straight for us. He swung and Rapide barely swerved out of the way. I hadn't realized he was also carrying a large, steel wrench in his other hand. He threw it and although I ducked, it hit a glancing blow to my shoulder. I yelped in pain, but I turned Rapide and rode straight at him. He leaped aside, then swung the crowbar and hit Rapide on his already lacerated rump. Rapide let out a pained whinny, and as we turned back, the guy pulled out a gun. I had only one possible weapon—my handie-talkie. I unclipped it and was about to fling it at him when Chien appeared out of nowhere, leaped and grabbed the guy's arm—not his gun arm—in his teeth. The guy screamed. I galloped closer and nailed him square in the middle of his forehead with the handie-talkie.

The gun went off, but the bullet whined by harmlessly as the shooter sank to the ground.

"Thanks!" I called to Chien, who barked, turned and headed out of the courtyard. I guess he only had time to save my life before he went back to fighting the other bad guys.

Overhead the dragon was still roaring and flames were pouring out. I jumped off Rapide and checked his condition. Blood was seeping out of the wounds on his rump, and I could tell from his eyes, that he was hurting.

"Go find Mother or Paul," I said. "They'll tend your wounds. I have to find Roger." I gave him a gentle slap on the withers. He neighed softly, turned and loped towards the gate. The gunman staggered away—without his gun.

I checked my handie-talkie. One corner was blunted from contact with the thief's hard skull, but when I pushed the button, it seemed to be working. I started up the steps in the keep. A number of weapons were strewn about and I grabbed a double-edged rapier and kept climbing, sword in one hand, handie-talkie in the other.

I stopped at the level where I had first seen the ancient weapons. The heavy wooden door had been knocked off its hinges—which was no easy task because the hinges were huge bronze plates that had lasted hundreds of years.

Inside, the racks were almost empty. All but a few of the spears, shields, knives and swords were gone. Still no Roger, but I was afraid to call his name because there might be someone with him—someone I didn't want to alert.

I climbed another level to Roger's apartment. That door was also open, and flickering light came through the outside window. I didn't hear voices, only a low, kind of scraping sound that I couldn't identify. I steeled myself and lunged inside, holding the sword pointed ahead.

Roger's books—the thousands in his collections—were scattered around, knocked off the shelves.

"Roger!" The name was torn from my throat.

Roger, gray hair flowing wild and long, was standing on tip-toe, gagged and blindfolded, with his back against rough stone, his hands tied to ancient, thick iron rings mounted high on the wall. He had been tied with his arms fully extended, nearly pulled out of their sockets, the toes of his shoes barely touching the floor. The scraping sound was caused by Roger trying to rub the rope that held him against the iron ring, hoping to fray and loosen it. He had a long way to go.

I slashed the ropes with the razor-sharp rapier. Cut free, Roger slumped to the floor, grabbing at his blindfold and tearing it off.

I pulled the gag out of his mouth and carefully cut his bonds.

His voice was hoarse. "Thank God you came, Willi," he said, rubbing his wrists. "I didn't know whether you had heard me."

"What happened?" I asked

"Tell you later," he said. He pushed himself upright, still wobbly from his ordeal. "We have to go up in the Dragon Tower and stop them."

Roger pushed a chest of drawers away from the wall and withdrew an automatic pistol from inside a stone niche. He slammed a clip of ammunition in the automatic and shoved it into his pants, then picked up the remote control he used to operate the exhibit.

As we started up the spiral staircase, we heard rumbling from the dragon and smelled acrid smoke. At the very top, the door to the balcony was open. Below us, in full operation, was the scale animated model he had built as a memorial to the World War II Normandy invasion. Allied ships shelled the coast, aircraft swooped through the skies, soldiers and marines splashed ashore, while Nazi gun emplacements poured withering fire down on them. The flashing gunfire and explosions sent torrents of sound, flame and smoke out through the dragon's mouth and eyes, creating the frightening scene that had terrified us until we learned its secret source. Even now, I involuntarily ducked when an exact copy of an American B-25 bomber buzzed by and bombs exploded in the countryside.

But Roger wasn't enjoying the scenery. Ahead of us, two men were forcibly disassembling the lighted console that controlled the exhibit. They didn't hear or see us immediately because of the noise and glare. As we approached they turned to look at us, surprised, and one of them reached into a shoulder holster for a gun. Before he could pull it out, Roger leaped forward and poked him in both eyes with his fingers. As the guy staggered back, Roger moved in, grabbed and pulled the thief towards him, slipped an arm around him, pivoted and straightened his knees. That forced the guy to turn over Roger's hip and leave his feet—landing on his back on the catwalk. Then Roger was on him, yanking the gun from its holder.

It would have been fun to watch if I wasn't facing the other man. He didn't have a gun, but he was carrying a large set of pliers which he raised over his head. I slashed his wrist with the rapier, and he dropped the pliers with a scream. He kept coming after me, and I hesitated, hoping to avoid stabbing him point-blank. Instead, I stepped back, while slashing the sword to keep him away. Fortunately for me, my blade sliced through his belt and his pants, and they dropped to his knees, tripping him. As he fell towards me, I kicked him in the chest. I think I broke some ribs because he yelped loudly and fell on all fours, moaning and scratching at his wounds.

Roger had subdued the gunman and held his arm twisted behind his back—his face contorted. Sometimes I forgot that Roger had been a tough guerrilla fighter in the secret French Resistance during World War II. I still tended to think of him as the supposedly wacky hermit who had hidden in the castle, or as the scholarly professor of Ancient History at the University of Paris.

My mother—I later learned with even great astonishment—had also been a brave soldier in the Resistance.

"Come on!" Roger said. "Let's get these guys out of the Dragon Tower."

I grabbed the guy I had kicked, still moaning, and pushed him ahead of me.

"Get us out of here in a hurry," he gasped. "*Please* get us out of here."

The other man said, "We can move faster if you let me go ahead of you. Hold a gun on me if you like." He was almost pleading.

Roger held his gun on both men as we hurried down the stairs. The one I had kicked, tripped and fell down an entire flight, screaming with the pain of his broken ribs, but he didn't stop, just dragged himself, bleeding and scarred, down the steps.

"What's going on with these guys?" I asked.

"Maybe they're scared of dragons," Roger suggested grimly.

"That's it!" I yelled. "Take my handie-talkie!"

I gave Roger the radio and started back up the stairs at a run.

"Where are you going?" Roger asked.

"Just get out of here!" I said, and kept climbing as fast as I could. I had remembered the dishonest mayor, Bersault, and Pêpe, the crook who had worked for him, setting explosives in the wall of the Dragon Castle. I was afraid the same thing was happening again.

When I reached the gallery over the exhibit, I ran to the console and almost immediately found a small packet jammed between it and the wall. It was silent, no ticking sound, no wires, but I knew it was trouble. I yanked it out, my heart thudding in my ears, and ran along the catwalk towards the jagged windows that made up the leering jaws of the dragon. But I was too far away, so I flung the packet towards the opening between the dragon's jaws. I twisted my body, trying to wish the packet between the huge teeth.

It soared across the space, spinning in the air as it approached the jaws. On the way out, it struck one of the teeth and bounced high, hit the roof of the dragon's mouth and dropped back inside. I threw myself down on the catwalk, just as the explosives detonated with a thunderous roar. Steel and stone and glass went flying everywhere. A large piece of metal came straight at me, but it only grazed my head. Unfortunately, the explosion crumpled the steel supports and the balcony sagged, slowly, but relentlessly down toward the great exhibit.

Sections of stone were beginning to break loose. I slipped over the side, jumped down a couple of meters, landing with a jolt, and scrambled over the exhibit, smashing ships and tanks and men. I tumbled off the Normandy coast, scrambled over the mountains, and out through a hole blown in the wall that opened onto the tower staircase. I ran down the stairs and outside in the fastest moves I ever made in my life.

♦ ♦ ♦

I was sprinting across the courtyard when another explosion rocked the Dragon Tower. The force of it sent me sprawling on the ground. As I was rolling away, I saw the dragon's bottom jaw sag sharply and then break loose, falling to the earth with a great crash of stone and glass and steel. Flames still poured out of the now gigantic opening where the dragon's fierce teeth had been, and smoke erupted from its now blind eyes.

I sprang to my feet and ran towards the gatehouse, vaguely aware of kids and parents and even the thieves, frozen in place, staring at the Crouching Dragon exploding with a fury neither its friends or enemies had ever imagined.

Chien came to me, a look of concern in his gold-green eyes.

"Let's get out of here!" I said.

We scrambled outside the walls, but when I turned to look back, a sharp pain stabbed in my gut at the sight of the Crouching Dragon without its lower jaw, flame and smoke curling through the gaping wound while crackling sounds and shooting sparks filled the night sky.

Then I heard another unwelcome sound. The thieves, taking advantage of the shock and chaos, had climbed into the first truck and started the engine.

"Stop them!" I yelled, but people seemed bewildered. I saw a pile of ancient weapons they hadn't yet loaded and grabbing the biggest sword I could find, ran to the truck and began slashing one of the front tires. It exploded suddenly, showering me with shards of rubber that knocked me to the ground—getting knocked down was becoming a bad habit. Meanwhile, Louise was slashing at the other front tire with another sword, while the driver cursed us both. Louise's tire only hissed as the air left it, but the great vehicle sank to the tire rims.

"Great!" I yelled to Louise, and she gave me the old "V for Victory" sign with her fingers.

Still, the driver put the motor in gear and the truck began to move, gaining momentum from the rest of its eighteen wheels, digging itself out of the ground on its front rims.

Then we heard a series of shots. Both Louise and I threw ourselves down, getting splattered by mud spinning from the wheels, but we soon realized it was Roger, using his service pistol to methodically blast the remaining tires of the truck. Slowly, like a wounded animal, it sagged to its knees, and began to sink into the mud.

The three thieves who had been inside the cab piled out, falling, scrambling, trying to run away. But they hadn't counted on Chien, who treated them like runaway cattle, and was barking, growling and herding them together against the wall of the castle. The sound of the shots had covered the hee-haw of the Peugeot driven by the local gendarmes, and four of them, led by our own Sergeant Phillippe, yelled at the thieves to halt.

Meanwhile, several local stalwarts had grabbed the thieves who were in the back of the truck. The heroes included my stepfather, Paul, who was controlling two men all by himself, and my loyal friend, André, working alongside his father, who had always been a cold man and a harsh disciplinarian. André had endured the greatest suffering of anyone at the hands of Bersault and his criminal friends. He had been beaten and left unconscious on the doorstep of his home, after merely walking his dog in front of the castle. André's leg was still crippled, but that didn't keep him from being as brave as any of us.

The two men Paul had subdued were sitting on the ground with their backs against the stone wall, afraid to make a move with Paul glaring at him. Louise's father, Desmond Donnet, who was now the mayor as well as the Latin Master at the Lycée, had captured another man. Odile and Denise had somehow captured a thief themselves, using ancient shields from the castle to pummel the guy, who was cowering in a crouch, hoping they wouldn't smack him again.

My mother had come up the hill with Paul in his truck, but I didn't see her until I found Rapide. She was using her shawl and a bucketful of water to cleanse his wounds. Rapide was standing quietly, appreciating the care.

Roger told the gendarmes (who looked grateful they hadn't had to fight with a gang of thieves themselves) what had happened.

Sergeant Phillippe questioned the brawny blonde man I had spoken to when I first rode up to the castle.

"Who are you?" he asked, "and where have you come from?"

The brawny man spat on the ground and yelled to the others, "Don't say a word! Don't tell them anything!"

"You would be wise to cooperate," the sergeant said. "These are serious crimes."

The brawny man spat again.

"The license plates are from Belgium," Paul said.

"The smugglers who stole our cattle for Mayor Bersault were also from Belgium," I said.

"You're right," the sergeant said. "Are you connected with our former mayor?"

The brawny man glared at me, but didn't answer.

"You lied to me," I said. "When I told you these treasures were the property of the people of France, you said you were going to take your share early."

The man almost smiled. The people began to mutter among themselves.

Mayor Donnet, who had been searching the cab of the lead truck, came down holding a fistful of papers.

"These are apparently forged documents, covering everything in the castle. I also found that man's passport"— he was pointing to the spitter—"he *is* a French citizen, despite the license plates. His name is Raoul Larron. There's an army discharge card, too, and a shield of some sort with a strange device on it."

Mayor Donnet handed the shield to Roger. It was about the size of a policeman's badge, enameled on the front in black and white with the design of a winged dragon, its jaws wide open, but with a sword driven through its body. The back was plain metal with a single phrase etched into it: *"Tueurs de le Dragon"*—DragonSlayers.

The townspeople were getting very restless again, mumbling angry epithets about crooks and thieves.

"These men are worse than thieves," Roger said, in what I thought was an extraordinarily calm voice considering the circumstances. "They viciously destroyed the exhibit in the Dragon Tower, and did terrible damage to the tower itself."

The crowd surged forward.

"Wait a minute!" Paul yelled, "We don't want to dirty our hands on these swine."

Paul—of all people—the same man who had been energetically knocking heads together only a few minutes earlier. The others, obviously impressed that Paul was counseling prudence, settled back.

Sergeant Phillippe, who had had many run-ins with Paul in the past, said "Thank you, Monsieur Montreux."

"What will you do with the thieves?" It was my mother, leading Rapide.

"Obviously I can't lock up twelve men in our little jail," the sergeant said. "We'll take them to Caen. Will some of you volunteer your vehicles?"

Every man in Bonville stepped forward.

The people began to laugh, probably as a kind of release from the tense situation.

Even Sergeant Phillippe, always so proper, smiled.

"Very good," he said, and knowing the people in the town well, he quickly chose three men who had sizable trucks.

"Four to a truck, and one gendarme—armed—with each group," the sergeant said. "Please get your vehicles and bring strong rope."

The chosen went loping down the hill.

◆　◆　◆

I don't think very many people went back to sleep that night. It took a while before the townspeople arrived with their trucks and the thieves were trussed and stowed on them. Several people said they would follow the trucks to Caen in their own cars to make sure the thieves didn't escape.

Louise and I walked back into the courtyard with Roger.

"Let's go up and see what condition the exhibit is in," I said.

Roger shook his head. "We'll wait until it's light in the morning. By then we should know if anything else is going to collapse."

If I had been the one whose years of work had been destroyed, I wouldn't have been so patient and reasonable. Roger had become my teacher, and there were still a lot of lessons to be learned from him—not easy lessons, either.

"You were going to tell us what happened," I said.

"The sound of the trucks woke me up," Roger said. "At first it just didn't make sense. I asked myself if the government was trying to violate our agreement, and that made me angry. Almost at once, I realized the government wouldn't send trucks in the middle of the night.

"Unfortunately, I had disconnected the radio control on the gate, and I carelessly decided to leave it open for one night.

"A whole gang of men entered the gate. I had my handie-talkie, but I didn't know whether you or Louise had yours turned on. Until now, I've stubbornly refused to install a telephone, so I couldn't call the gendarmes. I thought I had better wake up the town, so I used my remote control and turned on the displays in the Dragon Tower at full power, as bright and as loud as possible."

"It worked," Louise said. "You woke us all up."

"The thieves moved much more quickly than I expected," Roger said. "By the time I started using my handie-talkie, they were in my apartment. One of them ripped the radio from my hands and tossed it across the room, but not before I broadcast a help signal."

"I heard it," I said, "but it wasn't clear."

"Do you think Bersault sent the thieves?" Louise asked. "I'm sure he wanted to get even with us for uncovering his crooked operations."

"And pay back those gamblers in Belgium he owed so much money to," I added.

"But he's in prison," Louise said.

"That wouldn't stop a good criminal," Roger said. "Bersault is absolutely ruthless."

"Why did they hang you from the wall?" I asked.

"I put up a fight when they grabbed me, which made them angry, and as long as they were going to tie me up, they decided to make it hurt. Perhaps I should have gone for my weapon the minute I saw those men, but I haven't used a gun since the war, and as you know, I hate the damn things."

"I remember," Louise said, "how you smashed those cases of rifles when the mayor accused you of teaching us to use guns."

"Yes," Roger said. "I kept my weapons as a remembrance of our work in the Resistance, a time when we had no choice but to use them to defend our country against the Nazis. I never thought I'd use them again."

DAMAGE
CONTROL

The Crouching Dragon looked even worse on a chill, gray Normandy morning. In the darkness, lit only by the moon and dying flames, the Dragon Tower had still looked ominous, even with its lower jaw blown away. Now, toothless and blind, it seemed weak, ancient and lifeless.

We walked slowly across the bleak, empty courtyard, littered with shattered glass, twisted steel, broken boards and damaged stone blocks. A pair of lounging gendarmes contributed to the impression of a desolate battlefield, guarded against marauders who had long since disappeared. All of our work, our hopes and dreams seemed as empty as the sockets of the dragon's eyes.

We cautiously climbed the spiral staircase, avoiding fallen chunks of stone and wood, and clambered through the same hole in the wall that I had used to escape.

Roger shook his head sadly. Most of the steel catwalk had collapsed and fallen onto the replica of the Normandy beachhead, shattering many ships on the sea, tanks and trucks on land, knocking aircraft out of the sky and covering dozens of figures of soldiers and sailors under piles of debris.

Damaged sections of the control console had fallen from the catwalk and taken great gouges out of the carefully built beaches, cliffs and the other terrain.

"It's not that bad," I said, even though my heart had sunk as low as my shoes.

"Willi's right." Louise said. "Many of the ships are still

intact, and nearly all of the inland construction was barely touched."

"Barely?" Roger said.

"You wouldn't have to rebuild it alone," I said. "Now that the world knows about your exhibit, you could probably find skilled craftsmen eager to repair what's damaged."

Roger didn't respond.

"What about the console?" Louise asked. "Could you rebuild it exactly as it was?"

Roger waited a moment before he answered, and his usually strong voice was muted. "Because I was working in secret," he said, "I didn't want to be seen buying some of the advanced electronic equipment available. Most of the stuff I used was salvaged from old military installations."

"You see?" I said. "You can build an even better console today."

Roger was shaking his head again. "I promised the president a gift of this entire castle with the Dragon Tower intact and the exhibit complete and operational. It would take hundreds of thousands of francs to rebuild it."

"If the French government is willing to bear the cost," I asked, "will you do the work—or at least supervise it?"

Roger's expression was very thoughtful, his brow creased with concern.

"The Crouching Dragon is still a wonderful gift to the people of France," Louise said, "even in its damaged condition."

Roger was silent.

"In fact," I said, "if you were greedy, you could have sold the castle to someone who would have turned it into a resort, and you would have made more than enough money to pay off the taxes, with plenty left over for yourself."

At least he blinked his eyes.

"The Sûreté installed a temporary telephone line in your

apartment," Louise said. "Why don't you call the president?"

Roger stared at her.

"Never mind," I said. "I'll do it!"

◆　　◆　　◆

"Yes," I said, repeating my name to the operator at the Élysée Palace, "William Montreux."

"I am sorry, Monsieur," the operator said in a bored voice, "*Monsieur le Président* is very busy. I suggest you call back at another—"

"—Please explain that I am the young man from the Crouching Dragon. I know he will want to speak to me."

"The Crouching Dragon?" the operator said. "This is not the zoo."

"Tell him!" I said.

I heard a click and I thought the operator had hung up.

Louise and Roger stared at me as if I had gone mad.

"—One moment, Monsieur Montreux!" the operator said into my astonished ear.

Another click, and I heard a powerful voice that was familiar even over a telephone.

"General Montreux," the president said. "I understand that you have led French forces into another battle."

"Yes, *Monsieur le Président*," I replied.

"I believe I once told you, standing before the castle, that you were destined to live a complicated existence."

"Yes, *Monsieur le Président*. I remember your words very well."

"Once more, William, you and your friends, Professor Guiscard and the townspeople, have earned the thanks and the respect of the people of France."

"Thank you, *Monsieur le Président*. Unfortunately, the damage is very great. Professor Guiscard believes it will require—what did you call it—a supplemental appropriation?"

"May I speak to Doctor Guiscard?" the president asked.

I handed the phone to Roger, who seemed extremely reluctant to take it. I shook the receiver at him, and finally he closed his fingers around it as if it were a fragile and precious gem.

"*Monsieur le Président*," he said into the receiver. Then he listened for a minute.

"But of course, *Monsieur le Président*," he said.

Another pause.

"Yes, I am absolutely certain. If I can find skilled workmen and the necessary materials, it might be accomplished in one year."

Yet another pause.

"I fully agree. They are both outstanding young people . . . I'll put him on. My deep and fervent thanks, *Monsieur le Président*."

Roger, looking flushed, handed me the telephone.

"I repeat my earlier offer, General Montreux," the president said, "inviting you to come to Paris and complete your education here—where I can keep an eye on you."

"You are very generous, *Monsieur le Président*. I will give your offer very serious consideration."

"I shall not repeat it again," the president said, and then he was gone.

"William," Roger said, "I don't quite know how you do this to me. I will be totally convinced that I am not going to do something, and the next thing I know I'm doing it."

Louise and I laughed.

"I don't believe you ever do anything you don't want to, Professor," Louise said.

For the first time I saw a hint of a smile on Roger's lips.

"Do you really think Bersault conspired with those men?" Louise asked.

"It was just the kind of despicable thing he would do," Roger said.

"If those men were only thieves," I said, "they had no reason to use explosives. That was a vicious act, and it would take a vicious man like Bersault to order it."

BONVILLE

TOWN MEETING

Prior to the attack of the thieves, we had been working on plans to operate the Crouching Dragon as a public institution. The man Roger had chosen to be in overall charge was Jean Bourgeois, the Algerian who had been the major domo of the castle when Roger's uncle, Armand Moret, was alive. During the war, Moret, a famous international art dealer, had used tunnels under the castle to hide his own collections and those of many of his friends and clients from the Nazis.

Moret had also aided his nephew, Roger, and others in the French Resistance, including my mother, until he was betrayed to the Nazis by Antoine Bersault, and subsequently murdered.

As part of our agreement with President de Gaulle, he persuaded the French Parliament to provide funds for the restoration, and Victor Devereaux, a fine engineer/archeologist was assigned to the work.

But after the attack on the tower, Devereaux had to determine whether we could safely continue restoring the damaged structure—a noble tower that had survived intact since the eleventh century.

After intensive study, Victor reported, "The tower can be saved, but it will require difficult structural repairs, and protective scaffolding until the reconstruction is complete."

Victor told us that he was astonished by the president's continued support for our work. "He has so much more on his mind than restoring an ancient Norman castle."

"I think we better inform the local people," I told my friends. "After all, the Crouching Dragon is part of their landscape, and they ought to know what's going on."

Roger said, "We'll end up with days and days of meetings, plenty of yelling, and nothing accomplished, except that a bunch of busybodies will be poking around the castle." He no longer roamed about the castle and countryside in long hair, a ragged beard and torn clothing, but there was still something of the hermit in him.

"You're probably right," Victor said, "but it's usually best to have the community on your side, otherwise they'll find a million ways to delay your work."

Louise said, "I think my father can do a good job of controlling a meeting." Louise's father, whose principal position was as Latin Master at the Lycée, had been elected mayor after Antoine Bersault was arrested and removed from office.

"That's true," Roger said.

"If not," I said, "we can always get my stepfather to knock a few heads together."

I had never been able to laugh about Paul Montreux's strength and fighting ability before, but Paul was now a different man. He no longer got drunk at the bistro in the seaside town of Luc, and he hadn't started a fight with a local man or a gendarme in a long time.

The people of Bonville gathered in the sanctuary of the church of St. George, the usual forum for public meetings. The crowd was bigger than usual because there were additional groups from Luc and Lion, the two coastal resort towns, as well as from the rural areas near Caen.

Father Thomas had set some white flowers in vases by the altar and was fussing about like a host at a dinner party. He told me that this was the biggest crowd he had seen in the church since VE Day—Victory in Europe Day, May 9, 1944.

Roger, Louise and I, as well as Jean Bourgeois, Victor Devereaux and an associate of his, Bernard Louis, were seated on folding chairs at the front of the church. Devereaux and Louis had brought with them a large easel on which they mounted a corkboard with a drawing of the plan of the castle and a sketch of the Dragon Tower pinned to it.

Mayor Donnet called the meeting to order. He was tall and bald and almost always wore a suit, which was appropriate for a Latin Master. But he had proved his courage many times before: mental and spiritual as well as physical courage.

"I'm pleased so many of you have come. The Crouching Dragon has been our neighbor for over eight hundred years. There are no longer any knights or princes living in the castle, and there aren't any soldiers, either. Some of you may not have known the previous owner, Armand Moret, but he was a great and good man, and a brave one, too. His nephew, Roger, is with us today, and he's the one who gave the castle to France. We're all in his debt."

There was so much applause that Roger had to stand up and nod and say, "Thank you," several times.

The mayor continued, "We're all proud of our children, too—even if they did sneak out of our homes at night to build their own kingdom, a place where we wouldn't have the slightest degree of control over them."

Most people laughed. The school principal kind of "harrumphed."

Marc Vestien and his father George were sitting near the back of the church. Paul had fought hand-to-hand with George many times, usually winning, and George hated him. Marc hated me. He was a couple of years older than I was and a lot bigger, and he had bullied me for years. Then, when all of us kids were in the castle, we had our last and biggest battle, both of us on horseback, wearing steel helmets and breastplates, and carrying cloth-padded wooden poles as spears, just like knights in ancient days. To almost everybody's surprise, I had won, knocking Marc right off his horse.

Marc, humiliated and angry, had abandoned us at the castle and later ratted on us to the authorities. I knew he would take revenge if he could.

"Foremost among our young heroes," the mayor was saying, "are William Montreux and my own daughter, Louise." We both nodded (and blushed) while people applauded. Marc and his father weren't the only ones who didn't applaud. There was a man—I guessed he was in his thirties—with a thick head of gray-streaked hair who sat near the front of the church, arms folded with a frown on his face. He looked familiar.

"We all know about the terrible damage to the castle," Mayor Donnet continued, "and we're grateful to William, Louise and the others who helped lessen the destruction."

I wasn't so sure how much I had lessened the damage. If I had made a better throw with the packet of explosives, it would have exploded outside. Louise tried to reassure me, saying that if the explosives had exploded where I found them they might have totally destroyed the dragon's head. Still . . . .

"Also with us," Mayor Donnet said, "is the estimable Monsieur Jean Bourgeois, who was the gracious director of the castle during the ownership of Armand Moret. Monsieur Bourgeois has been appointed Chief Administrator of the Crouching Dragon."

There was some tepid applause for Bourgeois. I couldn't help wondering whether it had something to do with the fact that he was a dark-skinned man of Algerian heritage, and the conflict in Algeria was at its height. Native Algerians had sought independence from France, and when negotiations failed they had turned to violence. The French government had responded with brutal suppression of the insurgents.

I had no idea what Jean's position was on Algerian independence, but I was absolutely certain he would not be party to any violence or terrorism. Still, suspicion was rampant, with whites wary of natives, and dark-skinned people wary of Europeans.

"Today," Donnet said, "we also have with us two gentlemen from the French government who will describe for us the present condition of the castle and the plans for restoration. Monsieur Victor Devereaux is the chief engineer and archeologist assigned by the president himself to direct this effort. Monsieur Devereaux, please."

Polite applause; along with their other suspicions, the people of Normandy were nervous about people from Paris.

Devereaux was in his late thirties, of average height, sturdy, with a strong jaw and a fringe of brown curly hair around his balding pate. I could easily imagine him seated at a slanted drawing board, quite erect, drawing lines with swift sure motions. When he spoke his voice was clipped and staccato, but very clear and precise.

"*Messieurs et Mesdames,*" he said. "These drawings show the original design of the castle, with the damaged areas marked on them. The walls and outer towers do not require significant repair. Portions of the ramparts need attention, but we wish to preserve as much of the original construction as possible.

"At the bottom of this drawing you see the section designated 'secret gate.' Professor Guiscard had covered the original wooden gate with a stone veneer that made it seem to be part of the wall. It is my understanding that William Montreux made his first entry to the castle by means of a rope thrown over the ramparts, a technique he claims to have learning by watching American cowboy movies."

People laughed; Devereaux never cracked a smile.

"The public will require a more conventional kind of entry. Professor Guiscard had rigged the gate so that it was raised on pulleys operated by a small electric motor, controlled by remote radio control. The machinery still works, but we prefer to restore the gate to the original condition."

That surprised everybody, especially Roger, who rose and spoke: "Unfortunately Monsieur Devereaux," he said, "we no longer know what the 'original' condition was. Many generations have lived in the castle. Each succeeding group of occupants made changes—all of them destroyed some portion of what had gone before. In recent times, my uncle, Armand Moret, made modifications. Then the Nazis blew up some structures, including the entire lodge, which once sat in the keep."

Devereaux replied stiffly, "The structure Monsieur Moret built was definitely not part of the historic buildings."

"Very true," Roger said, "and I am not suggesting we rebuild it. But the motorized gate facilitates entry and provides security."

M. Henri, owner of the tiny three-room hotel in Bonville, stood up suddenly. "Is this not the twentieth century?!" he asked rhetorically. "Do we wish to employ men to pull the chains up and down?"

We all knew that M. Henri was hoping to build a larger hotel near the castle.

"Henri is quite right," said M. Charcute, the butcher. "While we intend to do everything with dignity, we do not wish to make it difficult for tourists to visit this place."

Devereaux said, "I agree that access should be easy. Would you agree to removal of the stone veneer," Devereaux asked, "exposing the underlying wooden doors which are old even though not original?"

Roger said, "Of course, Monsieur Devereaux. With a

new motor I can hide every bit of machinery and limit the sound to a very low, almost inaudible hum."

"Good!" Mayor Donnet said. "Let us go forward."

The familiar-looking man with the wavy gray hair sitting in the front row of pews did not seem to think it was "Good!" He was twisting in his seat at almost every comment, and he wore a steady and very angry frown.

"Very well," Devereaux said. "The most difficult part of the structural work will be reconstruction of the Dragon Tower. The entire lower jaw of the dragon was shattered beyond repair. We have learned that stone excavated from some of the tunnels leading to the Crouching Dragon was used to build the castle in earlier times. We hope to be able to quarry material from those areas and use it to restore the jaw.

"The glass is a different matter. We have learned the formula for replicating it, but the cost would be so extraordinary that I do not believe it would be worthwhile."

"There is a question of authenticity," said Madame Boulez, the mother of Stephen and Jules, sixteen-year-old fraternal twins. Jules was shaped like a dumpling, and next to him, his brother Stephen looked as narrow as a noodle; the kids called them the 'Chicken Soup Twins.' During the siege, the twins had behaved quite differently. Jules had stood by us, while Stephen had secretly abandoned his friends. However, both twins had accompanied their mother, and Jules no longer buried his chin in his chest, but instead sat up, strong and proud.

"We can use modern glass to replace that which has been destroyed," said Bernard Louis, Devereaux's associate, who had not spoken until then. "It will look so much like the original glass that only a laboratory test would make it possible to tell the difference."

Everyone seemed to agree that was a good plan, and

I began to think we would complete the meeting fairly quickly and successfully.

"Good," Devereaux said. "As you know, Professor Guiscard will be responsible for restoring the working exhibit of the Normandy invasion. He will—"

The frowning, wavy haired man in the front row leaped to his feet, interrupting M. Devereaux.

"—That is ridiculous," he said, speaking in a piercing voice. "What does an animated exhibit of a modern war have to do with a medieval castle? It shouldn't be rebuilt!"

I looked at Roger, who stared at the speaker with evident pain.

There was a lot of talking in the crowd, and several people were yelling: "You got a lot of nerve, Tony!" "We're proud of that exhibit!" "Get that man out of here!"

Mayor Donnet's voice rose over the others: "He's got the right to say whatever he pleases, but I disagree with him totally. The exhibit is not only a marvel, it is a magnificent memorial to all of the heroes who lived and died liberating France from the Nazis!"

A number of people cheered. One man said, "With your family's record, Tony, how dare you criticize Roger Guiscard!"

"Tony's right," George Vestien yelled from the back of the church. "This was a very happy town until that crazy Guiscard camped out in the castle and talked every kid in Bonville into lying to his parents and working for him free to rebuild the family estate!"

"Be careful what you say, George!" It was my stepfather, Paul, on his feet and looking ominous.

"Do you think you frighten me?" George responded.

"Or me?" Marc, his son, was also on his feet.

"That's enough!" Mayor Donnet said. "I've separated Paul and George before, and I don't want to have to do it again."

Paul was close to smiling—probably at the thought of

Donnet, brave but slender, stopping a fight.

"Don't worry, Desmond," Paul said to the mayor. "I've grown tired of beating George to a pulp. But I don't think Tony has any right to criticize Roger."

Many voices agreed, but "Tony" wasn't backing down.

"This is all nonsense!" he said. "These people are more like grave robbers than scholars, pretending they own property stolen from other people!"

I wondered what he meant by "other people."

Victor Devereaux was saying, "The castle belonged to Professor Guiscard's uncle and then to the professor himself. He has generously given it and everything in it to the people of France."

I whispered to Louise: "Who is that guy—Tony?"

She turned her luminous green eyes on me in surprise. "I thought you knew. He's Antoine Bersault the second, the son of the former mayor. He's taller and slimmer, but he has his father's strong, hard-edged features—and the same arrogant personality."

"That's for sure!" I said. I already disliked him intensely.

"My father says he's been in Algeria as an officer in the French Air Force," Louise said. "We think he's trying to use his military connections to get his father out of prison, but that's not likely with de Gaulle as president. Of course he hates de Gaulle, who brought the Sûreté down on him after the confrontation at the castle."

Tony was roaring again. "All that junk they brought in should be tossed away. I'm surprised that those so-called thieves wanted any part of it."

"That's ridiculous," Mayor Donnet said. "Experts say the property in the castle is worth tens of millions of francs."

Tony forced a laugh. "You claim to want a genuine, historic monument—filled with debris from Moret's gallery!"

"Why should the castle be returned to its former,

ravaged condition?" I said. "Monsieur Moret was a world-famous collector, and there is no doubt that all the tapestries, paintings and furniture are genuine."

"Are you going to listen to the 'Little American,' and the rest of these children?" Tony asked contemptuously.

A lot of people looked at me for a brief moment—I was the kid who had been called the 'Little American,' and it was definitely supposed to be an insult, but it no longer bothered me and I just smiled.

Tony attacked again: "Are you going to trust a man who was such a coward he hid in the castle for years?"

Jean Bourgeois said, "Professor Guiscard is a very private man, but he was a brave member of the Resistance, not a coward, nor the consort of France's enemies. He was the legal owner of the castle, and he spent many years protecting and preserving it, when everyone else stood by—or tried to steal it for their own enrichment."

"Who is this man to speak to me with such disrespect?" Tony said. "He was a paid lackey for the elder Moret and now he grovels before the nephew!"

"That's outrageous!" Roger said, on his feet once more. "Jean Bourgeois is a man of high intellect and outstanding character. He was loyal to his employers, but never compromised his honor!"

"He's an Algerian!" George Vestien roared.

"Algeria is part of France!" Donnet yelled.

"For how long?" Tony asked. "Men just like him have slaughtered white Frenchmen in Algeria. How do we know he's not one of them?"

Much of the crowd roared in outrage at Tony's words. Roger was on his feet, ready to go after Tony, but Jean grabbed his arm.

"Please?" he said. "Don't fight with this man on my account."

There was a lot more yelling, and when Tony tried to speak, he could barely be heard over the crowd. Then he roared, "It's not over yet! You'll hear from me again!" And, with almost everybody booing him, he stalked out of the church, swiftly followed by George and Marc Vestien.

Five minutes later the people unanimously approved the plans submitted by Victor Devereaux.

UNSOLVED
MYSTERIES

Being called the 'Little American' again was a prod to my memory.

I had taken a lot of abuse in school. Some of the kids, including Mark Vestien, called me names, like "Bastard" and "The Little American." They were saying Paul wasn't my real father—that I was the illegitimate son of one of the American soldiers who had landed in Normandy during the invasion that liberated France from the Nazis. I was forced to fight many times, and with an ox like Marc I almost always lost.

Eventually I confronted my mother and she told me my natural father was an American intelligence agent named Alan Stevens. He and another American, John Portman, had worked with her and Roger in the French Resistance. Mother and Alan Stevens—with John Portman and Paul Montreux as witnesses—were about to be secretly married in the Church of St. Pierre in Caen on the night of July 14, 1944, when a wayward shell from a British battleship hit the spire. The blast injured my mother and apparently killed Alan Stevens. Paul offered to marry my mother and accept her child as his own. Mother agreed, and I was baptized William Montreux.

Even before my mother told me the truth, I had found the grave she regularly visited, marked with the name Alan Stevens. It was on a rise of ground next to a plane tree in the civilian rather than the military section, even though Alan Stevens had been a military officer. Mother later told me nobody really knew what had happened to him, and they weren't sure who was buried in that grave. Paul was certain he was dead, but I firmly believed the contrary: Alan Stevens—*my father*—was alive and living in the United States of America. One day I would go there and find him.

On June 7, 1959, the day after we met President de Gaulle, I had felt the need to visit the cemetery again, even though there was great doubt my father was actually buried there. That afternoon, without telling anyone, I took a bus for the short ride to Caen. Along the way, I saw dozens of people visiting the various Allied cemeteries where many of the thousands who had died liberating France were buried. This had happened every year since the end of World War II, but the numbers were greater in 1959, the fifteenth anniversary of the 1944 invasion.

It was late spring, and Normandy was in fragrant bloom, with a fresh breeze gently bending trees and flowers. A single, many-lobed, pale green leaf had fallen from the plane tree and rested on the simple, gray granite marker, which bore only the name, "Alan Stevens." My emotions were conflicting: the name touched my heart, but someone else might be buried there.

From where I stood, the earth gently sloped downward towards a channel a few kilometers distant. I watched ships of considerable size ply the commercial canal, originally built in the nineteenth century, that paralleled the Orne River from Caen to Ouistreham where it emptied into the English Channel.

To the north, rose the huge, forbidding castle that William the Conqueror had built some years before he invaded England in 1066 and triumphed over the armies of King Harold. William, then Duke of Normandy, and his fleet had sailed from Dives, a few kilometers from Ouistreham and not very far from my home town.

I rested my shoulders against the trunk of the plane tree, the back of my head touching a pale, smooth place where the older bark had shed, then slid down to a seated position. The late afternoon sky was a brilliant, shimmering blue with wispy rows of cirrus clouds drifting by. A sudden strong gust shook the tree and a leaf fell and touched my shoulder on its way to earth; other leaves murmured softly as they fluttered by. What were they saying? Why were they falling in spring?

The wind died as suddenly as it had risen, and then I heard human voices close by. The trunk of the tree partially screened me from the speakers, a man and a woman, talking quietly. As they came closer, I realized they were speaking English with what seemed to be American accents, although still too softly for me to understand. Their long shadows stretched across the ground, almost parallel to my legs. I wondered if they could see me.

Out of the corner of my eye I saw a hand—a man's hand—holding a blue cap. As far as I could tell without turning my head, there was a gold design on it. The couple stopped speaking. They stood close to Alan Stevens' head-stone for several minutes, silently, unmoving. Then, the hand and the cap disappeared, and only the squeak of the grass told me they were walking away.

After a moment, I rose to my feet and turned to search for them. They were walking towards the entrance arch, hand in hand, both slim and tall, but I was unable to see their faces. I couldn't tell how old they were; based on their clothes and their pace, I guessed they were about my mother's age. After wavering for a minute, I suddenly had the urge to find out who they were and what they were doing near Alan Stevens' grave, but they were so far away I would have had to run through the cemetery, upsetting other mourners, and probably startling the couple, now dis-appearing from my sight.

Nevertheless, my mind was racing. Was the man Alan Stevens? Had I missed the chance to meet my own father? The urge to follow them overwhelmed me, but as I turned to run, I noticed something on the headstone—a blue cap with a gold design. That stopped me. The design was of a winged dragon perched on a globe, with the words "Flying Dragons" on it, and in very small print, "U.S. Air Force." Unlike the one on the DragonSlayers shield, this dragon didn't have a sword driven through it and it looked proud and triumphant.

I couldn't help myself; I grabbed the cap and ran, dodging headstones and leaping over graves, while the mourners stared. My feet were striking the ground so hard that I felt like I was digging into the turf, disturbing the dead. Still I ran—past the caretaker who tried to cut me off, through the arching metal gate and out onto the street. I looked about me wildly. There were a few people walking, a few automobiles moving.

Where are they?! I thought.

About a block away I saw the back of a man—like the one at the grave—as he slid behind the wheel of a small sedan.

I ran again. "Wait!" I yelled, hopeful when the car didn't start immediately.

"Wait!" I yelled again.

Then the red brake lights came on, and the vehicle began to move. I was waving my arms madly, yelling at the top of my lungs. People were staring at me, but I didn't care.

The sedan turned a corner into another street. If there was traffic in town, I still had a chance. I sped around the corner myself, and then stopped. No vehicle was to be seen; they had disappeared.

After a moment I realized I was still holding the cap. I lifted it against my chest—my heart. I didn't cry. Maybe the man had been Alan Stevens—which meant that my father was truly alive, and somehow I would find him.

Maybe a relative of Alan Stevens—or whoever was buried in the grave? Someone who could help me learn the truth—whatever it might be.

I took the cap and put it on my head and walked away—smiling.

THE ART OF
SELF-DEFENSE

After the town meeting, I finally had a chance to draw Roger aside and say, "I've wanted to talk to you ever since we captured the two guys up in the Dragon Tower."

Roger smiled broadly. "Judo," he said.

"Pardon me," I said.

"The techniques I used to subdue and control the thief in the Dragon Tower are based on a discipline called 'Judo.' It's one variation of a type of martial art invented in Japan in the 1880s."

"How did you happen to learn it?" I asked.

"Although I grew up to be a tall, fairly strong man," Roger said, "when I was a boy I was short, slim and weak. Perhaps because of that, I got into many fights in school and was often beaten up."

"I know what you're talking about," I said.

"My father," Roger said, "wanted to tell the school principal, but I wouldn't let him. He asked his brother, my uncle, Armand Moret, for advice. Uncle Armand had been sending his own son, my good friend and cousin, Gilbert, to a school of self-defense, and he recommended the same school for me.

"During one of Uncle Armand's many trips to Japan, a Japanese art collector told him about Jigoro Kano, a famous educator, who had developed a new and remarkable martial art, called Kodokan Judo. Fascinated, Uncle Armand contacted the master, who gave him the name of Moshe

Feldenkrais, who had a *dojo*—a studio—in Paris.

"Feldenkrais was not taking new students, but he recommended a master named Sadayuke Kawaishi, who accepted Gilbert for training, and later, me.

"Kawaishi was very strict, very formal, but he was a wonderful teacher. During the war, the Nazis shut down many of the martial arts schools—they didn't want the French to learn any combat techniques. Master Kawaishi's school remained open because the Nazis mistakenly believed he was a Japanese national and Japan was Germany's ally. Actually Kawaishi was a French citizen and loved his adopted country. He continued to teach me and his other loyal French students secretly, in his own home, which was against the Nazi occupation laws and very dangerous.

"It distressed Kawaishi greatly to teach the Nazis, and he hated the French collaborators even more. Ironically, many loyal French people detested him for training France's enemies.

"As you know, William, my parents, my older brother, and my aunt Chloe—Armand Moret's wife and Gilbert's mother—were killed in the first week of the Nazi invasion when their civilian train was bombed. I went to live with my Uncle Armand and my cousin Gilbert, and we mourned together.

"Later, when there were acts of sabotage against the Nazis by the Resistance, they retaliated by killing innocent French citizens, one of whom was my cousin Gilbert, machine-gunned to death right in front of Uncle Armand's gallery. That was when I joined the Resistance.

"Then, Uncle Armand closed his gallery and went to live in the Crouching Dragon, providing a hiding place for the art of French people and making the castle a base for the Resistance. I followed my Uncle to Normandy and Master Kawaishi came with me, abruptly closing his Paris dojo.

"It was in Normandy that I met your mother and Paul and the two Americans, Alan Stevens and John Portman. Master Kawaishi set up a secret studio in Caen where he trained members of the Resistance, including me. Eventually I earned a Black Belt."

"What's that?" I asked.

"When you practice Judo, you wear a *judogi*, a uniform consisting of a white jacket and pants and a wide, colored belt, which shows your rank. A beginner has no rank, so he wears a white belt. Boys and girls, ranking first through third *kyu* or class, wear violet belts; adults, brown. Then begin the *dans*, or grades. From first through fifth, you wear black. Sixth through eighth wear red and white, ninth and above wear a red belt. However, holders of the sixth dan and above may wear black belts if they prefer. I have earned the seventh grade, but I wear the black belt."

"I would like to study Judo," I said. "Does that man— did you call him Kawaishi—still teach in Caen?"

"No," Roger said. "He has reopened his studio in Paris."

"Is there another teacher?" I asked.

""The closest dojos are in Cherbourg and Le Havre," Roger said.

"I guess that leaves you, Roger," I said.

◆　◆　◆

"Louise? I wasn't expecting *you*," Roger said.

"I know," Louise said, "but when William told me about the Judo lessons, I thought it was a great idea. Will you please teach me, too?"

As we tramped down the curving stone steps to the cellar beneath the Dragon Tower, Roger shot me the kind of look I hadn't seen for a while. The last time was during the early days when we kids first secretly visited the Crouching Dragon. Night after night, more and more kids had showed up outside the gates, and Roger finally said, "One day we'll have every kid in the district inside the castle." As a matter of fact, his words were prophetic; by the time we were finally discovered by our parents and the authorities, almost every kid within a ten mile radius of the castle was part of our kingdom.

"Louise," Roger said. "I'm not even qualified to teach a young man, let alone a young lady."

"Treat me the same as Willi," she said. "I already have approval from my mother."

Roger, still dubious, began to pace the cellar. The ceiling was low, with extremely thick round columns spaced fairly closely together, carrying the slightly peaked arches that supported the level of the castle above us. Pale yellow light spread in overlapping circles from a couple of bare bulbs, and the stone walls and packed earth floor were damp, except where Roger had spread some old quilted mats on the floor.

For a long time, we kids hadn't even known there was a cellar because the Great Hall had an earth floor. Roger had eventually shown us that steps under the Dragon Tower led to a cellar and various tunnels that radiated out from the castle, one of them all the way into Bonville, where it surfaced to a secret trapdoor inside the church.

Roger was wearing a tired-looking, grayish-white judogi, consisting of thin, cotton, floppy pants that reached almost to the ankles, a wrap-around, long-sleeved, finger-tip length jacket and a black belt wound twice around his body and knotted in front with the ends hanging down.

For a moment, Roger stopped pacing.

"I have only this very old, shrunken judogi for William," he said, holding out a shabby white uniform with frayed cuffs and neckline and a shriveled white belt. "It was once worn by my cousin, Gilbert."

"Thank you," I said, feeling honored to wear his cousin's judogi.

Louise was carrying a duffle bag. "Willi's mother gave me this," she said, pulling out a judogi that looked just as white as Roger's and mine looked gray.

Roger began pacing again. He was probably one hundred and ninety centimeters—about six-feet, three-inches—tall, and the top of his head was only a few centimeters from the ceiling. He stopped suddenly.

"It's not enough for Helene Montreux to provide Louise with a judogi," Roger said. "She will have to work with you, Louise, while I work with William."

♦   ♦   ♦

I was afraid that we might end up with a whole army of kids in the castle. What advantage would I have if everybody in the district learned Judo? I hoped my mother would agree to work with Louise, otherwise I might have to do it. How do you throw around a girl—especially one you really like? It might sound sexy, but not to me. Fortunately, my mother agreed, although Paul thought the whole idea was crazy.

That meant that both Mother and Louise needed judogis. The problem was solved when Louise's mother used my mother's uniform as a pattern and made a new one for Louise.

The first thing I had to learn was how to wear my judogi. Pulling on the pants and tightening the drawstring was easy and so was slipping on the jacket and folding the left side over the right. The belt took getting used to. I had to hold it against my waist, then cross it behind my back, switch hands and bring the belt out front again, before I tied it in a kind of a square knot at my waist. When I did it right, the belt was snug around my body and the ends hung loose in front.

There was even a way to fold the uniform when you were finished. Judo has a lot of rules, but the rules are not just meaningless regulations—they help you become very efficient at Judo and in life.

When the four of us gathered at the Crouching Dragon, Roger asked me once again, "Why do you want to learn Judo?"

"Because I'm tired of getting beaten up by big guys or having to use some kind of weapon. I want to be able to beat guys up with my bare hands!"

"Wrong answer," Mother said.

I was astonished. "Both of you used Judo to take out Nazis."

"There are no Nazis today," Roger said. "Actually, the meaning of the word 'Judo' is 'the way of gentleness.'"

I laughed.

"Those are the words of the founder himself, Jigoro Kano," Roger said.

"You first give way," Mother said, "in order to gain victory. Judo is more than attack and defense, it is a way of life."

"When Professor Kano developed this technique," Roger said. "He followed one basic principle: make the most efficient use of your mental and physical energy. For example, when facing an opponent, use just the right amount of force, not too much and not too little."

Louise was nodding her head. All I had been thinking about was Roger tossing that guy over his hip.

Roger read from a book that looked worn and heavily thumbed:

" . . . let us say a man is standing before me whose strength is ten, and that my own strength is but seven. If he pushes as hard as he can, I am sure to be pushed back, or knocked down, even if I resist with all my might. This is opposing strength with strength. But if instead of opposing him I give way . . . withdrawing my body and maintaining my balance, my opponent will lose his balance . . . he will be unable to use all his strength. It will have fallen to three. Because I retain my balance my strength remains at seven. Now I am stronger than my opponent and can defeat him by using only half my strength . . . "

That sounded very good to me.

Roger put the book aside. "Now let us begin," he said.

About time, I was thinking.

"Before and after practicing," Roger said, "and before and after a match, opponents bow to each other."

"Why?" I asked.

"It's a matter of respect," Mother said.

"Do we have to do that if someone attacks us in the street?" Louise asked, with a sly smile.

"We are talking about good manners in the dojo," Roger said.

"You can bow either sitting or standing," Mother told us. "On entering and leaving the dojo you bow to your instructor and to those senior to you. For the rest, bowing depends on the phase of Judo you are engaging in. First, there is *kata*, which is a kind of prearranged practice. You work with a partner and follow an agreed set of exercises. It's almost like a play where you are following a script."

"I don't get it," Louise said. "What do you practice?"

"Throwing, grappling and striking techniques," Roger said. "Since each person knows what the other is going to do, they learn discipline."

"It sounds like a kind of dance," Louise said.

"It is, in many ways," Roger said. "Kata can be very beautiful to watch, but the partners are not just presenting a show, they are learning every kind of technique.

"There is also *randori,* a kind of free practice, when there is no pre-arranged plan, but there is no striking in randori, because it is too dangerous for fellow students to attack each other when the other person may not be expecting it."

"It's okay, isn't it," I asked, "to use the striking techniques if you are facing an attack outside of the dojo?"

"Even then," Roger said, "you are not to use more force than is necessary to subdue an opponent or make him run away."

"I don't know why I'm supposed to be nice to the bad guys," I said, "but I'll take your word for it."

✦   ✦   ✦

They taught us the basic movements, starting with the stances you take when you're beginning the practice. We learned the basic hold, which is the same for every posture. With your right hand you hold the opponent's left lapel near his armpit, and with your left hand you hold the opponent's right outer sleeve above the elbow. That was easy.

We learned to slide our feet on the mat, not lift them—except when you're close to an opponent, you're supposed to have one foot lead and the other follow.

Louise said to me, "Just remember that two-step your mother showed you when you were learning to dance."

"She didn't teach me to grab anybody's lapel," I said.

"She didn't teach you to step on my feet, either," she said.

"When do we learn some throws?" I asked.

Mother said, "Before you can learn the throws you have to learn how to fall."

"I see that surprises you," Roger said, "but in order to begin or complete many throws, you must know how to fall yourself, or you can be badly injured."

Mother said, "To use your strength most efficiently, you must break the other person's balance."

"The basic rule is very simple," Roger said. "If pushed, go with the force of the push and, keeping your balance, pull. On the other hand, if you are pulled, push."

"Yes," Louise said, "but it goes against your ordinary instinct. If someone pushes you, you want to push back."

Mother and Roger, working as partners, demonstrated the various ways to break an opponent's balance. It was absolutely astonishing to watch my own mother nimbly falling, spinning, turning, rolling. I had always thought of her as graceful and agile, but this was a revelation.

"Can we get started?" Louise asked. "That looks like fun."

"I'm tempted to tell you to try that forward roll yourself," Mother said, "but I think we better train you first."

"No, I can do it," Louise said, and without waiting, launched herself forward.

For a brief moment, she looked good, but then she fell off to one side, yelling an involuntary grunt. Louise sat up slowly, rubbing her neck.

Mother dropped to her knees beside her. "Are you all right?"

"I guess so," Louise said, "I bounced on my head."

"Watch me again," Mother said.

Roger explained, "She's rolling on her arm, shoulder and back, not her head."

As Mother's legs came down she slapped the mat, and in a moment she was standing upright again, smiling.

"Why slap the mat?" I asked.

"Because it gives you balance and the impetus for your next move."

"Okay," Louise said. "I'm ready to try again."

FRAMED

Louise and I watched André, my best friend, scramble at remarkable speed up the ladders that edged the steel and wooden scaffolding. From below, the framework looked like a child's construction that the Crouching Dragon was chewing on—and that André was about to be swallowed by the great creature. Odile and Pierre were leaning into the gaping void, working with Bernard Louis, the craftsman sent by the Department of Archeology of the University of Paris.

Bernard was a thin, wiry little man, with hawk-like features, piercing blue eyes and extremely strong hands at the ends of forearms knotted with ropes of muscle. He had wanted to work alone, but President de Gaulle had agreed that all of us who worked on the castle could participate in the reconstruction. Thus Bernard had reluctantly been forced to accept Odile, Pierre and others. He was a good teacher, and he swiftly trained them to remove the dangerous glass shards without cutting themselves or disturbing the remnants of the stone rims that had supported the windows.

Thirteen-year-old Odile told me, her still uneven teeth glowing, "We're helping as best we can, and I think he's beginning to like us."

André was carrying a bag of crisp bread, cheese and *jambon* (ham), plus bottled water for the kids, and a small bottle of red wine for Bernard. André could have sent lunch up on the hoist, but he wanted to share the meal and the view. From the top platform you could see our small town of Bonville, and farther on, the resort towns of Luc and Lion along the Normandy coast. On a clear day you could make out the thin line marking the English coast across the channel. I didn't worry about André; he could climb like a mountain goat.

An unpleasant damp wind was beginning to blow in from the coast, and the sky, crystal blue earlier, was closing down—a typical Normandy winter afternoon. The breeze was still rising and the clouds had begun chasing each other across the sky, like billowy dogs nipping at each other's heels, but André and the others didn't seem to notice, tearing off great chunks from the baguettes and stuffing them with ham and cheese.

While work was going on outside to rebuild the damaged Dragon Tower, other work was continuing inside the Great Hall. We kids had done our best to rebuild this large space while we were creating our little kingdom. At first we had worked with shovels and brooms to clear out debris left by the Nazis. One day Pierre banged his pickaxe against something that jarred the tool out of his hands and sent it flying upward. The edge of the axe cut a rope carrying a bucket of rocks and it fell towards the floor. I had shoved Louise out of the way, but got hit on the foot myself. My wounds weren't bad, and when I checked the site where Pierre had struck something, we uncovered several suits of armor that not even Roger knew about, which swelled his already substantial collection.

We built bases and mounted all of the armor around the Great Hall. We also repaired the roof, did some painting and mounted sconces to hold candles and light the space.

We hadn't been able to replace the tall windows in the hall, which were covered with ugly wooden panels. Now, with funds from the government and craftsmen supervised by Bernard, we were slowly, steadily rebuilding the stone framework of the windows, and would eventually have them glazed.

Bernard and the kids uncovered a few glass panels hidden in the cellar. For the rest, they contracted with the *Institut Vitrail* in Arras to create new windows. Some of them, still encased in protective covering, were arranged on a giant cartoon—an exact full-size pattern—on the floor of the Great Hall. Craftsmen were working on the stone splines that outlined large sections of the windows. In time, stained glass would be mounted, soldered and mortared into place. The colorful designs were based on Norman battles and sea-going adventures—scenes that included knights resplendent in armor, powerful kings and beautiful queens, as well as fierce enemies being conquered.

Pierre and Jules, the rounder of the Chicken Soup Twins, were assisting the skilled craftsmen rebuilding the stone framework. The two farm boys, the cousins Charles and Leon, were scrubbing centuries of dirt from the stone walls. One thing about the cousins, they were willing to do any useful work, and didn't care how filthy they got. As Charles once said, "You can't convince a farmer that dirt is bad."

Louise and I were surprised at the progress.

Pierre walked over, mopping his brow. "Just here to watch," he asked, "or are you going to help?" but there was a sly smile at the corner of his lips. When we first met, Pierre had seemed sullen, his typically glowering expression accented by his matted dark hair and heavy brows knitted together in a perpetual frown. But he had blossomed in our fantasy kingdom, surprising us when he turned up one day with a lute and sang for us in an extremely pleasant voice. I wasn't the only kid who had benefited from the creation of Kingdom of Guiscard in the Crouching Dragon.

"You're doing a great job," I said.

"Yeah," he responded, "we're pretty proud of it."

I stopped to watch the craftsmen skillfully re-cutting the stone splines. They worked swiftly, their faces covered with metal-and-glass masks to keep splinters out of their eyes. Other men were climbing up the scaffolding, setting the splines and mortaring them into place. Still others were glazing each section.

I had a vague feeling that something wasn't quite right. The men on the scaffolding stopped working and began climbing down. Perhaps they were breaking for lunch, like my friends on the scaffolding outside. I was about to ask, when Louise came running into the Great Hall. I had been so absorbed watching the glass workers that I didn't realize she had gone out into the courtyard, until she rushed back in, shouting, "Willi! Pierre! Charles! Leon! Everybody! Come outside! *Hurry!*"

We raced after her.

In the few minutes since we had gone inside, the wind had become a roar and a driving rain was pouring down at a sharp angle; the glass workers had stopped because the wind had made their work dangerous.

Louise, already drenched, long hair plastered to her face, was pointing upward to the platform where André, Odile, Pierre and Bernard were huddled together. The scaffolding had broken free from the Dragon Tower and was swaying in the heavy wind, first creaking away several feet, then slamming against the tower. Splinters were falling off and dropping to the ground. It looked as if the scaffolding might collapse and crash to the ground at any moment.

I hurried over, planning to climb up to where I could help my friends, but Jean Bourgeois appeared, yelling at me.

"No!" he shouted. "Don't try it!" and grabbed my arm.

"Let me go!" I said. "I can help them get down!"

"It's impossible!" he shouted, his voice cutting through the strong wind. "The ladder has broken loose!"

"I'll climb the framework. I can make it!"

But Jean was stronger than I was. He pulled my hands off the framework and literally knocked me to the ground. Angry, I scrambled to my feet, but he surprised me by expertly twisting my arm behind my back.

"Let go! " I screamed, unable to break his grip.

There was a terrible cracking sound, as if every board in the scaffolding had snapped at once. Jean let go my arm and gave me a powerful shove away from the framework.

"Get out of here!" he yelled, and began to sprint away.

I hesitated, still thinking of my friends, and then started to move, but it was too late. I looked up to see a tangle of steel and wood crashing down over my head. Even as I put up my hands in a futile gesture, a steel angle hurtled through the sky and smashed into me. In that fleeting second I thought I saw a face—a leering, glaring, staring face. I knew that face. But then everything was blotted out in a crash of stars and lightning . . . and blackness.

STRANGE ENCOUNTERS

Whirling clouds, gray and black, swirling about me. Flashes of red lightning, jagged arrows slicing through my brain, eyes rolling in my head, unable to focus; sharp jolts of pain through throbbing drumbeats that pulse harshly again and again— sharper, faster, and louder, pulling screams from my throat, my arms flailing about as if disconnected from my body, spinning wildly, rag limp, fingers splayed and gigantic, unable to grasp my skull and stop the pounding, roaring, screaming hell.

And then I am awake, eyes bulging from my head, arms and legs motionless, unresponsive to my commands, head rigid, fixed. A metal frame! I'm contained, held, helpless. A scream gathers in my throat, but I am filled with phlegm and my voice is drowned, buried. I'm dying. I'm dead . . . .

"Good. You're awake."

The voice is unfamiliar. The colorless face that goes with it—bland, pale, watery eyes, thin mouth—is unknown to me. My fear grows, expands, fills my perception.

"I'm Doctor Genet. You've had a bad accident, which might have killed you, but did not. You've been unconscious for nearly twenty-four hours."

He showed little expression and he was not reassuring.

I tried to speak, but my voice came out broken, guttural, unfamiliar. "My head . . . . " That was all I could say.

"You're in a rigid steel frame as a precaution. We're not

certain what damage there may be to your spine, your nervous system."

"Willi?" Another voice.

A face levitated into view.

"Mother?"

"You're going to be fine, Willi. A broken leg and arm, broken collar bone, but no breaks in your back."

"May I speak to my patient?" The doctor's tone wasn't actually disapproving, but it stopped my mother from speaking further.

A grunt. Strangely, I recognized the grunt: Paul. Actually, it was a friendly grunt, a clearing of the throat. It simply meant, "I'm here, too."

"Your radiography (I later learned that meant x-rays) is negative," the doctor said, "except for the bone breaks to which Madame Montreux referred (not "your mother," but "Madame Montreux"). We'll have to repeat them to make certain. In the meantime, you must rest."

My voice came out as if each word was a rough-edged stone scraping against other rough-edged stones: "Where am I?"

"Caen, the General Hospital on the Rue George Clemenceau," Doctor Genet said. "You were brought here in an ambulance."

I couldn't remember any of it. There was a question I wanted to ask, but I couldn't put my mind around it.

The doctor didn't change his expression. He looked at Paul and Mother and said, "You can come back tomorrow morning."

Mother kissed me again, Paul touched my hand. I had many questions, but my head felt like a brick and my eyes were beginning to close.

⋆　　⋆　　⋆

I awakened a couple of times during the night. The room

was quite dark, except for the glow of what I took to be a night light somewhere—I couldn't move my head to find out—and I dozed off quickly each time.

A sharp pain. I feel like I can't breathe, as if my throat is in a vise. My eyes pop open and I realize that someone has his hands around my neck. I can't see who and I can't cry out. My head is in the steel frame so I can't move away from my assailant. I try to grab the guy, but my hands are weak and I can't pull his hands away. My body is twisting, but my head is held fast.

In desperation I try to push him away, but he's too big. I grab his throat and try to squeeze. There's a grunt, and the pressure lessens a bit, but not much. I'm gasping for breath, trapped in a device that is supposed to be saving my life.

This is it. Everything is at stake. I struggle again to pull his hands away. I try to punch him in the throat with the side of my hand—a judo strike—but I miss and my blow glances off his shoulder. My only reward is another grunt. I'm fading now, the pain is terrible and I'm choking on my own vomit. An idea. A desperate idea. I shove with all my remaining strength and push him away a little. Then, as he lunges back, I pull him toward me sharply, surprising him, banging his head against the metal frame. His hands loosen a little and he tries to lean back, but then I pull him against the steel as hard as I can. He cries out in pain. Even though I still can't really see him, I aim to poke him in the eyes with my fingers. I sense that he is staggered.

With my throat free, I yell as loud as I can, which isn't much, but the guy is woozy from the blows against the frame and the poke with my fingers. I think I hear steps, someone running. My assailant slams me with his fist, and it hurts.

But then he is moving away, staggering towards the door.

The door opens—a light is switched on. I have a brief, gasping look at my assailant from behind and a sliver of profile.

"What's going—" a voice begins.

Then there is impact between the person with the voice and the guy who attacked me. I hear a yelp of pain, a body hitting the floor, a weak call for help, the sound of other voices and footsteps.

I'm breathing a little easier now, but the pain from the hands squeezing my neck is still sharp. My fingers and arms hurt from the jolts when I yanked him against the steel frame. Maybe I'm breathing too hard, too fast. I black out.

◆　◆　◆

When I came to, the doctor was there—what was his name?—Genet. Mother and Paul were close to the bed, looking anxious. I wanted to tell them everything was okay, but I knew I couldn't quite speak. I blinked my eyes trying to signal . . . something.

"Is William all right? Mother asks.

"'All right' is not the precise description," the doctor said, "but I think he'll live."

◆　◆　◆

It was morning. They had checked me from head to foot, x-rayed me top to bottom. A lot of lacerations, they said, and my voice would be whispery for a while, but no new major injuries. Mother and Paul both tried to smile.

"I'm okay," I whispered. Which I didn't believe, but what else could I say?

There were three other people in the room—the doctor, a policeman, and a man in a suit. The man in the suit was tall but chunky, neck and chin spilling over his shirt collar, tie loosened, tips of his collar soft and turning up.

He spoke in a droning monotone, "I am Inspector Rochefort. We must ask you some questions."

My voice came out in a ragged whisper. "What happened to the guy who attacked me?"

The inspector sighed. "He knocked out the doctor on

duty and escaped. The doctor could not give much of a description. Can you?"

My first impulse was to shake my head, but of course I couldn't.

"I think he was tall," I said.

"Why?"

"Where his head hit this steel frame."

I thought the inspector was impressed with my observation.

"Why would someone try to . . . hurt you?" the inspector asked.

"I don't know."

He stepped closer to the bed. His eyes seemed hard. "Have you any enemies?"

"Obviously I do."

"Which of your enemies would try to . . . hurt you?"

Paul said, "You make that sound like an accusation."

"It's very unusual," the inspector said, still staring at me, "for someone to enter a public hospital and attack a patient." He turned suddenly on Paul. "Do you have a blood feud with someone?"

"I am not the most popular man in Bonville," Paul said, "and I've had fistfights with a few men—"

"—We've learned that you once started a brawl with several men in a bistro in Caen," the inspector said. "And the gendarmes in your own village are not unfamiliar with you."

"That's unfair," Mother said. "At no time has Paul ever threatened the life of anyone. And he has made peace with certain people since the events at the castle."

"George Vestien?" the inspector said, expressionless.

Paul almost smiled. "George and I have been brawling for years, but mean as he is, George would never come to a hospital and attack William."

The inspector turned back to me. "You fought with the son, Marc Vestien."

"Marc and I had many run-ins," I said, trying to choose my word carefully, and pushing my voice so I could be heard clearly. "But I can't imagine him coming to Caen and attacking me in the hospital."

"Someone damaged the scaffolding that fell and caused your injury," the inspector said. His mouth moved, and his voice came out normally, but his eyes never wavered, boring into me. I don't think they ever blinked.

"I thought it was an accident," I said, very surprised.

"What about the former mayor, Antoine Bersault?" the inspector asked.

"He's in jail," Paul responded.

"We're aware of that," the inspector said coldly. "He was connected with a gang of international smugglers. Someone—perhaps the same people—made an attempt to steal valuable property from that castle, the Crouching Dragon as they call it, but you and the townspeople thwarted them. Could their associates be seeking revenge for your actions?"

"You might ask the Sûreté," I said.

"I am the Sûreté," the inspector said.

The French secret police? I thought. *What was this all about?*

The inspector spoke to Paul again. "You were a soldier in the war. Did you—do you have friends in Algeria?"

"Not that I know of."

"Enemies—here or there—men who are unhappy with the president's policy?"

Paul straightened. "I think the president is the greatest man in France, and therefore in the world," he said. "I support his policy, whatever it may be. But I have not fought with anyone because of that."

"What about the men in the bistro in Caen?" the inspector asked.

Paul looked surprised. "That—that was different."

The inspector stared at Paul for a long moment. Then he said, "Let us know if any of you remember anything that might explain this attack—anything." He left the room without another word. The policeman in uniform followed, not having spoken at all.

✦ ✦ ✦

After the inspector and the policeman left, Doctor Genet approached the bed.

"When you spoke to the inspector I noticed something, young man," he said. "Despite the steel restraint, I believe I may have detected movement. I'm going to loosen the clamps. For the moment, don't move. You understand: *Don't move!*"

I would have nodded if I could. What I could see of the doctor's hands was reassuring. His fingers were lean, long and looked strong. If he was loosening something, I couldn't feel it. Pang of fear.

"I'm working slowly," he said. "You won't feel anything for the moment." He had understood my fear; he actually seemed to acknowledge that I was a human being—with feelings. I heard scraping, almost like someone was turning an opener on a tin of tuna. I yearned to move my head, but I was afraid to contradict the doctor, afraid to try moving in case I really couldn't. It seemed like an hour before the doctor spoke again.

"Slowly, I mean *very slowly*, and without lowering or raising your head, move your chin one centimeter to the left."

I tried to move my head as I had been told. Nothing happened.

"You're moving your eyes, not your head. Move your head."

I tried again.

"Good," the doctor said. "Move it a little further."

I wasn't aware I had moved at all. I tried again. This time I felt my neck creak. But it was moving. A great feeling of joy began to well up inside me.

"Easy! Now very slowly, and stopping if you feel any pain, move as far to the left as you can."

I ended up with the side of my face on the pillow. I heard somebody crying. It must have been my mother. It was also me. In a few minutes, the doctor had removed the metal restraints. After appropriate warnings about caution in moving and bed rest, he quickly disappeared—even as I was thanking him, which he didn't acknowledge. Then it was time to hug my mother (carefully) and gravely shake hands with Paul.

◆　◆　◆

It was difficult to ask the question, and I was gut-wrenching afraid of the answer. "What about the others?" I asked.

They exchanged glances. "Jean Bourgeois had only minor cuts and bruises. Odile has a few cracked ribs, but they will heal, and Pierre has both legs in casts and is walking with crutches. The two of them clung together and although the scaffolding was breaking, they rode the platform to the bottom. It seems to have partially cushioned their fall."

"André?"

Paul answered. "He's in this hospital; he's been in a coma since the scaffolding collapsed."

"Yes?" I said, unable to put my question in words, feeling the tears welling in my eyes.

"They don't know yet. President de Gaulle, who was informed of what happened, sent a team of doctors from Paris. André is receiving the best medical care."

"Can I visit him?"

"When you feel a little better," Mother said.

"What about Bernard?"

Yet another pause, and then Paul said, "A section of the scaffolding almost exploded as it fell. Metal braces were driven through his chest. He didn't survive."

I felt a deep sense of despair. "I saw the storm coming," I said. "If only . . . " I couldn't finish the thought.

"It's not your fault, Willi," Mother said.

Her choice of words struck me. "Whose fault was it?" I asked.

Paul said, "The police found that several bolts had been loosened and wooden posts had been almost sawed through, then filled to hide the cuts. When the high wind came up, they gave way."

I almost leapt out of bed. "Who would sabotage the scaffolding?—the mayor is in prison, isn't he?"

They nodded.

"The thieves we caught at the Crouching Dragon are in jail, too, aren't they?" I asked.

Again they nodded.

An image came back to me. "As the scaffold collapsed, I thought I saw a face. It seemed familiar, but I didn't know who it was, then or now."

"Willi, you should rest as the doctor said."

"I don't know if I can. What about the project?"

"Too early to tell," Paul said. "Some people now believe it should be abandoned."

That made it certain I wouldn't sleep. I didn't realize that a policeman, the silent one who had accompanied the inspector from the Sûreté, was stationed outside the door to protect me.

❖   ❖   ❖

I stared at André. My friend was lying totally still, attached to many tubes, looking as pale as the sheets and pillows, his eyes closed. They had shaved his head and there was a bandage around it, clean and white and neat. What did it cover? How much of my friend was still there?

I pulled the metal chair closer to the bed and touched his hand, which was very cold. It was very quiet in the room, and I didn't know whether or not I should whisper. At first I did.

"André," I said, "it's me, Willi."

There was no reaction. I curled my warm fingers around his cold fingers, hoping he would respond. He didn't. I tried to speak in a normal voice, but it almost seemed as if a hand were still clutching my throat.

André had suffered more than anyone from the continuing series of mysterious events at the Crouching Dragon. He had been attacked by people we later learned had worked for Mayor Bersault when he chanced upon them killing cattle while chasing his dog near the castle. André was found unconscious and badly injured. In fact, his leg had never recovered from the beating and he still walked with a limp. Now, once again, totally innocent, he had been injured, this time even more seriously. It was so unfair.

"Come on, André, wake up. It's okay. You're okay. Open your eyes. Please."

I thought his breathing changed a little, and I got excited.

"That's it, André! Open up!"

"Shh!" I had almost forgotten there was a nurse in the room and she startled me.

"Sorry." I was back to whispering. But that wasn't right. If I wanted André to be normal, I had to act normal, myself, didn't I? "We have to get back to work on the castle," I said. "We've lost a lot of time and we really need your help." I was straining, trying to hear any change, trying to feel any movement whatsoever. "We're going back to town in a little while, and it sure would be great if you'd come with us."

It was the loudest silence I ever heard. But I wouldn't

allow myself to be discouraged because I was afraid that somehow my discouragement would reach André and he would feel disheartened, too.

I talked to him for a few minutes, saying trivial stuff, hoping the sound of my voice might get through. After a little while, though, the nurse touched my shoulder and gestured towards the door.

When I left, I noticed there was another policeman walking the hall.

✦   ✦   ✦

Odile, Pierre and I, wearing our various casts and bandages, limping and shuffling along, went to inspect the castle along with Louise, the only one outside when the scaffolding fell who hadn't been injured.

A policeman posted at the gatehouse asked us for our identification. While we were fumbling for it, Victor Devereaux came striding up.

"These are the very people who were injured by this vile action," he said, annoyed at the identification procedure.

The policeman drew himself erect and said, "It is my responsibility to—"

"—I'll vouch for them," Victor said, glaring at the policeman, who backed away.

Feeling vindicated, we followed Victor through the gateway.

"I hope you all feel better than you look," he said.

"I'm sorry," I said, "about your friend Bernard."

"He devoted his life to this kind of work. I shall miss him very much."

Victor accompanied us into the ward. A few workmen were collecting debris under the direction of Jean, who waved a somber greeting, then came over and gravely shook hands with us.

"When will you resume work?" I asked.

Jean deferred to Victor, who said, "We're waiting for word from Paris. The government is considering interrupting the reconstruction, at least for a while."

"That would dishonor Bernard, André, and everyone else who worked here," I said.

"I agree," Victor replied. "But it's not in my hands."

"I'll speak to the president," I said.

◆   ◆   ◆

First, I checked with Roger, since it involved him very deeply as well.

"Of course I want the work to continue," he said. "However, I think you should consider the present political situation in France, and ask yourself whether now is the time to ask for the president's assistance"

"Okay," I said. "Help me understand."

"Since 1954—you were nine or ten years old," Roger began, "the native population of Algiers has been seeking independence. They were encouraged by the success of the guerrilla movement in French Indo-China, which defeated France on the battlefield and caused the division of the country into North and South Viet Nam.

"Most European powers built colonial empires in Africa and Asia during the late nineteenth and early twentieth centuries. Some of those peoples were freed voluntarily, and others won their independence by armed struggle. Since the end of World War II, over one hundred new nations have arisen from the colonial empires."

"Do you think Algeria will end up the same way as Viet Nam?"

"Perhaps," Roger said. "There is a world-wide upheaval. In the United States, African-Americans are struggling for the right to vote, the right to unsegregated public schools, and other civil rights. Their movement is non-violent, but the reactions are often brutal."

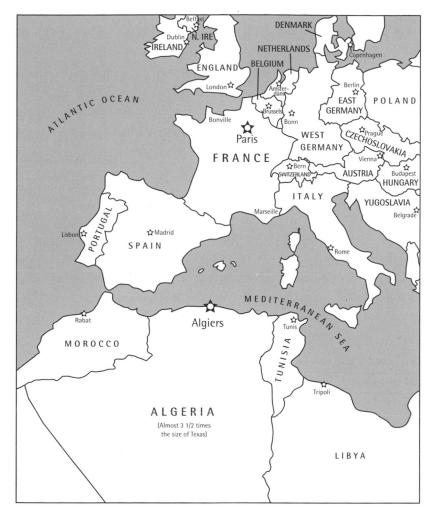

EUROPE & AFRICA - 1961

"Like in France and Algeria," I said.

Roger nodded. "De Gaulle came into power because he offered the hope of a new and stable regime. He traveled to Algiers in June of 1958, seeking the support of the settlers. They gathered by the tens of thousands and thundered, 'Algérie Francaise!'

"De Gaulle replied, 'I have understood you.' The settlers thought that he supported them, but he was only saying that he had heard them. He tried to negotiate peace with the Front Liberation National, the FLN, but failed. After his inauguration as president in January of 1959, de Gaulle instructed General Challe, his military chief, to win the war. Challe commanded a horrible campaign, crushing the rebels with terrifying efficiency and brutality. The campaign was an apparent military success, but it was a political failure. Thousands have been killed—a million people were sent to concentration camps."

"Concentration camps?" I said, incredulous. "I didn't know that."

"They are called 'regroupment camps,'" Roger said. "But whatever the name, de Gaulle has recognized that the war is futile."

"That's why he announced in September that Algeria would have self-determination," I said.

"Exactly, William," Roger said. "However, extremists among the white settlers formed a paramilitary group known as the Front National Français, the FNF—a parallel organization to the native Algerian extremists, the FLN.

"There were daily skirmishes in Algiers—a period called the "Barricades Week"—when settlers and students clashed with the gendarmes, some of whom were massacred, but the military did not intervene. General Massu of the Air Force told a German interviewer that the majority of French officers would not unconditionally obey President de Gaulle."

"I heard the president speak on television in January," I said. "He said he wouldn't give in to would-be usurpers—otherwise France would become a 'poor, broken plaything adrift on a sea of chance.'"

"Yes, but even though the people and military units responded patriotically and the immediate crisis ended," Roger said, "the unrest and violence continue."

"I guess I've been too involved with my own problems to realize how dangerous our situation is in France," I said.

"The point is," Roger said, "at this critical time do you wish to ask the president for help with the Crouching Dragon?"

I hesitated, going over in my mind everything Roger had said.

"To do nothing—to accept the situation," I said, "would give a clear victory here at home to the extremists—the Bersaults, the DragonSlayers, the FNF. I'm going to call the president and let him decide the proper course of action."

✦   ✦   ✦

It was against this background, of which I had been only vaguely aware, that I called the president of France to help with an ancient castle in a small town in Normandy. We had no telephone in our home, so I asked Mayor Donnet if I could use the one in the *mairie,* our tiny town hall in Bonville. Monsieur Donnet readily agreed.

Everyone was surprised at how swiftly I was put through to President de Gaulle. He was courteous, but curt. "Of course the work must go forward," he said. "We can't allow the enemy to thwart us. I must speak to the superintendent of the project."

"One moment, *Monsieur le Président,*" I said.

Victor Devereaux took the phone with obvious trepidation. He said very little, just listened to de Gaulle. "Of course,

Monsieur le Président, everything shall be done as you say. Thank you, I'll put him on."

Silently, but smiling now, he handed the phone to me.

"Are you well enough to travel?" the president asked in his awesome voice.

"Yes, *Monsieur le Président*."

"No bandages or visible scars?"

"No, *Monsieur Le Président*. I don't think so."

"Yes or no?"

"No."

"Good. Then there is no reason you cannot come to Paris."

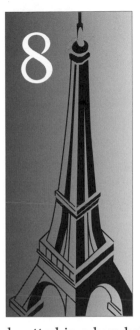

HONORS FOR US

It was the fifteenth of February, 1960, a couple of weeks after my fifteenth birthday. Roger, Louise and I waited in an anteroom, dressed in our best clothing. Louise looked very dignified in a dark green, high-necked and long-sleeved dress that complemented but could not match her emerald eyes. With her luminous black hair pulled straight back from her forehead and knotted in a bun behind her head, she was very striking.

I had seen Louise in pretty clothes before, but never Roger in a suit, white shirt and tie—with polished black shoes. He had also cut his iron-gray hair much shorter and trimmed his beard. Roger actually looked like a professor, very tall and slender and distinguished—not the wild-eyed, wild-haired, scraggly-bearded hermit in a flowing shirt and baggy trousers we had first met.

Mother and Paul had bought me a blue suit—the first new suit I had ever owned—just for this occasion. Louise said the color brought out my blue eyes. Since I knew that her green dress accented her green eyes, I couldn't argue with her. I had struggled to comb my hair flat and neat. Months earlier, just before Louise and I had raced through the tunnel leading from the Crouching Dragon into the town of Bonville through the hidden floor panel in the Church of St. George, the kids had lopped off my hair. They weren't being mean—they did it so the crooked mayor of our town, Antoine Bersault, wouldn't recognize me when we tried to stop President de Gaulle's motorcade. The kids had done a rush job, and even though it was more than six months earlier, my hair still tended to stand up in uneven blonde spikes.

Mother used a funny-smelling pomade to help me look neat.

"This stuff smells like bear grease," I told her as she applied it vigorously.

She just laughed. "You've never been near a bear in your life," she said.

"I figure this is how one would smell," I answered.

"Better to smell like a bear than look like one," she said.

I had wanted to trim my hair down to a very short, even, "brush cut," but mother wouldn't let me, and Paul wasn't going to argue with her, so there I was with my hair parted in the middle and pounded flat on either side. I thought I looked like an ugly, painted toy.

Standing in the anteroom, we could see into the great semi-circular chamber of the *Assemblée National*—the French National Assembly—with its vast white-and-gold ceiling curved like the inside of an egg. Well, half an egg. From the lowest point in the hall at the assembly president's desk, widening, concentric semicircles of wooden benches rose sharply, almost touching the shell.

Mother and Paul were supposed to be sitting in the visitor's gallery along with Louise's parents, M. and Mme Donnet, but I couldn't see them from my viewing angle.

Voices were raised in the Assembly, time and again. The President of the Assembly was a short, vigorous looking man in a black robe, with thick, brown hair, matching brows and a strong nose that came straight out of his forehead. His voice was nasal and penetrating, and he used it often to control the debate.

"Algeria must be free!" a tall, swarthy man standing in the well of the Assembly called out.

A pale, white-haired man with a ponderous belly rose in the third semicircle. "Algeria *is* free!" he cried. "As free as any other department of France—as free as Paris or Marseilles, and fully represented."

The first speaker replied, "The gentleman from Marseilles is subject to delusion. There are eleven million people in Algeria, and less than ten percent of them wish to remain part of France. The world is changing, Monsieur. Like all the great colonial powers, France stole Algeria from its native people one hundred years ago, and now those people want their homeland back."

The pale, white-haired man waggled a finger. "We brought you from primitive beginnings into the twentieth century, gave you railroads and highways, good schools and honest government. One million French have migrated from the mainland or been born in Algeria. What will you do with them?"

The swarthy representative smiled grimly. "You came to us because we had what you wanted. We did not want or need you. You can go or stay as you wish, but Algeria will be free!"

Another white man rose to his feet. "Never!" he cried. "*Algérie Francaise!*"

A brown-skinned deputy in the fifth row rose and responded, "The Vietnamese drove you out of Indo-China, and if you will not give freedom willingly, the Algerian people will drive you from their homeland!"

"War!" Another delegate cried.

"Insurrection!" roared another.

"Treason!" cried yet another.

Dozens of deputies were on their feet, yelling and gesturing. The President of the Assembly was gaveling for silence, and reporters in the press gallery were taking so many flash pictures, the hall seemed to be alive with a glittering, electric, silver-blue light.

The sounds came to us in waves, the voices sometimes clear and sometimes incomprehensible, as the speakers yelled simultaneously.

"Do you think this is a good day for us to be here?" Louise asked.

Roger laughed. "It is often like this. The deputies of the National Assembly rant and roar, but they seldom shoot each other."

"That's not very reassuring," I said.

"Don't worry," Roger said. "I believe the debate is winding down. It's a waste of time anyway. De Gaulle will get what he wants in the end."

There was another roar from the Assembly, as if both sides were responding to Roger's words.

A slim, elderly bald gentleman with a thin fringe of white hair, wearing a severe-looking black waistcoat, appeared in the anteroom.

"It's time," he said. His voice was low and resonant, and there was something frightening and prophetic about it, coming from this man with hollow cheeks and deep set eyes.

✦ ✦ ✦

"*Docteur Guiscard,*" said the Assembly President (in Europe, college professors and other distinguished people are often called "Doctor." They may or may not hold an advanced degree from university, may or may not be medical doctors). "You have done your country an invaluable service by preserving the great collections of the castle known as the Crouching Dragon. You taught young people the historic value of the castle and its many treasures, ancient and modern. Using remarkable engineering skill and great artistic creativity, you designed and built an amazing simulation of the Allied Landings on the 6th of June, 1944, using light and sound and animated scale models of great authenticity. Evil men have since damaged both the tower and your display, but they are being repaired and rebuilt. You, personally, were physically assaulted, but survived the attack and participated in the capture of those villains, with the help of your young comrades.

"You are the fitting heir of your uncle, Armand Moret, one of the greatest collectors of art in all the world, and the friend and associate of the Resistance in World War II, who gave his life for France. You also served with distinction in the Resistance and risked your life for the cause of the nation's freedom. Now, with great generosity, you have given the castle and all its wealth to your country. Doctor Guiscard, the nation accepts this gift with deep thanks, and promises to continue the great work you have begun. We, the members of the National Assembly, and all the people of France, salute you!"

With that, the entire chamber erupted in cheers, members standing and applauding and calling Roger's name. He was an humble man, and this great outpouring of honors and appreciation was overwhelming.

"*Salut! Salut! Salut!*" they cried, again and again.

Two men appeared wearing long formal jackets and white waistcoats, carrying a great parchment scroll, which they slowly unwound.

"We present you with this scroll as a token of the thanks of the French people. It is inscribed with the story of your great work and it has been signed by the President of France, by myself, and by every deputy from every *département* in the nation!"

Again cheers rose. Roger was trying to say "*Merci*," and you could understand the words from the curve of his lips, although you could not hear a sound in the great din of cheers and applause. The president raised his hands and asked for silence, and after a while the chamber subsided.

"We honor here, today, in addition to Doctor Guiscard,

two fine young French citizens, William Montreux and Louise Donnet."

The assembly began to cheer again, but the president waved them to silence.

"These remarkable young people aided Doctor Guiscard in excavating the Crouching Dragon, discovering highly valuable artifacts unknown even to him. They worked together with the youth of the area to establish a virtual kingdom of honor and achievement while rebuilding and restoring the castle.

"Of course," he said, pausing to give us a playful shake of the head, "they did all this without, shall we say, disturbing, their parents or the local authorities. But in the end they understood their responsibilities. They negotiated with President de Gaulle—and believe me, it is no mean feat for mature and trained adults, let alone teenaged youngsters to negotiate with *Le Grand Charles*—a splendid settlement, which led to the gift by Doctor Guiscard of this wonderful castle and all its wealth to the people of France.

"Recently, when criminals tried to steal the treasures and destroy the Dragon Tower, both of you fought bravely and helped capture the marauders. Yet another attempt was made to damage the castle: a leading engineer, Bernard Louis, was killed, several workmen and young people were injured—including you, William Montreux. You were hospitalized and viciously attacked again while you lay almost helpless, but somehow you managed to drive off your attacker. Monsieur Montreux, I do not see how you and your friends could have done any more for the Republic. You and Louise Donnet and all the others are heroes of France!"

Cheers rose again. It was a good thing that Roger had his hand on my shoulder to keep me steady. Louise positively glowed.

"In addition to everything else," the president continued, "the young people discovered a large and sophisticated ring of smugglers which had been stealing livestock. They rescued hundreds of animals and were instrumental in the arrest of the ringleader, the infamous Antoine Bersault."

Angry cries arose from the Assembly, and the name of Bersault was coupled with words I had never expected to hear in such a place.

"This despicable person," the president said, "is now in prison, and we can be sure that the great judicial system of France will guarantee him long occupancy."

At that, a man leaped to his feet in the top row of the hall and cried, "*Vive La France, Vive Antoine Bersault!, Vive Algérie Francaise!*" To our great surprise, the man was Tony Bersault.

For a brief second there was silence in the chamber, and then many deputies rose to their feet. Some were yelling, "*Insult!*" "*Disgracie!*" "*Ignoble!*" But others took up the cry, "*Vive la France!*" and still others, "*Algérie Francaise!*" so that there was great commotion and some pushing and shoving.

Tony was yelling "*Vive Antoine Bersault!*" again and again. Finally, two guards began to drag him away. A couple of deputies actually tried to help Tony, but the guards held them off.

As Tony neared the exit he forced the guards to a momentary halt and cried out, "You will pay—all of you will pay!" But then the guards reasserted themselves and dragged him through the doors. Even after they slammed shut, I thought I could hear him yelling, "You will pay!" and I felt his eyes burning into me.

"*Cellat suffit!*" the president called, once again pounding his gavel.

"I apologize," he said to us, "for this unfortunate interruption. I repeat, France is proud of you, Louise Donnet and William Montreux. We have authorized suitable scrolls for you both. The Assembly has further decreed that a fine bronze plaque shall be affixed to the walls of the castle bearing the thanks of France to all three of you. Then he raised both hands, and cried, *"Vive William Montreux, Vive Louise Donnet, Vive Roger Guiscard, Vive La France!"*

Cheers, more cheers and even more cheers. The President of the Assembly embraced us, we embraced each other, and the flashbulbs popped again and again and again. I couldn't help it as a tear forced itself from my left eye. Louise was not as restrained as I, and she was crying freely.

◆　◆　◆

We were standing on the sidewalk outside the National Assembly with Roger, my parents and Louise's parents. A number of people stopped to congratulate us, and a young male reporter from the great French newspaper *France Soir* asked for an interview.

"I understand," the reporter said to Roger, "that you have been nominated by President de Gaulle to be a *chevalier* in the Legion of Honor."

"You didn't tell us!" I cried.

"It's not certain," Roger said humbly.

"Believe me," the reporter said. 'If the president nominates you, you will be elected."

We all laughed, and Roger mumbled something.

"Speak up," the reporter said. "I need an interview I can use."

With that, he drew Roger aside, near the vast staircase that mounted to the great Greek facade of the National Assembly and began questioning him. Roger looked very uncomfortable.

"Don't worry about him," a lean, severe-looking young woman said, approaching us with a grim expression. "I want to interview young people." A photographer, a rather scruffy guy, was following her, and he was snapping pictures from so many angles that it looked as if he were doing a demented dance. I couldn't help laughing.

"Who are you?" My stepfather, Paul, demanded of the young woman.

"*Le Monde!*" she answered.

"That left wing rag!" Paul exclaimed. "There is no way I will allow you to interview my son!"

"Don't be silly!" the woman said, and tried to brush past him.

"I warn you," Paul said. "There will be no interview today. And if you don't stop that man, I will personally destroy his camera."

"This is a free country!" the reporter said. "You can't do that!"

But Paul was clenching and unclenching his fists, cords stood out in his bull neck, his color was growing red, and even through his suit jacket you could tell how thick his arms were. The reporter seemed to hesitate.

M. Donnet, smiling, took Paul's arm. "Perhaps some other time," he told the reporter. "Please permit our families to enjoy this moment."

"Wait a minute," I said. "What is the harm in answering a few questions?"

My friends and family stared at me, astonished.

"Roger is giving an interview," I said, "why shouldn't we?"

I think I was dazzled by the attention, the flashing lightbulbs—whatever—I was enjoying the entire adventure, and I didn't want it to end.

The reporter was smiling. "What about you," Mademoiselle Louise?"

"Come on, Louise," I said. "We'll do it together."

Louise gave me a long look with those brilliant emerald eyes. "No thank you," she said to the reporter, but she was still staring at me. Everyone was staring at me.

"Okay," I said, "I'll give the interview alone."

"Good for you!" the reporter said. "You are a hero in every way!"

That should have forewarned me, but it didn't.

"My name is Genevieve Artois," the reporter said. "You can look for the interview, along with your photograph, on the first page of the paper tomorrow."

I couldn't help it—the idea of being on the front page of one of France's most prominent newspapers was very exciting.

"Over here, please," Mlle Artois said, "next to the statue of Colbert. Do you know who he was?" The photographer was snapping away.

"I've heard his name, but I don't know much about him," I said.

"A great minister of King Louis the Fourteenth," she said. "He believed in a very strong central government, like your friend, President de Gaulle."

"I wouldn't refer to the president as my friend," I said.

"You don't like him? But he speaks so well of you," she responded, grinning wickedly. Before I could protest, she said, "It's remarkable that you can keep escaping from people who are trying to harm you. Maybe those attacks weren't as serious as you claim."

"I might have been killed when the scaffolding fell on me!"

"But you weren't," the reporter said, still smirking. "You're very lucky, don't you think?"

"You think it's lucky, having thieves trying to shoot me, a building falling on me and somebody trying to strangle me in a hospital bed?"

"It does sound suspicious, doesn't it?" she said.

"You're darn right!" I said. "If you're a good reporter, why don't you find out who's responsible?"

"But if it hadn't been for all these strange and 'suspicious' events, including your fortuitous meeting with President de Gaulle at that castle—what is it called, the spineless dragon?"

"The Crouching Dragon!" I said, my voice rising. I wanted to end the interview, but I didn't want to run away or act like a fool.

"Of course," the reporter said, now giving me a winning smile in place of the smirk, "the Crouching Dragon."

The photographer was still buzzing around me, snapping pictures, occasionally blinding me.

"That so called castle," she continued, "was actually a luxurious chateau owned by a French millionaire, Armand Moret—isn't that right?"

"I suppose so," I said reluctantly, "but it was a real Norman castle."

"With modern plumbing, fancy furnishings and garages for expensive cars," she said, laughing.

"I don't know about the garages," I said.

"Why should the government spend millions restoring an old chateau when there is a civil war in Algeria?" she asked.

"I thought you wanted to hear about my award from the National Assembly," I said.

"You think that's more important than the people dying in Algeria?" she asked, her smile gone, lips pulled back over feral teeth. I realized I was in way over my head.

I started to walk away, but she wouldn't let up. "You think you're too important to answer my questions?" she said.

Roger stepped between us. "That will be enough!" he said.

Mlle Artois gave us a harsh laugh. "I've learned all I need to know," she said and turned away. Her photographer was still clicking as he followed her, moving backwards. He stumbled once and almost fell, but never stopped taking pictures.

"What did she say to you?" Roger asked.

"I—I'm not sure. She was much too quick for me, and I probably gave stupid answers."

"Let's not let anything spoil this great day," Louise said. "Not Tony Bersault and not some crafty reporter."

"Maybe I'm crazy," I said, "but I thought that when Tony said, 'You will pay—all of you will pay,' he was looking straight at me."

"And me," Louise said.

"Why not me as well?" Roger asked. "Why not all of us? The Bersaults were trying to steal the Crouching Dragon and we joined forces to thwart them."

"Yes," Paul said, "and the young people helped get Bersault arrested."

"He had to sell his huge estate in Normandy to pay his debts," Louise said.

Mme. Donnet said, "You humiliated him in front of the president of France and the whole town of Bonville."

"Very true," her husband said. "There are plenty of reasons for them to hate you."

"Now," Roger said, "the Bersaults are fearful that if Algeria becomes independent, they will lose their Algerian property. I'm sure they're connected with the FNF, the paramilitary organization that has been brutalizing the natives."

Paul was getting excited again, saying, "What about the terrorist organization of native Algerians, the FLN? The violence in Algeria was begun by them. The white settlers are only acting in self-defense."

"These strange alphabet names drive me crazy," Louise said. "How is one supposed to tell them apart?"

"By the color of their skin," Paul said.

Mother shook her head. "That's unfair, Paul. In the Resistance there were many whose skin color was not white, and there have always been many Arabs and Berbers loyal to France."

"Jean Bourgeois is one," Roger said.

"I don't understand," I said. "If the French Army is fighting terrorism, why do the settlers need their own army?"

"It's an old story," M. Donnet said. "If you want to do something despicable, something your regular government wouldn't do, you form your own army. Depending on which side you are on, you may be considered a terrorist or a freedom fighter."

"One need not do something despicable to fight for freedom," Roger said, suddenly aroused. "On that basis you might consider the Resistance to be mere terrorists."

"Unfair!" Mother said. "The situation is not the same at all."

"We didn't kill civilians," Roger said.

"You see?" M. Donnet said, "That's the problem. The situation looks different to each of the parties involved. And by the way, there have been very strong rumors that the French Army itself has been guilty of torture and other crimes."

"I certainly wouldn't take Tony Bersault's threat lightly," Roger said. "We know that the elder Bersault is a ruthless man. Tony has a similar reputation."

"Perhaps President de Gaulle can help us," Donnet said. "He certainly has taken a deep interest in the three of you and the Crouching Dragon."

Louise turned to me, and said, "The president offered to bring you to Paris to complete your education under his guardianship. Perhaps now is the time to accept his offer."

I glanced at my parents. "I told him that I preferred to complete my studies at the Lycée in Bonville," I said.

"It was a wonderful offer," my mother said. "I was surprised when you refused it."

"The truth is, I was afraid to leave my home town and take on the big city. Paris is so vast, anonymous and . . . sophisticated. I'm just a country kid."

"I think you can do it, Willi," Louise said. She smiled

with those deep green eyes and lovely mouth in that perfectly oval-shaped face, framed by shimmering black hair. I
never could figure out why a beautiful, intelligent girl like
Louise took such an interest in me, but I wasn't about to
complain.

"Don't worry about us," Mother said. "We only want
what is best for you—and being educated here is the very
best thing that could happen."

"I agree," said Paul.

"William can stay with me," Roger said, "at my apartment in the Rue des Écoles. It's certainly not luxurious, but
there's ample room for the two of us. I'm certain that I can
arrange a program at the university that will enable William
to complete his secondary schooling and take additional
courses in the faculties of arts and sciences of the Sorbonne."

"I've decided I want to be an engineer," I said. Although
the words slipped out of my mouth, I had been thinking
about my future for a while—especially since I found the
cap on the gravestone marked "Alan Stevens," the one that
read "Flying Dragons," and "U.S. Air Force." Maybe my
father was a pilot, and to be a pilot you should be an engineer. Maybe that would help me find my real father when I
finally managed to travel to America.

I know I surprised Roger when I said I wanted to be an
engineer. I'm sure he had expected me to become a historian
and an archeologist like him.

"You'll have to do better at mathematics," my mother said.

"You don't have to make the choice now," Roger said
mildly. "You will be required to take courses in language, art
and literature no matter what your ultimate profession."

"That's fine," I said. "I want to take some courses in history and archeology."

Roger laughed, knowing I had said that for his benefit.

Paul said, "I'm having second thoughts. William is very

young. I don't know if we should put this much pressure on him."

This was the new Paul, quite different from the man who had spent so many evenings drinking in bars and bistros, and far too many knocking me around.

"I agree it will be a great challenge," my mother said, "but I think that William has the intelligence and the energy necessary to meet it."

At that moment, Louise said, "Perhaps my parents would let me study in Paris."

That really got me enthused. "I'm certain the president will help you, too," I said.

The Donnets glanced at each other. M. Donnet, the Latin Master, spoke for both of them: "My wife's sister, Arlene DuBois, lives near the Sorbonne. She and her husband Emile are traveling in the United States, or they would have been here today. We believe the DuBois' would happily agree to having Louise live with them during the school year. If Professor Guiscard can arrange a suitable program, we are in favor of this move."

"I am certain I can arrange it," Roger said.

No one said anything about the Bersaults and the danger to all of us. Would we really be safer in Paris than Bonville?

"I believe," Roger said, "that we should inform President de Gaulle of this decision."

PRESS AND PRESIDENT

We all remained in Paris that night—the Donnets, including Louise, had access to the apartment of her aunt and uncle during their travels, Roger stayed at his own apartment, my parents and I found a modest room at the Hôtel du Louvre.

Roger telephoned the Élysée Palace to request a meeting for us with the president the following day. We had barely checked into the hotel when a messenger arrived carrying my invitation—handwritten by the president on embossed and engraved stationary. Minutes later, Louise called to say that she, too, had received an invitation.

It was difficult for me to sleep that night, and not only because I was resting on a lumpy, rollaway bed. I was very worried about my decision to move to Paris. I had never lived away from home—except during the siege at the Crouching Dragon—and then I was surrounded by dozens of my young friends. I would be staying with Roger, but I knew virtually nothing about Paris, and I would be following a very difficult curriculum.

I also kept replaying in my mind the interview with the reporter from *Le Monde*. I came up with much cleverer replies, which only made me feel worse.

Our families had agreed that in the morning we would meet for breakfast at the dining room of the hotel. Mother and Paul and I were sitting at a table waiting when M. and Mme Donnet and Louise walked in. M. Donnet was carrying a newspaper, and he handed it wordlessly to my parents. Mother and Paul reacted with shock. After an eternity they handed the paper to me.

My photograph was on the front page—in profile next to the statue of Colbert. It looked like I was comparing myself with the powerful minister of the Sun King. Of course, I just looked childish and silly.

The headline read, "YOUNG 'HERO'—DE GAULLE NOT MY FRIEND."

I almost gagged, and I didn't have anything in my mouth. I scanned the article with increasing despair. The reporter referred to me repeatedly as a "hero," but always in quotation marks, and went on say that I had "admitted" that my account of the "alleged" attacks on the castle—even the attack on me in the hospital—sounded "suspicious."

I was described as "young, callow, uninformed and confused," but quite "boastful." What I admired about Colbert was that he had ruled with an iron hand—like de Gaulle. Mlle Artois pointed out that Colbert had been responsible for France's first great wave of colonization, and that like de Gaulle, he didn't want to give up foreign overseas territories.

I sat, head down, staring at the newspaper, but not really seeing anything except how asinine I looked, posturing in front of the National Assembly.

Paul spoke with barely contained fury. "She twisted everything you told her," he said. "She made you sound like a foolish child!"

That didn't help.

"You mustn't blame yourself, Willi," Mother said. "You had no way of knowing she would invent such nonsense."

Louise said, "It's all lies and distortion."

"It's an outrage," said Mme Donnet. "How can they get away with such a thing?"

"I fear," M. Donnet said, "that this sort of thing happens every day."

"I'm going to telephone the newspaper and tell the editor this report was entirely false," I said.

"That won't do any good," Mother said. "They won't admit a thing."

"But this is terrible!" I said. "I'll contact another newspaper and give them an accurate report."

"Do you really want to speak to another reporter?" Paul asked.

I had never felt so frustrated. "How can I dare ask the president to sponsor me in Paris?" I said. "This is how I repay his generosity—giving a stupid interview that casts doubt on the Crouching Dragon and all of our wonderful plans?"

"Perhaps we should speak to Roger," Louise said. "He might know what to do."

"Roger!" I said, almost involuntarily. "What will he think when he sees this garbage?"

"He will say, 'Be as brave as you always are, Willi. Don't let them intimidate you!'" It was Roger, looking stern but resolute, advancing on our table.

"I'm so—"

"—Don't say you're sorry, Willi!" Roger cut me off.

"But how can I face the president?" I asked.

"Now it is even more important that you keep your appointment," Roger said. "You will face the president like a man, not the 'young, callow, uninformed and confused' child the reporter described!"

◆　　◆　　◆

Louise and I walked from the hotel to the palace along the Rue du Faubourg- St. Honor, Paris home of the shops of Gucci, Hermes, Lanvin, Yves St. Laurent, Versace, and other elegant shrines of high (expensive) fashion. We soon reached the tall, arching, black wrought-iron and gold gates of the Presidential Palace. The guards wore dashing uniforms: tall, curving helmets decorated with gold and red feathers, fitted short, red jackets dripping with gold braid and buttons, black jodhpurs and highly-polished black boots. And carrying swords. And rifles. There were about three dozen of them. They weren't smiling.

I handed both of our letters of invitation to the officer at the gate. He accepted them with no expression on his smooth young face, examined them until we began to wriggle nervously—and then returned them to us with a nod.

We entered the stone-paved court, flanked by the low, gray limestone wings of the palace (this was before the entire city had been cleaned and the original soft, sandy tones of the stone revealed), and marched slowly to the columned, pedimented portico that fronted the three story main structure with its tall, mullioned windows and smaller windows in the gray mansard roof. We had barely climbed the steps to the portico and reached the tall, glass doors when they were opened, and an officer in a dazzling uniform appeared. His jacket was black, but the epaulets were edged with gold and rows of colorful ribbons edged his chest. The officer was tall, handsome, with a fine, thin mustache and—a familiar face.

"Major Alain Gerard, at your service."

"You were with the president at the castle—the Crouching Dragon," Louise said, almost shyly.

The major nodded and smiled. I allowed myself to be hopeful because he was smiling.

—"You were a captain, then," I said.

"I have been promoted," the major said, "but I am still the personal aide in charge of personal security for the president." He bowed slightly to Louise and extended a hand to me. I did not know that a handshake could be so formal and yet personal. I almost bowed myself.

"The president will speak to you soon," Major Gerard said. "I assume this is your first visit to the Élysée Palace, and if you so desire, I can give you a brief tour of the public rooms."

"We'd appreciate that," Louise said.

"The room we are in," the major said, "is known as the 'Vestibule of Honor,' where the president greets foreign dignitaries, especially heads of state."

Louise and I glanced at each other, thinking, *What are* we *doing here?*

It was an austere, columned hall with limestone walls and a checkerboard floor paved with white and red marble. We passed through the wood-paneled Salon of Tapestries with its elegant, bright-colored hangings, deep-carpeted floor and glittering chandelier of Bohemian crystal.

Next, the major led us to the Salon Napoleon III.

"Many state dinners are held here," he said.

The walls and the high ceilings were elaborately worked in plaster images, painted and gilded. Enormous, tiered chandeliers hung from individual circular glass cupolas opening to the sky, the ponderous fixtures reaching closer to the floor than the ceilings. The entire floor was carpeted in a rich, glowing floral pattern. Gilded, upholstered chairs ringed the walls, the entire vast ensemble echoed in twenty-foot-high mirrors.

"The next hall," the major said, "is called the 'Winter Garden.' It is no longer exposed to the elements; now it is covered with a greenhouse-style roof, the metal framework painted white. A few austere bushes in white planters are reminders of the hall's past."

Beyond was the great Festival Hall with the same imperial carpeting as the Salon Napoleon III, a high, coffered and intricately-worked ceiling, grand chandeliers, huge historical tapestries, and arched windows high in the walls admitting bright sunlight. The large room was filled with circular tables covered with white tablecloths, and garnished with forests of glassware and plates.

"Tonight," the major said, "there will be a state dinner in this room for the Prime Minister of Great Britain."

He led us through the Salon of the Aides-de-Camp ("named for those in my position," the major said), the Salon des Ambassadeurs, ("where foreign ambassadors are received"), the Salon Pompadour, the Portrait Salon, the Salon Cleopatra ("all for various sized meetings and receptions").

We had a quick glimpse through the palace windows into a walled park with formal shrubbery, sculpture and fountains that backed onto the Champs-Élysées. Then the major led us up a steep, narrow, marble staircase to the private apartments of the president. We entered a relatively small room, which had a modest, coved ceiling and was rather simply furnished, except for the elegant, marble-inlaid round table where the president sat, half-turned toward us, wearing a patterned silk robe over shirt and pants, reading glasses perched on his nose as he wrote with long, powerful strokes of his pen.

This was the first time I had seen the president since the sixth of June, 1959, when I met him at the Crouching Dragon. I had spoken to him on the telephone a few times, reporting on the progress of the restoration and my own progress at school, in which he seemed interested. At his request, I had sent him copies of my school reports from the Lycée in Luc every term. He actually wrote brief notes on some of them, such as "Good work, your understanding of France's international role is developing well," but also, "Please review this material again. Your comprehension is not bad, but your grammar is terrible." I shared some of the notes with Louise, who had been sending reports to the president herself. His comments on her work were always very complimentary. I didn't show her the note about my grammar.

As we entered the room, I was struck by the fact that the president's face seemed more drawn than before, his brow furrowed. My brow was probably furrowed, too, because I wasn't sure how we would be received. Several newspapers were piled neatly on a low table next to his desk; *Le Monde* was on top of the pile.

The major saluted. The president rose to his full, awesome height, returned the salute and—smiled at us. He bowed to Louise, who curtsied, then took my hand in both of his huge hands. His grip was strong, but almost gentle.

"*Monsieur le Président,*" I said.

"*Monsieur le Général de la Château,*" the president responded, slowly releasing my hand and directing us to the gilt armchairs opposite him at the table. The major remained standing, his feet apart, hands held behind his back.

"You look well, William," the president said, "despite your terrible experiences."

"I'm feeling well, *Monsieur le Président,* especially after the wonderful honors conferred upon us by the National Assembly."

"Well deserved," the president said.

"I apologize for the terrible article in the newspaper," I said.

The president smiled. "Even you have come to learn the high risks of dealing with the fourth estate," he said.

I knew enough to understand that the "fourth estate" referred to the press.

"I feel very foolish," I said. "I didn't say most of the things the reporter said I did, and the rest she distorted. For example, I wasn't trying to say you weren't my friend, but rather that I didn't believe I had the right to claim you—the great president of our country—as my friend."

"You may do so, William," the president said, "and I trust I may claim you and Mademoiselle Louise as my friends as well."

"Thank you, *Monsieur le Président*," I said. "I am greatly honored."

Louise was smiling. "I, too, feel deeply honored."

"We hope," I said, "that the newspaper interview won't create any problems with securing funding and continuing the restoration of the Crouching Dragon."

The president said, "After the deplorable attacks on you and the castle, and the sad loss of the gentleman who died during the collapse of the scaffolding, it has become all the more important that the work continue. Sabotage involving a project of the government is a most serious crime, and attacks on citizens involved in the project are even greater ones."

I braced myself for the most important question, but before I could ask it, the president spoke again.

"Because of your integrity, your intelligence and your achievements, and for many other personal reasons," he said, "I am happy you both have decided to come to Paris to complete your education."

I was stunned. Louise said, "How did you know that, *Monsieur le Président?*"

The president smiled. "For a government to succeed, it must have access to superior intelligence—not only the intelligence that comes from trained investigators, knowledgeable analysts or even from spies, but the intelligence that comes from experience with and understanding of other human beings."

"We are happy that you have understood us," I said.

The president looked at me sharply, realizing that I had chosen to use the same phrasing he had used when speaking to the Algerians before he was elected president.

"William," he said, "that is precisely the kind of intelligence I was referring to, but it is rare to find it in one so young. You may rest assured that we will do everything possible to further your studies and to make your life here as pleasant as possible."

We both said, "Thank you very much, *Monsieur le Président.*"

"However," the president continued, "I did not realize, when I originally made the offer, that your personal jeopardy might be this great. In addition to the risks of attempted retribution by the Bersaults, in or out of prison, there is additional danger arising out of their connection with certain elements in Algeria who are our implacable foes, and now, yours as well."

"Do you think they are looking for revenge against all of us?" I asked.

"Perhaps," the president answered. "You must be protected by our security forces."

"Oh, no," I said. "That would be a great embarrassment."

"Injury to you, or to mademoiselle, would be a greater, 'embarrassment.'"

"Forgive me," Louise said, "but I agree with William."

"You assume the security will wear red and gold uniforms like the formal guards of this palace and march beside you. Believe me, you will never know they are there."

We were silent.

The president seemed to brighten. "But I am sure your time here will be very pleasant and valuable. Have you decided what courses of education you will seek?"

Louise said, "I am interested in joining the Foreign Service, but in the meantime, I'll take a basic curriculum in the arts and sciences."

"We both plan to continue our courses in Judo," I said,

"with the famous teacher, Sadayuke Kawaishi."

"The study of self-defense is always wise," the president said. "Judo is now part of the training of our military. But surely you don't intend to make a career in the martial arts?"

"No, *Monsieur le Président*," I answered." I am planning to be an engineer, preferably an aeronautical engineer. I would like to design and build airplanes."

"Very good," the president said. "I have always been acutely aware of the uses of aviation, both civilian and military. I assume you also would like to learn to fly."

"Yes," I said. "Perhaps I'll find a way to take flying lessons."

Louise said, "I hadn't really thought about it before, but I'd also like to learn to fly—someday."

The president offered what seemed, to my surprise, to be a conspiratorial smile.

"Major Gerard," he said. "Do we know anyone who might be qualified to teach these young people to fly aircraft?"

For a moment, I thought the major looked stricken. Then he seemed to rally.

"Of course, *Monsieur le Président*," he said.

The president said, "Perhaps you have not noticed that above the dazzling rows of ribbons—well earned—on the major's chest, there is also a pair of wings. The major was originally in the Air Force, detached from that service on the recommendation of the chief of staff. At the time, I believe he was not terribly happy at being assigned to administrative duties here."

"Quite true," the major said, "but I have never regretted this assignment."

De Gaulle smiled. "Very loyally spoken. When in the Air Force, the major was a highly qualified instructor, both in propeller and jet aircraft."

"There is a squadron at Le Bourget field, and training

aircraft are based there," the major said. "If the president authorizes your lessons, I would be pleased to be your instructor."

"I shall issue such an order immediately," the president said. "I hold you personally responsible for their safety, Major. At times William can be a very rash young man."

The president stood up and took my hand in both of his. His voice was more gentle than I had ever heard it before.

"We are soldiers together in a very different kind of war. It is our responsibility to be brave and intelligent. May God bless you."

"Thank you, *Monsieur le Président*," I mumbled in a slightly uneven voice. "I promise to do my very best."

Then he took Louise's hand and astonished her by bending low and brushing it with his lips.

SORBONNE

Paul drove me into Paris in his beloved truck. We entered from the southwest through the Port de St. Cloud, immediately crossing the Seine and traveling alongside it into the city. We were on the "Left Bank" of the river, meaning that we were heading "upstream," the flow of the Seine towards the coast being opposite to our direction.

At one time there had been *quais*—wharves and piers—along the river, and there still were some at the southwest end of the city. But now these were primarily "quais" in name only, with walkways and roadways, but little marine traffic, except for the occasional barge and the sightseeing boats—for example, the *Bateaux Mouches.*

We passed the Eiffel Tower, that three-hundred-meter-tall concoction of soaring, interlacing steel that looks like a child's erector set gone mad. Although many of the greatest cultural figures of the time detested it, the Eiffel Tower has been the symbol of the city since it was erected for the *Exposition Universelle* in 1889. It has no grand scientific, cultural or societal value, except that it is graceful, provides wonderful views of the entire city, and now functions as a beacon for low-flying aircraft—and carries the antennae for radio, television and telephones.

Paul drove us past the Palais Bourbon, home of the National Assembly, and turned into the Boulevard St. Germain. Repeatedly thwarted by one way streets, we finally pulled up in front of No. 45 Rue des Écoles. We were in the Latin Quarter, so called because it was the original Roman part of the city. Around us were random groupings of the various faculties of the University of Paris, the Sorbonne—named for the canon, Robert of Sorbon, who had persuaded King Louis IX to found a college for poor theology students some seven hundred years earlier. All of the buildings were built of the same, now dirty-gray limestone, most five or six stories high, except for the soaring, rounded chapel dome. I felt that I had entered into a mysterious stone paradise.

Facing the sidewalk were double wooden doors, carrying innumerable coats of paint, but now a heavy green, wide enough to admit an automobile. A smaller door for people was fitted into one of the large doors. We pushed the buzzer next to the name Guiscard (there were six names—one for each of the apartments on each of the floors), but almost immediately the large doors swung open and Roger came rushing out, all smiles and handshakes and hugs. The arched passageway led to the building entrance and a small parking area behind it.

Roger hefted one of my bags, keyed open the wood-and-glass entrance door to the building, and led us into a tiny vestibule. To my surprise there was an elevator that rose in the center of an open staircase spiraling up around it. The stair railing, the framework that enclosed the elevator and the elevator itself, were of ornately-woven, wrought-iron and steel, which gave the construction a light, airy feeling, but wasn't reassuring from the standpoint of sturdiness and safety.

Roger pulled open the glass and wood doors of the elevator, and we entered the steel cabin. A push of a button and we jolted up, swaying and occasionally banging on the surrounding metal framework—the wheels, pulleys and weights squealing.

"Probably needs grease," Roger said. "I'll speak to the landlord."

Paul was silent, probably trying to hide his apprehension as the elevator banged and rattled its precarious way upward. A long time later I would learn that was the first time he had ever been in an elevator. I had been in one before, at the Hall of Records in Cherbourg, when I had traced the ownership of the Crouching Dragon to Roger, but it was enclosed in solid walls, so you didn't feel as if you were suspended in a casually swinging birdcage. Also, the Cherbourg elevator was operated by a human being; this was my first *automatique.*

Roger's apartment was on the sixth level—called the fifth floor because the lowest floor was called *Le rez-de-chaussée,* the ground floor, and only the upper floors were numbered. Brass buttons had been rubbed to a smooth, glossy finish by the pressure of many hands, so that the panel and buttons seemed surprisingly bright compared to the dull black metal cabin. The wooden floor was slightly warped.

When we exited onto a small landing at the top of the stairs, I noticed that to reach the roof you had to use iron rungs built into the wall with a little hutch and an access panel above. That didn't seem important at the time.

There was neither a name nor a number on Roger's apartment. Dark-brown-toned, double wooden doors opened from the landing into a tiny vestibule intersecting a long hall, which bisected the apartment from front to rear. The stairs, landing and elevator shaft took a notch out of the space on each floor.

Opposite the front doors and opening onto the long hall was the small kitchen, which had a single, double-hung window that opened onto an air shaft, itself notched into the building. Next to it was the lone bathroom with a glazed window that opened onto the same blind shaft. The wall of the building next door as seen through the windows was solid brick, but if you leaned out and looked up, you could see a small patch of sky, partially obscured by an antenna.

Walking towards the front of the apartment, there was a small dining room next to the kitchen, and across from it a small bedroom, or office. The hall ended at the parlor, which covered the entire street-width of the building, and boasted four tall windows and wrought-iron balconies.

To the rear, past the kitchen, the hall widened into a small vestibule, leading to two side-by-side bedrooms with windows that opened onto the back courtyard. The larger bedroom—three windows—was Roger's; the smaller bedroom—one window—was to be mine. There was a fire-escape outside of Roger's windows. The building across the courtyard was one story shorter, so there was a view from our windows across the roofs and chimney pots of Paris all the way to the tops of bell towers and the spire of the Cathedral of Notre Dame.

When Louise saw the view she said she was immediately reminded of a movie she had seen based on Victor Hugo's nineteenth century novel, *The Hunchback of Notre Dame*. A few years afterwards, I saw a movie derived from a book by an English writer, P.J. Travers, called *Mary Poppins*. The story took place in early-twentieth-century London, but the scenes on the roofs and the lines of chimney pots reminded me of my room in Paris.

The furnishings of the apartment were simple: a large padded sofa and three unmatched, upholstered armchairs, plus a couple of low tables and floor lamps completed the parlor. From the narrow wrought-iron balconies there were interrupted views of some of the structures that comprised the Sorbonne. Through one opening, I saw the dome of the Pantheon, where many French heroes were buried. In the street below, students and faculty trooped to and from their lycées and colleges.

"This is great," I told Roger.

"You won't have much time to enjoy the views," he answered, and Paul nodded vigorously.

Every room of the apartment was filled with books, some on shelves, many piled on the floors. Even the kitchen had books piled under a small table. In Roger's bedroom books and papers were stacked as high as the ceiling—in some places, three tiers deep. Hundreds of books were piled randomly in the front parlor, and there really wasn't a usable dining room, because the space was almost completely filled with books, many perched on the dining table and chairs. Although I couldn't detect any order, Roger would often go directly to a pile, remove a dozen or more books, and grab exactly the one he wanted.

The room opposite the dining room had been converted to an office, with a drafting table for a desk, and many drawings and photographs piled here and there. And books.

I shouldn't have been surprised at the number of books. Roger's living quarters in the Crouching Dragon had been filled with thousands of them. But those were stacked on shelves; in the Paris apartment, there weren't any.

"I've been meaning to build shelves," he told me, "but there hasn't been time, what with all the research I've been doing under the city and the classes I've been teaching."

I didn't know what he meant about researching "under the city," but it sounded ominous.

I hadn't brought much with me to Paris; I didn't have much. Mother and Paul had bought me a couple of pair of pants, a jacket and another pair of shoes to go with the rest of my slender wardrobe—which featured the fine blue suit they had bought me for the ceremony in the National Assembly. I also carried a few books that I had cherished for a long time, including the tale of Roland, the great French hero of medieval times, and French translations of books by J.R.R. Tolkien: the *Hobbit,* and the three books of *The Lord of the Rings.* I had been studying English in school, and I hoped to re-read those books in their original language, but my English wasn't good enough—yet.

Roger had told us he had enough bedding, sheets, towels and such, so I didn't bring any. He had also said he owned cooking utensils and dishes. In fact, he had four plates, four bowls, four forks, four knives and four spoons. Well, there were only two of us and we weren't going to give any big parties. Oh, and I forgot, he did have eight fairly large glasses and three coffee mugs—no saucers

I was surprised at the simple, spare quality of Roger's belongings because I assumed he had inherited some good things from his wealthy uncle, Armand Moret. However, the Nazis had carried off most of the valuable items. When he gave the castle to France, Roger had included anything of historical worth that was left.

◆   ◆   ◆

"You'll take most of your courses at the Lycée de Paris and a few at the colleges," Roger said. "You've got a lot of work to do to catch up with the students who are entering the university after completing their baccalaureates."

In appearance, the Lycée was indistinguishable from the other buildings that made up the district of the Sorbonne. Five stories, with no elevator, wide stairways, high ceilings and clad in the usual limestone. All of the classrooms seemed to be identical rectangular wood and plaster boxes, with blackboards on one wall, many wood and wrought-iron seats and wooden desks, windows high (and usually dirty), chandeliers, but not much light.

Roger introduced me to the Director, Monsieur Rideau, who was courteous but curt. Soon I was established in classes in Literature, Social Science and Mathematics. The students came from all over France, her colonies and former colonies. There were boys and girls with black, brown and yellow skin and many shades in between. French was spoken with some variation in accents, but less than I expected. I was surprised that some students from East Asia spoke a purer French than those from Marseilles with their broader southern rhythms, or others from Alsace who spoke in harsher, Germanic tones.

The work was even more difficult than I had expected. In the literature classes they were reading translations of Shakespeare's plays from the English, Goethe from the German and Dante from Italian.

In mathematics, I had to take remedial courses in Algebra and Geometry because the other students were deep into calculus, statistics, and other subjects I hadn't even heard of.

Louise was registered in some of my courses, although her math was far advanced over mine. Louise was taking more university courses than I was, including college-level physics and chemistry. I wasn't ready for the advanced science classes—the ones I would eventually need if I was going to be an engineer.

I took a survey course in archeology, which Roger taught to first year college students. Fortunately I knew the teacher, who gave me additional instruction in the evening.

◆　◆　◆

We were waiting impatiently to hear from Major Gerard about flying lessons. In the meantime, Roger took Louise and me to the studio of the great Judo master, Sadayuke Kawaishi. His dojo was located in a loft on the top floor of a building on the Rue Clovis, near the church of St- Etienne du Mont, not far from the Pantheon. The studio was much larger than I expected, with a ceiling six or seven meters high. Most of the light came from rows of fluorescent fixtures that cast an even glow over the entire room. No columns interrupted the space, which was approximately fifteen meters wide and thirty meters long. The walls were wood-paneled, with windows above them on both the front and rear walls.

Except for a wooden margin, the entire floor was covered with mats. At least two dozen students were engaged in one exercise or another, some in remarkable unison, others in free patterns. All wore the judogi, the plain white costume, although they were distinguished by many colors of belts.

Along the street side, there were tiers of wooden benches with people eagerly watching the floor exercises. Except for slapping sounds as some struck the mats, and a few grunts, the room was almost totally silent. Even when the people engaged in practice spoke to each other, it seemed like a silent movie; you could not hear their voices.

Roger led us around the wooden margin to a single door in the far wall. A handsome young man in a judogi appeared, smiled, and opened the door for us. I felt like I was entering a religious shrine.

Inside, kneeling on a mat, was a very small, very old man, with wispy white hair arranged neatly on his head and a long, iron-gray mustache with drooping ends, wearing a crisp, white judogi and a black belt. His face was heavily seamed in a precise pattern that seemed to radiate in concentric rings from his oval eyes, which were black and penetrating, even though hooded by smooth lids. He seemed frail and powerful at the same time.

The three of us bowed from the waist, touching our fingers to our legs above the knees, and the *Sensei*, the Master—for it was obvious that this must be Sadayuke Kawaishi—bowed forward, placing his hands on the mat.

When he again sat upright, he gestured to us that we might kneel on the mat as well, which we did.

"Welcome," the master said, in a voice that was gentle, but projected strongly. Although the single word sent new circles radiating from his mouth and eyes, his expression was warm and youthful.

We bowed again, this time from the kneeling position to the mat, and then Roger said, "Thank you, Master, for permitting us to meet with you."

"Doctor Guiscard," the master said, "are your young friends trained in the Kodokan Judo?" He spoke very precisely, in French that was easily understandable, despite a sibilant murmur underneath each word.

"This is Mademoiselle Louise Donnet and Monsieur William Montreux," Roger said. "Yes, Master, they have had some very basic training, and they are most anxious to continue their studies under your illustrious guidance."

Kawaishi Seinsei smiled, a fleeting smile, but it lighted all the niches and crevasses of his face. "Their names are not unfamiliar to me. I am aware of their exploits, worthy indeed of you as their mentor, Doctor Guiscard."

Roger bowed and responded, "Their accomplishments have little to do with me, although I am always happy to aid in furthering their education."

"You know," the master said, "that I no longer participate actively in the instruction of students, although I supervise the work of my teachers. I must observe these young people in the kata so that I may make appropriate recommendations. I will arrange judogis for them."

He signaled almost imperceptibly, and two assistants, one male and one female, appeared, and bowing, led us to the dressing rooms. In the men's dressing room, the young man silently assigned me a locker and proffered a freshly laundered uniform. Then he disappeared. I dressed quickly, and, going into the hall, met Louise, who looked perfect in her judogi. I realized that she had probably anticipated the test, because her hair was already tightly knotted in a bun on her head when we arrived at the studio.

We smiled at each other, and returned to the master's office in silence.

When we entered, Master Kawaishi rose from the kneeling position simply by rocking back on his feet and standing up. His posture, unsurprisingly, was erect, but relaxed. He walked easily, athletically, with a stride that belied his seventy-plus years.

As we entered the dojo there was immediate, total silence and every activity ceased. It was amazing to see so many figures frozen in graceful poses, any one of which would have made a powerful sculpture. Kawaishi nodded and the activity resumed—as if a motion picture freeze frame had started up again.

It wouldn't be accurate to say that I was frightened, but I certainly felt apprehensive. Louise and I were going to be on trial. We couldn't even be certain the master would accept us as students.

Until then I had hardly noticed the appearance of the male assistant, but now I saw that he was approximately my size, though a few years older. His eyes were brown, his features were even, regular, and his black hair was clipped short; I guessed that he was of European heritage, but he had as yet said nothing, so I couldn't evaluate his French.

I glanced quickly at the female assistant, and it took only a single look to see that she was an extremely pretty young woman with Asian features and black hair as lustrous as Louise's. I wondered when, if ever, the four of us would be introduced.

We all bowed appropriately. The master told us what exercises we would perform, and as we progressed, he added instructions. We began with a series of falls from various positions, and then we each performed a number of throws, both as initiators and the accepters of the action. Lastly, we engaged in grappling.

I was aware that others in the dojo were watching. They had not stopped to stare; that would have been rude and totally contrary to the rules of Judo, and I was concentrating so hard that everything else was crowded out of my consciousness.

I didn't stumble, or miss a hold, or grimace, or fall except when I was supposed to—at least I wasn't making humiliating mistakes. It seemed like the test went on for an hour, but Roger later told us that it took only fifteen minutes.

When we had completed our assignments, I anxiously awaited the master's evaluation. At his signal, the young man I was working with bowed and told me that his name was Jacque Rouen—and his accent was definitely French.

The young lady who had been working with Louise identified herself as Mai Pham (I learned to spell their names later). Her French seemed as pure as Jacques.'

The master said, "Please work out a schedule together—not more often than twice a week, but you may practice yourselves on other days if the dojo is not filled."

He bowed, we bowed, and—that was that.

Roger, who had been watching quietly, walked over to us, smiling.

I couldn't resist asking Jacques, "How did I do?"

He cocked his head, smiled slightly and said, "You have promise."

Mai said approximately the same thing to Louise.

Roger sensed our disappointment. "It is a great privilege to train in the dojo of the Sensei," he said.

"Jacques and I were watching television on the day you were honored by the National Assembly," Mai Pham said.

"When we heard that you might be coming to the dojo, we requested the assignment of working with you."

"That's flattering," I said. "I hope you don't expect too much of us."

Mai gave me a surprisingly warm smile. "Judo will enable you perform even greater acts of heroism."

I think I blushed, but I sure didn't know how to respond.

Roger said. "You may want to arrange your sessions for a time before your classes start."

On most days our classes began a little after eight in the morning, so the idea wasn't thrilling.

"I like that," Louise said. "How about you, William?"

"Well," I said, feeling trapped. "On Tuesdays and Thursdays my classes don't start until 9 A.M."

"My classes begin at the same time," Jacques said. "I can be here at 7:30."

I wanted to groan but I didn't dare.

"That would also be a good schedule for me," Louise said. "It's up to Mai."

Mai gave me a quick look before she replied. "I know I can rearrange my schedule to fit yours, Louise. So it's settled."

"You still don't recognize me," Jacques said to me.

That was really embarrassing; it's a terrible feeling when someone says you know them, but you don't.

"I'm sorry," I said.

"I'm in Doctor Guiscard's 9 A.M. Archeology classes on Tuesdays and Thursdays," he said.

That was really embarrassing; I think I turned purple.

Roger was laughing. "I have students from many different grades."

Mai was laughing, too, but in a somewhat different way. "There are others who would like to meet you," she said, staring first at me, and then turning to Louise. "Perhaps at the break we can meet in the corridor outside."

"We should get dressed," I said.

Roger said his goodbyes, and we went back into the dressing rooms to put on our street clothes. Jacques told me the locker would be assigned to me permanently and the judogi was a gift from the master. I dressed hurriedly, curious to know who wanted to meet us—particularly if there might be other girls as good-looking as Mai.

At the break, Mai and Jacques led us out into the corridor. To our surprise, there was a row of young people standing by the outer wall of the building—smiling.

"May I introduce our friends?" Jacques said, and then spoke a series of names. There was a Robert and a Thomas, a Marie and a Nina, a Mohammed and a Marcel. I think I also heard Richard, Nicolas and Félice. I bowed so many times that my head was almost rocking in its socket.

After the introductions, the line broke and our new friends surrounded us.

The questions came one after another and some on top of the others. "Tell us about the Crouching Dragon," "Did you get to see the president?—What is he like?" "Where do you live?" "What do you think of the master?" and on and on.

"Hold it!" Mai said. "They don't even know who we are? Shouldn't we explain?"

Jacques said, "We have heard and read so much about you, that we believe we are familiar with you, which we aren't."

"Some of us," Mai said, "like Mohammed, Marcel and Richard, attend classes at the same school as you do, the Lycée de Paris. Others—Robert, Thomas and Marie, are already students at the Sorbonne."

"And some of us just work for a living," a guy said, "like me. I'm Richard—Nina, Marie and Nicolas also have full time jobs."

"But we all have something in common," Jacques said.

"We're members of a group we call *Le Clandestin*—the underground. That was another name for the French Resistance during the war. Each of us has relatives who were active in the Resistance, and we consider ourselves the Resistance, Second Generation. But we use the name Clandestin because it sounds more secret and mysterious."

Louise said, "We should have used that name when we were secretly occupying the Crouching Dragon."

"Exactly!" Mai said. "That's one reason we though you might want to join us. But let's go to our favorite bistro, *Le Dragon Enragé.*"

"The Raging Dragon?" I asked.

"Yes," Mohammed said. "Your dragon crouches and ours rages, but a dragon is a dragon."

"Just a minute," Louise said. "Willi's mother and even his godfather, Roger Guiscard, were in the Resistance, but no one in my family was part of that honored organization."

Jacques said, "Because of your close relationship with William and Professor Guiscard, we are prepared to make an exception."

"Yes," Mohammed said. "You will be considered an honorary member of the Resistance."

"And," Marcel said, "a fully qualified member of Le Clandestin!"

✦ ✦ ✦

My experience with bistros was limited to three: one in Bonville that Paul had been barred from, another in the seaside town of Luc, where Paul had gotten drunk night after night, and started fights with the patrons, and the last in Caen, where Paul was arrested for fighting with the owner and some customers. As a result I wouldn't have been very enthusiastic about going to one in Paris, except that the name intrigued me.

The Raging Dragon was located in the Place St. Michel,

within sight of the Seine and the famous island named Ile de Cité that bore the Palace of Justice, the Conciergerie, the exquisite chapel known as Sainte-Chapelle and the great cathedral, Notre Dame. I soon learned that the square was filled with students, night and day.

Above the door to the bistro hung a wooden sign with a dragon painted on it that looked very much like our Dragon Tower on the night of the explosions, with flames roaring from its mouth, eyes glaring, body coiled for the attack—except it still had a lower jaw.

"Just like home," Louise said, and I agreed.

"We chose this place," Jacques said, "because there was a violent scuffle in the square in 1944 when students connected to the Resistance confronted Nazi troops."

"That's true," Mohammed said, "but mostly Jacques chose it for the pretty girls who gather here."

"Speak for yourself," Jacques said.

"I am," Mohammed answered. He was a tall, rangy,

young man with smooth, *café au lait* skin, large, crinkly brown eyes and a wide mouth that displayed perfect teeth in a dazzling smile. Later, I learned that he was only a year older than I was, but he seemed much more grown-up and sophisticated. He was: his father was a high-ranking French diplomat of Berber heritage, who had been posted by the government to many countries, and Mohammed, his mother, and his sister Chérie, had traveled with them. He spoke several languages, including English, Spanish, Arabic, and Vietnamese from their days in French Indo-China (later Viet Nam).

The street facade of the Raging Dragon, about fifteen meters long, was framed in waist-high, bright-green metal panels, topped with small, mullioned windows. The front door was usually blocked open, and the flow of people, mainly students, was continuous. As you entered, on the left was a U-shaped dark wooden bar, with patrons three deep, and on the right, many small, spindly metal tables with wooden tops and skinny, metal chairs. Every seat was occupied and people were standing everywhere. Laughter rang through the bistro, and the sound level verged on uproarious. Unfortunately, the air was filled with cigarette smoke.

The bartenders seemed as young as the patrons, and instead of uniforms they wore white, short-sleeved shirts and a motley assortment of pants. There was no table service; food could be ordered at a high, narrow wooden counter in front of the kitchen, from which a variety of dishes was conveyed at a rapid rate to a line of patrons that often stretched to the door. The food smells were good—they would have been better if there wasn't so much smoke in the air—and despite the pace, the servings looked ample and appetizing.

Mai took my arm and worked me through the crowd to a door at the back of the dining area. She pushed it open and yelled (something obscene?) at a couple of kids drinking beer with their feet up on a table. They hurriedly grabbed their beers and got out of the room.

"Perfect, isn't it?" she asked, encompassing the room, maybe six meters square, with such an expansive gesture you would have thought it was a vast auditorium. She was laughing and so was I. It was nice to laugh with Mai, who had a truly engaging smile that narrowed her oval eyes, but did not extinguish the sparkle.

Louise and the others were now inside; a couple of them already held beer bottles or wine glasses, and I wondered how they managed to get served so quickly.

"Now that you're safely here," Mai said, "I'm going for a glass of wine. One for you, too?" she asked me.

I was fifteen years old, and I sometimes had wine with dinner at home, as most French kids did. On a few occasions, I had gone to a restaurant in Caen with my mother and stepfather and been allowed a glass of wine, but I had never been in a bar without my parents, let alone had an alcoholic drink.

"No thanks," I said.

Mai shrugged and left the room.

"We meet here every couple of weeks," Jacques said.

"How many of you are there in the group?'" Louise asked.

"Oh," Jacques said, "about a hundred."

"A hundred!" I said, looking around the room, which seemed crowded with less than a dozen.

"Jacques is talking about total membership," said a pert, round girl, named Nina. "About three dozen are active, and the real core is the group that attends the studio of Master Kawaishi."

Mohammed said, "About twenty of us attend the dojo on different days of the week. A few go to the studio of

Master Kim, who teaches karate, similar to Judo, but more offense-minded."

"May I ask why you have formed this organization?" I asked.

"At first," Jacques said, "there were just a few of us who met socially because we attended schools and colleges in the neighborhood. Later, we learned that each of us had a relation who had been in the Resistance. Then we discovered we had something else in common—an interest in Judo. My uncle was a student of Kawaishi Sensei, and he told us that the Master had been a good friend of the Resistance and trained many of them, so we transferred from our other dojos."

"In time, the group grew in numbers," Mai said. "Robert de Cotte is the oldest of us, an ancient twenty-nine."

Every one laughed, including Robert, an angular-faced man with a shaved head, quite tall, with very broad shoulders and a powerful chest that was accented by the tight t-shirt he wore.

"I'm one of the founding, uh, fathers," Robert said. "I began meeting with a few others ten years ago. Mai, who is seventeen, is the youngest. The others are almost all the ages in between."

Mai had returned, carrying two glasses of a red wine, and handed one to me.

I didn't see how I could refuse, so I set it down on the table. She was sipping her wine, staring at me over the top of her wine glass. I decided to change the subject.

"Do you have any other purpose other than social?" I asked. "I mean, what is there to resist these days?"

Most of the kids were laughing, but a guy named Nicolas said, rather stiffly, "The government."

"Nicolas claims to be a communist," Mai said, "but he lives in a huge apartment on the Boulevard St. Germain, and his father is a powerful industrialist."

"All the more reason to resist!" Nicolas said.

"Who?" Jacques asked, "Your father?"

Nicolas turned red, stood up, and marched out of the room.

"Hey, come back," Mai cried after him, but he didn't return.

"He's a pretty good guy," Robert said, "but sometimes he gets very self-righteous."

"Let's be fair," Nina said. "A lot of people in the French Resistance were communists—including Jean Paul Sartre."

"Yes," Jacques said. "However, then we were fighting the Nazis together. There's no reason today why we should be fighting each other."

"Are you forgetting Algeria?" Félice asked.

"What has that to do with communism?" Robert asked.

And then an argument began. Louise and I sat, listening. We had never heard some of this stuff before, and had no idea who—if anyone—was right.

"Time!" Robert cried out, and everybody stopped talking.

"We can argue these political matters as much as we like," he said, "but we haven't answered William's question."

The others agreed.

"This isn't a debating society," Robert said, "and the reason we call ourselves Le Clandestin is not because we are plotting against the government—ours or anyone else's. Aside from drinking and laughing together, we have formed a private association to show our respect for our relatives who fought so bravely by doing public service of our own. We volunteer during emergencies, as when there is an accident in the Metro, or a very bad storm and help is needed. We work privately, without seeking recognition. The Resistance had many heroes, and few of their names were known. We make no claims and seek no credit."

"That sounds good to me," Louise said. "Why the Judo?"

"We never know," Robert said, "when some people may attempt to take advantage of an emergency by looting or other violent acts. We want to be ready to stop them if the police or the army isn't there."

"There is another aspect of our work," Nina said. "One of the important things the Resistance did was to provide a means of communication, unknown to the Nazis, where information could be shared and people in danger could be forewarned."

"Robert," Jacques said, "has provided us with short-wave radios and other equipment so that we can communicate in an emergency."

"You all have radios?" Louise asked.

"Not all," Robert said. "We have nine main locations, which we call bases, where there are radios. The Clandestin in charge of those radios know how to reach the others, if only by running and knocking on doors."

Louise asked, "Have you ever had to deal with an emergency?"

"The older members have handled many," Mohammed said. "But even I, a recent member, have been able to help. Last autumn there was a sudden storm that flooded the Marais section. It's one of the oldest parts of Paris, and some of the streets collapsed. Emergency vehicles couldn't get through, but we were able to use our little radio network to direct individual health workers to where they were needed. We may have helped avoid an epidemic from dangerously polluted water."

"Who knows?" Nina said. "Maybe some day we'll be able to do something really important."

✦ ✦ ✦

When Louise and I finally left the Raging Dragon a few hours later, we were quite happy—pleased to have been accepted by Master Kawaishi, and excited about making new friends. Mai had paid me considerable attention, sitting very close to me. That didn't mean much; the place was so crowded that you couldn't sit or stand anywhere without touching someone. But I was flattered by the attention of a pretty woman—an "older" woman.

At the same time, I was all too aware that Jacques was taken with Louise. He was too old for her, wasn't he? A twenty year old with a girl of fifteen? I was the one who finally said, "Louise and I are late."

In fact, Louise and I weren't quite ready to go home. After leaving the Raging Dragon, we turned, without saying a word, to walk along the Seine. Louise tucked her arm in mine as we strolled. It was evening and the winter sky was clear and sharply black, filled with a luxurious throw of stars. The little hutches selling cards, drawings and *objets d'art* were closed, shuttered for the night; the painters and pastellists were gone; but there were many strollers along the promenade. Light from the jewel-faceted street lamps filtered through the spare branches, and here and there a match flared as someone lit a cigarette. Along the Quai de Montebello we were enthralled by the vision of Notre Dame, silvered by powerful spotlights. The great arches and buttresses, towers and spires, were filigreed like lace against the sky; the great cathedral seemed to be an artist's shimmering overlay on a dark canvas.

I said, "I feel as though I could reach out and lift the cathedral from its frame, roll it up carefully, and carry it away with me."

Louise gave me a brief kiss. "There's a touch of a poet in you, William Montreux."

"On a night like this, with a woman like you, there would be a poet in any man," I said.

And then we embraced and kissed. Of course, we weren't alone. Paris, especially along the banks of the Seine, is famous for its lovers. The thought gave me pause: Love. Was that what I felt for Louise? Of course. But what kind of love? I had known her since childhood, but only very casually until our adventures at the Crouching Dragon. Were we affectionate friends—or more?

Louise moved away, very slightly, and pointed across the street to some large, illuminated windows.

"That's the world famous restaurant," she said, "called *Tour d'Argent.*"

"The silver tower?" I said. "A lovely name, but why?"

"Perhaps because of the glorious view of the cathedral of Notre Dame—illuminated as it is now."

"Of course," I said, but I would later learn that it was because of the champagne stone with a silver reflection of which the restaurant building was built—the same stone used for the Notre Dame.

"One day we'll have dinner there," I said

"It has many Michelin stars and it's very expensive," Louise said.

"That won't stop us," I said, crossing my fingers.

THE DESERT FOX

❢❢"The Desert Fox."

We were standing on the tarmac at the fenced-off military aviation section of Le Bourget Airfield, just a few minutes southwest of Paris. There were several huge hangars in a long line and many aircraft in camouflage tones of green, gray, beige and brown. Some were jets—swift-looking pursuit planes and bombers; some were propeller aircraft, including large cumbersome cargo planes. All wore the French Tricolor, three vertical stripes of red, white and blue, the gold *fleur-de-lis,* and mysterious sets of numbers and letters.

"I've seen aircraft like these in movies," Louise said, "but standing here, so close to them, they seem really ominous."

"They are warplanes," Major Gerard said. "They are designed to look ominous." But he said it mildly, not as if he were trying to impress or frighten us.

At that moment, a flight of jet fighter aircraft roared so low overhead it seemed I could touch them, the noise deafening, shaking the air and the ground, leaving black clouds and an acrid smell behind them. "How long before we can fly those?" I asked.

The major laughed, then turned to the aircraft beside us and repeated what he had said before: "The Desert Fox. Its name is actually *Fennec,* which is a small animal. We think of it as a fox—our enemies as a rat. I flew this type of aircraft on reconnaissance missions in Algeria. It was fitted with weapons, but we seldom had to use them. Armed with guns and bombs it was very effective."

"Is the tan and brown desert camouflage?" I asked.

"Yes," the major answered. "Now, of course, we use this aircraft as a trainer, but I asked that it not be repainted."

"Did you fly this particular plane?" Louise asked.

"Pure chance, but I know this lady very well."

"Are you going to introduce us?" I asked.

"I call her Roxanne," he said.

"Like the lady in the play, *Cyrano de Bergerac?*" Louise asked.

"Well, yes," the major said. "But, in fact, there was a young woman I knew in my home town, Avignon, in the south of France. That was the Roxanne I had in mind."

I was thinking to myself that this plane looked very powerful, but it was not sleek and pretty. I wondered about the original Roxanne, but I was not about to suggest any comparisons.

"The cockpit has two seats, one behind the other," Louise said. "I thought the instructor and the student would sit side by side."

"In some trainers, yes, but tandem is probably better. The student sits in the front and he is not distracted by someone sitting beside him, so he has the sense that he alone is responsible for the aircraft. It's like riding as a passenger in an automobile with an awkward or dangerous driver. You find yourself tightening up, even stepping on the brakes that aren't there."

Louise and I laughed.

"You see what I mean," the major said. "The student pilot is always wondering what the instructor thinks of him, and he may not be fully concentrating on flying."

"I will be behind you, with a second set of controls, and I will take over the aircraft from you if necessary. Learning to fly an airplane isn't easy, and you will certainly make some mistakes. Everyone does. I repeat: Everyone does. What is important is to learn from your mistakes. I will see that you do."

His voice had taken on a more serious tone.

"First," he said, "a quick walk-around."

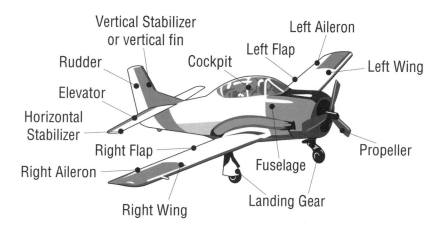

He pointed to the main body of the aircraft. "The fuselage," he said, "and although I don't have to tell you which are the wings, you may not know the names of the hinged extensions on the wings. The ones closest to the fuselage are called flaps. When lowered they change the flow of air over the wings, which allows you to fly without stalling. The outer ones are ailerons and they control the rate of roll."

We followed him around to the nose of the plane.

"This engine is very powerful, over eighteen hundred horsepower. It's called a radial engine because the pistons are installed in a circle around the shaft, rather than in line, from front to back. The propeller has three blades and they are slanted and curved so that they, shall we say, 'pull the air,' like a motorboat or ship's propeller. The Desert Fox has a top speed of almost five hundred kilometers per hour and a cruising speed of approximately three hundred twenty.

Maintaining the cruising speed instead of the top speed gives you greater range before you run out of fuel."

We continued to circle the aircraft. "Civilians call that tall, angular shape at the back of the plane the tail, which is correct, but we think of it as the vertical stabilizer. The hinged section at the back of the tail is the rudder—sort of like the rudder on a ship. When used with the ailerons it helps you make smooth, coordinated turns.

"As you have guessed, the section of the tail assembly that looks like smaller wings and is set at right angles to the vertical stabilizer is—the horizontal stabilizer, and the hinged parts that go up and down are called elevators. Again, an elevator in a department store is not exactly the same as elevators on an airplane, although they both take you up and down."

He helped us up on Roxanne's wing so we could see the inside of the cockpit. There were a lot of dials, and they seemed very complicated. The major climbed inside the rear cockpit and sat in the instructor's seat—almost identical to the front seat, where each of us would sit.

"This control between my legs is called 'the stick.' Watch! When I push it forward both elevators on the horizontal stabilizer hinge down. When I pull it towards myself, they hinge upward. If I move the stick to the right, the aileron on the right wing angles down, while the one on the left one angles up and we roll right—and if I move it in the opposite direction, we roll left."

We watched eagerly, trying to remember everything.

"These pedals are for the rudder. Step on the right one and the rudder goes to the right and the plane noses right; on the left one, and it noses left. When you are on the ground, the rudder pedals steer the nose wheel like the steering wheel of an automobile."

"The pedals on top of the rudder pedals are for the brakes, and as you have figured out already, you don't just step on the brakes to stop an airplane in flight, although you do use them after you have landed and are rolling along the runway. It's a good idea not to have them on when you land because you'll immediately blow your tires.

"This handle is the throttle. If you add throttle, you increase the r.p.m.'s of your engine. Throttle back and you decrease them—just like a car. There's more to it, of course, but for now I just want you to be observant. Later, it will all make sense."

"I hope so," I said.

"So do I," said Louise.

"You need to be flexible and resourceful," the major said, "and you'll soon be able to respond correctly."

We both nodded, but I had a hunch that each of us had enough ego to think that our quickness and agility would set us above the average student. We had a lot to learn.

The major showed us the instruments: the altimeter, which would show us our height above sea level; the vertical velocity indicator, that would show how fast we climbed or descended; the airspeed indicator, which would give us our speed "through" the air, but not necessarily our speed over the ground; and the artificial horizon, which would show us what angle our wings were in comparison to the horizon—the line between earth and sky. Of course, there were fuel and oil and engine temperature gauges and other, more mysterious dials that Major Gerard said we didn't have to know about yet.

By that time we were getting pretty antsy. It was all very interesting, but we wanted to get up into the air. Further, we were wearing our jumpsuits and although it was March, it was an unusually warm day, especially with heat radiating off Roxanne's body.

The major told us he would do the flying the first time, and we would only watch and listen. He helped Louise into her parachute pack, and said, "Mademoiselle Louise," and pointed to the front cockpit.

She threw me an uncertain smile which said, "I hope you don't mind if I go first?" and I had to smile back.

✦ ✦ ✦

It was difficult standing alone in the bright sunlight, squinting as Roxanne roared down the runway and took off. Her "tricycle"—three-point—landing gear included a nose wheel, so taxiing and takeoffs were easier than on the older "tail-dragging" type aircraft because she didn't have to lift her tail while taxiing. In just a few hundred meters, Roxanne was airborne, easily clearing the power lines at the end of the field. She soon disappeared into the haze.

Meanwhile, many other planes were taking off and landing at Le Bourget, which at that time was the busiest airport in France and one of the busiest in Europe. There were commercial liners, most of them with jet engines, a few turboprops—with jet engines driving propellers—and some with plain old petrol-fired engines. A few military aircraft were in action, too. Each plane had its own sound, and sometimes the smaller aircraft seemed to make the most noise.

Then I noticed a four-engine propeller aircraft taking off bearing United States colors and markings. I assumed it was a cargo plane and was about to turn away when I saw a powerful symbol on its side: a winged dragon perched on a globe of the world—the same symbol as the one on the cap I had taken from the headstone marked "Alan Stevens." Almost involuntarily, I ran towards it across the tarmac. I could barely make out the words "Flying Dragons" inside the symbol, and then the plane raced out of my range and took off into the sky. At first I had a sense of loss, but then I realized it was another clue to aid my search for my father.

I hadn't told anyone, even my mother, about the cap, and I wondered whether I should try to trace the airplane I had just seen. And how I would do it.

I sighted Roxanne again, flying pretty high, and I was

startled as she made a funny dipping motion, and began to spin, quickly dropping hundreds of meters. I knew flying could be dangerous, but this was happening too soon. I could feel my chest tighten, as the plane spun lower and lower. Then her nose pitched down, the spin stopped and she began to climb.

In a few minutes, Roxanne landed and taxied to the tarmac in front of the hangar. Louise came leaping out of the cockpit, pulling off her helmet, hair flying, with a smile the size of Paris itself.

"I flew Roxanne!" she said.

"Were you flying when the plane dropped like a bird hit with a stone?" I asked.

She didn't even frown. "Major Gerard wanted to show me how my intuition could fool me, and it did," she said, "but he told me what to do and I pulled out of it. This is the most fun I've ever had!"

The major helped me into my parachute pack, and then I climbed up into the cockpit, pulling on my helmet with the built-in radio microphone and earphones. I plugged it into the jack in the aircraft as I had been instructed.

I had never been in an airplane before. I don't mean that I had never been a passenger, or sat in a cockpit. I had never been inside a plane—ever. Paul had told me about being taken up in an old biplane at a carnival in Caen before World War II, a light airplane with one wing at the bottom of the fuselage and the other on struts on top. Other than that, I don't think anyone in our little village, Bonville, had flown in an airplane. Several men had served in the military, all in the infantry or the cavalry. During the war, the army had actually used horses, although the cavalry also included tanks.

So there I was, as the major revved up the engine and we started down the runway.

"Note the windsock," his voice told me through the

earphones, "it's aiming our way."

I looked at the windsock, a circular, open-ended cloth bag shaped like a conical hat, which pointed towards us.

"We're taking off into the wind, which is the proper way. It helps provide lift and means we can take off in the shortest possible distance."

Roxanne trundled along the runway, gathering speed, her tail already high because of the tricycle gear, and suddenly I could feel the plane climb—at first slowly and then, after a slight dip to accelerate our airspeed, faster and faster. We were climbing at about a thirty-degree angle above level ground. Pretty soon I couldn't see the ground, the hangars or the trees as we sliced through the air. I was so thrilled, I forgot to be scared. A part of me noticed that the controls were moving and the gauges and dials changing, but I was too excited to concentrate on anything.

Gradually, the plane leveled off and accelerated, moving serenely through the sky, affected only slightly by little gusts of air. Major Gerard reduced the power.

"Where's the horizon?" he asked.

Without even thinking, I said, "Below us?"

"Aren't you looking?"

I looked ahead to the line where the earth met the sky and was surprised. "It's our level, almost eye level!" I said.

"I'm going up again," The major said. "See where the horizon is when we're two hundred meters higher."

Soon, after another thrilling surge of power, we leveled off again.

"It's in the same place!" I exclaimed.

"Surprising, isn't it?" Gerard said. "Even if we went up to ten thousand meters, the horizon would appear to be at the same level as your eyes. Do you see that barn straight ahead? It seems to be lower than the horizon, which means it is lower than the level we're flying at, and we can safely pass over it. But look at that line of hills ahead. They are above the horizon, so if we continue at this same altitude we will very likely bump into them.

"Did you watch the stick as we were climbing and leveling off?" he asked.

"Yes," I said. "When we were climbing it moved back towards me, and when you leveled off it went back to the middle."

"Correct, I was adjusting the elevators on the horizontal stabilizer," he said.

"The throttle moved, too," I said. "And, of course, the engine roared louder, as you added throttle."

"Okay," he said, "Now you fly the plane! Take the stick when I say, 'You have it.' You say, 'I've got it,' and when you shake the stick I'll relinquish my control and she's yours."

For the first time I felt a pang of fear, but not for long, although I was holding onto the stick pretty tightly.

We didn't fall out of the sky.

What a relief! The nose moved up a little and our vertical velocity indicator said we were climbing, but when I pushed forward on the stick, the nose came back down. A little too much, so I pulled back—just a little to achieve level flight.

I was flying the Desert Fox—Roxanne. It was unbelievable. There I was, fifteen years old, never having been inside one of these things, and I was flying it.

"Give her a little more throttle," the major said.

I added throttle, and the engine sound became a little louder. The plane seemed to rise a bit, so I lowered her nose to level using the horizontal elevators on the tail.

Then I saw it and also felt it in the seat of my pants as the plane tilted down a little to the right, so I moved the stick to the left. The aileron on my right wing hinged upward, and the one on the left wing hinged down. Again, I had over-corrected—and it was scary because I thought we might end up upside down, but with a little adjustment we came back to level.

"What have you learned?" the major asked.

"First, to keep the plane level requires constant attention to the horizon. To climb up or down you pull back or forward on the stick, raising or lowering the nose, and to keep the plane level side to side, you move the stick from side to side, adjusting the ailerons."

"In time you will learn that the throttle is the control that gets you up or down, and the elevators control your attitude and speed," the major said, "but that's good enough for now."

"How fast are we going over the ground?" the major asked.

I glanced at the airspeed indicator. "Two hundred twenty kilometers per hour."

"Are you sure? We're flying into a wind? How fast is it blowing?"

"I don't know," I said.

"From experience I would guess about thirty kilometers per hour. So our net speed over the ground is one hundred ninety, right?"

"Yes," I said. "I guess so."

"Of course, if a thirty kilometer wind was behind us," the major said, "our ground speed would be two hundred fifty. If it was blowing sideways or crossways that, too, would make a difference. The number on your airspeed indicator is not necessarily the rate at which you are flying across the earth. It shows you how fast you're flying through the air."

Something else to think about.

"Now," the major said, "please turn the plane and take us back to Le Bourget."

I decided to make a right turn, so I stepped on the right rudder pedal. The aircraft did begin to move a bit to the right, but it was also moving to the left! As if we were skidding through the sky! I turned the rudder even more, but the slipping motion became even more pronounced. We were yawing badly and now the plane was nosing down. I pulled back on the stick to lift it. Her nose came up, our airspeed dropped, and she began to roll, with her left wing higher than her right—and then to spin. I panicked. The plane was spinning with her nose down and the earth moving wildly below us in strange patterns of rapidly rotating roads and fields and trees.

"You have it!" I yelled.

The major put in full rudder opposite to the direction of spin and pushed the stick forward. Our nose pitched down, but the spin stopped. He pulled the stick back and added power. We were flying level again.

The major's voice was calm. "I told you on the ground that the rudder is not the primary control for turning an aircraft. Pay attention to what I do as I turn to the right. First, I bank the plane to the right by moving the stick to the right. The left aileron comes up, the right moves down. I use a little rudder to coordinate the turn—to prevent yaw."

The plane was now at roughly a forty-five degree angle to the horizon. She seemed to turn to the right even though the rudder pedal barely moved.

"Notice how I pull back on the stick to lift the nose to compensate for the reduction in our lift."

As he did so the aircraft continued to turn smoothly to the right. Then the major reversed his controls to level flight, and we were headed back in the general direction of Paris.

"I see," I said, "but you did use the rudder, except you stepped on the right pedal instead of the left one."

"I moved the rudder in the direction of yaw to prevent the yawing movement caused by the ailerons as they roll the wings," he said.

"Now you understand that you use your ailerons, rudders and elevators to turn," the major said. "I also added throttle to maintain constant speed and attitude as we turned."

Soon afterward the major contacted the tower at Le

Bourget, was given permission to land and a runway to use, as well as information about other flights taking off and landing at the field.

He circled the field counter-clockwise and then turned to approach the runway from about three kilometers distance. Just before we reached the runway, the major eased back on the stick, raising the nose to slow our descent and reduce our speed. The two main wheels touched the runway simultaneously, and then he lowered the nose and pushed on the tops of the rudders to apply the brakes.

◆   ◆   ◆

We taxied up to the hangar where Louise was talking to a man in a military flying uniform with officer's picks on his epaulets. With the engine turned off, I realized that Louise was arguing with him. As we approached, I saw on the back of his flight jacket, the black and white shield of the DragonSlayers.

"Look who we have here," Louise said, her voice raised, her eyes fierce.

The officer turned to face us, smiling: Tony Bersault. I struggled to keep myself from slugging him.

Louise said, "Do you see the symbol on his uniform?"

"The DragonSlayers," I said.

"My flying squadron," Tony said, still smiling.

"The leader of the thieves had a shield in his wallet with the same symbol!" I said. "They worked for you!"

Tony shrugged. "Don't be ridiculous. A man—who knows what man—carries a symbol like mine. So what? Even if he were in my squadron, what does that prove? There were dozens of men attached to our flying group, including mechanics and support personnel. Am I supposed to be responsible for all of them?"

I was drawing back my arm to throw a punch—at the moment I had forgotten all about Judo—but Major Gerard stepped between me and Tony, took my arm, and held it firmly.

"How dare you present yourself here?" Major Gerard asked in a voice so cold and hard I thought it might slit Tony's throat.

But Tony was smiling, teeth bared in a nasty grin, eyes as cold as the major's voice. "I finished my tour of duty; I come here regularly to fulfill my reserve requirements."

"I think," the major said, in that cutting-edge voice, "the president can persuade your superiors to relieve you of such onerous duties."

Tony began to laugh; that was too much for me.

"You hired those criminals to blow up the Crouching Dragon!" I said.

Tony raised his hands, palms outward. "What is this young man talking about?"

"No one but you had any reason to try to blow up the Dragon Tower," Louise said.

Tony maintained his innocent expression. "Have you any evidence of that?"

I started to lunge for him again, but the major's grip tightened and I couldn't reach Tony, although I did pull the major forward a step.

Louise said in a hard, angry voice, "You were probably the one who tried to kill Willi in the hospital."

Tony, clearly enjoying our anger, said, "Did such a thing really happen? I hadn't heard a word about it."

"That is enough!" Major Gerard said. "I shall speak to the president this evening."

"Don't bother," Tony said smoothly. "I'll resign my commission soon; I do not desire to remain in the military under this . . . regime."

Major Gerard said nothing. Tony snapped off a salute—which the major did not return—and stalked away.

ROXANNE

"Isn't there anything we can do about Tony?" I asked the major.

"One thing we *can't* do," Major Gerard said, "is have you attack him physically. Some day he'll make a mistake and we'll be rid of him, permanently, but legally."

"That guy is so slimy," I said, "he slips away every time we try to grab him."

"The intelligence services are working very diligently, trying to connect him to many crimes," the major replied, "but the Bersaults are very crafty, and they have a surprising number of supporters."

"The connection is obvious, now that we know the name of his squadron," Louise said.

"I'd rather not be in the position of defending Tony Bersault," Major Gerard said, "but anyone could copy that symbol and use it for any reason."

"I don't believe it," Louise said. "The whole thing is too suspicious."

"Our friend, André, is still in a coma," I said. "We don't know what his future will be. And this man swaggers about, untouched."

"I'll give you a moment to calm down," the major said. As he strode towards the hangar, he gave a hint of a smile— to Roxanne.

Louise said, quietly, "I think Major Gerard loves that airplane."

"He looks at Roxanne as if she were a beautiful woman," I said.

"Frankly," Louise said. "With such a thick middle and big nose, I think the plane looks more like a fat cigar."

I laughed. "The wings seem pretty stumpy don't they? And the cockpit has a hump in the middle so it doesn't look sleek despite all the glass."

Louise said, "Roxanne is no beauty."

"Perhaps not compared to you, Mademoiselle."

It was the major. We hadn't noticed him approaching us out of the deep shadows in the hangar.

He placed a hand on the skin of the aircraft and said, "If a lady has protected you when you were in very dangerous places, and brought you safely home even though badly hurt herself, you tend to think of her as very, very lovely."

◆　　◆　　◆

"There is one piece of history I have failed to share with you," the major said, "and it involves this airport."

"You mean about Charles Lindbergh?" Louise asked.

"Then you do know," the major said.

"Only that he made a famous flight from America to France a long time ago," she said. "That's all I heard."

"In 1927, Charles Lindbergh was the first man to fly non-stop over the Atlantic Ocean. He performed that remarkable feat solo, in a single-engine monoplane, named 'The Spirit of St. Louis,' taking off from Roosevelt Field in New York, and landing here at Le Bourget Field on May 20, 1927. The flight covered 3600 miles and took thirty-three hours."

"Thirty-three hours!" I couldn't help exclaiming.

"Yes," the major said. "What a jet aircraft can now accomplish in six or seven hours, took Lindbergh thirty-three—without sophisticated instruments, or even a radio. He spread a map on his lap and flew by the seat of his pants. But virtually the whole world was watching—reading the newspapers, or listening by radio for reports of him. When Lindbergh landed, he was mobbed by over one hundred thousand French people. Overnight Lindbergh became the most famous man in the world. He was only 25 years old."

I loved the story, of course. It provided a dramatic link with my father, Alan Stevens, an American who had fought in France—and may have been a pilot himself. Having the U.S. Air Force cap with the Flying Dragon's symbol added to my dreams.

"If you ever travel to the United States," the major said. "you may wish to visit the Air and Space Museum of the Smithsonian Institution in Washington, D.C. Lindbergh's aircraft is one of the major exhibits."

That made it even better.

◆   ◆   ◆

"Angle of attack!" Major Gerard said firmly. "The angle of attack is almost everything in flying."

We had learned that angle of attack hadn't anything to do with war; it was the angle at which the wing of an airplane meets the air.

"That is how the plane flies," he repeated patiently. "The wing is nothing but an air deflector—it is an inclined plane, cleverly curved and streamlined to change the air moving over it. That's why Roxanne is called an air-*plane*. The wings are more or less flat on the bottom and curved on the top, so that the air going over them travels faster than underneath. This difference we sometimes call lift. The arching air over the top seems to suck the wing upward and keeps the plane aloft."

I didn't much like the technical stuff, but I knew I had to master it if I was going to be a good pilot.

◆　◆　◆

The most fun, of course, was learning while flying. The major drove us to Le Bourget at least twice each week, sometimes three times, and we were very happy to have so many opportunities. However, between Judo and flying, we were up early four or five times a week.

Major Gerard had us fly many turns, using the elevators, ailerons and rudder properly so that the aircraft turned smoothly, without slipping and sliding. We learned how steeply we could climb without separating the air flow over the wings and stalling.

We were surprised to learn that when a plane had stalled and was falling through the air, the answer was not to pull the stick back to lift it up, but to push it forward and regain speed and lift.

"You must understand the concept of 'relative wind,'" the major said. "It's seems apparent when you're flying that the air is moving past the plane, while actually, it's your own motion *through* the air. It's just like a boat in a river—you have to consider the current to get where you want to go."

◆　◆　◆

Despite the added time required for our flying lessons, I was still doing pretty well in my classes. Louise, as usual, was handling everything just fine. We were also making good progress at the dojo. Jacques and Mai were very young, but they had been trained by the master, Sadayuke Kawaishi.

"How long did it take you to earn your black belt?" I asked Jacques.

"Three years," he said, which almost deflated me. "However," he continued, "the first two years I practiced at another dojo. Once I started at this one, I made much faster progress."

Sometimes, instead of working with Mai or Jacques, we practiced with other members of the Clandestin at the dojo. I particularly enjoyed training with Mohammed Almedienne. He was highly skilled, but always patient, and clearly explained what I was doing wrong.

"You ought to be an instructor, yourself," I told him.

"Thank you," he said. "I try to help some of the younger people at the Foreign Office, although the administration frowns on it."

"But your father *is* the administration—he's the head of the Algerian Section."

"Yes," Mohammed said, "but I think he feels there is something undignified about the training—at least for the son of an official."

"You defy him?" I asked.

"No, never," he said. "I always ask permission, and it is always granted, although reluctantly. I believe my father expects me to decide for myself that this is not proper training."

"Have you ever wondered if he is right?"

Mohammed laughed. It was a deep, rippling laugh and it lighted his face. He was a very handsome young man, with strong, clean-cut features and glowing skin. I had seen many young ladies eyeing him in the dojo, on the streets and at the Raging Dragon.

"I respect my father very much," Mohammed said, "but I don't see how it can be wrong to learn to defend yourself, whether or not you are a Muslim, or the son of a dignitary."

◆　◆　◆

Louise and I enjoyed meeting our new friends at the

Raging Dragon and elsewhere. The group took us on a tour of their nine "bases": the apartments, offices and shops where they had set up radios and antennas to communicate with each other and the outside world.

"I often listen to the British Broadcasting Company," Robert de Cotte said. "The BBC gives me a different view of world affairs than the French stations."

"Treason!" Nina said, and we all laughed.

"For English language broadcasts," Marcel said, "I prefer the Voice of America."

"You just like their music better," Marie said. "The BBC is too old-fashioned for you."

"You're right," Marcel admitted. "You don't hear 'Mack the Knife' or 'Itsy Bitsy Teenie Weenie Little Yellow Polka Dot Bikini' on BBC. You certainly don't hear Elvis Presley or any rock and roll."

The others didn't seem impressed with Marcel's taste in music.

"I'd rather listen to Edith Piaf sing *'La Vien Rose,'*" Robert said, "or Yves Montand sing anything than listen to that booming junk you like."

Marcel just laughed.

Robert was an architect, and he invited us to learn to use the short-wave radio in his office on the top floor of a commercial building near the Arch of Triumph. The office opened onto the roof and the views were sensational. Drawings and photographs mounted in the studio showed many famous buildings, which surprised us, because Robert seemed to be such a casual guy.

He showed us the transmitter, earphones, etc., and pointed out the tall antenna mounted on the roof. Robert claimed he had the best reception in the Clandestin network.

"We broadcast on one of two frequencies," Robert said, and jotted them down for us. "We test our equipment at least once a week to make sure our little network is ready for any emergency."

He spun the dial, and in a few minutes taught Louise and me how to tune in and adjust transmission and reception. Then we spoke to Nina and Marcel at their bases. We felt pretty proud of ourselves.

"You're naturals," Robert said, with only a hint of a smile.

◆　◆　◆

One day at the dojo, Mai made a point of telling me she had her own apartment.

"Aren't you kind of young to live alone?" I had asked.

"I'll be eighteen in a couple weeks," she said. "When my mother was eighteen she was fighting against the Japanese in French-Indo China, carrying a gun just like any man."

"She must have been very young when she had you," I said.

Mai blushed furiously. I didn't know what I had said wrong.

Fortunately, she rallied quickly and said, "Young people often don't have complete freedom. I'm determined to choose my existence, not have it chosen for me."

How could I argue with that?

"I'd like to practice with you," Mai said.

"Why?" I asked.

"It's good to work with someone who is bigger than you are."

"How about Jacques?"

"I'd prefer you," Mai said. She was staring at me so intensely I had to look away.

"The master won't let us practice together in the dojo," I said.

"My apartment isn't large," she said, "but there's room for a couple of mats in the parlor." She handed me a small piece of folded paper. "This is my address and telephone number."

"I have to go to class," I said, jumping up and heading for the dressing room.

"I'll be home after 6 P.M.," Mai said, giving me an exceptionally winning smile.

I thought about it all day, trying to figure out her motivation.

Don't be silly, I thought. *She probably means exactly what she says. All she has in mind is Judo practice.*

Still, meeting a pretty woman at her own apartment was an exciting prospect. My experience with girls was next to nothing. The only girl I had ever been interested in was Louise, and all we ever did was some hand-holding, hugging and kissing. That had been enough for me, mostly. Far, far, back in my mind was the idea that she was my girl, and that maybe some day we would get engaged, and then married.

Would I be untrue to Louise if I went to see Mai? We had never discussed limiting our dating. In fact, we didn't have many real dates, except for occasionally going to the movies together, and then we usually went with a group of friends.

That afternoon when I was in the library, I saw Louise sitting at another table. I was about to go over and talk to her, when I realized she was sitting next to one of the Clandestin, Richard Bruant. He was a pretty good looking guy, a few years older than we were. Richard was saying something, and Louise was laughing and kind of leaning towards him. They seemed to be very friendly.

What was wrong with that? Nothing. But now I had a little different perspective.

◆　◆　◆

Roger looked at me quizzically. "Why are you packing your judogi?" he asked.

"We're going to practice Judo," I said.

"On a school night?" he asked, patiently.

"I won't be there long," I said. "Can you give me directions to Mai's apartment? Her address is 88 Rue du Moulinet, and there's a note that reads, 'Tolbiac metro station.'"

"That's south of the Place d'Italie," Roger said. "The fastest way is to take line number 10 east from Cluny-La Sorbonne to Jussieu, then switch to line 7 south, past Place d'Italie to Tolbiac. It's only a short walk from there."

I thanked him, made myself a sandwich, drank some coffee and started out around 6:30 P.M. I didn't want to get there too early.

♦   ♦   ♦

When I climbed to the street level at Tolbiac, I was surprised to see so many Asian faces. The Rue Tolbiac and intersecting streets were lined with shops boasting signs in various scripts I couldn't read. Until then I didn't know there was a so-called Chinatown in Paris. Other Asians were also drawn to the district, and it had become a thriving area with many nationalities represented, among them the Vietnamese. Viet Nam had once been a French colony, and French culture was still in evidence, especially in urban architecture. Saigon, the southern capital, was often referred to as Little Paris. After the partition, many Vietnamese migrated to France, and they congregated in the area where Mai lived.

It was a very lively neighborhood. The sidewalks were filled with people and the chatter of voices, sometimes in French, usually in other tongues, often with a chant or sing-song pattern. Unfamiliar music—reedy, metallic, percussive—drifted from shops and apartment windows; unusual, often tangy, food smells mingled in the streets.

Less than half an hour after leaving Roger's apartment I was standing on the sidewalk in front of number 88, Rue du Moulinet, wondering again what I was doing there. But I brushed asides my doubts and rang the bell next to the name Mai Pham.

Her building was a typical Parisian apartment structure, distinguished only by a gaudy sign over the windows of the first floor shop, filled with a jumble of (to me) exotic artifacts. Mai's apartment was on the first (not the ground) floor. The smells in the corridor were alien, but subtle and pleasant.

She was waiting in the doorway, glowing. Instead of a judogi she was wore a revealing black body suit. I had not realized just how round she was.

"Hi," she said, pulling me towards her and giving me quick kisses on both cheeks. That was very European, but with her pressed against me it was very personal.

Mai took my hand and drew me into the apartment. It was very neat, very clean, with starkly modern furniture, not obviously Asian. She led me around, showing me the tiny kitchen with its modernist dishes and glasses and astonishingly industrial-looking pots on the stove. I didn't expect to see the bedroom, but that was part of the tour.

"That's my bed," she said, pointing to a white thick mat lying on the floor, with a white comforter on top. "Do you know what it is?" she asked.

I shook my head.

"It's called a futon, invented by the Japanese," she said. "When I heard your voice on the intercom I thought I'd unroll it and show you. Come here," she said, and slipped down to the mat, trying to pull me down with her. I resisted and she laughed.

"I have my shoes on," I said (lamely).

"Take them off. You should have removed them the minute you came in."

I quickly slipped out of my shoes, and while I was off balance, she drew me down on the futon, lying next to her.

Mai smelled awfully good—a flowery smell, reminiscent of the jasmine my mother carefully nourished in a sheltered, but sunny corner of our garden.

"Comfortable isn't it?" she asked, rolling towards me.

"Not bad," I said, getting up quickly.

She kind of shrugged and stood up, too.

"What's in the bag?" she asked.

"My judogi," I said.

She laughed again. Mai had a musical laugh that tinkled up and down the scale. It was pleasant and suggestive.

"You actually brought your judogi," she said. "William, you're wonderful."

She gave me another kiss, this time on only one cheek, but closer to my mouth.

"Your parlor is just like you said," I mumbled, "mats and all."

"Are you surprised?" she asked. The top of her head came about to my eye level, and with her head tilted up, her oval eyes seemed dark, mysterious, and inviting. I became aware that the room was lighted with candles, not electricity, and in the soft glow, her features were both sculptured and hazy.

"Tea?" she asked, and drew me down on one of the mats, next to a low, black lacquered table, which did seem Asian, although the teapot and cups were stark and modern.

Mai knelt before me, pouring the aromatic tea into a cup—so slowly it seemed like a sensual ritual. She poured her own in a similar manner and then offered me a plate of small cakes.

"Thank you," I said, "but not before exercise."

This time her laugh was throaty, but she didn't take a cake herself.

I sipped politely at the tea, which was minty in flavor and smell. When Mai sipped, it looked like a kiss.

Mai suddenly said, "Let's practice."

"I'll put on my judogi," I said. I picked up my bag and marched into the bathroom and shut the door. There was no lock, and I had never undressed and redressed so fast in my life. I took a very deep breath, opened the door and walked back to the parlor.

"I'd like to do some grappling," Mai said, speaking in a very matter-of-fact voice. "We'll start with you on your back on the mat." She gently pushed me down; I gave little resistance. "We'll try hold-down techniques first."

So there I was, lying on my back, with a pretty woman hovering over me. I wondered if my pounding heartbeat was visible through my judogi. I was also swallowing—again and again

"The scarf hold is the easiest," Mai said. She grabbed my right outer sleeve with her left hand and pulled me against her, clamping my right arm in her left armpit. Naturally, that meant that my arm was pulled tight against her chest.

"Now," she said, "I'm going to put my right arm around your neck—like a scarf—and place my fist on the mat." She brought her right thigh against my body hard. She was bending her left leg and stretching it back, and her head would soon touch the mat. We were about as close as a couple of people could get.

Mai went through a sequence of moves that developed from the first hold. Although we were in close contact, she moved so quickly and decisively that I was thinking more about escaping than enjoying her pliant body and heady scent. I began to think that maybe she was serious about practice.

We tried some variations of the scarf hold and then worked on shoulder holds, first with Mai as the "aggressor," and then with me. When I started, I was a little tentative.

"I'm not breakable," she said. "Treat me as if I were Jacques."

"That's not easy," I said.

Since we were practicing the kata, our moves were pre-arranged, and there should have been no surprises. Except that at one point when Mai was on top of me, she moved unexpectedly and kissed me firmly on the mouth.

Then her cheek was next to mine and she whispered in my ear, "That was a reward for your excellent work."

"I didn't know that in Judo you are supposed to kiss your opponent," I said. At that moment I believe I could have thrown her off of me, but I didn't want to.

Her lips were sliding along my cheek and she turned her head so that her mouth was on mine again. My whole body was beginning to respond.

Somehow, with a great exercise of my wobbly will, I managed to slip out of her grip and sit up.

"I think that's enough practice for one evening," I said. "It's been more than educational."

"Next time," she said, "we'll try some more challenging moves."

◆　　◆　　◆

Louise was the first to take off in Roxanne, and her maneuvers looked perfect to me.

"I was scared," she told me. "But actually, it was pretty easy. This plane has plenty of power, and although I pulled up a bit too quickly, she didn't stall."

I expected the major to let me take off right after Louise, but he didn't, and I didn't ask why, because I wasn't sure I was ready to hear his reasons.

A few days later, when we were aloft, he allowed me to continue flying south until we approached Orleans, over one hundred kilometers from Paris. Compared to Le Bourget, the runways at Orleans looked really small, and there were trees and power lines all around the field. Major Gerard took over the controls and guided the plane to a perfect landing.

After we had refueled the aircraft—the smell of petrol

was becoming very familiar and almost pleasant to me—the major said, "Take the controls; you're going to guide Roxanne into the sky."

I swallowed hard and said, "The runway is pretty short. Do you think I'm skilled enough to get Roxanne over the trees and power lines?"

"We will soon see, Monsieur," he said. "Remember: as you are approaching the end of the runway and it seems you will not clear the trees, don't try to climb too steeply—we don't want to stall. Just do what you have learned in your lessons."

I nodded—almost fiercely. I was even more excited than I had been on the mat with Mai. The major radioed for clearance. Once cleared for takeoff, I opened the throttle and started down the runway, feeling every bump in the uneven paving, grateful the wind was aiming right in our faces. I had expected my first takeoff would be from one of the big, wide and long runways at Le Bourget, not at a cramped provincial airport, but I was completely focused on the takeoff. I consciously relaxed my shoulders and gripped the stick firmly, but not too tightly. In a few moments, we were airborne.

As we raced down the macadam, it looked as if we were about to run out of space. I wanted to pull back on the stick to lift the plane up over the trees, but that was the reflex the major had told me not to follow. I held the stick steady, climbing at a constant speed, and we soared over the trees. I was so thrilled I thought I would swell up to fill the cockpit.

Très bien," the major's voice said in my earphones. "A very good *first* try."

◆   ◆   ◆

Louise and I had both noticed how much heavier we felt when we were making turns and spins and whenever we came out of a dive, than in ordinary, level flight. Major Gerard had told us from the beginning that gravity was trying to bring the plane down, just like the engine and wings were trying to keep the plane up. But the extra weight we felt in turns was even stronger."

"Centrifugal force," the major said. "We call it a g load and it can be many times the ordinary force of gravity. Coming out of a dive you might pull five or more g's, which means the force of gravity is several times 'normal' so that you and the aircraft become five times as heavy. And the plane has to overcome that extra weight. In a fast jet fighter, the g's seem to pull you apart.

"I think I'll wait awhile to fly jets," I said.

The major raised his eyebrows as if to say, you don't have to worry about that, young man.

He kept reminding us that stalling didn't always have to do with speed. A plane stalled when it was flying at an "excessive" angle of attack—for some aircraft not more than eighteen degrees. Whenever the angle is too sharp, the air flow over the top of the wing burbles and breaks away, and then—a stall.

The major also told us, "You must learn to fly with more than your eyes. Be alert to the sounds of the engine, the feel of the stick, even the seat of your pants."

And he taught us how to look. We thought we knew, but he trained us to keep moving our eyes so that we took in as much as possible all around us.

We had to learn to deal with cross winds and up or down drafts. The air wasn't always smooth; sometimes it was rough and we had to understand how to deal with that—to respond but not to over-control.

"I don't want you to be tense," he said, "but you must be alert. Relax, even while you're paying attention. This is fun—and it will be even more fun, after you have trained yourselves to react to the many different situations you'll encounter."

Despite this encouragement, I privately told Louise,

"Sometimes the stuff he teaches us makes me dizzy. I worry that I'm not going to remember something important.

"Me, too," Louise said. "But we can't be too hard on ourselves. I think we're doing well. If we weren't, I'm sure the major would tell us."

I was also worrying about Tony Bersault. "I thought he was going to resign his commission, but I think I caught a glimpse of him at the terminal."

"You did," Louise said. "Yesterday, while you were flying with the major, he spoke to me."

"What did he say?"

"It was kind of personal."

"Tell me," I said, beginning to smolder.

Louise took a deep breath. "He said I was getting prettier every day—that it was hard to believe I was only fifteen years old."

Louise was blushing; I was furious.

"Be careful," I told her. "He's unpredictable—and totally evil."

✦　✦　✦

Our classroom at Le Bourget was in the hangar where Roxanne lounged when she wasn't flying. In the far corner was a fenced area where tools and supplies were stored. In front of the metal link barrier sat a few folding chairs and a rectangular table that Major Gerard used to spread drawings, books and maps.

"In some ways," the major said one day, "the airspeed indicator is the most important instrument. However, it's really not a speed indicator but a pressure gauge, measuring the pressure built up on the plane as it advances through the air. It is correct only near sea level when the temperature is mild. At high altitude or when it's hot, the dial will understate your speed. But when it's cold, you will think you are in a much faster plane."

"I thought you said the airspeed indicator can warn you about a stall," Louise said.

"Yes," the major agreed, "if you know the speed at which your aircraft will stall—for Roxanne, it is approximately one hundred twenty kilometers per hour. That will be the stalling speed at any temperature and any altitude; it has nothing to do with your real speed over the ground, just your speed through the air.

"I want you to understand where true danger lies. Flying low and slow is very dangerous—no room for error. Low and fast is safe if you pay attention and don't fly into a barn. But flying high and fast, which most people think is very dangerous, may be the safest of all. Why?"

"Because," Louise said, "at high altitude you have lots of room to make up for an error, and at high speed you're not as likely to stall—or if you do, you have more room to correct your error."

The major smiled.

Some lessons couldn't be taught well in the hangar. One of those was how to deal with a cross wind. The major had taught me that on the day we flew almost due south to Orleans. The wind was coming at us from the southeast—from our left at a forty-five degree angle, and he told me not to fly directly south but head into the wind. I was surprised at the results, of course.

"Tell me what you see," the major asked.

"I'm aiming into the wind, but we're moving towards Orleans," I said, "We're moving like a crab over the countryside."

"Exactly," the major said.

"When I was aiming straight south," I went on, "and the wind was coming from the left, it seemed like there was more pressure on that side of the aircraft and less on the right side."

"Not true," said the major, "You might want to think of

the air you are flying in as invisible soup. If you were a noodle floating in consommé, the soup would be all around you, pressing on all sides of you. And if someone moved the bowl across the table, it wouldn't change the pressure on the noodle. The body of air we're flying in is like the bowl of soup being moved—and we're the noodle."

Major Gerard often asked us questions which seemed to have obvious answers—but didn't.

"Why does the aircraft have a horizontal tail fin—a stabilizer?" the Major asked.

"To hold the tail up," I said, thinking that was obvious.

"Exactly wrong," the major said. "The horizontal part of the tail is meant to keep the tail down and the plane level. It's a wing just like the main wing, but at the right angle of attack the main wing is trying to lift the plane, while the horizontal stabilizer keeps the nose where we want it. Above the horizon and we'll climb, below and we'll dive."

"'I don't get it," Louise said.

"You're forgetting that the tail isn't sitting up in the air alone," the major said. "It is operating in what we call the downwash from the wings—the tail's angle of attack is downward.

"You see, an airplane like Roxanne is brilliantly designed to maintain stability in flight. The horizontal part of the tail, balancing the wing, does just that."

✦　✦　✦

On a sunny spring afternoon at Le Bourget, just when we thought Tony Bersault might be out of our lives, he appeared at Roxanne's hangar in civilian clothes as we completed our final lesson of the day.

"I've come to say my goodbyes," he told us, with a tight-lipped smile. "I shall miss you, Major. You have a certain rigid, military charm that can't be ignored."

Major Gerard merely stared at him.

"And you, too, Monsieur 'Willi' and Mademoiselle Louise. I've taken a position in private industry with an aerospace company known as *Orion Systêmes Aéronautiqe*. I have been assigned to their office in the United States and I will leave tomorrow. Sadly, I presume I will not see you again soon— unless you are planning to visit America. Is that possible?"

Neither Louise nor I gave him the satisfaction of responding.

"Of course, OSA must be where, shall we say, the action is? Yes, in the throbbing heart of the United States government—in the capital, itself—Washington, D.C. Have you been there, Major? It is a very lovely city. Difficult to realize that it's merely a glittering façade for the raw power of the most dangerous country on earth."

"Have I been to Washington?" the major said. "No. Will I be there? Yes. At the completion of my present enlistment, I expect to be reassigned as military attaché to the French Embassy in Washington."

We were shocked.

Tony laughed. "What a wonderful surprise!" he said. "I'll ring you up for drinks sometime."

"Don't bother," the major said.

"And how about you, Willi and *cher* Louise? Wouldn't it be perfect if all of us could meet at the top of the Washington Monument?"

Louise said, "You'd probably set a bomb and blow it up!"

"What cruel words from such an elegant looking woman!" Tony said. "I am shocked. Before I become too emotional, I will take my leave."

He gave us a little bow, and with a departing leer at Louise, he swaggered away.

As soon as he was out of earshot, I said: "What is he up to Major—why is he going to Washington?"

"Bersault, the younger," he said, "is part of an evil

conspiracy that has eyes and ears everywhere. It is virtually impossible to keep a secret from these people. In consequence, there is almost no one you can trust." He gave us a wry, sad smile. "Even me."

We both protested, but he waved us off. "I am simply trying to warn you that you can take nothing for granted. Be on your guard at all times."

"Please tell us about your re-assignment." Louise said.

"I don't believe this is a military secret," the major said. "The president is considering a separate nuclear force to be built and operated by France alone, what he calls *La Force de Frappe*. The United States and the other members of the North Atlantic Treaty organization—NATO—want France to remain within the Alliance's nuclear deterrent, controlled of course, by the United States. Negotiations on this are very important, very fragile, and the president wants me to be in Washington to assist our ambassador. Of course, I am far down the list of those in military and diplomatic authority on this matter, but I have the confidence of the president."

"How do you feel about this assignment?" Louise asked. It was one of the few personal questions either of us had ever addressed to him.

His answer was a little stiff: "I have many reasons for preferring to remain in France, but I am a military officer and as such, accustomed to go where I am assigned."

"We think of you as a true friend," I said, "and we'll miss you."

He smiled "I am your friend, and I hope that our friendship will continue for a very long time."

Despite the smile, there was an edge of sadness in his voice.

SOLO⊙

The ignition was on. I checked the flaps, the ailerons, the elevators and the throttle. I studied all of the instruments and dials.

"Aircraft FT28-72 requests permission to take off, runway number 3."

"Cleared for takeoff, Roxanne."

I smiled. Even the tower knew Roxanne; ground control called her by name.

I ditched my smile immediately, revved the engine and taxied forward to the end of the tarmac. I had traveled this route many times, but this was different. The major wasn't sitting in the rear cockpit, ready to take over if I made a mistake. I turned the aircraft and started down the concrete runway. I was alone—about to solo. The moment every pilot in training aims for. My tongue was a bit dry.

The runway, one of the longest and widest in France, had never look so narrow and short. I added full throttle and accelerated steadily down the runway. Only a light, left cross wind was blowing at a slight angle against the aircraft. I used a little left aileron and right rudder to keep the nose straight. The stick felt a little, well, sticky. As the major had taught me, my eyes were focused on the runway, but I was also aware of everything around me.

When I reached one hundred thirty kilometers of airspeed, I eased the stick back. Liftoff. The plane began to climb, the engine roared. Climbing free of the earth, free of the limitations that had restrained man for so many millennia, soaring into the sky, elated but concentrating, delighted but focused. Retract the landing gear and the flaps.

More than four kilometers past the end of the runway, still climbing, now up to nearly five hundred meters, on my way to my assigned altitude, seven hundred. Banking Roxanne for a planned left turn. Stick to the left, rudder slightly left, a little bit of back pressure to keep the nose up. Thirty degrees of bank, the land below me to my left, under the side of the aircraft. Smooth. No slip; no slide.

Heading one hundred eighty degrees, I rolled the wings level and stopped the turn. Eight or nine kilometers from Le Bourget. Airspeed up to two hundred fifty kilometers. Little wind, little crabbing, easy to correct. Now at assigned altitude. Level flight. All serene. Other aircraft in the sky. Many aiming for Le Bourget from all parts of France. The largest airport, the most flights.

"Tower, FT28-72. At assigned altitude of seven hundred meters. Circling the field."

"We read you, Roxanne. Diverting all other aircraft in the area to Marseille."

He was joking, of course. But that didn't mean I wasn't aware of other planes.

I had passed Le Bourget to my left and had begun to circle counter-clockwise, which would take me over Paris; no time for sightseeing. I was to circle the field, then land in the same direction I had taken off—into the slight angling breeze—on a parallel runway.

Roxanne was purring through the air, responding promptly to every command. Louise might think she looked like a fat cigar, but not to me. On this bright, sunny morning she was an elegant lady, and she was giving me the ride of my life. I radioed for permission to land.

"FT28-72, cleared to land, Runway 7 left."

Nose slightly down, descending smoothly through the air lower and lower. Landing gear down, flaps down. The airport coming up at me rather quickly now. I slowed my descent by raising my nose, but not too much—have to keep coming down. As I crossed the end of the runway, I reduced the power to idle, easing the stick back so the airspeed slowed to near Roxanne's stalling speed.

What a place to solo! God bless Major Gerard. He had been tough, but persistent, demanding but understanding. He taught us well.

I notice a four engine cargo plane lumbering along a feeder runway approaching runway 7—then, inexplicably, entering the runway.

The tower yelling, "Touch and go around!" But too late. I will hit her. I will crash. I will die.

Aiming straight at the cargo plane, but fighting the urge to pull up abruptly, I add full throttle, trying to tug Roxanne back into the air. Cargo plane so large she fills my windscreen, but we are beginning to climb.

Thump! Roxanne veers to the left, but I bring her back. Has my left gear hit the cargo plane? Later—now fly the plane! We are up, free of the field, soaring to safety. The tower is talking to other aircraft, changing their approaches to avoid me as I rise to pattern altitude again.

"FT28-72 requests permission to land," I say, hoping my voice sounds normal.

"You have a slight problem, Monsieur Montreux. Your left wheel is lying on the end of Runway 7."

The voice isn't the voice of the traffic controller. It is Major Gerard.

"You must circle the field again, William. We will check to see that your other landing gear has been retracted."

It's bad enough that one wheel has been knocked off. If the other wheel didn't retract, it will be virtually impossible to land safely. I will have avoided one death on the runway to face another when I return. My heart is pounding so hard

I think it will leap up and hit the roof of my mouth. I can't swallow at all. I wonder how all the moisture can have left my face.

The lights on the instrument panel indicate that the gear has retracted. The way the plane is flying gives me no indication of drag in one direction or another. But . . . .

The major's voice comes on again. "An Air France pilot tells us that your gear is fully retracted. Good news.

"William," the major says calmly, "The airport has cleared Runway 4. Without landing gear, you will have to land on your belly. You'll need to be just above stall speed. You will skid along the runway, of course. Your brakes are useless. Are you following me?"

"Yes, Major."

"Good. Now turn for your landing."

It had all seemed so easy and perfect just minutes earlier. I turn the aircraft and head for Runway 4.

"Slower, but above the stalling speed I taught you . . . throttle down slowly."

The familiar sound of the engine fades. The propeller slows.

"Gently back on the stick . . . Good, you are settling in control . . . Keep your airspeed above stall . . . Full flaps! . . . Nose a little higher."

The earth is coming up at me with sickening speed.

"Good," the major says. "You're over the end of the runway.

"Calm, William, calm. When the skid begins, use your rudder to control your heading. Keep her on the runway if you can. The impact will be louder than normal. Don't go rigid against it—bounce with the aircraft. When the aircraft stops, open your canopy, unhook your parachute, and jump out of the plane as soon as you can. Fire trucks are waiting, but the fuel may still explode."

I do as I am told, trying to keep my body from tensing up.

Lower, then lower, then IMPACT! A screaming roar as the metal fuselage hits the runway. A bounce and a skid. A bounce and another skid. Pain shooting through my entire body, a scream from my lips. The plane fishtailing, spinning about, impossible to control the rudder, a wing crumpling, the fuselage screeching beneath me.

Then, a sudden stop. Roxanne noses over and almost stands on end, jolting me hard against my seat belt, knocking the air out of me. I unbuckle the belt, and I am spilling out of the cockpit, climbing over the crumpled wing—leaping off and running. Running and stumbling and falling and rolling over and over, trying to get away from the plane.

The sound of sirens and motors and aircraft overhead. Everything loud and unreal and the blast about to shatter me. I hunch my body into a ball and wait.

And wait.

There is no explosion. The sirens are still jawing. I roll over to look. Roxanne is very badly damaged, but still largely intact. Firemen are spraying her with foam. She has settled down and back, no longer on her nose. She accepts these indignities with grace and restraint.

An ambulance skids near me. Men run up with a stretcher. I may have some broken bones. I don't know. But I'm not going to die. I have landed Roxanne, somehow. I wonder if that qualifies me as a pilot—or disqualifies me.

I begin to laugh. The guys with the gurney look at me as if I am crazy.

◆　　◆　　◆

I was getting tired of waking up in hospitals. This time I wasn't in a coma—although the doctors were afraid I might have brain damage when the ambulance crew reported they found me laughing after crashing an airplane at Le Bourget.

They insisted on taking me to the nearest hospital; Major Gerard and Louise insisted on riding along. The major told the driver he was an aide to the president, and that got their attention.

"I'm fine," I kept saying during the race to the hospital.

They checked my pulse and blood pressure and weren't able to find anything except a cut on my forehead where I scraped it on the canopy when Roxanne tried to go over on her nose. I had scrapes and scratches from bouncing around and climbing out on the wing and scrambling across the ground. I think I disappointed the ambulance crew, who seemed to believe I should at the very least have had the decency to break a few bones in such a spectacular crash landing.

"We'll x-ray you from head to toe at the hospital," one said, as if I had to pay for cheating them out of a chance to apply some splints.

The ambulance nurses were very suspicious.

"Why were you laughing?" one asked.

The other made a derisive gesture. "Shock," he said, dismissively.

Which made me laugh again, and upset them all over again.

"Shock for sure!" I said. "Shock that I managed to land the plane without killing myself!"

"You were wonderful!" Louise said. "Wasn't he wonderful, Major?"

The major sighed. "It was an exceptional landing under the circumstances. I have been flying for twenty years and I don't know how anyone could have done better."

"Thank you!" I said, genuinely thrilled.

"There are a few things we can discuss for future application," the major added, "but they are trivial."

"Does that landing qualify? Am I considered as having

soloed? Can you certify me so that I can get a flying license?"

The major smiled. "That's what you were laughing at, wasn't it? You were thinking about whether a crash landing was a qualifying event?"

I nodded, not taking my eyes off him.

Now, both he and Louise were laughing.

"I believe," the major said, "that unorthodox as it may be, landing a crippled aircraft safely and without loss of life—or apparently even serious injury—may be certified by me as fully complying with the requirements."

I smiled as broadly as my cracked lips would allow and Louise kissed me.

"That," the major said, "is the ultimate certification."

Still, the medics insisted that I be admitted to the emergency room, x-rayed, and examined by several doctors, seeking for any kind of injury, internal, external or otherwise. They checked my heart, lungs and brain, scanning every millimeter of me. There were the usual jokes about finding nothing in my brain, and other similar remarks. Still, they insisted that I must remain in the hospital overnight, which I found very annoying.

"You know," I told them. "The last time I was in the hospital someone tried to kill me."

The doctors stiffened. "There is no possibility that any of us will do you any damage whatsoever."

"It wasn't a doctor," I said. "At least I don't think so."

After a while, there were nice messages from Roger and even the president. I spoke to my mother over the telephone and reassured her that I was perfectly well.

"You probably won't want to fly planes after this," she said, "at least for a while."

In fact, I could hardly wait to get back up in the air, but I was smart enough not to tell her that. After I hung up, I told Major Gerard, "I want to fly again as soon as possible."

He said something like "Hmm."

Which brought me to another difficult question: "How is Roxanne?"

He sighed. "I'm afraid the lady is not as anxious to fly again as you are."

"I'm sorry," I said.

"She doesn't blame you," the major said. "Roxanne has been badly treated by pilots who forced her go faster and dive more steeply than she wished, who flew her in the desert where it was sandy and hot, and at high altitudes where it was freezing cold. Sometimes they starved her for fuel, and at others they failed to make certain she had her regular bath. On many occasions, when pilots engaged their enemies—not hers—she was shot at and even hit. Most of her wounds healed, but Roxanne still remembers. All in all, I think she has had enough of human company— although I'm sure she would have preferred to make an exception for you, Mademoiselle Louise, one lady accompanying another—but I believe that she has reached an age where graceful retirement seems attractive."

"I'm sorry," I said, "that I should be the one—"

"—You mustn't think that at all, William," the major said. "In fact, she may choose to remember that you brought the last, shall we say, thrill, into her life."

◆　　◆　　◆

I managed to get out of the hospital the day after they finished my tests. Louise and the major were waiting with a black staff Citroen, and they escorted me back to Paris.

"Neither of you has discussed this event with anyone, is that correct?" the major asked.

Louise said, "We followed your orders and told no one."

"Good. The press was informed that the airplane which crashed was piloted by an air cadet, and they will not be allowed to question him."

"I'm happy to hear that," I said. "I wouldn't have known what to tell a bunch of reporters."

When we reached the Élysée Palace, guards came out to escort us in. Most of them were smiling, and they invented a little ceremony with crossed swords that we walked under. I guess the way that Major Gerard had told the story, I was viewed as some kind of hero—not just a dummy who smashed up a perfectly good airplane.

The president and Madame de Gaulle greeted us in their private suite. The president shook hands gravely, and Madame gave us both a hug.

"You have again justified my belief in you as a courageous and resourceful fellow," the president said to me. "The ground controller who cleared the cargo plane into your path has been suitably punished."

I felt terrible. "I'm sorry. I didn't want to—"

"—William," the president said, interrupting me. "Apparently you are not aware that the aircraft that caused your problems was deliberately sent onto the wrong runway."

That left me speechless.

"Major Gerard was pressed into service at the control tower because it was necessary to immediately relieve and place under arrest the controller who had intentionally created a potential disaster."

"Was it Tony Bersault?" I asked.

"The controller refuses to answer questions," the major said. "As for Bersault, he was on a commercial airliner flying to the United States on the day it happened."

"We never catch him," Louise said.

"Was there a sign of the DragonSlayers?" I asked.

"We didn't uncover any," the major said.

"I'm very lucky the major was at the tower to talk me down," I said. "Again, I thank you for saving my life."

"I was only fulfilling my duties," the major said.

"Somehow," the president said, "Major Gerard is always where he is most needed."

◆　　◆　　◆

A week later, the major convinced the commander of the base to loan us another Desert Fox for additional training. This one had been named Lionel for the father of one of the pilots who had flown her in Algeria.

"I have obtained permission to rename 'Lionel' as 'Roxanne 2,'" the major told us. "With all due respect to the previous pilot, an aircraft should never be given a masculine name. It flies in the face of history and nature."

The day of Louise's flight was chilly and cloudy, with gusting winds.

"We can postpone this," the major said.

"No, I'm ready," Louise said.

I had the urge to kiss Louise before she climbed into the cockpit, but that wouldn't have been, as the French say, *comme il faut*—suitable—so I gave her the same handshake that Major Gerard did.

We watched her taxi along the feeder ramps and onto the main runway. She would be taking off with a cross wind striking the plane at almost exactly a ninety degree angle.

"Not more than eighteen kilometers per hour," the major said, reading my mind.

She started down the runway, accelerated smoothly with just the right combinations of ailerons and rudder to control her direction, and soared into the sky. We watched her as long as she was in sight and counted minutes until her expected return.

"There!" I said. She had just entered the outer limit of our vision. I caught sight of her flying above a British Airways jet coming in to land. *Those people better stay out of her way,* I thought.

I lost sight of Roxanne 2 as she circled the field, but the major, with his practiced eye, pointed her out as she began her descent. Louise turned the plane slightly into the breeze to follow a straight course down to the runway; there was no wobble, little movement of ailerons and elevators, little movement of Roxanne up and down in the sometimes tricky currents.

Then she was low over the runway, coming in with nose slightly down, flaps extended, smoothly, smoothly, smooooooothly. The two main wheels touched a fraction of a second before she lowered the nose wheel. We saw a tiny bit of smoke as the brakes took hold, but her rollout was very straight and even.

"You see, William," the major said. "That is how it should be done."

◆　　◆　　◆

A few weeks later the major advised me of another exciting piece of information: the design of the Desert Fox was based on an American aircraft, the North American T-28, which had been modified for the French Air Force. Perhaps Alan Stevens had flown in exactly the same type of plane.

THE RIOT IN THE
RUE ST. MICHEL

Our friends in the Clandestin were very interested in our flying lessons and they asked us about them day after day.

"Can you take me up in your plane?" Jacques asked.

"It's not my plane, Jacques," I said. "I don't think Major Gerard will let me carry a passenger in a military aircraft."

"William is very careful who he flies with," Mai said, with something like a smirk on her face.

Later, when I was in the Raging Dragon having a cup of coffee with Mohammed, he told me that he knew how to fly; his father owned his own private twin-engine aircraft.

"Now that you've soloed," he said, "maybe you'd like to learn to fly our Dassault Spirale Turboprop."

I think my eyes bugged out. All I knew about turboprops was that the engines were jets with turbine-driven propellers that added power to the jet exhaust.

"Thanks," I said, "but I'm barely qualified on a single engine plane—I can only fly under visual flight rules. Don't you have to be trained on instruments to fly a plane like yours?"

"Well," he said. "I have been certified, although I've never had to fly by instruments in an emergency."

"If you turned over the controls of your plane to me," I said. "you'd automatically have an emergency."

We both laughed.

I liked Mohammed a lot—he was a good student, but

very relaxed and easy-going. We attended several classes together, and often met at the Raging Dragon. He was the perfect "drinking" companion for me because he was a Muslim and didn't drink alcoholic beverages.

Mohammed and I often discussed politics; he knew much more than I did, having lived in so many different places, and having a father in the French Foreign Office. The subject of Algeria was on everybody's mind. I tried to learn as much as I could, reading newspapers of the left and the right, talking to Roger and questioning Mohammed.

"Where do your sympathies lie?" I asked him.

"You must understand," he said, "that the Algerian question is very difficult for me. Because of my father's position I must be very diplomatic and careful not to say anything that might embarrass him."

"I'm not going to tell anyone what you say unless you give me permission, Mo (that was the nickname he had approved). What is your personal opinion?"

He sighed. "The flow of history is toward the independence of former colonies of European countries. The French like to say—and many of them really mean it—that Algeria is no longer a colony, but rather an integral part of the nation."

"Isn't that true?"

"Up to a point," he said. "But native peoples feel they have been subjugated by settlers and that is also correct in some ways. There doesn't seem to be a middle path—those who try to take a position between the native peoples and the settlers are shouted down."

"We understand there has been much violence on both sides," I said.

"I believe the FLN has been guilty of great brutality in some instances, but decent people are also astonished that torture has become a standard procedure for the French military. Few people in France are willing to justify that, even if they want to hold on to Algeria."

I couldn't help noticing that he had said, "hold on to Algeria," which seemed to me to be an indication of his own feelings.

"Most of the students seem to be in favor of independence," I said. "They march in the streets and carry posters opposing the torture, urging separation. Have you ever been tempted to march with the student union, the UNEF?" I asked.

Mohammed leaned forward. "If I did, there would indeed be a split—a split in my head from my own father."

I laughed.

"Even if I agreed with the student groups," he said, "I distrust them because some of the students are prone to violence and I hate to see that in the streets of Paris."

"According to the newspapers, the opposition to independence is headed by prominent politicians who seem almost as hard-headed."

"Yes," he said, "the trade unions and the communists favor separation, but many French people—not all of them rightists—feel the opposite."

"What do you think will happen?" I asked.

"I'm not a prophet or a seer," Mohammed said, "but I think separation is inevitable. The only question is whether it will be peaceful or violent."

◆   ◆   ◆

In September, 1960, there was a trial of people who had supported the FLN, the National Liberation Front of Algeria, which the government considered a terrorist organization.

"The intellectuals on the left are outraged," Roger said. "They can't understand how France, the champion of the rights of man, can fight a war against people who wish to form an independent state."

"I've been reading *Le Monde*," I said. "Famous people are

saying that soldiers should disobey orders and desert rather than continue fighting the native Algerians."

"So far," Roger said, "there have been few desertions and no mutiny, but the intellectuals have issued a manifesto against the war, signed by 121 leading scholars, artists, writers, movie stars—such people as Jean-Paul Sartre, Françoise Sagan, Simone de Beauvoir and Simone Signoret."

"I hear there's going to be a student demonstration today, but I promised Mohammed I would meet him at the Raging Dragon."

"Phone your friend," Roger said, "and postpone it."

"I'll meet him at the bistro and we'll immediately go somewhere else," I said.

The streets were quiet. Here and there, the remains of a torn anti-war poster littered the walk or were stuffed into a trash can. The Place St. Michel wasn't crowded, although the Raging Dragon was busy.

I saw Mohammed the moment I entered the Raging Dragon.

"There are rumors of a major demonstration in the place," he said. "Let's get out of here."

But it was already too late.

We heard yelling from the square, and the customers in the Raging Dragon were on their feet and trying to squeeze through the doorway.

Mohammed, who was taller than I was, stood on his toes looking into the street. "The square is filled with demonstrators," he said.

I was anxious to see what was going on. Gradually, we were squeezing through the funnel of people and tables into the Place St. Michel.

"*Algérie Libre! Algérie Libre! Algérie Libre!*" The chant was taken up by dozens of voices.

A couple of times I heard *Vive de Gaulle*, but that didn't

seem very popular, even though the president had supported self-determination. For these young (and not so young) people, any kind of authority was suspect.

Students were carrying posters, yelling for Algerian independence, cursing the military, sometimes cursing each other. The scene was colorful, although the primary color was red. Some demonstrators wore red shirts, others red bandannas, a few carried red flags or banners, with the occasional black hammer and sickle. But those were accents. For the most part, the students—some in their thirties—wore a disparate mélange of shirts, pants and jackets. There were as many women as men. It was September and the air was brisk, but a couple of the demonstrators had ripped off their shirts. I wondered if they were protesting the wearing of clothes.

Many police were in the place, attempting to channel the marchers away from the storefronts and to keep traffic moving. Automobile horns were blowing along the Boulevard St. Michel and the cross streets, but there was no movement. The cacophony had a throbbing quality, as if the yelling and horn-blowing were orchestrated.

Counterpoint was provided by protestors singing the "Marseillaise," the French national anthem, while others sang "Meadowlands," a communist anthem. Despite the yelling, most of the demonstrators didn't seem angry. Some of the people were clearly outraged, others seemed to be out for a good time.

"Doesn't look too bad," I said to Mohammed—or rather, I yelled in his ear.

"Look at the bridge," he replied.

A large band of men was marching across the Pont St. Michel, some bearing signs that read *Algérie Francaise*, others carrying the French Tricolor. None of them were smiling. I wondered who they were—although they had looked brawny, I knew that the unions had joined the students in supporting Algerian independence.

The students gradually became aware of the men approaching them. Both groups began to surge together. I would have preferred to slip away, but we were being shoved forward by a group waving red banners and yelling friendly greetings like "Rightist Pigs," "Capitalist Dogs!" and other more obscene remarks.

In a moment the clash began, despite the police brandishing clubs and police cars hee-hawing. The grim-looking men were also swinging clubs and banging the wooden supports of their posters on the heads of the "students." The students used their posts and their clubs to respond. Fist fights were going on all around us. The very sound of the blows, wood on wood, wood on skulls, fists on jaws, feet on streets, created an ugly and distinctive rhythm.

Mohammed and I were dodging and twisting, holding our arms high to block blows, ducking as many as we could. We were about to spring free at the edge of the crowd, when a tall, muscular man with a shaved head and fierce black eyes grabbed Mohammed.

"Algerian dung!" he cried, and smashed him across the head with short, round stick.

Mohammed reeled backwards, blood spurting from a cut over his eyes, but the man raised his club again, yelling guttural oaths. I grabbed his arm from behind and shoved him off balance. He roared and swung around, screaming at me. I gripped his club arm, pulled him forward and threw him across my hip, so that he went crashing into another man.

Mohammed was kneeling in the street holding his bloody face. Another guy began punching him in the back of the head. I left my feet and kicked the guy in the ribs. He yelled in pain and crumpled down.

Other men surrounded us, trying to punch or kick us.

Mohammed had managed to get up and was doing his best to fend off the blows. I was using everything Roger and Jacques (and Mai) had taught me, and I kept surprising the attackers, who were expecting punches and clubs, not Judo. But there were too many of them, and they rolled over us.

We were about to be beaten senseless when a couple of policemen arrived, swinging their own truncheons and clearing most of the mob. That left Mohammed and me and two of the thugs.

"Bring them all in!" a policeman yelled, and they began dragging the four of us to the wagons.

◆　　◆　　◆

I tried to tell the police that Mo and I were innocent bystanders, but they wouldn't listen. We were shoved into the wagon with the guys who had attacked us; there were already several surly men inside. Nobody was saying anything, but we were all staring at each other warily.

Mohammed was trying to wipe away the blood with a handkerchief, but not doing a very good job.

I spoke to the policemen who were guarding the wagon. "Can't you see the man is bleeding?" I asked. "He should be taken to hospital."

One of them reached under the prisoner's bench in the wagon and threw me a white box with a red cross on it—a first aid kit. That was the first time I had ever seen such a thing. I opened it gingerly and found some antiseptic, swabs and a bandage.

"Hold tight," I told Mohammed, as I cleaned his wounds. The chemical was very astringent and he flinched.

"Sorry, Mo," I said.

He gave me a weak smile. "If my father ever finds out, I'm finished."

As I cleaned the wound, I was relieved to see that the cut was long, but not deep. However, Mohammed's left eye was bloodshot and swollen, and the flesh around it was rapidly turning an ugly color.

I found a pad and an adhesive bandage and bound up the cut. It looked clumsy and amateurish, and later Roger told me it would have been better to leave the wound exposed to the air.

Meanwhile, the sounds of battle gradually diminished, and through the open doors of the police van we watched the crowds gradually dispersing. Police were still dragging combatants to their fleet of wagons. I saw a couple of flashes and assumed that reporters were covering the demonstrations. I wondered if the lady from *Le Monde* was there. Later, I learned that she had been one of the marchers.

"Why don't you let us go?" I asked the policeman who was guarding us. "We weren't even in the demonstration."

He shrugged. "I was told to guard you," he said. "That is what I am doing."

"Not much of an answer for a clever Frenchman," I said.

The policeman, who was a young fellow with smooth, clean features, smiled a nice even smile with nice, even teeth.

"As far as I'm concerned—" he began.

"—Don't let these commies trick you!" the man who had first hit Mohammed yelled.

The young policeman, eying the bully, said to me, "How did you get involved with that moron?"

The "moron" eyed him fiercely and started to stand up, but the policeman's hand went to the truncheon in his holster, and the guy sat down.

"We're not with them," I said. "We were walking along minding our own business when this guy started beating Mohammed on the head."

Speaking of Mohammed, the gendarme said, "He's an Algerian, right?"

"I'm a Frenchman," Mohammed said, straightening. "I

had nothing to do with these thugs."

That set the bullies grumbling again.

"Can I speak to you a minute?" I asked the policeman.

He allowed me to step down from the wagon and we walked a few steps away.

"Mohammed's father is an official in the Foreign Office. He'll be in a lot of trouble and his father will be deeply embarrassed if this becomes public knowledge."

The policeman drummed his fingers on the handle of his truncheon, then gestured to Mohammed, who wearily climbed down from the wagon.

"Both of you," the policeman said, "start walking—slowly—but get out of here as soon as you can."

"Thanks," I whispered.

Mohammed and I started walking away, the most innocent possible expressions on our faces.

"Wait a minute!" the thug yelled from the van. "Those commies are escaping!"

KILL ALL
THE BOOKS

Mohammed thanked me over and again for saving him from the bullies, and helping him make a graceful escape from the police.

"Go home, and take care of your wounds," I said. "If you're exiled from Paris, I can hide you in the Crouching Dragon."

He grinned and shook my hand and hurried away.

I headed for Roger's apartment, but I couldn't resist going by way of the Raging Dragon. Something was obviously wrong: on the sidewalk lay the damaged sign of the Raging Dragon, which had been torn from its frame and smashed to the pavement. It was split in the middle, as if a sword had been driven through the body of the dragon. Like the sign of the DragonSlayers. My blood began to boil again.

Two men I recognized as waiters were working on the sign.

"What happened?" I asked.

One of the waiters said, "A couple of men with pruning hooks—like the kind you use on fruit trees—pulled down the sign and trampled it. They were yelling '*Algérie Francaise!*' and 'Death to traitors!' and 'Kill the commies.' By the time we got outside they were gone."

"Did they say anything about DragonSlayers?" I asked.

"So that's what they were yelling," the second waiter said. "Who are the DragonSlayers?"

I didn't want to get into that. "Can you fix the sign?" I asked.

"I don't know," the second waiter said. "The parts don't quite fit together as you can see, and if we patch it, the sign won't look right."

"Maybe that's how it ought to look," I said. "It would be a symbol of the dragon overcoming its enemies."

They looked at me with surprise, but then smiled.

◆   ◆   ◆

Roger said, "You have a knack for getting in harm's way, William."

I grinned. "I'm totally innocent. These things just happen to me."

"Why didn't you stay inside the bistro?"

While I was mulling that over, Roger said, "Don't answer. I want you to remain William Montreux, not some-one else. However, it's obvious that the Sûreté doesn't have you under twenty-four hour surveillance."

"I couldn't live with that," I said. "Anyway, I have my friends in the Clandestin, and I still have you."

Security was an issue that Roger and I had argued about before. The first night in Roger's apartment, he had shown me a rifle, automatic pistol and ammunition he kept under lock and key in a sturdy armoire. He gave me a key to the armoire as well as a key to the apartment.

"I used them in the Resistance," he said, "and I hope I'll never use them again, but I believe you should know where they are, just in case. Would you like to learn how to fire these weapons under strict training conditions?"

I hesitated for only a moment. "No," I said. "Not now." I was thinking, *Not ever, I'll never touch a gun*, but I didn't know what crises life would later bring.

◆   ◆   ◆

In the past I had seldom walked to and from the apart-ment with Roger. But after the demonstrations, he often made excuses to keep me company. One afternoon, he came to find me in the Labrouste Reading Room of the great library known as the BSG—the Bibliotheque Sainte Genvieve of the Sorbonne—where I often studied. There were over two million books in the collections, and the reading room contained row after row of tables and chairs, under a high, double arching ceiling framed with surprisingly slim steel columns and girders.

"Come on," Roger said. "We're going home early."

In the past, we had often visited some of the sights of the city on the way to his apartment, but now Roger was being extremely cautious, and we walked directly to 45 Rue des Écoles.

The elevator wasn't on the ground floor, and when I pushed the call button, nothing happened. We looked up to see it stationed on our floor. Roger was exasperated.

"Out of service again? Come on, we'll walk."

We trudged up the stairs.

"Look," Roger said, as we approached the top floor, "the doors to the elevator are blocked open. Is it out of order?"

Then his expression changed. He pointed to the door to his apartment. It, too, was propped open with a small piece of wood.

"No one should be in the apartment without my permission!" Roger said. He marched inside, then threw out his arms and stopped me.

Ahead of us in the kitchen, pots and pans were strewn about, broken glasses and shattered plates covered the floor. The door of the small refrigerator had been ripped off and leaned crazily against the kitchen table.

A glance back towards the bedrooms revealed the doors open and books and papers scattered and torn. We heard the sounds of ripping and tearing to our left, and we ran towards the parlor at the front the apartment.

Two men wearing black pants and jackets and black ski

masks were trashing everything in sight, making so much noise they didn't hear us approach. One tall, big-chested man was wielding a small axe; the other, short and round, was swinging a crowbar. It was the Crouching Dragon all over again.

The tall man was leaning over a large folder lying on the floor with engineering drawings spilling out of it, while he held the axe poised over his head. Roger lunged at him, grabbed his axe arm with both hands and bent it savagely backward. The man staggered back, his arm almost breaking, as he crashed into the wall. Screaming, he dropped the axe.

The short man hurried toward Roger, swinging the crowbar. I grabbed the first thing I saw—a plate—and threw it at him. The plate shattered against his head with a roar, and the man stumbled, but didn't fall. He turned to face me, still holding the crowbar, while blood shot through the nose and mouth holes of his mask.

Roger and the tall man were wrestling, hand-to-hand, falling over a table that gave way beneath them, crawling over chairs, bouncing off the windows, shattering a few panes. Roger was adept at Judo, but the other guy seemed to know a martial art, and he was fending Roger off.

The guy with the crowbar was obviously groggy, but he was stalking me. I didn't see anything to use as a weapon, but I knew I had to stop him before he gathered his strength. I spun and kicked at his hand, and fortunately knocked the crowbar away. Then I jumped on him, but he managed to step aside and, although I hit his shoulder, I bounced off and crashed to the floor. Sometimes I forgot everything the Judo masters had taught me.

He was on me, so close I could see his gray eyes through the mask and the fierce leer that spread his lips— and the knife in his hand. I reached desperately around, grabbed a book and thrust it forward as he struck. The jolt nearly took my shoulders out of their sockets. As I pulled the book back to block another blow, I saw that the knife was stuck deep into it. I had yanked it out of his hands as I pulled the book away.

He kept coming, falling on top of me, swinging his fist so that even as I turned my head, the blow glanced off my chin, hard enough to make me feel the lower part of my face was going to separate from the upper.

But now I could grapple. I grabbed his arm and used the force of his swing to shove him in the same direction his arm was going and rolled away, so that he hit the floor. I grabbed the hilt of the knife stuck in the book and yanked as hard as I could. The guy was on his feet, coming at me again, when he saw I had the knife. I took a wide stance, holding the blade up in front of me as I had seen in a movie.

The guy hesitated, broke away, and began running down the corridor.

Roger was now giving the tall guy a pretty good beating, using the edges of his hands and his fists according to Judo protocol, and the tall guy also broke away and ran down the corridor.

"You stay here!" Roger yelled, at me pulling his automatic pistol from the cabinet in a quick, almost blindingly fast move, and shoving it into his waistband.

"No way!" I yelled and ran after him.

I thought the intruders would use the stairs, but they didn't. The sound of metal on metal turned us around and we looked up, just as the access panel over the metal rungs that led to the roof slammed shut.

"Stay here!" Roger yelled again, as he began to climb quickly up the rungs.

I didn't even bother to disagree; I started up the rungs behind him. At the top, Roger pulled out his automatic just as he shoved open the access panel. We heard the sound of feet running on gravel.

Roger clambered through and I followed him. Ahead, the two men reached the end of the roof and leaped across to the next building.

"They'll run out of roofs soon!" Roger yelled. He had apparently accepted my participation in the chase.

We both leaped across to the next building, which had a copper rather than gravel roof; I skidded on the surface, but recaptured my footing.

"Stop!" Roger yelled at the two men, holding his automatic aloft.

They never slowed their pace, even as they approached the next building, which was several feet lower. They both leaped and we heard a yelp as one of them apparently landed badly. When we reached the edge, they were running again, although the round guy was limping.

"Stop! I have a gun!" Roger yelled.

They hunched over, but didn't stop.

Roger glanced at me for a second, shrugged, stuffed his gun into his waistband and jumped down to the lower roof. I followed.

The impact didn't seem to bother Roger at all—I had been concerned that since he was an "old man" of forty, he might come up groaning. He didn't.

I landed a second later, having bent my knees to absorb the impact, and rolled over as the Judo masters had taught me.

"There's construction scaffolding at the end of the building," Roger called out. "They're going to climb down to the street!"

We ran even faster, watching as the two men jumped onto the scaffold and swung over the side. By the time we reached the framework, they were half way down, sliding along the circular uprights, clambering down the cross-bracing. As we followed them, we saw masks discarded on a platform and then jackets. They were out of our view now, and we didn't even know what they looked like.

At the bottom, we ran into a crowd of people at the intersection of the Rue des Écoles and and the Boulevard St. Michel. The evening rush hour was beginning. We stared about, trying to locate the intruders.

"There!" Roger yelled and started off towards the Boulevard St. Germain. He cut across the crowded sidewalk onto the street and began running. At that instant I saw a tall blonde man running ahead.

"It's him!" Roger called out, puffing a bit, "Raoul Larron, the man who led the thieves at the Crouching Dragon."

I wanted to yell that he was in jail, but maybe he wasn't.

Drivers were incensed to find the two of us running along the gutter. Horns blew, drivers shouted, and brakes screamed as we slithered along the curb. We were rapidly approaching the intersection with the Boulevard St. Germain.

"Metro!" Roger called back over his shoulder, cutting sharply across the street, dodging car after car. I was too scared to stop or think—I just followed him. At the entrance to the Metro, I saw Larron and a short, chubby, dark-haired man running with him.

By the time we had crossed the intersection, they had disappeared down the steps. When we reached the steps, they were lunging down the escalator, pushing people aside. We hurried down as fast as we could, slipping between people, raising their ire and earning sharply-worded protests. The French are very gifted at swearing, and their epithets cover many generations and large parts of the animal kingdom.

I was carrying my student Metro pass and Roger had his faculty pass so we barged through the turnstiles side by side.

Then we were on the Cluny-Sorbonne platform, the walls of tile and concrete arching over us, the crowds moving every which way, trains roaring through the tunnel, whistles blowing, speakers droning, lights flashing.

"They've jumped the platform!" I yelled, watching the two men avoid the electrified third rail and clamber up on the opposite platform. Roger never hesitated—leaping down, toe-dancing to avoid contact with the third rail, climbing up on the other side.

People were yelling at us, a policeman blew his whistle. Our quarry dodged into another pedestrian tunnel. The smaller man banged into somebody and knocked him off his feet. The injured party yelled an unprintable name, while the short man scrambled after Larron.

The guy who had been knocked down got up and unwittingly stepped into Roger's path. Roger crashed into him, knocking the man down once again. Roger merely spun around and continued the chase. I jumped over the fallen man, who groggily reached up and caught the heel of my right foot. I was airborne for a second, arms windmilling, and then I hit the pavement, stumbled a few step and kept running.

"Line 4!" Roger screamed. Three underground Metro lines criss-crossed in that station, and Roger had chosen number 4.

The men we were chasing leaped over a set of turnstiles, drawing protests from a guard, but he didn't follow them. We used our passes, which slowed us a little. We reached the platform level, but the north and south lines, although adjacent, were in separate tunnels, divided by walls. The signs told us north was Porte de Cligancourt, south was Porte d'Orléans. Which way?

Roger seemed to have no doubt, racing towards the southbound platform after a train about to leave. The doors to the last car were still open, and Roger pushed his way aboard. The sliding doors grazing my arms as I squeezed inside.

We looked about trying to locate the intruders, but didn't see them.

"We'll have to go through the cars," Roger said—the noise of the running train was so great I almost had to read his lips—and we started forward.

Not without resistance. No one, of course, was prepared to move out of our way voluntarily, and we had to force out way through the crowd. Fortunately, most people simply yielded to the pressure.

A few—more women than men—resisted physically, or at least frowned, but no one said a word, and we kept moving, searching ahead and from side to side. It was slow going. The trains reached St. Germain des Prés before we entered the next car, and then we had to deal with the press of people exiting and entering.

It was hot and sticky in the car, and bouncing off people was beginning to wear on me, but Roger kept resolutely pushing forward. We made stops at Saint-Sulpice and St. Placide, then passed through the huge multi-level station at Montparnasse Bienvenue, where lines 6, 12 and 13 intersected with line 4. When our train halted and the doors opened, people were shoving in every direction, and in with the crowd came the sounds of trains squealing, people yelling, loudspeakers wailing, and a jack-hammer throbbing somewhere.

Roger yelled, "If those rats get off at this station, we'll never notice them."

I yelled back, "I thought you knew where they were going?"

Roger scrunched his eyes and responded, "Maybe I don't know enough about the criminal mind."

The train lurched into motion. The track made a ninety degree angle swing to the left after the station and soon reached Vavin. We finally reached the rear end of the front car, without a sign of our enemies. Perhaps they had disembarked long ago.

Once again we were in motion, and in a couple of minutes the train stopped at another large station, Raspail. We had almost reached the motor car, meaning we had searched the entire train. There was a glass partition between the passenger compartment and the engineer's compartment, and it was obvious the engineer was riding alone. There was no place to search and we hadn't found them.

I sagged, and Roger did, too. As we hesitated, the doors closed and the train began to move, gliding along the platform.

"Look!" I yelled. Roger followed my pointing hand. On the platform, grinning, or rather, leering at us, were the two men, standing nonchalantly in a sea of hurrying travelers. Larron, the big blonde guy, was making an obscene gesture.

Roger lunged against the doors, but it was too late. We were well underway.

"They got away," I said, dejectedly.

"Don't be too sure," Roger said, surprising me. "We'll have a nice, quiet ride to Denfert-Rochereau."

I was flabbergasted.

"Close your mouth, Willi," Roger said. "Relax. Now we're ahead of them. Whether they walk or take the next train, we'll get there before they do."

"Get where?"

"To the catacombs."

A chill went through me. "Where they buried people?"

Roger nodded, "Seven million, give or take a million."

The train finally reached Denfert-Rochereau, and I followed Roger onto the platform and up the escalators to the street.

"There," he said, pointing to a pair of three-story, lime-stone buildings with gabled roofs and triple arches that flanked the Avenue du Général Leclerc. "They were orginally built by Claude-Nicholas Ledoux as tollhouses in the late eighteenth century. No. 1 houses the entrance to the catacombs."

"Why don't we wait and capture them here?" I asked. I didn't want to go down into the catacombs. "In fact, if there's time, maybe we should call the police."

He smiled. "I don't really want to capture them. I want to follow them and see what more I can learn about the DragonSlayers. However, we can wait here and see if they come down the street or up from the Metro."

I asked Roger a question that had been bothering me since the first time we had seen the mark of the DragonSlayers: "While I sure hate the guys who use it, I don't understand what's wrong with the symbol itself—a sword thrusting through the body of a dragon."

"You seem to believe the dragon is the bad guy," Roger said. "It's true that in most of the western world, people think of dragons as evil and destructive. In Bonville, almost everyone feared the Crouching Dragon, and your local church is named for St. George, the knight who killed a dragon. But think about it: the Crouching Dragon was a place where you and your friends created a wonderful fantasy kingdom. You learned lessons of courage and friendship under the glaring eye of the Dragon Tower. Eventually you discovered that I had built an animated model of the Allied landings on the Normandy beaches. Recently, you and I were both honored by France for saving a national treasure and donating it to the people. Do you still think of the Crouching Dragon as evil?"

"No," I said, "the Crouching Dragon has been good to my friends, my town and the whole country."

"In other parts of the world," Roger said, "especially in Asia, the dragon is respected as a sign of prosperity and well-being—a force for good. I think the DragonSlayers hate what is good and want to destroy it."

Of course, there was another matter bothering me. "Did they really dig miles of tunnels just for a cemetery?" I asked.

"No," Roger said. "For almost two thousand years, limestone quarried underground was used to construct some of the buildings in the city. Eventually, the quarries were abandoned. They might have been forgotten, except that they kept collapsing. During the eighteenth century the authorities decided to locate all the quarries and shore them up.

"They ended up with over three hundred kilometers of galleries, unintentionally creating a maze where it was possible to hide from the police and to smuggle people and objects into and out of town. However, this network proved to be the solution to a pressing problem. In the late eighteenth century, many epidemics were traced to city cemeteries. Someone had the ingenious idea of closing the worst cemeteries and re-interring bodies and bones in the tunnels. In one fifteen month period, they transported millions of bones and rotting corpses in huge carts by night from the unsanitary city cemetery at Les Halles."

The whole thing sounded pretty horrible to me. "Are bodies still brought there to be buried?"

"Not legally," Roger said, "but who knows? The catacombs have become a playground for the adventurous, for young people in search of thrills, or close encounters with the occult."

Roger suddenly pulled me into the shadows. Across the street, Raoul Larron and his confederate came out of the Metro station, walking rapidly, but without looking around. Apparently they believed we had given up the chase. They crossed the street to the entry, where a set of metal, arched panels and a modest nameplate read *"ENTRE DES CATA-COMBES."* The two men disappeared through the doorway.

Roger said, "Let's wait one minute."

Exactly sixty seconds later we hurried across the street and entered the doorway, where Roger greeted the uniformed guard inside.

"Bonjour, Pierre," Roger said. "This is my friend, William."

"Mon plaisir," Pierre said.

"Do you want to take your flashlight?" Pierre asked, reaching to open a metal storage cabinet.

"Of course," Roger said. "I appreciate your kindness in keeping it here for me."

Pierre shrugged in a typically French way.

We began to descend a long spiral staircase with a round metal railing affixed to the stone walls. I guessed the bottom was twenty or twenty-five meters below the surface. We entered a tunnel—I couldn't quite touch the walls on both sides and the arching ceiling was a little higher than I could reach. The lighting was very poor—it was a good thing Roger brought his flashlight—and the air felt heavy and old. The walls were not quite dripping, but they were cold and damp to the touch.

We heard footsteps ahead of us, and Roger paused for a moment and held his fingers to his mouth, then began moving forward cautiously. We came to a junction, and Roger pointed left. We had entered a maze of rock quarries. Some walls were natural stone, occasionally showing the marks of quarrying. Others were built up of stone blocks, most set in neat, regular tiers, some in haphazard fashion.

Suddenly a couple of kids, a boy and a girl, maybe ten or twelve years old, appeared out of the gloom, walking towards us. They grinned, a little uncertainly, and soon passed us, moving towards the entrance.

It seemed that we were descending gradually. We turned to the right and suddenly I heard the crunch of wet gravel beneath our feet. At that amount, a light flashed briefly, a voice yelled something unintelligible, and then we heard the sound of feet running away from us. We started running, too.

Roger, ever the professor, whispered as we ran: "This is the underground entrance to the Ossuary of Denfert-Rochereau, for which the Metro stop is named."

Strange plaster and stone square columns with crown-shaped capitals marked the entry. Inside the crypt, bones and skulls were piled to the ceiling as far as Roger's flashlight let us see. Many skulls consisted of merely the cranium, missing their teeth and lower jaws.

"It looks as if the walls are quilted with bones," I whispered, shuddering as we loped along.

We could still hear the pounding feet of our adversaries as we ran through chamber after chamber. The skulls became a blur of grinning, sightless heads, and the bones might well have been kindling.

Roger whispered, "Remains from Trinity cemetery."

The arrangements were more haphazard than in the previous crypt, although the stone walls were built so neatly that they contrast weirdly with the remains of the dead.

There was a crude stone altar with words incised into the stone. In the flash of Roger's light, I read, "Man, like a flower of the field, flourishes while the breath is in him, and does not remain nor any longer know his place." Very comforting.

There was a sharp flash of light from ahead, and Roger yelled, "Down!"

I hit the slimy floor and rolled to one side. Immediately there was another flash—a different, flaring, reddish dart—then a loud report, and something whistled by my head so closely that my hair parted. A row of skulls shattered into shards, fragments striking my face, arms and chest.

Instantly, Roger was beside me, tearing off a piece of his shirt and wiping my face. There was blood from many tiny cuts, but I could see all right.

"Just scratches," Roger said. He was blocking my body from the tunnel, but I clearly heard our assailants running away.

"This time I won't be so gentle," Roger said through clenched teeth, as he got to his feet, pulled his automatic out of his pocket and started running.

As usual, he called, "Stay here!" There was no chance of that.

We descended further, following the corridors as they slanted deeper under the city, racing past a sign reading, "Cemetery of St. Nicolas des Champs, 1804." Bones were strewn about and the area was extremely wet. Water dripped on us from the ceiling, stalagmites of limestone were forming overhead, and the drippings were slowly cementing the bones together with a shiny glaze of limestone.

A couple of elderly men were sitting on a torn blanket, sharing a sandwich and a half bottle of wine. They looked at us incuriously and returned to their meal.

Roger braced at every opening, every angle, his gun at the ready. We continued to hear running feet, sometimes smacking on solid stone, sometimes a crunching sound.

"They're crushing the bones!" Roger said, swearing under his breath.

The next sign read, "Gilbert's Tomb." There were neat stone monuments and columns, and wooden fences blocking off some empty space.

Next we saw some crosses and more tiers of skulls and bones. A sign read, "Bones from the riots of 1788." We reached a chamber with a paved floor—a large gallery with a ceiling more than ten meters high, reinforced with sprayed concrete, constructed with a masonry arch and a masonry wall. The angles were strange and wavering, and at times I was afraid the walls would fall on me and I would be buried in tons of bones and skulls. A two-hundred-year-old man might be more deadly than a bullet.

Cautiously, we entered a bell-shaped hall where the limestone had eroded "upwards," accounting for the height and the strange shape. No bones, a simple bench, sprayed concrete. Emptiness. Roger looked around frantically, but there was no one to see. Or hear.

We mounted a staircase with a metal railing, and near the top I saw a slice of street. Then we were out on the sidewalk, exiting a blockhouse of a building, fighting the glare after the darkness of the grave. The street was empty except for a few parked cars.

Roger was breathing hard. "Where are they?" he asked, almost desperately. "Did we pass them on one of the turns—down one of the galleries?"

"Until a minute ago," I said, "we heard them running."

He put a hand on my shoulder. "I don't know what to do. I probably should have alerted the police to arrest them when they came out of the Metro station."

"You didn't shoot back when they fired at us," I said.

"I never had a clear target, and I didn't want to blast bones and skulls for nothing."

"Instead, you put your body between me and them."

"I promised your parents I would protect you," Roger said. "If I had thought your life was still in danger, I wouldn't have hesitated about using the gun."

"How did you know they would lead us to the catacombs?"

"A hunch," Roger said. "When they took the Metro south, I recalled all the stops on the line, and thought of Denfert-Rochereau and the catacombs."

"If they had a gun," I asked, "why didn't they use it in the apartment?"

Roger looked startled. "You're right, Willi," he said. "Maybe someone else fired that shot. Come on—we're going back!"

"Where are we going?" I yelled, as he started down the steps.

"The Nazi Bunker!" he responded. "I should have thought of it sooner!"

We raced up one corridor, down another, until Roger stopped about a meter from a dark crossing. He held his hand over the lens of his flashlight so that it glowed only enough to allow us to follow the angles of the corridor.

After about twenty meters, the corridor widened and the ceiling was higher. Roger let a little more light escape from his flashlight and I saw a metal pipe running along the ceiling with a few boxes intersecting it. I guessed the pipe was conduit for electrical wiring and the boxes were connections for lighting fixtures, now gone.

The corridor widened again, this time into a rectangular room, with benches and shelves cut into the stone. Roger suddenly flashed his light on, full force. Set into the far wall was a large metal door, with a riveted surface and a large metal wheel—like a steering wheel—mounted on it.

"Damn!" Roger said.

Thick metal bars crossed the door and were bolted into the stone on either side. A large black-on-white paper sign was pasted across the door, reading *Accés Interdit*— Access Forbidden. Two black-on-yellow signs read *Défense D'Afficher!*, which only meant posting signs was forbidden, but of course, there were graffiti all over the door.

"I didn't realize the government had closed the Nazi Bunker," Roger said.

He shoved his gun in his waistband.

"The shot came from somewhere else," he said. "I have no idea where."

"If the door wasn't barred," I asked, "could you turn that steering wheel and open it?"

"If you look closely you will see a keyhole in the middle of it. I have had that key for years, but I haven't used it since the war. I was hoping that if our enemies were in the bunker, it might be open anyway, but now . . . ."

His voice trailed off.

I LOVE PARIS

It took almost two weeks to catalog Roger's torn and shattered books. Many of them had been in the collections of his parents, his brother and his uncle, all slain by the Nazis. Others, he had collected himself and folded into the group. He had gathered and protected them for much of his life.

Even when Roger had taken refuge in the Crouching Dragon, he transferred his books there, load by load, month after month, almost always under cover of night. All of those books, and more, had been transferred to Roger's Paris apartment. Now, we had the job of cataloguing and cleaning them, saving those we could, and disposing of those we couldn't. We also found some oily rags and matches, and we guessed that the thieves might have planned to set a fire.

"If we had arrived a little later," Roger said, "Larron and his friend might have destroyed everything."

After our battle, the intruders had abandoned their axe and crowbar. When I picked up the axe, I noticed a design carved into the oval end of the wooden hilt—a shield in black and white with an angry, winged dragon on it, a sword slashed through its body.

"Look at this," I said.

Roger took the axe from my hand and stared.

"The DragonSlayers design that haunts us time and again," he said.

"They're fanatics," I said. "They were not only going to tear and smash your books and mark them with their symbol, they were going to burn them, too."

"But they're not just a group of vandals out of control," he said. They're people with a plan, a program and their own set of perverse principles."

"It has to be Tony Bersault."

"Maybe, but it's bigger than that," he said. "The guys who did this didn't leave Tony's name—they left this mysterious symbol."

◆　◆　◆

Demonstrations and disputes about Algeria continued through the autumn months. During the same period, Nikita Khrushchev, boisterous and outspoken chairman of the Soviet Union, had appeared at the United Nations in New York City, removed his shoe and pounded it on his desk. It was crude and embarrassing, even for Soviet diplomats, but it indicated to the world that Russia was increasingly aggressive, and the threat of a nuclear confrontation between east and west was in the forefront of everybody's thinking.

Nevertheless, on the fourth of November, President de Gaulle announced, "Algeria for the Algerians," which implied that he was on the side of independence for the former colony. That softened the position of the left, but infuriated everyone else.

That same month, a major election was underway in the United States. John F. Kennedy, a Democrat, was running against Richard Nixon, a Republican. Kennedy accused the previous Republican administration under Dwight Eisenhower of permitting a "missile gap" to exist between the U.S. and Russia—something he would remedy if elected. In fact, the United States' nuclear arsenal far exceeded the weapons available to the U.S.S.R. in number and sophistication, but Kennedy's statements were widely believed in America and the rest of the world, which made Khrushchev's belligerency seem even more dangerous.

Almost all of my friends and I favored Jack Kennedy—young, handsome, charming and articulate. Nixon projected a glowering, awkward image to students and intellectuals—not to mention France's communist-controlled unions. His anti-communism sounded false and strident.

The televised debates between Kennedy and Nixon were re-broadcast in France with French translations in subtitles. Louise and I watched the debates, struggling to follow the sometimes complex arguments, but it was a great way to improve our language skills. Naturally, we all thought that Kennedy had demolished Nixon.

On the ninth of November our wishes were granted: in a very close election, John F. Kennedy was elected the thirty-fifth president of the United States of America. We hoped that would help keep the world at peace, but we didn't think it would solve the Algerian problem.

In early December, President de Gaulle went to Algiers to speak in favor of Algerian independence. He escaped four separate attempts on his life—presumably by European settlers—while the Muslims demonstrated on his behalf, shouting, "*Vive de Gaulle.*"

On December 14, the United Nations General Assembly adopted a Declaration on the Granting of Independence to Colonial Countries and Peoples, and on December 20, President de Gaulle announced a referendum on whether independence should be granted to Algeria, to take place the following January 8.

Louise and I were sitting in the Raging Dragon soon after the announcement, and we discussed the issue with Mohammed.

I said, "I think people should be free to have the kind of government they want, but there are many people in Algeria—not all of them like the DragonSlayers—who want to remain part of France."

Mohammed smiled and said, "We're too young to vote. We don't have to decide that question."

"True," Louise said. "but I think we should stand up for our principles anyway."

"Would you go to war to keep Algeria part of France?" Mohammed asked.

"There's been a war going on for years," I answered. "What do you think will be the result of the referendum?"

"My father," said Mohammed, "believes that the voters will favor independence."

"What will happen to those who want to remain part of France?" Louise asked.

"They'll retain their citizenship in France," Mohammed said. "They can always live on the mainland."

"That could be costly and heartrending for hundreds of thousands of people who built their lives in Algeria."

"Yes," Mohammed said, "but my father says the real problem is whether or not the settlers will accept the results of the referendum."

"If it's up to the DragonSlayers or the extremists on the other side," Louise said. "I'm afraid the slaughter will resume."

◆ ◆ ◆

Meanwhile, Louise and I were deeply immersed in our studies. We especially admired one of our teachers, Mademoiselle Simone Louvois. She was a tall, graceful lady, extremely slim, with a generous fall of thick, wavy brown hair, flashing brown eyes and a vibrant, outdoorsy complexion. Her lips were full, her mouth wide, and her nose rather long and narrow, but some considered that a sign of elegance. She spoke with great animation, had a rippling laugh, and dressed more fashionably than most of the teachers at the Lycée—her taste running to slacks and blouses more than was usual for sedate "ladies" in that era.

"You've made excellent progress," she told our class one fine afternoon, "and as a reward I am going to assign a project I know you'll enjoy. The subject matter is the city of Paris in art, music, literature and film. Even native Parisians are often unaware of the multitude of ways the city has been portrayed in our culture. Of course, you will be required to view a number of motion pictures."

There was a cheer.

"You are fortunate," she said, "that Paris has as many or more movie theatres and as broad a selection of films as any city in the world."

There were twenty kids in our class, and Mme. Louvois divided us into ten teams. Louise and I managed to pair up. All the teams were given the same list of famous places in Paris. We had to visit each one and study books, plays, music and films about them.

Louise and I decided to begin with the Paris Opera House, because both of us liked Gaston Leroux's early twentieth century novel, *The Phantom of the Opera.* Mme Louvois arranged passes that would permit students to inspect the building both during and after a performance.

The Garnier Opera House was a grand confection of a building that stood on the Place de l'Opera facing the avenue of the same name. When we arrived on the evening of a performance, Louise and I circled the building, well-lit by flood lights. We knew that the design was by a then unknown thirty-five year old architect named Charles Garnier, who won an architectural competition in 1860. They began building it in 1862, but didn't finish until 1875.

"It's easy to see why it took so long," I said.

"Yes," Louise said. "The architect and the artists he commissioned covered every inch with some design or figure."

"It has an incredible number of elements, but no character," I said.

"Don't say that too loudly," Louise whispered. "They say the people of Paris absolutely love this place."

The sidewalks, the entrances and the vast Grand Foyer and Grand Staircase were crowded with people. Many were so elegantly dressed that I felt awkward in my plain blue suit, white shirt and very dark red tie. Louise wore the blue dress I remembered from the school dance the past year, but she had—how shall I say it—grown into it.

We entered the foyer, which soared several stories above us, framing the broad marble staircase, ornate columns, arches and balustrades, the gilt figures and cascades of chandeliers. Marble in the foyer was arrayed in many colors—white, pink, blue, red, green, and many shades between, quarried from many parts of France.

The scene was alive with hundreds of operagoers, ushers, and sellers of programs—light reflecting, bouncing and refracting off or through chandeliers, bronze and gilt statues, an avalanche of varied marbles, clothing, jewels and eyeglasses; especially jewels.

Some day, I thought, *I'm going to buy a beautiful necklace for Louise.* What a strange thought; until then, I had never bought her anything more than a cup of coffee and a roll.

"Is the building too ornate for you?" Louise asked. Her eyes were shining; she thoroughly enjoyed being in this special place among so many fashionable people.

"It's overwhelming—but I like it. Just standing here and watching is an adventure. It's hard to believe it's real: all the glittering people, marble, stone and gold. And it keeps flowing, as if according to plan—like Roger's animated exhibit in the Crouching Dragon—everything is operated by remote control, gliding, turning, rising, into one magnificent cascade of sound and light."

I frowned, thinking about what I'd said. "Did I sound too much like an engineer?" I asked.

Louise squeezed my hand and said, "More like a writer."

We mounted the staircase to our seats near the top of the house. Once inside we found the auditorium equally dazzling: four towering tiers of flamboyantly-carved, gold-covered balustrades, framing scarlet-upholstered walls, draperies, boxes and seats. The audience—especially the women—matched the hall in vivid colors.

"Twenty-two hundred seats," Louise said. "Madame Louvois says many opera houses are much larger."

"I keep looking at that great chandelier," I said. "All the light flashing off the facets of cut glass. Remembering *The Phantom of the Opera*, I wouldn't like to sit under it. According to the program it weighs eight metric tons—over seventeen thousand English pounds."

The opera we watched was Puccini's *La Bohème*, which was about some starving artists who lived in Paris. I liked the music well enough; Louise loved it. When the heroine died, she actually shed tears.

After the performance, we were allowed to visit the interior of the opera house—including the huge backstage areas—with the help of a young usher, Diane, who was a student of music at the Sorbonne. First, she took us into the basement.

"Garnier wasn't permitted to begin construction until he solved the problem of dealing with a spring right under this building," she said. "Look through this grating—you can see the waters are still flowing, but channeled in such a way they don't harm the structure.

"In Leroux's book," she continued, "he described a lake beneath the opera. In fact there really is one, now channeled. The great sewer systems of Paris also criss-cross beneath here, and the Metro lines intersect, so that there is, actually, a thriving city beneath the opera house, a fitting site for the mysterious story of the phantom."

Our voices echoed in the chambers as we spoke; it was just dank enough in the bowels of the building to be more than a little scary.

Backstage, the space was very deep and amazingly tall, threaded and crossed with catwalks, ropes and pulleys. Scenery for *La Bohème* was still in place. Up close it wasn't very convincing, but from the auditorium it had looked quite real. A few sections were being lifted high above the stage into what Diane called, appropriately, the "flies." Huge pieces—made only of cloth stretched on wooden frames and painted—bent and swayed as they rose, and the whole setup looked flimsy and dangerous. Maybe these opera people were braver than I had thought.

We were taken into the service areas and dressing rooms. Performers were still bustling about, removing makeup and costumes, chatting, laughing—even singing—and sometimes complaining. They didn't seem to notice us.

Diane led us from the wings, out onto the stage in front of the huge, velvet curtain.

"It's difficult to imagine performing in front of a couple of thousand people," Louise said.

"I've done it," Diane as, "as a member of the huge chorus in the opera, *Aida*. I was surrounded by dozens of people singing their lungs out, so I certainly didn't have anyone's eyes focused on me. I was never so frightened in all my life, but after a few performances, I almost got used to it."

Diane then took us into the seating areas of the auditorium.

"I can't look up at that chandelier," I said, "without imagining it crashing on my head."

"It has never happened," Diane said, smiling. I chose to believe her, but Louise had lingered along the edge of the seating.

Afterwards, we thanked her warmly for showing us around and then left the opera.

"I'm happy we were allowed to see a performance," Louise said. It makes everything come alive. Otherwise, I'm afraid we would just have considered the opera house an awesome lump of stone, marble, bronze, glass, gold and paint."

◆   ◆   ◆

We used the resources of the Bibilotheque National—the great national library—and several newspapers to track down movies that involved the Garnier Opera House. A small theatre in Montparnasse was showing a 1925 American film starring the fearful Lon Chaney as the phantom, and another house in Montmartre ran a 1940s picture that starred Claude Rains.

Later, I said to Louise, "Lon Chaney is more frightening."

"But Claude Rains is so elegant, so mysterious," she answered.

"I don't know," I said. "For me, the fact that the earlier picture is in black and white makes the film more ominous."

"Nothing could be scarier than that huge chandelier crashing down in full color," Louise said.

◆   ◆   ◆

Our next choice was Les Halles, the vast wholesale market area known as "The Belly of Paris," after the name of a novel by Emile Zola, built on a site where foods and other wares had been sold for eight hundred years. The architects used iron girders painted deep green and skylight roofs to span block after block, including the covered streets, where every conceivable food product was sold. Beneath the buildings were vast cellars, but we didn't see them.

Arriving at the best time, before dawn, we found the market throbbing with activity—buyers and sellers scurrying everywhere, yelling and gesturing. We strolled the streets, corridors and aisles, buying an apple here, a banana there, a sprig of lilac (my first flowers for Louise) and pastries of such melting beauty it seemed wrong to swallow them. But we did.

As we wandered, I caught sight of a man walking ahead of us in a dark suit, carrying a bag under his arm. Something about his size, his strutting walk and his wavy, iron-gray hair seemed familiar.

"Louise!" I said. "Doesn't that man look like—"

"—Tony Bersault! Louise said.

We hurried down the corridor. The man turned the corner, out of sight, but as soon as we turned the corner we saw him again. It was difficult making progress through the crowded market, and there were a thousand places to disappear. Fortunately, Louise and I were agile, and we slipped in and out of the throngs.

Again we lost sight of him, stopped and stared around in all directions.

"There!" I yelled. I had seen the man disappear into a draped area within a stall.

"If he goes down into the cellars," Louise said, "we'll never find him."

We approached the stall where the man had disappeared. There was movement behind the drape, and then it was pushed aside and the man came out. It was him!

He was tall, with wavy, iron-gray hair, pulling on a smock, and he strongly resembled Tony Bersault. But he was—a butcher.

He immediately noted our inquiring expression, and asked with a fine smile, "Can I help you?"

We sadly shook our heads and walked away.

"It's getting pretty bad," I said. "I'm beginning to see Bersault everywhere."

We sat down at an open cafe for a cup of coffee.

"I'm glad we came," Louise said. "This place won't be here very long—they're going to relocate it outside Paris."

"I know," I responded. "They'll tear this all down and build modern commerical buildings with a public park and gardens on the top."

"It just won't be the same," Louise said.

The only novel about Les Halles we found was the book by Zola. We weren't lucky finding films either, although we were told that the Americans were planning a comedy-mystery movie starring Cary Grant, Audrey Hepburn, Walter Matthau and James Coburn, which would include scenes in Les Halles at night. Years later, we saw that film, called *Charade*, but not in Paris.

We couldn't drop everything else to follow the easy and delightful Paris project, but Mme Louvois had given us ample time to complete our work. Some places were easy. We went to the gardens of the Tuileries, picked out a bench, sat there and read books from our other courses.

We found many references in books and movies to the Tuileries—virtually every movie about Paris, and there were dozens of them, has a scene or a tracking shot of the famous gardens.

Our favorite spot was the large, circular stone pond near the Arc de Triomphe du Carroussel, the great marble arches erected by Napoleon, surmounted by a mythical goddess in her chariot, racing bronze horses. From underneath the central arch there is a spectacular view, along the axis that runs from the Louvre through the Tuileries, Place de la Concorde, the Champs-Élysées, the great Arc de Triomphe, the Avenue de la Grand Armée and beyond to the area known as La Defense, after a monument that marked an historical defense of Paris. Future plans for La Defense included a major business section with high rise towers, until then forbidden within the city.

The circular pond was less grand, but more fun. You could rent small, sturdy sailboats and set them going in the pond. Often, there were many small children playing around the pool, shoving their sailboats with wooden sticks, yelling and running.

Louise and I chose a cloudy late afternoon when most of the children were gone, and we could sail a boat in virtual seclusion. We didn't rent metal chairs, which offended the lady who rented them. Instead, we sat on the concrete rim of the pool and watched our sailboat bend to the winds.

"You first," I told Louise, handing her the wooden prod.

"Is this a contest?" she asked. "Do we want to see who can get the boat to travel the farthest?"

"That's a good idea," I responded.

"Okay," Louise said.

The little boat, blue-hulled with a green stripe, one red sail lashed to the wooden mast, set out bravely. It bumped against the concrete only a few meters from where she launched it.

Sadly, she handed me the round stick, and I began working on the boat.

"What are you doing?" she asked.

"As a skilled seaman, I'm adjusting my sails and rudder."

I had a rubber band and a toothpick in my pocket, which I used to set the sail.

"No fair!" she said.

I ignored her, judging the breeze and setting rudder and sails to get full benefit of them. When I pushed the little boat away from the rim, the wind took it on a circular course, parallel to the curving edge of the pond.

"You've already won!" Louise said. "I want another chance."

I held up the stick and waved it like a wand. "Patience," I said.

The sailboat had now reached the point where the wind was no longer driving it, but in fact, was against it. That pushed the sail the other way and knocked off my little controls. The boat began to wobble and shake, driven one way and then another, leaning over so hard that I feared the sail would end up in the water. Happily, the boat took an erratic course across the widest part of the pond, eventually bumping the rim.

Louise was smiling. "You really gave the little guy a ride," she said.

I gave her a mock haughty look. "I'm going to be an engineer, you know."

We both laughed. Louise declined another try and we brought the boat back to its owner.

"Not bad," the frayed-looking, gray-haired lady said to me gruffly. I hadn't even realized she was watching. "But next time, no bands or toothpicks."

I took Louise's hand and we strolled through the park, now darkening quickly. The breeze was fresher and the plane trees were bending and whistling in the wind. Along the Rue de Rivoli, the fashionable street that margined the Tuileries on the north, automobiles were massing for the drive home, their yellow parking lights lit.

Other lights were coming on in the row of buildings that edged the street, and a soft glow illuminated the air. I put my arm around Louise and held her closely as we walked. As we neared the Place de la Concorde, I kissed her. We clung together and kissed again, as the breeze carried Louise's fragrant hair against my face. Life was absolutely perfect.

✦　　✦　　✦

On the eighth of January, 1961, a few weeks before my sixteenth birthday, our friends gathered at the Raging Dragon to listen to Radio France announce the results of the Algerian referendum.

" . . . an overwhelming victory for President de Gaulle," the announcer said. "The vote in favor of Algerian independence is decisive."

Most people in the bistro cheered.

"Not all Frenchmen are pleased," the radio voice continued. "It is rumored that disaffected settlers have formed a new, supposedly secret organization, known as the "OAS", the *'Organization Armée Secrète,'* but it is obviously no secret."

"It's a joke," Jacques said. "Secret army indeed! There are one million settlers and ten million native Algerians—don't they realize they're outnumbered?"

"Not if the army is on their side," Mohammed said.

"De Gaulle will control the army," Robert de Cotte said.

"I don't know," Mai said. "They challenged him before."

"And lost!" I said.

◆ ◆ ◆

Until our Paris sojourn, Louise and I had avoided reading Victor Hugo's masterpiece, the novel, *Les Miserables,* because it was so long—over fourteen hundred pages in a small-type paperback edition. However, when we read it for our Paris project we both found it engrossing.

We felt sympathy for Jean Valjean, the simple man who was sent to jail for ten years because he had stolen a loaf of bread to feed his starving family. We also loved poor Fantine and hated Javert, the cruel police inspector who followed the hero implacably.

For me, the scenes in the Paris sewers were the most compelling because of my experiences in the catacombs and tunnels and other parts of the vast underground world beneath Paris, including the Metro.

We were astonished to learn that no less than a dozen films based on *Les Miserables* had been made in France, the United States, Mexico, Egypt, Italy, Japan and Germany between 1911 and 1957. Not all of them were available in Paris, and we finally settled on watching first, an American production from 1935 with famous actors Frederic March and Charles Laughton; then, a later American film, 1952, with Michael Rennie, Robert Newton, Sylvia Sidney and Debra Paget. Just to be loyal, we watched a 1957 French film starring Jean Gabin, a great star of our cinema.

Should we actually visit the sewers?

"Doesn't it smell down there?" Louise asked.

"Not bad," Roger said. "And, this will surprise you, there are regularly scheduled tours under the auspices of the city government."

The public entrance to the sewers was near the Pont de l'Alma, one of the major bridges crossing the Seine. There was a small museum, where we dutifully learned the history of the two thousand kilometers—almost thirteen hundred miles—of sewers that lay under the pavements of Paris.

Descending the stairs, we became aware of the smell.

"Don't wrinkle your noses," Roger told us. "They treat the entire system with disinfectants and deodorants—you only think you smell the sewage."

There were only a few visitors walking on the ledge above the waters for a short distance. They soon turned back and exited the sewers.

Roger had arranged a tour on one of the small maintenance boats, which had no enclosure above its flat bottom, and ran on a quiet electric motor that barely stirred the waters. The "captain" was called—just that, "Captain." He wore a yachting cap and a naval jacket and said very little. We glided almost soundlessly into the dimly-lit world.

"Above us," Roger said, "you see freshwater mains, compressed air pipes, telephone cables, power lines and pneumatic tubes. Most of the utilities serving Paris are carried in the tunnel, along with the waste waters beneath us. There is a slight current in the tunnel as millions of cubic feet of water are sent through the sewers to be processed by a plant in a Paris suburb north of here, Acheres."

The Captain pointed out the overflow outlet, the sand filtering basins, and some reservoirs, which made me think of the "lake" under the opera house. When we spoke, our voices echoed through the halls.

"It's fascinating," Louise said, "following the streets, going through intersections, seeing blue and white street signs just like the ones on the surface."

"Yes," Roger said. "You can find the pipes and lines that run to every building at every address in Paris."

On a steady basis, we watched waste being discharged from above. I think I was turning green, but in the dim lighting, I hoped I didn't show it.

We reached one of the tunnels that served the Champs-Élysées.

"Take the Avenue de Marigny," Roger told the Captain. "We're going to visit the Presidential Palace—in a manner of speaking."

As we approached the Rue de Faubourg St. Honore—this time underground—something caught my eye.

"Look," I said, half rising out of my seat.

Everyone turned to stare. A large loop of cables and wires branched up through the tunnel. Below it, a sign was scrawled in chalk.

"The DragonSlayers!" Roger said, obviously startled. "We must report this at once. Captain, please take us to the nearest exit!"

◆   ◆   ◆

Roger phoned Major Gerard, who thanked him profusely, and a day later, received a scrawled note from him. But nothing further.

"When we first heard about the OAS, some people laughed," Roger said, "but since then there have been several bombings. People have been killed, property destroyed. Every day the crisis deepens. The military is repeatedly at the edge of mutiny, and demonstrators take to the streets time after time."

Roger threw up his hands, but I was too angry to give up.

I told Louise, "We have to do something ourselves. We know the Bersaults are connected to the DragonSlayers and others who would overturn the government."

"What are you thinking?" Louise asked.

"Paris is the heart and the mind of the country," I said. "The government is here and the major military installations are not far away."

She smiled. "Are you going to run for the French parliament?"

I laughed. "I'll be the youngest French leader since Joan of Arc."

She stopped smiling. "Joan of Arc was burned at the stake."

"I'm hoping to avoid that fate," I said.

"Then what?" she asked.

"I have a feeling that Madame Louvois has set us on the right path, but we didn't recognize it. We know the DragonSlayers are active in Paris. They left their mark when they tore up Roger's apartment. We chased them into the catacombs and they shot at us, but got away. During the anti-war demonstration one guy who attacked the students carried the symbol. Somebody tore down the sign of the Raging Dragon and split it, just like a sword. In the sewers, we found the Dragonslayers emblem near the Élysée Palace. Tony Bersault was lurking around the airport, and someone tried to get me killed.

"We have to learn to know the city better—and we have to do it quickly. The more alert we are," I said, "the more likely we'll discover something that will help us stop the DragonSlayers."

"How can we investigate a city of several million people?" Louise asked.

"I believe that if there's going to be an attack, it will involve the major axes of the central city—east-west from the Arch of Triumph to the Marais district, north-south, from Denfert-Rochereau to Montmartre."

Louise was shaking her head. "To cover that territory would take weeks, maybe months."

"We have to start somewhere," I said. "It's better than merely sitting around, wringing our hands. We'll complete the project Madame Louvois gave us and check out the major tourist sites in Paris—we've already begun."

I wasn't sure that I had convinced Louise; I thought the plan might seem desperate, myself, but my instincts told me I was on the right path.

"Good," Louise said. "How do we begin?"

"We'll pretend we're tourists. What will we want to see?"

"Let's start from the west, probably from the Bois de Boulogne."

"Do we expect to find traitors conspiring at the racetrack at Longchamp?" I asked.

"Very funny," Louise said, "but we hear that the French paratroopers have divided loyalties. If they parachuted into Paris, the Bois would be an obvious place to land."

"All right," I said. "What then?"

"Of course we must visit the Arc de Triomphe and the Champs-Élysées." she said.

"To shop?"

Louise ignored me. "Every tourist visits the Eiffel Tower," she said, "and the École Militaire and the Invalides are not far away."

"If we stay on the left bank," I said, "there's the National Assembly, which we've seen, and the Quai D'Orsay—the Foreign Ministry. But let's assume Mohammed's father is alert to anything there."

"Yes," Louise said. "We should consider the Luxembourg

Palace and Gardens, the Latin Quarter and the Sorbonne, plus the Pantheon."

"We must cross the Seine," I said, "and see the Conciergerie, the Sainte-Chapelle and the Cathedral of Notre Dame. Shall we go as far east as the Cemetery Père-Lachaise?"

"We'll think about it," Louise said. "So many famous people are buried there—and not all were French."

"Is it possible the dead would rise up in rebellion?" I asked.

"Not funny. Remember, this is your idea, not mine."

"Is this all going to be so serious?" I asked. "Can't we have a little fun along the way?"

"Of course, but cemeteries don't make me laugh."

"Very well," I said. "Obviously we will visit the Marais district and the Place des Vosges."

"We'll go to the Louvre Museum," Louise said. "Then we're close to Palais Royale, the Place Vendome and the Opera."

"We've 'done' the Opera," I said.

"After that we'll look at the Church of the Madeleine and return to the Place de la Concorde."

"We should also go up to Montmartre and the Cathedral of the Sacré-Coeur."

"Okay," Louise said. "I guess that covers the city."

"Wasn't that easy?" I asked. "Now we're experts on Paris."

"I wonder how much time we'll have."

"Tourists try to see Paris in two, three or four days," I said. "That's impossible, but you can get some of the flavor of the city. We should pretend we're tourists with only a few days."

"All right," Louise said. "We'll call Major Gerard and postpone our lessons. We'll also have to give up the dojo for a few days. I'll phone Jacques and you can call Mai."

"You have it backwards," I said. "I'll call Jacques."

◆   ◆   ◆

We started our speeded-up tour at the Eiffel Tower. The

choice ultimately proved fortunate because we saw something that didn't impress us at the time, but later gave us an
important clue.

After standing in line to buy tickets from the cashier,
we got into line for the north elevator, the one nearest to
the Seine.

As we waited, a group of tourists came up from the quais
along the Seine, escorted by a guide. They were all men, and
all wearing dark-colored outer garments. The guide, similarly
dressed, spoke rapidly and we couldn't hear what he was
saying. However, the tourists only glanced up at the tower
briefly as the guide directed their attention through the legs of
the tower to the vast great open field of the Champs-de-Mars,
and across it to the École Militaire, and perhaps to the dome of
the Invalides church, glistening in gold, a bit to the east. He
seemed serious, not making jokes as tour guides often do, and
the tourists were listening intently—a few making notes. But
the guide must have said something because they hurriedly
shoved pads and pencils into their pockets.

All of the tourists carried black bags, probably given to
them by the travel agency as souvenirs, although they were
considerably larger than the usual totes.

"They must be carrying laundry in their bags," I said.

I was vaguely curious; I figured we'd see them up close
in the elevator or on the tower. A few minutes later, when I
looked around for the tour group, they were gone.

"What happened to our friends?" I asked Louise.

"They marched off toward the Seine."

"Without going up in the Eiffel Tower?"

"Maybe that wasn't in their budget."

In a moment, the great steel and glass elevator reached
bottom, discharged one load, and we got on, lucky to find
places along the glass windows.

The elevator glided quietly upward, ascending at an

angle through a forest of girders, or rather a lacework. The pattern seemed fragile and strong at the same time, and I had the impression we were floating in the sky, and the intricate iron framework just happened to surround us.

We got off at the first platform. A breeze was blowing, and lovely, cumulus clouds were unrolling like bales of cotton unraveling across the sky. Louise took my arm.

We began to stroll around the perimeter, some fifty-seven meters above the ground. The pattern of the city was beginning to emerge, the many circles with streets radiating from them, the serried residential areas, the famous parks and buildings punctuating the plan.

"Let's go higher," I said. "I want to feel really important."

In a few minutes we were rising to the second platform, approximately twice as high. Louise dragged me over to the railing.

"Look," she said, pointing to a spot near the Pont de l'Alma.

"The entrance to the sewers," I said. "We were there."

"So are our friends—that's what attracted my attention."

The tourist group with the black bags was entering the structure leading to the sewers.

"Hmm," I said. "They go underground, but not up in the tower."

We weren't sure why that deserved our attention, and we soon re-entered the elevator and headed up to the third platform, two hundred seventy-six meters above the city.

"Do you feel the tower swaying?" Louise asked.

"Maybe. They say that at the top it never sways more than a hands-width."

The great undulating arcs of the Seine flowed below, separating the city into two vast playgrounds. It's a cliché to say that people, buildings and vehicles look like toys from great heights, but for us at that moment Paris was a huge amusement park, and we temporarily forgot there were bullies out there ready to break up our games.

The sun was beginning to set, and the clouds were streaked with rays of brilliant yellow, red and orange against a glowing, milk-toned sky. The tops of the clouds were jagged, but the undersides seemed geometrically even and parallel to the ground, as if they were resting on an invisible table. Some of the soaring tops were stretching into ringlets of angel's hair, while others looked like castles made of cotton candy.

We stood together in the fast-chilling wind, each with one hand on the railing, one around the other. As the last rays of the sun faded in the sky, and the clouds turned gray and ominous, I tilted Louise's face up to mine and kissed her, at first gently, and then more insistently. I was aware there were other couples on the platform embracing as we were, but they didn't exist. Neither did Paris or the sky or the Eiffel Tower. There was only Louise and me.

I knew I was in love with her, but I had never said so, and I didn't that day. I had no experience nor any knowledge of love, let alone any skill at expressing it. Louise returned my kiss and my embrace, but she didn't speak either. After a moment, we both pulled back and smiled. People were right: Paris was the City of Love.

Then, as the darkness fell rapidly, Paris lived up to her other name, the City of Light—evening version. Street lamps, vehicles and buildings sparkled, as thousands, perhaps millions, of lights were turned on.

"How can you describe it?" I whispered.

"People talk about diamonds sprinkled across the landscape," Louise said.

"Not bad," I answered, "but it's been said so many times."

"Have you a better image?"

"Some day I'm going to write a book about us," I said. "Maybe then I'll find the words."

DEEPER AПD DEEPER

While Louise and I were touring, Roger had received a call from the Sûreté, and he had set up a meeting at his apartment for the next morning.

The officials, ordinary looking men of medium height, medium build, medium age and medium dress, informed us their names were Monsieur Le Blanc and Monsieur Noir—Mr. White and Mr. Black. They wanted to hear about the DragonSlayers.

We told them everything we knew, but it was obvious that, with minor exceptions, our information only repeated what they had already learned. They seemed intent on drawing as much information from us as possible, but provided very little information to us in return.

"We thought Raoul Larron was in prison," I said.

M. Noir said, "Unfortunately a magistrate agreed to set him free on bail. Now he has disappeared."

"Disappeared?" Roger said. "We run into him all the time—where are you?"

Both men shifted uncomfortably.

"Larron is only a tool," I said. "We feel that the Bersaults are the culprits."

M. Le Blanc said, speaking in an undistinguished voice with a neutral French accent, "We are not certain about the connection between these events and the people in question."

"We are continuing to investigate," said M. Noir.

"*Merde!*" said Roger. "Their tentacles are everywhere.

Everyone in the Calvados knew that the Bersaults collaborated with the Vichy government of Marshall Petain during the war, and that they betrayed my uncle, Armand Moret, to the Nazis."

Le Blanc and Noir nodded, but didn't comment.

Roger continued, "There's no question the Bersaults are furious at the three of us."

Once again the men nodded; in unison.

I said, "Is it mere coincidence that Tony Bersault was in the DragonSlayers squadron in Algeria?"

After a moment of silence, with not even any nods from the two men, Louise said, "You must know much more than you are saying."

Finally, M. Noir spoke: "We have authority to give you information on a related subject."

We waited.

"As you know, Doctor Guiscard," M. Noir said, "in 1942 your cousin, Gilbert Moret, was shot dead by the Nazis in the street, in plain sight of your uncle in his gallery."

"Yes," Roger said. "The bastards shot several young men in reprisal for actions of the Resistance."

"That is true—in part" said Le Blanc. "But we have also learned that your cousin was *not* selected at random. The records of the German command in Paris indicate that the execution of Gilbert was deliberately planned, and that the murder of the others was used to cover that execution."

"But why?" Roger asked, in evident anguish.

"The murders were done by the Gestapo at the behest of a favored collaborator."

Roger suddenly rose to his feet. "Who was that collaborator?" he asked.

"In the Gestapo records," M. Noir said, "we could not find that actual name of the collaborator, but his code name was 'DragonSlayers.' We have reason to believe that

DragonSlayers was the code name of Antoine Bersault, the father."

Roger's eyes were brimming with tears. "Is there to be no end of this evil?" he asked.

✦ ✦ ✦

"I hope we're not wasting valuable time," Louise said to me, "sightseeing all over Paris."

Despite our doubts, we decided to continue our tour, but to accelerate it as much as possible. We began at the former Royal Military Academy—Le École Militaire. The classic main façade, hundreds of meters long, topped with a fine dome, faced the Eiffel Tower across the Champ-de-Mars. In front was an equestrian statute of Marshall Joffre, a hero of the First World War.

"This was a barracks for poor soldiers?" Louise asked.

"Napoleon was a cadet here," I said.

"Did he get good grades?"

"His evaluation report said he would make a good sailor."

Louise laughed. "You always know these facts about famous heroes."

"I guess Napoleon was a hero. Not everyone thinks so."

"He certainly thought so," Louise said. "He crowned himself emperor."

"Not for long."

We circled the building until we reached the semi-circular "square" on the opposite side. To the north stood various ministries; to the south, built in an irregular shaped "Y," was the practically new headquarters of the United Nations Educational Scientific and Cultural Organization—UNESCO.

"I can't imagine any greater contrast," Louise said. "The formal, eighteenth century neo-classical École Militaire and the ultra-modern UNESCO."

"Opposites," I said. "One memorializes war, the other stands for peace."

We had started toward the main entrance to the Military Academy, when I noticed something and grabbed Louise's arm.

"Are those our friends?" I asked quietly.

Ahead of us, standing outside the courtyard, was a group of tourists toting large, black bags.

The guide was speaking earnestly, directing the group's attention, not to the UNESCO building or the École Militaire, but to the nondescript ministries across the street. After a moment, they marched off along the Avenue de Lowendal towards the Hôtel des Invalides.

"Let's follow them," I said. 'The Invalides is on our itinerary anyway."

"One thing about the French," Louise said. "They built glorious buildings for poor soldiers and sick ones," referring to the École Militaire and the Hôtel des Invalides.

"We build glorious buildings for everyone," I said.

Louise smiled. "Chauvinist."

The group was moving faster and we accelerated to keep up with them.

"Strange tourists," Louise said. "Who do you think they are, and why are we following them?"

"Something Roger once said about anybody, any time, any place."

As we reached the Avenue de Tourville in front of the Invalides, two of the tourists left the group and turned toward the west; the others continued without them.

"Cut through here," I said, drawing Louise with me. "I think they may have spotted us."

We hurried up the block to the Avenue de Segur and then turned back towards the place Vauban and the Hôtel des Invalides. The group was standing in the walkway beside the garden, the great golden dome of the church rising above them.

"Aren't they going in to see Napoleon's tomb?" Louise asked.

They didn't go in, and instead began walking along Avenue de Tourville. I noticed a black bag sitting alone on the pavement in front of the Invalides.

"One of them left his bag," I said. "Let's be good citizens and return it."

We hurried towards the bag, then saw that the group had stopped. One of the tourists was returning.

I made a quick decision, and picked up the bag, which felt as if it were loaded with bricks.

"Is this yours?" I asked the man, who was running as he approached us.

"Put it down!" he yelled, but before I could, he grabbed it out of my hand, glared at me, and turned quickly away.

"I was only trying to help," I called after him. The others in the group were arguing with him.

I spoke to Louise: "Let's go see Napoleon's tomb," I said.

Louise and I headed for the Invalides, not looking at the group.

"That thing weighed a ton," I muttered under my breath as we walked.

The minute we were out of their sight, I stopped.

"Did you see that?" I asked.

Louise shook her head.

"On the bag—the emblem of the DragonSlayers."

✦　✦　✦

"You're sure it was the same design?" Roger asked.

"Positive," I said. "I saw something else." Some letters above the symbol. I thought they were a B, a T, and an A."

"If there really is a tourist agency," Roger said, "maybe that's the name."

We checked the business pages of the telephone directory to see if there was one with the name "BTA." The minute we saw the caption for that sector, Louise and I said, simultaneously, "Bureau de Tourisme!"

"Good!" Roger said. "That takes care of the B and T. Now what about the A?"'

We soon found a listing—just a single line—for "BTA." There was no street address; only a telephone number.

Roger quickly dialed the number. After a moment he began to frown, then slammed down the telephone.

"There is only an answering machine. No explanation, only the message, 'Please leave your number.'"

"How can we track them down?" I asked.

Roger's face brightened. "I'll call my friend at the telephone company. There is a reverse directory, and if you have the telephone number, they can give you the street address."

Roger called his friend, who checked the records while Roger waited. Again he frowned.

"Thank you, anyway," Roger said and hung up the telephone. "It is what they call a restricted listing. The address is not available, even to telephone company personnel."

"What about the Sûreté?" Louise asked.

Roger rummaged in his desk for the card M. Noir had left us and dialed the number. Once more, he frowned, but before hanging up he left his own telephone number and a brief message.

"Another answering machine!" Roger said. "This world is giving in to machines. One day they'll do all the talking and we'll be kept silent!"

The phone rang. Roger grabbed it. *"Allo, oui?"* he said. "Ah, Monsieur Le Blanc," and then he told them what we had seen. After a minute, Roger held his hand over the phone and said, "They're checking."

Several minutes passed. Then Roger was listening again. After a minute, he said "Goodbye" and slammed down the phone.

"They have no access, either," he said. "Le Blanc told me that someone very powerful is blocking the records and refusing to allow them to tap the phone."

"Too powerful even for the Sûreté?" I said.

"We mustn't get discouraged," Louise said.

"You're right," I said. "If we continue to frequent the major tourist sites in Paris, we'll probably see the group again. Then we can follow them back to their office—*if* they have an office."

"Okay," Louise asked. "Let's get going."

"Let me do the surveillance," Roger said.

"No," I answered, "you're too tall and you also seem to be a primary target. Besides, it will take two people to work effectively. I have another idea. Our friend Jacques has a small sedan, a Renault. If he drove us around, we could cover more territory more quickly."

"Can you trust him?" Roger said.

"He belongs to the Clandestin and I think he is very honest," I said.

"Very well," Roger said. "I can help in another way."

He opened a cabinet in his office and produced two small gadgets. "At the Crouching Dragon, you used two old fashioned handie-talkies," he said. "Now I have these little beauties, lighter, more compact and with greater range."

◆　◆　◆

Jacques promptly and enthusiastically agreed to help us.

We decided to return to the Eiffel Tower, and Jacques drove us there in his little, green Renault four-door.

"I'll leave you at the tower," Jacques said, "You can pretend you're tourists, and I'll cruise the quais looking for a group with big black bags."

"Good idea," I said. "We'll leave one handie-talkie with you."

We strolled towards the tower, gaping as if we had never seen it before. The lines were fairly long, and there were a lot of people walking by, but no groups with black bags. We were carrying our school bags; it wasn't unusual for teenagers to be sightseers in Paris.

"There's no point going up," I said. "They didn't."

"We should look like real tourists," Louise said.

"All right," I said. "Let's buy ice cream cones."

Louise liked that idea, and we purchased cones from the vendor at the base of the tower. We sat down on a bench and tried to eat very slowly, but the ice cream didn't cooperate, even on this chilly winter day, and we devoured it.

"I couldn't help it," I said. "It would have melted."

Louise laughed, throwing back her hair, which always seemed to return to the same perfect alignment every time.

"Okay," I said. "Let's study our map."

And so we did, pretending to be searching for something. Time passed, but our quarry didn't appear. Jacques had circled many times.

Louise finally said, "Let's call Jacques on the portable radio."

"I don't think we should stand in the open," I said. "I'll wait here and you go over in the shadows of those trees, and make your call."

Louise walked casually into the shadows. She pulled the radio from her tote and spoke into it. A couple of minutes Jacques arrived, and we got into his car.

"I didn't see anything," he said. "Did you?"

"No," Louise said. "Let's go on to the École Militaire."

"This time," I said, "I'd like to try the handie-talkie from both inside and outside the building."

Jacques gave me the unit he had been carrying and I

stuffed it in my school bag. He let us out in front of the main portico, and then drove away.

"First, let's experiment outside," I said. "Want to take a little walk?"

Louise strolled down the block, while I walked up to the main entrance. I looked around and seeing no one near, I pulled the radio from my bag and pressed the talk button.

"Hello," I said, "Conqueror calling." That was the code name I had chosen. I know, it was corny—William the Conqueror—but I liked it.

"Perfect," Louise answered, her voice quite clear, with little crackle. "Princess reads you loud and clear."

"I'm going inside," I said.

I entered the chapel, following a group of children and their teacher. As soon as they moved on, I radioed again.

"Not as clear," her voice came back, "but I can hear you well enough."

A half hour passed and we didn't see our quarry.

Jacques hadn't seen anything either, so he drove us the short distance to the Hôtel des Invalides. This time I went inside to view the lovely Église du Dôme, the beautiful circular church with its gold dome, topped by a gold lantern, and five radiating chapels, one of the masterpieces of Hardouin-Mansart, begun during the reign of Louis the Fourteenth in 1677. Many great soldiers were buried there.

The focus of everything was the great crypt in the center. It had been constructed one level below the main floor, but completely open to the church and the soaring cupola, and it contained a huge, red porphyry sarcophagus on a green granite base that held the emperor Napoleon's tomb. Massive bronze statues guarded the entrance, and twelve colossal marble statues served as columns that encircled the tomb. It was not a modest construction.

There were a number of tourists, and I had to wander

through the chapels a few times before I called Louise. I reached her and she immediately responded. It seemed that the little radios were going to work.

I walked further into the sanctuary that joined the Église du Dôme to the Soldiers' Church, the church of St. Louis. It was not as awesome as the Dome church, but very lovely, cool and somber. Again, I reached Louise, but I had nothing to report.

The complex also housed several museums. I couldn't resist visiting the Army Museum, especially the arsenal, with forty complete suits of armor, one thousand helmets, hundred of pikes and spears, swords and rapiers, projectiles and firearms. The firearms were not that interesting to me, but for many years I had loved to read the history of France and heroes who wielded steel weapons in hand-to-hand combat. At the Crouching Dragon, we had discovered many valuable suits of armor and created our own chivalric kingdom inside the walls.

The museum also housed arms and armor from Persia, China, Japan, the Ottoman empire and Russia. I found an empty gallery and called Louise again. This time she sounded less clear, but still understandable. I hurried outside.

"That took a long time," Louise said. "I began to worry that you had run into Tony."

Our next stop was the Luxembourg Palace and the gardens, as impressive as any in Paris. The palace, which had been German headquarters during the war, was now the seat of the French Senate.

"Why don't you park," I said to Jacques, "and come with us this time?"

Unfortunately, the Senate was not in session and we couldn't get into the chamber. The gardens, however, were splendid and available. Napoleon had decreed that they should be dedicated to children, and they had become one of the greatest draws in Paris. There were nannies and young mothers with small children and many students. The park contained playgrounds, tennis courts, and courts for the game of *boules,* and a pedal-car circuit. Close by was the Odeon Theatre, and on the grounds was a famous marionette theatre.

Near the Senate building was the narrow rectangular pond with the renowned Medici fountain—mythical characters, grottoes and all—shaded by plane trees.

The main area of the garden was laid out in strict geometric fashion around an octagonal pond, with semicircles and rectangles radiating from it. The pond, known as the *Grand Bassin* was crowded with sailboats like the ones Louise and I had sailed in the Tuileries gardens.

"I like the Tuileries better," I said.

Louise smiled. "I want to watch the marionettes," she said.

We followed a gaggle of young theatre-goers to the little building, where the puppets portrayed characters familiar to most French people, including sad Pierrot and happy Harlequin. The kids were entranced, but the show didn't last long, and the minute it ended the spell was broken and the kids began yelling, laughing and running, with their mothers and nannies following doggedly behind.

As we walked away from the theatre, Louise said, "Isn't that, Mohammed?"

On a flat open area nearby, several young people were kicking a soccer ball. One of them was Mohammed. He moved across the field gracefully, running swiftly but under control, guiding the ball with effortless ease, avoiding defenders with smooth, unexpected maneuvers.

He caught sight of us and waved, left the game and came over to see us.

"Great legs," Louise whispered to me.

Mohammed was wearing a tight, white pullover that showed the fine definition of his chest, and very brief blue shorts. All in all, he looked very fit.

"Do you play soccer?" he asked.

"Not much," I said.

"I played at the Lycée," Jacques said, "but not since I started university."

"I don't play at all," Louise said. "Do you come here often, Mohammed?"

"My uncle lives on the Rue Guynement. Sometimes I look for a soccer game here when I visit him."

"We're working on our Paris project for Madame Louvois," I said.

"Have you seen the movie, *Paris Holiday*?" he asked. "There are many shots of these gardens."

"We'll look for it," I said.

Mohammed's expression became serious. "You told us about the mayhem at the professor's apartment," he said, "but not whether the culprits were found."

"No they haven't been," I said.

"Your friends from Clandestin are worried about you," Mohammed said. "We'd like to help, if we can."

I realized that I probably should have talked to Mohammed about the DragonSlayers before. As an Algerian and with his family connections he might have useful information. I was thinking about asking him when Louise said, "Is there anything you know about the people called the DragonSlayers?"

"In Algeria," he said, "they're rumored to be the most vicious members of the Front Nationale Francaise—and the OAS, if there is any real difference between them. All we're certain of is that some paramilitary group tortured and killed people we knew."

"I'm sorry," I said.

"I lost a cousin, about my age, a couple of months ago," Mohammed said. "A bomb killed him and several members of his family. They were not necessarily the targets of the bomb, but they are just as dead as if they were."

I couldn't help thinking of Roger's cousin, Gilbert.

"Did the killers leave the DragonSlayers emblem?" I asked.

"We think that's what it was," he said, "but the bomb blast left such tiny fragments that we couldn't be sure."

"Maybe you could help us, Mohammed," Louise said. "What do you know about a travel agency with the letters BTA in its name?"

"Bureau de Tourisme Algérie," Mohammed said calmly.

"Are they friends of yours?" I asked, warily.

Mohammed laughed. "They hate us—and everyone else with a dark skin."

"Then you know they use the DragonSlayers symbol on their tourist bags," Louise said.

"Yes, and I've often wondered what was in those bags."

"Who runs the company?" Louise asked. "Is it the Bersaults?"

"There's some connection," Mohammed said. "The Bersaults actively oppose Algerian independence, and they've been seen with people from the BTA."

"Where did you learn that?" I asked.

"My father, as you know, is in the Foreign Ministry. But I'm telling you this in confidence."

"Of course," Jacques said.

"Do you know specifically how he got the information?" I asked.

"That, he doesn't tell me," Mohammed said. His back seemed to stiffen. "I can assure you my father is a loyal Frenchman."

"We're not questioning that," Louise said.

"We've been trying to track the BTA tourist groups," Jacques said. "Learning the name of the agency will help."

"I can take you to their office," Mohammed said. "I

know the location isn't listed in the telephone book."

• • •

We all climbed into Jacques' little Renault. Mohammed directed us to the Avenue Bosquet, and there, in an ordinary apartment block, was a storefront with a small sign in the corner of the window reading, "BTA." Jacques parked a couple of hundred meters down the block.

Jacques and Mohammed stayed in the car, while Louise and I approached the storefront, trying to act like casual window shoppers. There were a few, dusty, folded maps and brochures in the window, nothing more. Through the streaked and dirty glass we saw a woman sitting at a desk set at right angles to the window, typing. There didn't seem to be anyone else in the office.

"Let's cross the street," Louise said. "There's a small café. We can get some coffee and wait."

"I'll tell the guys."

The front of the café was open, so we picked a table just inside the shadows where we couldn't be seen clearly. The four of us ordered coffee and tried to relax.

Mohammed said, "My father was the source of the information about BTA, but I was involved, too. One day, while having lunch in the school dining room, I overheard a student from another North African country say that there was an Algerian travel agency located in the Avenue Bosquet. I told my father, who was surprised. He thought he knew the names of all the agencies that specialized in travel to Algeria—even the small boutiques. Later, when he had trouble getting space on the flights he wanted, he sent his secretary to see if, by chance, that agency was holding any reservations he could use. His secretary was treated very rudely by the personnel in the office. My father then made discreet inquiries and learned that it was alleged to be a front for the FNF, and now the OAS."

"What about the Bersaults?" I asked.

"I've heard that the son was seen here, but that doesn't mean very much."

"We'll just have to follow those people," I said, "and find out what they're up to."

◆   ◆   ◆

"Mohammed Almedienne's father Georges," Roger said, "has an excellent reputation as a man of fine intelligence, capability and honor. Jean Bourgeois speaks very highly of him. By the way, I've spoken to Jean in the past concerning the DragonSlayers and he knows nothing about them."

"What about the Sûreté?" I asked. "Should we inform them of our surveillance of BTA?"

"These days, William, it's very difficult to tell what side anyone is on," he said. "The military is split down the middle—caught between their duty to obey the civilian government, and their desire to keep France and France's army together."

"What about the police?" I asked.

"The same," Roger said. "This country is famous for such divisions. The French Revolution was only one example. The violence men did to each other in that era was as despicable as both sides have been guilty of in Algeria. During the last war, there were many more collaborators than we French want to admit. Marshal Petain was a traitor to France, and he had been considered one of our greatest men."

"Should we inform the president?" Louise asked.

"We need concrete evidence," Roger said. "There's no point disturbing the president with fears and rumors."

Everyone agreed that the four of us would have to stake out the BTA office ourselves, but I had another suggestion. I said to Roger, "I learned from you that during the war my mother was very active in the Resistance."

"She was the bravest of the brave," Roger said.

"Did she spend any time in Paris?"

"What are you getting at?" Roger asked.

"Isn't it obvious?" Louise said. "William thinks his mother might be willing to work with our team."

Roger looked at me sharply, and I nodded.

"Amazing," Roger said. "This time the child is recruiting the parent."

THE NEW
RESISTANCE

Roger didn't give Mother a complete description of our plans over the telephone, only telling her that we were planning to do some surveillance on behalf of the president, and that her experience in the Resistance would be very helpful. She was absolutely thrilled by the suggestion, but Paul wasn't. Nevertheless, he drove with her into Paris to meet with us.

When we met, Paul said, "This is crazy. Helene was a brave soldier in the Resistance, but that ended over fifteen years ago. I don't see her as a sharpshooter any longer."

"We don't need sharpshooters," Roger said. "We need intelligence agents to track the enemies of our country. Helene need never touch a gun."

"You see?" Mother said.

Paul wasn't convinced. "I'm sure it will be dangerous, Roger, but that doesn't stop you from involving William and Helene, not to mention Louise."

"And others as well," I said. I went back to Roger's bedroom, collected my friends and brought them to the parlor. "Mai Pham, Jacques Rouen, Mohammed Almedienne, I would like you to meet my mother, Helene Montreux, and my stepfather, Paul Montreux."

Paul was obviously surprised by the arrival of all of my friends, but his eyes fluttered between Mai and Mohammed.

"Who are you?" Paul asked.

"We're all friends of Louise and William from the Lycée and the Sorbonne," Mai said. "We're pleased to meet William's parents."

Helene smiled and shook hands with all of them. Paul nodded.

Jacques said, "We're members of the Clandestin, an association of younger relatives—the next generation—of former members of the Resistance."

"Including this young lady and this young man?" Paul asked, pointing to Mai and Mohammed.

"Is it possible, Monsieur Montreux," Mai said, dark eyes flashing, "that you are unaware that Vietnamese and Algerians were in the Resistance?"

"We carefully verified their heritage," Jacques said, his tone serious, but there was a hint of a wicked grin on his face. "Both of their fathers have perfect credentials."

"Had," Mai said coldly. "My father was a French army officer who died fighting the insurgency in Indo-China—now known as Viet Nam."

"I . . . I'm sorry," Paul said.

"I knew Mohammed's father briefly in the Resistance," Roger said. "He is a close friend of Jean Bourgeois, now the director of the Crouching Dragon."

"What is your interest in this matter?" Paul asked Mohammed. He wasn't quite ready to give up.

"My father is the head of the Algerian Section of the Foreign Ministry."

"Isn't he in favor of independence for Algeria?" Paul asked.

"Yes, but so is de Gaulle," Mohammed said. "The president is a great and wise man. Do you think he didn't know how the voting would turn out? By authorizing the referendum, he virtually guaranteed the result."

I looked at Mohammed with new respect.

"Isn't anyone interested in my credentials?" Jacques said. "Or is my white skin credential enough?"

Mai and Mohammed laughed; everyone else, except Paul, smiled. He looked sheepish.

"Very well," Paul said. "but I still don't understand what you are trying to accomplish."

"Mohammed and Jacques helped us track down the DragonSlayers' headquarters," I said.

Paul blinked again. "DragonSlayers?—like the symbol the thief carried at the Crouching Dragon?"

Roger showed him one of his books marked with the symbol, and then told him about our discovery of the men in the apartment, our struggle with them, and the ensuing chase.

Both Paul and Mother were giving me accusatory looks.

"This is even worse than I thought," Paul said. "Why haven't we been told?"

"We didn't want to worry you unnecessarily," I said.

"And now you are worrying me *necessarily*?" Paul said. "Wonderful!"

"Paul," Helene said, with an entirely innocent expression on her face. "You can come along and protect us."

Even Paul laughed. "I'm the perfect spy," he said. "Tall, big, with black hair and a black mustache. No one would ever notice me."

Helene said, "You could—"

"—Not a chance! I will never shave off this mustache!"

"We should explain," I said. "Many people are unhappy about the referendum, and there is talk of an uprising— rumors of certain elements of the military attempting a coup against President de Gaulle. We know the DragonSlayers are associated with the white settlers in Algiers, and they may be involved in such an attempt."

"We think," Louise said, "that the DragonSlayers were

interested in more than stealing treasures from the Crouching Dragon and attacking Roger and William."

I said, "Maybe the attempted theft from the castle was part of a plan to raise money to support the DragonSlayers' operations in Algeria and mainland France."

Paul looked uncertain. "Isn't this a problem for military intelligence?"

"We can't be sure who is on whose side," Louise said. "Everyone knows the president has enemies in the military."

Paul said, his voice rising, his fists clenched, "I hate anyone who opposes *mon général*, the great president of our country. But I don't understand what a professor, a few students and some former Resistance fighters are going to do about it."

"For the moment, we only intend to gather information," Roger said. "If we find evidence of a plot, we will inform the president."

Paul looked unconvinced, but he said nothing more.

Roger said, "Paul in his truck and Jacques in his sedan can take turns driving us around the city. That will leave six of us—Helene, Louise, Mai, Mohammed, William and I—to actively stalk our quarry. I can supply portable radios for everyone. There is nothing sacred about the frequencies on which the radios operate—our enemies may be able to listen in on us."

Paul was shaking his head—again. "If these guys are as bad as you say, you might all be killed. What about the Sûreté?"

"They've been no help," Roger said. "We also informed Major Gerard, the president's personal security chief, of the break-in at the apartment. He informed us of the president's sympathy, but that was the end of that."

I realized that nothing would convince Paul that our operation wasn't very dangerous, and in fact he was right. But we had to go forward.

"I think we should begin," I said, "by systematically trailing people from the agency. We have many other friends in the Clandestin. They all know how to use shortwave radios and most are trained in Judo. If necessary, we can ask them for help. If it seems we're getting in over our heads, we'll have to inform the authorities."

"Excellent," Louise said, as if that settled the matter.

Mother had taken Paul's hand, and maybe that reassured him more than our words.

♦   ♦   ♦

The following day, Mohammed and Louise began by "staking out" (I got that from an American detective story) the storefront on the Rue Bosquet, sitting in the café across the street. They reported that a number of people had entered the agency at different times and from different directions, and later left in a group, all carrying the DragonSlayers bags.

Jacques and Mai immediately picked up the trail and followed them until they reached the Eiffel Tower, then got into Paul's truck and drove away. Mother and I were waiting at the tower—we had guessed it would be on every itinerary. After a few minutes, two of the "tourists" left the group and entered the Bir Hakeim Metro Station. We followed that pair, while Jacques and Mai circled back to watch the main group.

The two men we followed took the train on line number 6, and got off soon after the subway crossed the river, at the Trocadero station. They switched to line number 9, but got off at Alma Marceau, walked a few blocks and then went back down at the same station, Alma Marceau, and boarded a train on exactly the same line. I had begun our trip wearing a cap, but took it off after a while, hoping I looked different.

The tourists got off again a few stops later at St. Augustin and then walked towards the station, Gare St. Lazare. We crossed the street, so we wouldn't be seen exactly behind them. They stopped to look in a tobacconist's window. We sensed they were checking to see if they were being followed, so we actually passed them on the opposite sidewalk, pretending we were on our own errand.

"I wonder if they noticed us?" I asked.

"I doubt it," Mother said. "I don't think they really suspect they're being followed. They're just using standard techniques."

"They're walking again," I said. A tilted store window had given me a view back across the street between cars and walkers and buses.

They entered the great iron-framed station and went to the platform for trains from the west—Normandy and Brittany. We waited in the main concourse. After a while, they came back out—with two other men, all four of them now carrying the familiar black bags.

"Boat train from Le Havre. Four men, four bags," Mother said into her handie-talkie. "Heading for main exit, Rue de Laborde."

Roger was driving Jacques' little Renault, which wasn't easy because Roger was so tall that his knees came up behind the steering wheel.

We watched them exit the station from just within the doors. As they reached the curb, a dirty, gray van appeared. The four men got in quickly and the van drove away.

Mother spoke into her radio: "Gray van, license number ARC145—where are you?"

"Sorry," Roger said. "Traffic blocked me."

◆   ◆   ◆

When we gathered again at Roger's apartment, Mai and Jacques reported their quarry had crossed the Pont d'Iena, and entered the Metro station in the square.

Louise and Mohammed followed a group along the Avenue de la Bourdonnais. Two left at the École Militaire station; two more disappeared somewhere in the Invalides. Four went into the Varenne station. They broke off surveillance there.

I couldn't help expressing my frustration. "What did we learn? Nothing. What are they doing? Who knows?"

Paul, who had returned to wait at the apartment, said, "It's only the first day, William. You must be patient."

That from Paul, who had seldom shown patience in the past.

Roger was studying one of his many maps, spread on the remains of a drafting table. The intruders had knocked off a leg, but Roger had propped the board on a pile of books. It wobbled, but he didn't seem to notice.

"Bir Hakeim, Tour Eiffel, Pont d'Iena, École Militaire, Invalides, Varenne," he said." Do you notice anything?"

Mohammed said, "There are tunnels or sewer entrances adjacent to all those locations."

"*Exactement!*" Roger said, "Precisely! Something is going on underground, as we have long suspected. Tomorrow, we'll know even more."

The next day, Paul and Louise were designated to wait in the café. Yes, he had decided to actively participate. Paul didn't cut off his mustache, but he put on a workman's cap that almost covered his thick, black hair. They alerted Mother and Jacques, who followed the group to the Metro at Bir Hakeim, where Mohammed and I took over. They switched from line to line.

"We're losing some of the tourists as we go along," Mohammed said.

"If only we had more people," I said. "Except then they might notice us."

We noted the departures, two at a time, at Chatelet-Les

Halles, Strasbourg-St. Denis, and Poissonniere.

"Let's stay with the main group," I whispered to Mohammed.

After a while, I said, "The next big stop is the station, Gare du Nord. I'm calling Roger."

But the handie-talkie didn't work underground.

After a couple of more switches, the guide and half the remaining group got off at the Gare du Nord.

"Should I stay with the ones who didn't get off?" Mohammed asked.

"Good idea."

I followed the guide and his group. Once above ground, I was able to reach Roger. "Gare du Nord. Stand by," I radioed.

The group split and pairs went to different platforms.

I radioed Roger for orders.

"Stay with the tour leader," he said. "I'll be outside the station, waiting for you and them."

The leader and two other men met two additional men disembarking from a train that had originated at Calais, another port city. Black bags of course. All five of them left the station. The same van I had seen at the Gare St Lazare picked them up, but this time we were ready, and I jumped into Paul's truck, which Roger was driving in place of Jacques' Renault.

The van moved swiftly through city traffic, just escaping lights turning red. At the opera house, the van slipped through before we reached the crossing. Roger banged his hand on the steering wheel. We waited for the light to change, and then started again.

Fortunately, the van, too, had been caught in traffic and we reached the next intersection while they were still waiting at the light.

"I don't think they've seen us," Roger said.

The van turned right into the Boulevard Sebastopal, raced

along it, angled right into the Rue Turbigo, then right again into a side street, the Rue Artaud. Suddenly, they turned into a driveway of an apartment house, under an archway. But as we reached the driveway, the gate was slammed shut. We double-parked down the block, and I walked to the gate.

The door in the gate opened and a man peered out.

"What do you want?" he asked crossly.

"Sorry," I said. "I have the wrong address."

The man glared and then slammed the door shut.

I walked to the truck, marking the address on a pad of paper, 26 Rue Artaud.

The radio crackled. "We're following a group in my Renault," Jacques said, "but I think they've spotted us. We're going to turn off at the Rue Turbigo." The handie-talkie went silent.

"They're right around the corner!" I said.

"Let's get moving," Roger said. "We'll circle the block."

We drove slowly around the block until we saw several people with black bags turning into the Rue Artaud, walking very quickly.

"Don't stare," Roger said. "I'm going to pass them."

Roger was studying the sideview mirror on the curb side of the truck.

"There's no doubt in my mind they're heading for number 26," he said, and accelerated away.

◆   ◆   ◆

Mohammed, Louise, Mother, Paul, Jacques and Mai reported their findings. They were disappointed because the tourists, by repeatedly fragmenting their group, had prevented them from following all of the units to their eventual destinations.

"We do have the Metro stops," Mai said.

"Roger and I were fortunate," I said. "We followed two groups—including the one that Jacques and Mother were tailing—to the same building in the Rue Artaud. That must be a safe house."

Roger was plotting the Metro stations the others had named. "We're paralleling tunnels and also some of the main entrances to the sewer system," he said.

"That's all very well," Mother said, "but time is passing, and we still don't know what these people are up to."

◆   ◆   ◆

The following day we decided that additional tourists would probably be coming from one of the other train stations. The next in rotation would have been the Gare de l'Est, but since most traffic into that terminal would probably not have originated at a port, we guessed that the Gare de Lyon would be the best place to watch. Sure enough, the guide was there and met a train from Marseille, France's second city and major port on the Mediterranean.

In succession, we staked out the Gare d'Austerlitz and the Gare Montparnasse. We switched pairings and followed the "tourists" as well as we could. Sometimes we lost them in traffic, other times they simply disappeared into Metro stations. In many cases, they separated into groups that went off in several directions and we couldn't follow them all.

"Dozens of these people have come in," Mother said. "Surely they are planning something big."

"Yes, but what?" I asked.

"We haven't even tried to cover the airports," Roger said. "Who knows how many of them are coming in by plane?"

"We should have taken more of the members of Clandestin into our confidence," Jacques said.

"Yes," Mohammed said, "but the more people, the more difficult it is to coordinate the effort, and the greater danger of someone unintentionally revealing our secrets."

"The news from Algeria is getting worse," Mother said. "There are rumors that a brigade of paratroopers will be flown to Paris any day now and take over the city."

Nobody came up with an answer, and then it was late and time to quit for the night. Jacques, Mohammed and Mai left. My folks were sleeping on my bed, and I was sleeping on the sofa in the parlor.

"I'll walk you to your aunt's apartment," I said to Louise.

"That's not necessary," she said, but I was helping her on with her coat and opening the apartment door.

As soon as we were outside, I said to Louise, "I've got a crazy idea. Do you want to take a chance and go somewhere with me?"

"Okay. Where to?"

"The catacombs."

"Now?" Louise was incredulous. "Won't it be locked?"

"Only the formal entrance at Denfert-Rochereau," I said. "Roger told me there are over one hundred other access points. We'll use the one that Roger and I used after chasing the intruders."

"Won't it be dark?"

I grinned and pulled a flashlight out from under my jacket.

◆   ◆   ◆

We waited until the street traffic cleared and then slipped inside. Using my flashlight, we trotted down the circular staircase into the damp gloom of the tunnels, moving rapidly through the vast empty hall with the high, arching roof and stone pillars.

"Okay," Louise whispered. "How about telling me where we're going?"

"I was studying the locations Roger plotted on his map, and I thought I saw a pattern—with the Nazi Bunker at the hub."

"You said that when you and Roger went to look at it, the bunker was barred and closed."

"Right," I said. "That's why I felt silly about bringing it up again."

We had traversed another corridor. Now we were in a space where rows and rows of skulls were piled to the ceiling on both sides of us. When my flashlight illuminated them, they looked like they were leaning towards us. Light flickering through empty sockets made the eyes seem to be staring at us. The echo of our own crunching footfalls sounded like the skulls and bones were coming after us.

Louise put her hand in mine.

I was traversing the corridors from memory, aiming for the Nazi Bunker. At one point I chose the wrong tunnel, but I realized it almost immediately and doubled back.

A couple of minutes later we reached a turnoff that I recognized as the one that led to the bunker.

"We're almost there," I whispered.

I let go of Louise's hand and covered the lens so that it glowed with only enough light to follow the corridor. The rows of bones now had an even stranger look, shifting into and out of my vision, as if they were appearing and disappearing—and grinning at me.

There was a rattling sound. I grabbed Louise and pressed us both back against the wall—except we weren't leaning against limestone, we were up against a wall of skulls, which were digging into our backs.

The sound was louder, a funny, scratchy sound right at my ear. I stepped away and flashed my light directly at the noise—at a skull—at an ugly, furry thing leaping out of the nose cavity.

Louise screamed; I threw up my hands to hold it off. It struck my arm and I dropped the flashlight. In the flare I saw it—a rat. A snarling rat, who was just as frightened of me as I was of him. He leaped to the floor and scurried away. At least, I thought he scurried away. My flashlight was off and the corridor was pitch black. Shades of the tunnels from the Crouching Dragon.

"Are you all right?" I asked in the echoing darkness.

"Disgusted, but okay," she said.

"I'll find my flashlight," I said. I hoped it was still working. "Stay near me, Louise."

I crawled along the damp corridor on my knees, reaching blindly from side to side. After a couple of minutes I felt the cold metal cylinder. "I've got it," I said. I slowly stood up and pushed the switch.

Louise yelled again, I stood frozen.

In the sudden glare, a huge, angry creature leaped off the wall at us—red, orange and yellow—with glaring eyes, enormous jaws and a reptile's tongue. It was a dragon—a furious dragon with a bloody sword shoved through its twisted body.

A painted dragon. On a shield.

We whispered the word together: "DragonSlayers."

"In full color," Louise said, "not just black and white."

Still frightened, I scanned the rest of the area with my flashlight. We were in the chamber in front of the Nazi Bunker, with its empty shelves and heavy, riveted steel door with a wheel on it.

"The bars are gone," I said. "There were heavy steel bars across the door."

I shined the light back on the dragon, which even then seemed ready to attack.

Louise whispered, "It isn't directly on the wall," she said. "It seems to be painted on something."

"It wasn't here before," I said.

I handed Louise the flashlight and reached for the wheel. It didn't turn. Apparently it was still locked.

"Let's get out of here," I said.

I gave the dragon one last, nervous look before we started running out of the catacombs.

✦   ✦   ✦

"I should have realized there was something funny about those bars across the entrance," Roger said. "In all the time I've been studying the catacombs no one told me the Nazi Bunker was locked."

Mon Dieu," my mother said. "They seem to have encircled the city."

"Do you think they're planning a coup?" I asked

"Perhaps," Roger said. "But we can't do any more by ourselves. We must share this information with President de Gaulle."

"Not yet," I said, "All we can tell the president now is that we've seen some people acting suspiciously, that they may come from Algeria and that they use the same DragonSlayers symbol. If the president asks us to describe these suspicious actions, what will we tell them? They visit the historical sites in Paris, but don't usually go in; some of them disappear— probably into the sewers or tunnels of the city. That we found a DragonSlayers symbol in the catacombs?"

Everyone was silent; no one disagreed with me. I had almost hoped they would.

"That doesn't mean there's nothing we can do," I finally said. "Why don't we 'stake out' the old Nazi Bunker and see what we learn?"

Roger opened his armoire, rummaged inside, and then held up a large, iron key.

"I've been holding onto this for seventeen years."

✦   ✦   ✦

Paul waited in his truck near the main entrance to the catacombs, Jacques in his Renault near the other exit; both had radios. Roger and I entered first. Then, ten minutes later, Louise and Mohammed. Last, Mai and my mother.

Each pair had a handie-talkie radio, although we didn't know if we could communicate down deep in the tunnels. The kids carried tools in book bags. Roger carried tools as well, but he also brought his automatic pistol. We rendezvoused a little ways into the tunnel, and then continued together, single file.

The air in the tunnels, as usual, seemed dense, damp and heavy. I was surprised to hear myself breathing. The only other sounds were the footsteps of my friends, causing a sucking sound where the floor was smooth and a scrunching noise on the gravel. Somehow, the steps didn't seem to echo. The occasional bulbs provided fragile illumination.

As we approached the chapel of the Trinity cemetery, Roger flicked on his flashlight and there was a smothered scream. I tensed, then saw a young man and woman entwined on the bench in front of the altar, fixed in the glare. They scrambled up, and dashed past us into the tunnel.

Roger grinned. "I don't think they're DragonSlayers."

"They weren't carrying the right tourist bags," Louise said.

We resumed our progress through the chapel area and then back into the narrow corridors of the tunnels.

"We'll take the next turnoff," Roger whispered.

As we were about to turn from the main corridor into the bunker tunnel, we heard running feet. Roger hurried us past the opening and we huddled against the wall.

The footsteps grew louder, and a light bounced up and down on the floor and against the blank wall of the main corridor opposite the bunker tunnel. Louise was close beside me—standing on my foot. I didn't dare make a sound.

In a second we heard voices. Two men ran into the main corridor and turned—away from us and back along the route we had traversed. I caught a brief glimpse of a rugged profile and a clump of blonde hair—Raoul Larron.

Instinctively, I started after him, but Roger grabbed my arm and held me.

In a few moments, the light and the sound of running feet faded and disappeared.

"That was Raoul," I protested to Roger.

"How did he get out of jail?" Mother asked.

"Someone bailed him out," Roger said. "That's the only information about him we actually learned from the Sûreté."

"You can blow up a building, and still get out on bail?" Mai asked.

'Yes," Roger said. "and destroy hundreds of books."

"There's something wrong with the system," Paul said.

"Back to business," Roger said. "William and I will go on ahead to the bunker. Louise, can you whistle?"

"Of course," she said, smiling, "loud enough to blow out your ear drums."

"I prefer high and piercing," Roger said, "so that it carries a long way."

Louise obliged with an example, and the rest of us stepped back in surprise.

"Perfect," Roger said. "You and Mai go on ahead about two hundred meters toward the rear exit and wait. If you see or hear anyone, first signal us with your handie-talkie. If we don't respond immediately, run back to this branch of the tunnel and favor us with your whistle."

Mohammed said, "I can ululate like my forbears in the desert. It sounds like an animal baying and it carries a long way." He was about to give us an example, but Roger held up his hand.

"I believe you, Mohammed." he said. "You and Helene go back about two hundred meters towards the main entrance— the same way those men went. If you hear or see anyone, first try the handie-talkie, and if not hurry back here and ululate.

"As soon as either of you signals, by radio or otherwise, all of you must run away in the opposite direction from which you hear noises. Clear?"

We all nodded, and Roger turned to enter the branch.

"Wait a minute," Mohammed said. "What if you run into someone in the bunker?"

"If you hear any noise—even shots—split up and go in opposite directions and call the police."

"We should come back and help you," Louise said.

"You'll help me best by following my instructions," Roger said.

We started down the tunnel, with me a couple of meters behind him. Roger, as usual, was shielding the lens of his flashlight. The skulls were still grinning at me, but they almost seemed familiar. Almost. Listening for another rat, I heard something I hadn't noticed before: a low, background sound, as if the skulls were slowly settling into their places—or getting ready to pounce.

Just before we reached the bunker, Roger held up his hand to stop me, and he opened his fingers to let his flashlight illuminate the space.

The wall was cold, blank stone. Where was the DragonSlayers symbol? Roger looked at me questioningly.

I was confused, but only for a second. I pointed towards the ceiling—something was rolled tight against it. Roger unrolled it enough to satisfy himself that it was the hated symbol, then carefully put it back into its original condition.

He turned his eyes to the riveted metal entrance door. There were still notices splashed on it and two heavy bars crossed it. He jiggled the end of one so that it came out of the stone, and laughed under his breath. Together, we lifted first one bar, then the other, off the door and set them on the floor.

Roger pressed the side of his head against the door,

listening. Then he handed me the flashlight, set his tool bag down and slowly extracted the key. It was a very large, old-fashioned key, forged of steel, with a thick barrel. I held the flashlight on the door while he carefully inserted the key into the keyhole. He twisted it slowly and pulled. The key slipped out of the opening so easily that he almost staggered. Roger tried once more, not turning the key as far as before, but trying to shove it further in. This time the key did not come out, but it didn't open the door, either. He tried several more times, but the door remained shut.

Roger removed a sharp, pointed tool—an awl—from his bag and dug into the keyhole, prying loose a chunk of plastic that had apparently blocked his key.

Again, Roger inserted the key and turned it. Satisfied, he gripped the metal wheel with both hands and turned. There was an unpleasant grating sound of metal on metal. With an eerie, creaking sound, the door began to swing open on rusty hinges. Roger gestured to me to hand him the flashlight, which he immediately turned off.

In the last glimpse of light, I saw that he was holding the flashlight in his left hand, his automatic in the other. The door was swinging farther open on its own.

The flashlight suddenly turned on, illuminating Roger standing in the opening, holding his weapon high. Then he disappeared inside, and all I could see were flashes of light. After a few nervous moments, he appeared again.

"Nobody here," he said.

The bunker was much larger than it seemed from the outside corridor, with several rooms and many concrete bins and shelves. Light fixtures had been stripped from the ceiling, but there were a couple of floor lamps and a small motor, with thick, black extension cords plugged into it.

"Electric generator," Roger said, wrinkling his nose. "You can smell the fuel, even though they vented it. The

Nazis had a bigger generator, despite being hooked into the Paris power grid."

There was a wooden table with a drafting lamp affixed to the top and a couple of stools. Papers were spread on the table, but Roger continued into the bunker.

"Herter—Major Wilhelm von Herter. This was his command post," Roger said, pointing to another room that opened off the central corridor. In it was a table, a chair, and a wall of lockers, but Roger didn't open them.

"You even knew his name?" I asked.

"We knew everything about them," he said. "Our headquarters was only a couple of hundred meters away, although they didn't even know it existed. Every once in a while we'd interrupt their electric service. They'd call for an electrician, and we would slip one of our people in to fix the power. He'd tap on the fuse box, we'd reconnect the power line and he'd throw the switch. Meanwhile he was collecting information. The Germans liked things to be orderly, and they had lists and names posted."

"They never found out where you were?"

Roger laughed. "We scared the hell out of them, tapping on walls, setting off tiny explosions. They'd come charging out of the bunker, but we'd be gone. Their usual entry was under the Lycée Montaigne, next to the Luxembourg gardens.

"Eventually, the Nazis became afraid that they'd get blown up in their own bunker. They finally vacated it and we had the whole tunnel system to ourselves. After the war, I took one of the keys as a souvenir."

At the end of the central corridor was another metal door. Roger yanked it open, still holding his automatic.

"Will you look at this!" he said.

The room was large and in it were racks of weapons— submachine guns, rifles, automatic pistols, grenades and crates of ammunition. I was so surprised I just stood there, mouth open.

"These guys are almost as neat as the Nazis," Roger said, checking one of the automatic weapons. "French—same kind the army uses today."

Roger opened a large locker. He reached in, grabbed something and tossed it to me.

"A beret," I said, puzzled.

"Not just any beret. Look at the markings: French paratroopers. At least they've got the uniforms and the weapons."

It was all beginning to fit together in my mind. "They've got people already here. They won't have to fly them in from Algeria."

"Exactly," Roger said.

"Look!" I said. "A pile of black tourist bags!"

"That's what those 'tourists' were carrying," Roger said. "Weapons and uniforms!"

"We should alert the authorities," I said.

Roger pulled something from his tool bag and held it to his eye. When it flashed, I realized it was a very small camera.

"Just taking inventory," he said, clicking pictures in room after room.

In the Nazi major's office, he opened the lockers and revealed two tall metal tubes.

"Bazookas," Roger said. "You could stop a tank with them."

"How many people could they arm with all this stuff?"

"A few hundred," Roger said, still clicking away.

"You couldn't take Paris with a few hundred men," I said.

"You could if dozens of paratroopers suddenly appeared at key locations, and their supporters poured into the streets and disrupted traffic, and everybody thought the city had been surrounded by the military."

"Especially if they managed to capture the president," I

said. "Let's start removing this stuff!"

"We're going to leave everything just as we found it," Roger said. "We don't know what else they have stashed in other places. If we move too quickly we may not be able to control the situation."

Roger carefully photographed the documents in the office, page by page.

My handie-talkie crackled. I thought I heard Louise.

"Come on!" Roger said. "Let's get out of here!"

We closed the metal door and Roger keyed it shut. Next we replaced the metal bars. Then we raced down the corridor. When we reached the main tunnel, we saw Louise and Mai running towards the far exit. After a couple of hundred meters, we found Mohammed and my mother.

"You were supposed to run!" Roger whispered fiercely.

"We couldn't just leave you there," Mother said.

Louise hushed all of us as we heard the sounds of people approaching. Roger raised his weapon, motioned the rest of us against the wall, and turned off his flashlight.

The steps grew louder and louder and I tensed for a fight. But the sound diminished—they had turned into the bunker tunnel. After a moment, we heard a creaking door.

We all began to run.

◆　　◆　　◆

We piled into Paul's truck—Mother and Mai in the cab—Roger, Mohammed, Louise and I in the canvas-covered van. I radioed Jacques to meet us at Roger's apartment.

As we hurried along the street, we passed many automobiles with their horns blaring. Groups of people marched along the sidewalks, singing and waving the French Tricolor.

Louise asked, "What's today's date? Is this a holiday?"

"It's the twenty-second of May," Roger said. "If this is a holiday, it's a new one."

◆　　◆　　◆

Jacques were waiting when we reached Roger's apartment. "Listen to this," he said, turning up the volume on Roger's radio.

The announcer was speaking in a clipped, emotionless voice: " . . . army claims to be in control of Algiers and the Sahara. We have unconfirmed reports of armed confrontations between the military and the FLN in the capital city. President de Gaulle has declared a state of national emergency. Rumors continue to reach us of paratroopers preparing to fly from Africa to Paris and surround the city . . . "

Roger turned off the radio. "Come on, Mohammed," he said. "Let's make pictures."

The rest of us discussed what we had found in the bunker while Roger and Mo developed photos in the bathroom, which they were using as a darkroom. It seemed only a few minutes before they grimly showed us their work: two dozen black-and-white prints hanging, still wet, on a stretched clothesline.

Roger said, "We must get our information to the president as soon as possible."

"First," I said, "we should alert our friends in the Clandestin. They're pretty tough, they know Judo and they can communicate by radio. We may need them to subdue the DragonSlayers."

Paul said, "Two or three dozen kids won't be enough to control several hundred battle-hardened men."

"We have almost one hundred members, most of whom don't go to the Raging Dragon, but we know how to reach them."

"Some of them have guns," Mohammed said.

"You call them the Resistance, second generation," Mother said. "Let's not forget the first generation."

"Brilliant!" Roger said.

"We'll alert our friends," Jacques said, "and they'll alert

their relatives who were in the Resistance."

"How many will that be?" Roger asked.

"On short notice," Jacques said, "we can probably reach almost everybody who's in town—each member contacting several others. Let's say seventy-five, and the same number of relatives, about one hundred fifty in all."

"The DragonSlayers aren't expecting us," I said. "With the element of surprise, we'll overcome them."

Louise said, "We must speak to the president."

THE COUP

He stood very tall and silent, methodically examining the drawings—there were five of them—individually mounted on back-lighting boxes against the wall in the Security Room. In sharp contrast to the elegant public rooms and private apartments of the palace, this room was stark in design: beige walls and ceiling, brown wainscot and brown-patterned tile floor. Although the space was large and well-lighted, his presence filled it, even though his bald head was bare, tiny reading glasses were perched on the end of his ample nose, and he wore a simple, dark suit with a dark tie and dark shoes. The only sound in the room was the impact of his leather-soled shoes on the textured floor as he walked from drawing to drawing.

After viewing the drawings, he moved to the two dozen enlarged black-and-white photos pinned to a corkboard. When he leaned close, an aide snapped on a flourescent light above the display.

When he had finished examining all of the drawings and photographs, he stood for a moment with his back to us and then turned slowly around.

"Please tell us your interpretation of what you have found, Doctor Guiscard," he said.

"Thank you, *Monsieur le Président*," Roger said. "Inside the old Nazi Bunker we discovered the cache of arms and matériel shown in the photographs. An inventory is mounted on the corkboard.

"The drawings depict the catacombs, connecting tunnels and the Metro. Markings were added, each consisting of an object and a number. Comparing markings from the bunker with markings for the other locations, it is evident that the symbol of a bullet stands for ammunition, a notched circle represents the magazine on a submachine gun and thus the weapon itself, and so forth, for rifles, pistols, grenades and plastic explosives. The number, of course, stands for the quantity of each.

"There are no symbols for the paratrooper uniforms. Our count in the Nazi Bunker was two hundred uniforms. If we assume that the proportion of uniforms to weapons in the other locations is similar to that in the bunker, we estimate that there would be weapons, supplies and uniforms for approximately seven hundred men."

Major Gerard asked, "How certain are you of these numbers?"

"There can be no certainty," Roger said.

"*Monsieur le Président*," I said, "the number is probably increasing because our surveillance indicates that additional men are coming to Paris every day. We have not been watching the airports and so the number could be far greater."

M. Noir, the official representative of the Sûreté, said, "We do not think the numbers arriving by commercial airlines can be substantial, *Monsieur le Président*. We have been checking the airports since the military uprising two years ago, and we have a complete roster of everyone from Algeria who has entered the country since then."

My friends and I exchanged surprised glances.

"The only persons connected to the military," M. Noir continued, "or to any paramilitary organization or protest group are the handful of officials and officers on the list we provided you this morning. The so-called 'tourists' presumably used ships and trains because they knew we were *not* scrutinizing those modes of transportation."

"How did they know that?" Roger asked.

Noir shook his head. "It was an unfortunate error," he said.

We had always assumed that Noir was not his real name, but only that morning we had learned that he was, in fact, a *commissaire* of the Sûreté and that his real name was Reginald Surat. Nevertheless, even in this meeting, he was referred to by his pseudonym, Noir.

"What about military transport?" the president asked the other man in the room, who had been completely silent until then: General George Richelieu, who wore a crisp uniform, pressed to board texture, with endless rows of decorations on his chest and manifold stars and insignia on his epaulets. His close-cropped, iron-gray hair, narrow mustache and thin mouth seemed to frame a perpetual frown, and he held his kepi, his military cap, under one arm, where it remained for the entire meeting.

He spoke in a voice as crisp as his uniform: "We are unaware of any persons dangerous to the regime who have used military aircraft. However, our intelligence will immediately verify the data provided by the commissaire and the . . . others."

"No verification is necessary," the president said, "considering the impeccable sources who have provided it."

"Everything I have learned," Major Gerard said, "tends to confirm the intelligence furnished by Doctor Guiscard and Monsieur Montreux."

"When do you think they will strike?" the president asked.

"Tonight," I said.

The president seemed surprised.

"Tonight, at 8 P.M.," he said, "I am making a televised address to the citizens of France, here and abroad."

"Perhaps you should broadcast from another, secret

and secure location," General Richelieu said.

"I shall speak from the Élysée Palace. I will not give the people of France the impression that the enemy has forced me into hiding."

Major Gerard said, "We have ample personnel and facilities to protect our president, the integrity of the palace, and the broadcast."

"That won't solve everything," I said. "It's our opinion that the DragonSlayers will take advantage of this event to stage their operation. While the president is broadcasting to the nation, they'll set off explosives in various parts of the city, making it look like the president is not actually in control, even in Paris. People will be injured, perhaps killed, buildings will be damaged. Emergency crews will be racing everywhere, sirens blasting."

"That would be terrible," the major said. "But how will anyone reach the president?"

"They won't have to," I said. "In the confusion, the DragonSlayers will appear at multiple locations, in uniform and with weapons. It will seem as if the paratroopers have actually landed and taken over the city."

"The people will believe," Roger said, "that the regime has collapsed. I regret to say this, *Monsieur le Président,* but it will seem that your speech is a meaningless exercise, contradicted by the reality in the streets."

"They'll also be hoping," Louise said, "that the people will arise spontaneously and join them, perhaps even some military units and the police."

"We must send troops to capture these people immediately," the general said.

The president said, "The army, to its great disgrace, has announced that it is in control of Algiers. There are rumors of a paratroop attack on Paris. If the people see troops in the city, no matter what I say, they will believe there has been a coup. Your men will not have time to explain which side they are on. If they know."

"The Sûreté is not equipped to deal with this type of operation," M. Noir said, looking rather nervous and perhaps even frightened.

"With the approval of General Richelieu," Major Gerard said, "I was going to recommend that we call in the special forces, our commandos. A large unit is stationed outside of Paris. It will take only minutes to alert them."

"Will they arrive by helicopter, Major?" the president asked. "Will they wear masks and dress in fatigues? I am certain your intentions are the best, but without extensive preparation, using the special forces might end in disaster."

"We have a plan, *Monsieur le Président*," I said. "Louise, Mohammed, Mai and I belong to an organization known as the Clandestin."

"A group of young people," M. Noir said, "who are the sons and daughters, nephews and nieces and so on, of members of the French Resistance."

Evidently M. Noir was trying to impress the president that he had at least some useful information.

"Correct, Monsieur Noir," I said. "The Clandestin has nine bases in key locations around Paris, all equipped with shortwave radios. Since very early today, our friends have been contacting members of the group and their older relatives from the wartime Resistance—specifically, men and women whose loyalty to the president is unshakable—to instruct them to gather at these bases and await further instruction."

"How many people are you talking about?" the general asked.

"Approximately one hundred fifty," Louise said.

The general said, in plainly skeptical tones, "If there is such a plot as you describe—and I am not convinced there is—you are planning to send a cadre of children to stop a coup planned by supposedly seasoned and heavily-armed men. They would be slaughtered."

"The Clandestin are not mere children," Mohammed said. "They are strongly motivated young people who have been training for emergencies for many years. Virtually all of our people, young and not as young, are skilled in the martial arts."

The general seemed to smirk. "They will conquer with their hands and feet."

"Those from the Resistance have weapons," Roger said, "just as I do."

Mai added, "Many of our young people also have weapons and training. My uncle, a military officer who, like my later father, served with the counter-insurgency forces in Indo-China, trained me to use rifles, handguns, automatic weapons, even bayonets and garottes."

"This all sounds very unprofessional," the general said.

"Perhaps that is why it will succeed," the president said. "No clumsy bureaucracy and no military units of uncertain loyalty. I have heard your description of your personnel, General William Montreux, but not your plan of action."

"There are twelve locations, call them cells, where the DragonSlayers have stored arms and uniforms," I said. "We will split our forces into teams and assign them to subduing individual cells—timing the operations so that they commence simultaneously two hours before your address. The largest team, divided into two units, will converge on the largest cell, the Nazi Bunker, attacking from opposite directions to prevent escape. Roger, Louise, Mohammed and I will join that group."

"You have given me your troop assignments and strategy, William," the president said, "but you have not described your tactics."

I couldn't help smiling. "We are discussing, *Mon Général*, some of the toughest and most imaginative people in France. I am confident they will devise the best tactics for each situation, improvising as necessary."

The president stared at me, and though he said nothing at that moment, I felt the warmth of his support and understanding.

Major Gerard asked, "Have you informed your groups of their assignments?"

"We came in two vehicles, my stepfather's truck and one member's sedan. Mohammed and Mai will deliver maps and assignments to the bases as soon as we have the president's approval."

Roger said, "We need your help in making multiple copies of the drawings marked with the weapons caches."

The president pushed a button on his intercom unit. An aide entered promptly and the president told him to make two dozen copies of the key drawings.

"There are boisterous crowds in the streets," the major said. "I have loyal men who can make your deliveries."

"It will be best if it is done by Mai and Mohammed," I said. "Our comrades won't know whether or not to trust your people."

General Richelieu said, "You've told us that your bases have shortwave radios. Why don't you simply radio them from here and describe their assignments?"

"Because," Louise said, "we don't have secure channels. Anyone might be listening. We can alert the bases that information is coming, but we don't dare broadcast their locations or our specific plans."

"This is a desperate venture," the major said. "I hope you will consider the other alternatives."

"This plan suits me," the president said.

In minutes, we had the requested copies. We had

previously decided which bases would subdue which cells, and we had prepared notes to write on each set of drawings. Roger, Mai, Louise, Mohammed and I used the long table in the Security Room to copy the notes onto the plans.

Mai and Mohammed gathered up the sets.

"Bon chance," I said, and then they were gone.

The major said, "I will take you to the radio room."

"I must prepare my speech," the president said. His voice was calm, and he seemed completely serene.

◆　◆　◆

The major took us to the radio room and instructed the operators to follow our instructions. I kept checking my watch; this was taking longer than I had expected.

"I must confirm security arrangements at the palace," he said. "I'll return shortly."

The operator assigned to us quickly found the frequency we wanted and turned the microphone and a set of headphones over to me. It took only a few minutes to advise our friends, who were standing by, that information was on the way. I told them to radio us as soon as they received it

"Mai and Mohammed should reach the closest bases in fifteen or twenty minutes," Louise said.

"The traffic may be very heavy," Roger said.

"There's no way it could take more than an hour and a half to reach even the most distant locations," I said.

"It's almost 3 P.M.," Roger said.

We sat and waited and paced and twitched and worried, taking turns on the headphones.

At 3:30 P.M., while Louise was on the headphones, Jacques radioed to ask where the couriers were. Louise told him they were on the way.

"I wonder," I said.

By 4 P.M., we had heard from all of the bases, everyone complaining they hadn't seen either Mai or Mohammed.

"I'm going to talk to the president," I said.

◆   ◆   ◆

The president's speech was to be broadcast from the large Salle Napoleon III, which would easily accommodate the television crew, staff and security personnel. It was unsettling to see television equipment rolling over the rich carpeting, but the exquisite furniture had been collected and roped off. The president was sitting behind his favorite table-desk, which had been carried from his private quarters, making notes in longhand on a large, lined pad, oblivious of the crew, which was running long, thick black cables and setting up cameras and microphones. The major was standing by.

"We haven't heard from any of the bases," I told the president.

"It's probably just heavy traffic," the major said, speaking irritably.

"We need a backup plan," I said.

The president waited.

"We're running out of time," I said. "If the major will take me to Le Bourget, the two of us can fly over the bases and drop canisters with the drawings in them."

The major laughed harshly. "Very dramatic," he said. "Why do you think we'll be able to get through traffic to the airport if your friends couldn't?"

"In a government vehicle with a siren going and lights flashing," I said, "we will get there."

The major was smiling, as if I was not to be taken seriously. "Suppose we reach the airport," he said. "We would need canisters with small parachutes attached of the type used to deliver small items on a battlefield. I have no idea where to locate such items on short notice."

I said, "I thought we could put the drawings in boxes or something and drop them without parachutes."

"Monsieur William," Major Gerard said, "if you drop

boxes from five hundred meters, the lowest permissible height over the city, you would never hit your target. In fact, you would probably kill someone." He was speaking patiently, as if talking to a small child. I had come to like the major a lot, but now he was beginning to make fun of me.

"Major Gerard," I said. "This is an emergency. The rules should not stop us. We could fly low, maybe fifty or sixty meters!"

The major seemed startled.

The president spoke softly, but firmly. "We may not have parachutes, but we have plenty of diplomatic pouches. With a skilled pilot like you flying at low altitude, Major, and William aiming carefully, it can be done."

It was obvious the major had never expected the president to give serious consideration to my wild proposal.

"Very well," the major said, "I'll contact Le Bourget and have a military pilot fly you over the city."

"I wouldn't feel comfortable with anyone but you," I said.

"I must remain here," the major said stiffly, "and supervise security."

"Major Gerard," the president said. "You can be back in ample time to fulfill your responsibilities. In any case, I'm confident that you have prepared your security staff for any eventuality."

"*Monsieur le Président*," the major began. I was certain he was going to voice another protest, but his facial expression changed suddenly. "Very well. We must leave at once!"

"Thank you," I said. "Let's get Louise and the drawings."

"Why do we need Mademoiselle Louise?" the major asked.

"She can help me mark the drawings and pack the pouches while we're driving to the airport," I said.

FLIGHT PLAN

Lights flashing, siren screaming, Major Gerard drove the black government van, with Tricolors flying, through the city. The traffic was very heavy and there was plenty of horn-blowing. We saw many French flags, but it wasn't clear which side the flag-wavers were on.

Police at intersections usually waved us through and held opposing traffic back, their white gloves flashing graceful and dramatic signals. A couple of times the major drove over a curb to get around traffic, sending bystanders flying out of the way, drawing many curses and some very explicit gestures. Despite the major's expert driving, we were losing time.

Louise and I marked the drawings and packed the diplomatic pouches in silence. The major's expression was very grim, his jaw set. I saw his Adam's apple working, and when he looked past me to check crossing traffic, his steely look was enough to slit a throat.

At Le Bourget, we were quickly waved through the military gate and raced to the hangar of Roxanne's successor, Roxanne 2. The doors were open, and the major actually drove part way inside. It was 5 P.M., and I was still feeling optimistic. The flight shouldn't take more than half an hour.

"Great driving," I ventured.

The major said nothing as he stepped to the tarmac. I helped carry some of the diplomatic pouches close to Roxanne. If the major didn't help us, it would take two more trips. We set down the pouches and turned to go back for more.

Major Gerard was facing us with a gun in his hand.

He spoke matter of factly: "Tony Bersault told me to kill you. I would prefer to lock you in the hangar, but Tony was insistent—he says he refuses to accept any further interference from you."

"What are you talking about?" I asked.

"Your friends did not reach their bases because we took them into custody a few minutes after they left the palace. With you out of action, they will have neither maps nor directions. The DragonSlayers will accomplish our coup without interference."

"But—" I began.

"—There's no time for conversation," the major said. "Move over to the storage area." He gestured with his gun.

We moved slowly, keeping our eyes fixed on him.

"It's difficult to believe you're one of them," I said.

"You're not like Tony Bersault," Louise said.

"Our goal is the same: Algeria must remain part of France."

"We thought you were loyal to President de Gaulle?" Louise said. Her voice was tight, very strained.

"I am loyal to France, not to one insufferably arrogant man."

I said, "We thought—"

"—In selecting me, the president trusted the recommendation of Air Force General Le Tourneau, a man who has now declared his allegiance to the generals who have taken control of Algiers. No one bothered to investigate the fact that I, too, had been a member of the DragonSlayers Squadron—in fact, Tony Bersault's squadron leader."

I wanted to keep the major talking as long as possible. "You served the president well," I said.

'Of course," the major said. "The better I served him, the more he trusted me."

He moved quickly to the enclosure, and still holding his gun on us, unlocked the metal gate.

"On the floor you will find a large dark-gray, metal container," he said. "Bring it out here, William."

The container was heavy, and I had to drag it across the concrete floor.

Louise asked, "What do you plan to do with the president?"

The major waved off her question. "William," he said, "open the container."

I fumbled with the latch, trying to delay everything.

Louise said. "We've always considered you our friend. You taught us how to fly—you saved Willi when the cargo plane on the runway almost crashed into him."

"Once William avoided the cargo plane," the major said. "I thought he had earned a safe landing. Tony was furious."

The expression on the major's face softened for a moment.

"I do like you," he said, "both of you. But you are too young to understand that you are on the wrong side of history. France will be reduced to a minor European power without Algeria."

His voice hardened again. "William," he said, "Take the coiled rope and handcuffs out of the container."

I moved as slowly as possible, realizing that he didn't intend to kill us in the hangar. He was going to truss us and take us to some other location. I didn't try to imagine our ultimate fate.

"Are you going to kill the president?" Louise asked.

That seemed to startle the major. "No," he said. "Tony and the other DragonSlayers wanted to kill him, but I refused to be part of such an operation."

I was thinking, *But you don't mind murdering a couple of kids.* Louise said, "You tried to kill him in Algeria many times. You've tried to murder him here, too. Why should we believe you?"

"Not me!" the major said. "I always disagreed with those tactics."

"What about tonight?" Louise asked.

"Tonight," the major said, "he will be prevented from making his expected speech to the nation. Our security will take him into custody at 7 P.M., *but he will not be harmed!* In fact, the result will be much worse than death—the president will be disgraced—humiliated."

The major's expression had changed again. His smile was very unpleasant. I realized the situation was growing worse every second. It wouldn't be enough for our friends to subdue the DragonSlayers in the catacombs; we would also have to disarm his enemies at the Élysée—and do it before 7 P.M.

"How can you be sure the president won't be harmed?" I asked. I was holding the handcuffs.

"It is not in our interest to harm him. The cameras will show the 'great man,' shackled and totally restrained. General Richelieu will speak in de Gaulle's place—with the president standing there, mute and helpless. We believe the people will rise spontaneously to support us."

"You're going to trust the general, a traitor, not to betray the president *and* you?" I asked.

The major seemed startled. "I must get back," he mumbled, releasing the safety on his automatic, clearly shaken by what I had said.

As I was talking to him, Louise had moved closer. In that moment of distraction, she spun and kicked the gun out of the major's hand. I lunged forward and swung the handcuffs against the side of his head. The impact jolted them out of my hand, but the blow staggered him, and I used his own weight to knock him to the floor.

He fell heavily, yelling in pain, while blood spurted from his temple. I was about to pin him to the floor when Louise called out, "Don't Willi! I have the gun!"

And indeed she did. Louise was standing, feet planted apart, holding the gun with both hands, aimed at Major Gerard's head.

"Don't move, Major," she said. "Don't move a centimeter."

The major was lying with one leg twisted unnaturally under his body, breathing heavily and bleeding profusely.

"I'll get the cuffs," I said.

When I had the cuffs, I said, "Roll onto your chest, Major."

The major painfully rolled over onto his chest, uttering little gasps of pain. I put the handcuffs on him and slipped the key into my pocket.

"It's too late," he was mumbling. "You won't be able to stop the coup."

"What are we going to do?" Louise asked.

"The same thing we came out here for, but you're going to fly and I'm going to drop the pouches over the side."

"Do you think they'll let us take off without the major's approval?" she said.

"We'll make him ask the tower for clearance."

"How will we get him to the radio?" she asked.

"Even if it hurts," I said, "he's going to walk."

"Okay, Willi, but then will we lock him up in the hangar?"

"No, we're taking him with us—I'll explain why later. Now, we're going to pull the seat out of the rear cockpit, make him climb in, tie him up, and I'll sit on him while I drop the pouches over Paris."

Louise almost smiled.

While I held the gun, Louise got into her jumpsuit and donned her parachute.

"Your turn," she said.

"No parachute," I said. "There's not enough room."

Louise held the gun on him while I dressed, collected the pouches and piled them on the wing. We had marked 7 P.M. on each map as the latest time for the assault in the tunnels; I hoped that would be adequate, but there wasn't time to re-mark them all.

I removed the bottom seat cushion from the rear cockpit, and then used a first aid kit to make temporary repairs on the major. After wiping his head, I applied sulfa powder and covered the wound with a bandage. Then I took the coil of rope out of the metal container.

"That's it, Major," I said. "Get up and get moving."

He mumbled, "My leg is broken."

I pushed against the leg with my foot. He screamed.

"Based on my experience with farm animals," I said, "I think your knee is only sprained. Get moving, Major!"

He slowly dragged himself to Roxanne.

"I can't climb up without help," he whispered.

"You're lying."

He pulled himself up on the wing and teetered beside the cockpit. I climbed up and wound the rope around his lower legs. I had learned some pretty good knots working with animals.

"All right, Louise, give me the automatic and you start the engine."

Louise handed me the gun, pulled the chocks, climbed into the front cockpit and started Roxanne, still in the hangar. We couldn't afford to be seen outside.

As soon as the engine roared, I pushed the major and he fell into the cockpit, head down, legs up; then I reached in and folded him into as little space as possible. I held the helmet next to his head so he could speak into the micro-phone and each of us could hear through one of the earphones. I plugged it into the control panel and turned on the radio.

"Your turn, Major. Make it good."

I pressed the mike button, but the major was silent, so I prodded him with the automatic and whispered. "Start talking!"

He said, "I will not be humiliated in this manner."

"You have a choice, Major: you can call the tower and ask for clearance, or you're dead."

I had the safety off the gun, and I hoped I looked fierce enough.

His voice was grim: "Open the mike."

I did.

The major spoke into the microphone: "Bourget Ground Control, FT28-74. Request taxi and takeoff instructions."

The ground controller said, "Major Gerard, when you phoned earlier, you said you had, shall we say, a mission in the hangar. Is there a problem?"

I nudged the major with the gun again.

"No problem," the major said. "A change of plans."

I whispered, "Tell him Louise is flying."

"Mademoiselle Donnet will be flying today," the major said.

Louise broke in: "Ground Control, FT28-74, taxi instructions for takeoff, *please.*"

"Taxi Runway 4 west, Mademoiselle. Wind zero-two-zero at one-two kilometers."

"Requesting eight hundred meters cruise altitude."

"What is your destination?" the tower asked. He sounded suspicious.

Louise looked back at me, a question on her face.

"Amiens!" I whispered. That was the first city north of Paris that came to mind."

"Destination, Amiens," Louise repeated.

"Cleared for takeoff on Runway 4—climb to and maintain eight hundred meters," the tower voice said.

"Thank you, Tower," Louise said.

I jammed myself into the cockpit, sitting on Major Gerard, who moaned now and then, and piled the pouches around me. I had to lean forward so my head wouldn't hit the canopy.

"Can you give me a flight plan?" Louise asked.

"Certainly," I said. "Take off, turn north and head for the Eiffel Tower."

"What altitude?"

"One hundred meters. The Eiffel Tower is almost three hundred, so don't fly into it."

Louise taxied expertly to the proper runway and added takeoff power.

"I'll need more power," she said, "because of the load."

Her takeoff was perfect, but instead of rising to eight hundred meters, she leveled off at one hundred and turned left to a three-hundred-sixty degree heading.

"FT28-74, Tower. Are you experiencing problems, Mademoiselle? You are leveling off at a very low altitude."

"That guy is beginning to annoy me," I told Louise, "I'm changing to the Clandestin frequency."

"Roger," she said. I always liked the fact that the typical radio message of approval was the name of our dear friend.

"Raging Dragon to Clandestin, all bases," I radioed. "We are making a special air mail delivery directly from Roxanne. Accelerate program if possible." They all knew the name of our aircraft, and I was certain they would understand. We had chosen the name of our operation—Raging Dragon—when we first alerted them.

Within a couple of minutes each base acknowledged the message.

It was 5:30 P.M., and our timing was becoming more urgent every minute. Still, I couldn't help being aware that there was still plenty of sunlight on this beautiful April day.

Paris was a lovely lady dressed in blue skies with white clouds as a wrap around her shoulders. The trees were showing the bright, light-green promise of spring, and the rows of gray buildings seemed to be lovers' arrows pointing to the heart of the city. Unfortunately, this wasn't a pleasure outing. I pushed open the canopy so I could sit upright.

"We have company," Louise said, pointing upward.

About two hundred meters above us was a loose, tactical formation of three fighters of *L'Armée d' L'Air.* They peeled off and began flying criss-crossing patterns, so that, despite their speed, there was always one directly overhead.

"They won't dare do anything," I said as bravely as I could. "They'd kill civilians."

The Eiffel Tower was looming up at us, looking gigantic compared to fragile Roxanne. It didn't seem like a steel filigree any longer—more like a fancy crowbar ready to smash us down.

"Give me a target, Willi," Louise asked.

"Champ-de-Mars station—Quai Branley. "

The Clandestin base was in a building at the intersection of the quai with Avenue de Sufferen, across from the Anthoine stadium.

"What airspeed?" she asked.

"You're doing fine," I said. I was afraid that if we reduced our airspeed further Roxanne might stall, and at an altitude of only one hundred meters, we would have plenty of trouble recovering.

I was kneeling on the major's back, braced against the fuselage, and leaning into the windstream. I thought I saw someone waving his arms. Just then Roxanne encountered some turbulence from a jet fighter passing close in front of us. I was bounced back to the other side of the plane, drawing a groan from the major.

"Sorry!" Louise said. "I'll make another pass."

"As low as you can get!" I yelled. Louise brought the plane down to not more than seventy meters.

I leaned out and dropped the pouch, leading my target.

"Oh no!" I cried. The pouch was headed straight for the roof of a bus. I couldn't help closing my eyes for a second. When I opened them, I saw the bus had turned the corner and the pouch had smashed into the pavement. Someone—I hoped one of ours—was running into the street, waving at cars.

"Next stop, Trocadero!" I yelled.

Louise deftly turned the plane, and moments later I was dropping another pouch onto the grass between the palace and the Seine. This time, the pouch seemed to sink into the earth.

"Champs-Élysées," I said.

A shadow crossed us. I flinched, then realized it was one of the jets, diving and trying to frighten us off. The jet pulled out, but he had seemed close enough to touch.

"Don't try to scare us, you bully!" I yelled into the void.

We approached the building where Robert de Cotte's office was located.

"Circle the base," I said.

Louise banked Roxanne into a tight turn. Sure enough, our guys were on the roof as expected. Did I dare drop the pouch there? What choice did I have?

"I hope they have a strong roof," I said.

"Can you hit that small a target?" Louise asked.

"Don't shake my confidence," I said.

Louise circled once more and I leaned out and dropped the pouch. As she continued the circle, I watched the pouch spinning and falling—onto the roof of the building next door. It bounced, but didn't go through the roofing. The Clandestin were leaping across to the next building. Close enough.

"Hôtel des Invalides!" I called.

Suddenly there was a piercing whistle, nearly deafening me. Someone was jamming our radio.

I yelled to Louise, "I've switched to the other frequency!"

We hoped that our friends were monitoring both frequencies. One after another, we made the rest of our drops near the Metro stations: Denfert-Rochereau, Pont d' Alma, Franklin D. Roosevelt, Charles De Gaulle-Etoile, Haussmann-St. Lazare. I had chosen a jagged pattern—I didn't want our enemies to anticipate our course.

I glanced at my watch; it read 6:15 P.M.

"We're out of pouches," I said. "And we finished in forty-five minutes!"

I tried to sound optimistic, but some of the Clandestin units would have less than forty-five minutes to organize, reach their targets, and neutralize our enemies. We had the same amount of time to land, get to the palace and protect the president. In fact, we should accomplish our mission *before* 7 P.M.—maybe 6:45. Half an hour and we weren't on the ground yet.

Louise gave me a thumbs-up sign from the front cockpit. "What now?" she asked. She was still circling Roxanne over Paris, and shadows of the jets crossed us at times.

"You've got to set her down."

"I'll head back to Le Bourget," she said.

"We're not going to Le Bourget," I said.

"Where?"

"I was thinking of the Champ-de-Mars."

"Whaaat?" Louise cried.

"But it's too far from the Élysée Palace, and the traffic will be terrible. There's open space between Les Invalides and the Seine—that would be pretty good."

"William," Louise said, "be serious!"

"I am serious," I said. "We still have a major mission to accomplish."

"Can't we just radio the palace and tell them about the plot?" she asked.

"I don't think we can trust the major's security staff," I said.

"Look!" Louise said.

To our left side, flying beside us, was another light plane, a four-seater with high wings. On the fuselage it read "*Air Police de Paris.*" The pilot was waggling his wing, trying to get our attention.

"What do you suppose they want?" I said.

"Be serious!"

"You keep saying that, Louise. They're signaling for us to get out of here, but I don't see any guns."

"You can be sure they have them," Louise said. "Do you think they'd shoot?"

"Same answer as with the military jets," I said. "Too many people would get hurt."

"They're going to buzz us!" Louise said.

Sure enough, the light-blue plane shot across our flight path, engine roaring, wings still waggling.

A voice came over our frequency—a calm voice, but firm: "FT28-74, this is Police FAP-201. Do you read me?"

"Ignore them," I told Louise. "Let's think about other places to land. The Luxembourg Gardens are too far away. There are too many trees in the Tuileries."

"Willi, please tell me the rest of your plan," Louise said.

"I will, Lou, after we set the plane down."

"We?"

"You."

The police plane kept radioing us. I turned down the volume, happy they weren't using a helicopter.

"I think I've figured it out, Louise."

I hadn't told Louise why I had chosen the particular order of drops because I didn't want her to be thinking too much about landing the plane in the middle of Paris.

"Tell me!" she said.

"Look below you. See that huge open space."

"The Place—"

"—It's the best chance we have. All of the grass areas are too soft from the April rains.

"You're crazy, Willi. I'm not going to land *there!*"

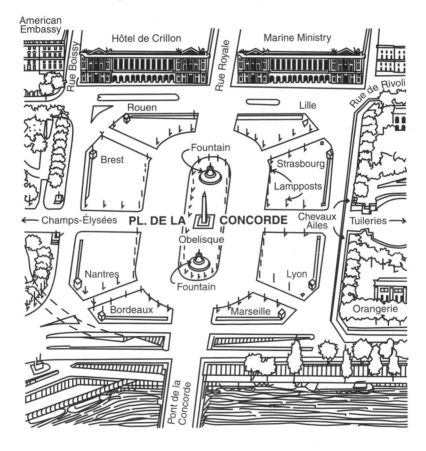

She was speaking about the spot I had indicated—the Place de la Concorde. It was the largest square in Paris, one of the largest in the world. Right now, it was filled with automobiles.

"Louise, we don't have a choice. If we land too far away, do you think we'd be able to hail a taxi and reach the palace on time? Of course not. Once the vehicles clear out, you'll have plenty of solid surface to land on."

"It's too short for a runway," Louise said. At least she wasn't screaming *"No!"*

"You'll have to land just above stall speed, but you can do it."

Louise was momentarily silent.

"Let's talk to our friends" I raised the volume on the radio. "FAP-201, FT28-74. Nice afternoon isn't it?"

The voice that answered was no longer calm. "FT28-74, FAP-201. You are ordered to return immediately to Le Bourget field."

"Do you have any means of enforcing that order?" I asked. There was a brief pause. "We are anxious to do what you want—that is, if you want us to get out of the skies of Paris."

"That is exactly what we want—what we demand."

"Take it easy, FAP-201. We're going to set down in the Place de la Concorde."

"We forbid this madness!" the policeman yelled.

"You see? You *are* dealing with madmen—excuse me, one madman and one madwoman, not to mention one unhappy major. We're going to land in the Place whether you help us or not. If you clear the area, many lives will be saved."

"I repeat what I said," the policeman continued. "Return to Le Bourget, *immédiatement!*"

"Okay, Louise, buzz the square," I said. "Just low enough for everybody to get the message."

"Willi," she said. "This is too dangerous."

"We have no choice," I said—again.

Louise pushed the stick forward, and swept down over the Place de la Concorde. Even over the wind noise and our engine, I could hear brakes squealing. Louise pulled up sharply at the Seine, freezing the traffic on the Concorde Bridge. She resumed circling, south of the Seine.

There was silence on our radio.

"They don't believe us, Louise," I said. "Let's do it again."

As Louise dipped Roxanne's nose again, FAP-201 came on the air.

"*Arrête!* Stop! We will inform the police on the ground to clear the square!"

Soon, white-gloved hands were waving and horns were blowing. Slowly, the square was clearing.

"What do you think, Louise?" I asked. "Based on the flags flying over the naval ministry, there doesn't seem to be any breeze."

"The longest approach is from the south," Louise said, "and the square is rectangular, longer north-south than east-west. But it isn't a straight run. I'll have to do some fancy taxi work. Shall I go right or left?"

"Let's go right," I said. "There's no use stopping at the Hôtel de Crillon. I can't afford the room rates." I didn't mention the Egyptian obelisk in the middle, or the fountains, or the streetlamps.

"Do you think they're simply going to let us walk away from the plane if we land safely?" Louise asked.

"We'll negotiate," I said.

The police radio crackled again. "Perhaps you should land aiming toward the Tuileries, so that you'll minimize the damage."

"Don't worry," I responded, "our pilot has force-landed this aircraft in even smaller places many times. Watch, my friends, and you will see a miracle of modern flying!"

Louise raised her fist for only a second, then circled back over the river to begin her approach over the Pont de la Concorde.

Major Gerard had tried to move many times during our flight. Now he twisted his shoulders, trying to bring his head up. I was afraid I was going to have to crack him with his own gun, but he spoke just a few words.

"What did you say?" I asked. Actually my attention was on the Place de la Concorde, coming up very quickly. Louise had throttled down to very low speed.

"Full flaps *NOW!*" the major cried.

"FULL FLAPS!" I yelled.

Louise closed the throttle and pulled back on the stick; we slowed our descent—airspeed just above stall. Ahead of us, the Hôtel de Crillon and the Marine Ministry suddenly looked huge, the obelisk a tremendous knife about to stab us. I didn't even hear car horns sounding or police whistles blowing. Except for the air slipping past the plane, there was almost total silence. The world consisted only of Roxanne, the three of us and the Place de la Concorde, never this empty in over one hundred years. I didn't dare breathe, move my head, or even my eyes. I was staring at the back of Louise's seat, trying to keep my body loose and relaxed. When would we land?

Bang! With a seismic jolt, the landing gear hit the pavement. Louise immediately cut the engine and stepped hard on the brakes. Tires squealed—the plane felt like it was coming apart. We skidded sideways, the aircraft teetering and tottering, and we spun around three-hundred-sixty degrees, while street lamps and statues and the obelisk flashed past. In a split second we would crash into the ministry. I closed my eyes.

A final jolting motion almost threw me out of the cockpit. Roxanne shuddered to a stop. Intact. Not even smashed landing gear, although I thought the right main tire had exploded.

A cheer. A great cheer rising from around the square.

Hundreds of French men and women, clapping and cheering. Horns blowing. People with flags were waving them. Paris was applauding Louise's flying—thunderously.

"You're great, Louise!" I said. "The best pilot in the whole world! The bravest person I've ever known!"

I thought I heard Louise mumble, "Thanks."

My watch read 6:30 P.M. We had fifteen minutes to get the job done.

Amid the blasting horns and the cheers, I heard another sound: sirens. In a second, Roxanne was surrounded by enough cops to fill a soccer stadium.

A voice spoke with amazing clarity over a hand-held loudspeaker: "Come out of the aircraft, one at a time, very slowly. If you have weapons, first throw them into the street. Any quick move, any aggressive action, will be your last."

"After all this," I said.

Louise was slowly climbing out of the front cockpit, pulling off her helmet very slowly and letting her lush black hair flow freely.

There was a cry from the crowd. Until that moment, I don't think anyone had any idea the pilot was a woman. Another cheer began, horns and all.

The loudspeaker roared.

"SILENCE! SILENCE IMMÉDIATEMENT!"

The silence came, but not *immédiatement*. Slowly the cheers echoed away, the horns ceased blaring.

I wasn't going to give up the major's gun—not yet. I jammed it into an inside pocket of my jumpsuit.

"Don't go away," I told the major, who grunted—angrily I thought.

To climb out of the cockpit, I had to step on him, and he let out a yelp, but I don't think anyone in the Place de la Concorde knew what the sound was. I took off my own helmet, wondering what response a blonde, sixteen-year-old male would get.

A few desultory cheers, but nothing like the accolade that had greeted Louise.

As I slid down off the wing, I noticed that none of the policemen were aiming their weapons at us.

One officer, a man with stars on his epaulets, stood apart from the others. Apparently the commander, he was very handsome, with sharp, fine features, and the kind of pencil-thin mustache that Frenchmen seem particularly apt at tending. His expression was stern, but not angry as he asked, "Are you all right—physically, that is?"

I glanced at Louise; we both nodded.

He continued in the same, almost pleasant, tone of voice, "We know who you are, Mademoiselle Donnet and Monsieur Montreux, and we are astonished that you have committed an offense such as this."

"*Monsieur le Commander*," I began.

"Colonel," the officer said. "Colonel Etienne Victoire."

The sound level began to grow in the Place. Having seen an unexpected spectacle, people now wanted to get home. Horns sounded.

"Thank you, Colonel," I said. "We have not landed this plane in the Place de la Concorde as a lark. We are on a most important mission, ordered by the president himself. We have already distributed certain pouches from the aircraft—"

"—We are aware of your flight pattern," the colonel said, "although we do not understand its purpose."

"The purpose, Colonel," I said, "is to save the republic by saving the president."

He remained patient. "Why have we not been informed by the government," he asked, "and why has the government chosen you for this mission?"

"I'm sorry, Colonel," I said, "but there is not time enough for explanation. We ask you to deliver us at once to the Élysée Palace."

Louise said, "Your patriotism and your courage are challenged today, Colonel. You will have to make the most important decision of your life."

"And," I said, "there is another person involved: Major Alain Gerard, formerly the officer in charge of presidential security, now a traitor to the Republic, is bound and trussed in the back cockpit."

The colonel blinked, then gestured, and two men leaped forward.

"Careful," I said. "He's injured."

The two policemen carefully lifted the major out of the cockpit and set him on his feet.

"I have the key to the handcuffs," I said, handing them to the colonel, "although I urge you not to release him at this time. It's probably safe to untie his legs—his knee is sprained and he can't run. However, it would be best if he came with us to the palace."

The colonel was staring at us, his mind obviously awhirl.

"This is the moment of crisis," Louise said. "The president is to speak at 8 P.M., but he will be under attack no later than 7 P.M. We should reach the palace by 6:45—it is now 6:35."

I could feel the colonel making his decision. His back was ramrod straight, but he seemed to grow taller.

"Very well," the colonel said. "We will leave at once!"

A weight came off my heart.

The colonel directed us into the back of his own vehicle and ordered the major held in a van. He gave crisp orders to other officers and then climbed into the front seat with his driver.

I looked back, somewhat sentimentally, towards Roxanne. A huge tractor of some sort, moving on tracks instead of wheels, had entered the square, and several men were running thick chains from it to the aircraft.

"I hope they treat her gently," Louise said.

"She's a brave lady," I said. "Just like you."

THE BROADCAST

"**B**efore we leave," Colonel Victoire said, "you must tell me what you intend to do at the Élysée."

I said, "Enemies of President de Gaulle, known as the DragonSlayers, a branch of the OAS, are planning a coup. Tonight, security men trained by Major Gerard, and supposedly loyal to the president, will instead take him into custody at 7 P.M. I believe they will offer him a chance to resign. He will, of course, refuse. General Richelieu will announce the coup on tonight's national broadcast—with the president standing there, shackled and humiliated. Richelieu will state that the army has taken over as a first step to new elections, and urge the people to support the change in government."

The colonel was staring at me as if I were insane.

"I am not insane," I said. "It is these traitors who have gone mad with their thirst for power."

"What about your flight over the city?"

"Our friends—the new and the old Resistance—are currently in the tunnels and sewers of the city, battling military men who have secretly come to Paris from Algeria and stored arms and uniforms. They planned to suddenly appear in the streets, dressed in their paratroopers' uniforms and heavily armed, to give the impression the city is under military control."

The colonel was shaking his head as he spoke. "This sounds like a fantasy. Is it true? Did the president approve of your plan?"

"You may ask him yourself, but only after we have disarmed the plotters who are about to subdue him."

"Driver," the colonel barked. "To the Élysée—at once!"

"Wait!" I yelled.

The colonel stopped his driver, and now looked even more confused.

"Sorry," I said. "I suggest we take Major Gerard in this vehicle with us, straightening his uniform and removing his handcuffs, but keeping him under control. When we reach the palace, we'll go in with a squad of your men, telling the guards we are working under the major's command."

"I see," the colonel said. "Once inside, we'll overwhelm the traitorous security contingent."

"Exactly," I said.

"What if the major protests, or informs the security people?"

"Shoot him!" Louise said.

The driver, the colonel and I were all surprised by her vehemence.

"She's right, of course," I said. "If you make that clear to the major, it may not be necessary."

The colonel hesitated for a moment. "Why do you trust me?" he asked.

"Frankly, Colonel," I said. "We have no other choice." It was the third time that afternoon I had said the same thing.

The colonel and his driver leaped out, and he proceeded along the column of vehicles giving orders.

Louise said to me, "When did you think up this plan?"

"When the colonel ordered his driver to go to the palace. I was making it up as I went along."

"You're good at that, Willi," she said.

The colonel returned with the major, who was wearing his military cap, cocked a little because of the bandage on the side of his head. The colonel and his driver got into the car with the major between them.

"Let's go," the police colonel said.

At that moment, I wasn't sure what side the colonel was on. Would he actually help us or was he planning to turn us over to the traitors at the palace?

The driver took the Rue Boissy at the far northwest corner of the Place de la Concorde to the Rue Faubourg St. Honore which led directly to the Élsyée. The roar of the sirens was so great that vehicles ahead of us scrambled to get out of our way, some actually driving up on the curbs. It seemed we had no more climbed into the police vehicle than we were screeching to a halt in front of the gates of the palace.

"Agree with everything I say," the colonel told the major, "or you are a dead man."

Major Gerard did not respond.

We got out of the vehicle, with the driver and the colonel flanking the major. I was certain the driver had a hidden weapon aimed at Major Gerard. Louise and I followed, escorted by a squad of police carrying automatic weapons. A dozen, heavily-armed guards met us at the gate.

The commander of the guards, a captain, saluted and then addressed a question to Major Gerard: "What is the meaning of this, sir?" he asked.

"We must see the president immediately," the colonel said.

The captain waited for the major to say something, but he was silent.

"Please, Major," the colonel said, "I know you are in pain, but nod your head so this foolish man will let us through without a pitched battle."

The guard commander recoiled, but the major nodded.

The colonel didn't wait; we closed ranks and marched to the entrance. It was 6:40 P.M.

A truck from the National Television Service was parked inside the gate, and long heavy cables were strung to and through the entrance, which stood partly open. In a moment, we were inside the Vestibule of Honor, facing another group of armed guards. They were checking their weapons, as if ready to begin action. An officer was talking to a man with the National Television trademark on the back of his uniform.

"Lead us to the president!" the colonel said. "This is urgent!"

The guards hesitated—a second too long. The police squad was on them at once, and in a moment disarmed them all. The television man just stared.

"There's an anteroom," Louise said. "One man could guard them there."

"What about me?" the workman asked.

"You can have a smoke with the guards," the colonel said. A corporal herded the disarmed guards and the workman into the anteroom.

"What now?" the colonel asked me.

Suddenly the major spoke. "The president usually broadcasts from his suite upstairs, but you can see the cable leads from the Vestibule through the Salon des Tapisseries into the Salon Murat."

Earlier I had seen seen the president in the Salon Napoleon III, but it was in the same direction.

"Follow the cable," I said.

Which we did. It was 6:43 P.M.

As soon as we passed through the Tapestry Salon and entered the Salon Murat, we were faced by several more guards, all armed. I realized the major had chosen this route because he knew guards were stationed in it, and we would be channeled into a narrow space by the huge conference table.

"Take them!" the major cried and threw himself down to the floor.

The police closed quickly. One guard got off a shot before being struck down—a shot that struck a policeman just in front of me. He spun to the floor, grabbing his chest, and as he fell I saw the man who had shot him—Raoul Larron. He was as surprised to see me as I was to see him. In that split second, I launched myself at him, throwing a rolling block into his legs and knocking him over backwards. I kept rolling and kicked the gun out of his hands. He was out of breath from the impact, and I could easily have controlled him with Judo, but my hand was raised and his head was beneath me. I couldn't resist—I punched him flush on the jaw. My hand hurt, but he was out.

Louise and a second guard were struggling on the floor, Louise using her Judo. I picked up Larron's gun and popped Louise's assailant over the head. He went limp. This was getting good.

The police overwhelmed the rest of the guards without another shot being fired. 6:47 P.M. I hoped there weren't any more guards. We had almost kept our schedule.

"Someone may have heard the shot," the colonel said. He sent the captured men back to the anteroom with escorts. They had to drag Larron because he was barely unconscious.

"Don't lose that guy," I said. "He's gotten away before."

The door to the Salon Napoleon III, held partly open by cable, was now completely open. A cameraman was swinging a television camera around towards us.

"Security operation!" I yelled, and shoved the door in the faces of the crew. I couldn't get it closed because of the cable, but the crew was frightened and fell back.

Major Gerard had remained on the floor; someone had kicked his sprained knee and he was holding it, moaning. I didn't feel sorry for him; he had tried to get us killed—again.

Louise was on her feet, dusting herself off.

My left leg felt very heavy, and I wondered if I had been

wounded. Then I remembered the major's automatic; it had slipped down inside my pants leg. I pulled it out and handed it to the colonel.

The colonel smiled, a quick, brilliant smile, flashing a remarkably white set of teeth. He looked like an American movie version of a French officer—maybe Cary Grant or Tyrone Power with a mustache and a kepi.

"*Encroyable!*" the colonel said. "The two of you are amazing."

"What is going on out there?" a strong voice asked from within the Salon Napoleon III.

"That's General Richelieu," Louise said.

"All right, Major," the colonel said. "It's time for you to meet the commander-in-chief."

His pulled the major to his feet, moaning audibly. His face was an ashen color, and his eyes were dead. There were deep furrows in his brow.

The police opened the door cautiously, weapons ready. After a moment, they waved us forward, and the colonel led us into the salon. The television crew had fallen back, far back from the door, standing silent and apprehensive. No armed men were visible.

A couple of rows of chairs had been place in front of the magnificent table-desk where President Charles de Gaulle sat, writing serenely on a pad, wearing the uniform of a brigadier general, his rank in the military. His military cap rested on the desk. Undoubtedly he had heard the shot, but Charles de Gaulle had been a battlefield soldier decorated for bravery under fire. He had been the target of dozens of assassination attempts. A single pistol shot and a scuffle obviously had no effect on him.

Facing us was General Richelieu. He also realized what had happened, and he changed before our very eyes, just like Major Gerard. This crisp, creased, arrogant man, granite-jawed, and heavy-browed, virtually dissolved. He remained erect, his shoulders square, but he looked like a scarecrow with unmatched clothing draped on his stick arms and body.

I whispered to the colonel, "Get the TV people out of here."

"Security check," he said to them, and they quickly filed out of the salon. The general, who had lost his compass, seemed ready to follow the crew, but the colonel said, "Not you, General. Please stay with us."

Louise and I and the colonel of police marched across the carpeted floor to the president's desk, flanked by General Richelieu and two policemen on one side, and Major Gerard, half-carried by two policemen, on the other.

We navigated through the maze of cameras and equipment and the rows of chairs and halted a couple of paces from the president. He set aside his pen, removed his glasses from his nose, placed his military cap—his kepi—on his head, pushed back his chair, and stood up.

President Charles de Gaulle was a very tall man, but as he rose from the desk, he reached greater height than I had ever seen before. The colonel saluted and the president returned his salute, firmly, but not theatrically. General Richelieu stood silent, ramrod straight and motionless, eyes fixed somewhere in the distance.

I thought we would have to tell the president in detail everything that had happened, but in that moment, looking into his eyes, I realized that would not be necessary. Charles de Gaulle understood everything. I felt a rush of emotion at the privilege of working with and for a man of such vast intellect and understanding.

The president turned his eyes on General Richelieu. Had I been Richelieu I would probably have fallen dead from the piercing assault of those icy eyes. If the president had torn the general's epaulets off his shoulders and ripped his ribbons from his chest, then pulled his clothes off his body, he could not have dismantled the man more completely.

General Richelieu saluted—the president did not return the salute—turned on his heel and marched out of the room. Later, I learned that the general promptly resigned his commission, placed himself under house arrest at a military base outside Paris, and awaited court-martial. The court-martial never came; the president did not even think he was worthy of a military tribunal. The general left the military, unnoticed, disgraced for ever.

President de Gaulle next turned to Major Gerard.

"You have betrayed my personal trust," the president said. His voice was flat, but I detected a note of personal pain. "To betray a friend while betraying your country is the ultimate combination of dishonor. Court-martial is too good for you; even death at the hands of a firing squad is more than you deserve. I will arrange your permanent exile to a place far distant from France."

There was a gasp from the major, but nothing more. The men guarding the major led him, stumbling and wincing, from the salon.

The president's expression changed. He looked upon Louise and me fondly. "You must tell me the complete story when there is time, General William and General Louise. I see that you have at last found a loyal man in Paris."

The colonel saluted again. "Many loyal men, *Monsieur le Président*," the colonel said. "I trust there are many more in France."

The president nodded. "Where are Doctor Guiscard and the others?" he asked.

"We are waiting to hear from them, *Monsieur le Président*," I said.

"We'll wait together," he said, and gestured that we should sit in the chairs arrayed before his desk. We chose the back row.

The president sat down at the desk, picked up his telephone and began speaking quietly. That was the outstanding characteristic of the very large salon: silence except for the murmur of the president's voice. Even as he spoke, he shifted the papers on his desk, and made corrections. When I next glanced at my watch it was 7: 15 P.M.

Aides came and went; the president signed papers and gave instructions. He did not smile when he spoke to his aides—neither did he give any indication he was facing a crisis.

Louise and I didn't speak. The colonel moved into and out of the hall, organizing security in the palace, maneuvering very quietly for such a large man. I struggled to keep from checking my watch every minute, but I couldn't avoid it entirely.

7: 20.

7: 30.

7: 40.

I yearned to move into action. What was happening to my friends and family? Shouldn't I be doing something to help them?

7:47 The door to the Salon opened and Roger strode in, accompanied by Paul, my mother and Mohammed. The president did not quite smile, as he indicated they should all approach.

Roger spoke first: "Mission accomplished, *Monsieur le Président*. There will be no false or traitorous paratroopers tonight in Paris. Unfortunately, we suffered some casualties, but all of the DragonSlayers are under our control."

I was shocked at the thought of casualties—who? How badly hurt? I wanted to know, and also wanted to ask about Tony Bersault, but the clock told me that 8 P.M. was fast approaching.

"I invite all of you to remain here during my broadcast," the President said. "Colonel, please advise the secretary that it is time for the ministers to enter, and instruct the television crew to return."

The colonel saluted and turned on his heel.

In a minute, several ministers entered—stern-faced and silent—and quickly seated themselves in front of us.

The television people came in tentatively at first, but then they began to hurry. The director gave orders firmly, authoritatively.

President de Gaulle sat at the desk, a microphone hanging over his head. A makeup artist approached and the president waved him away. The papers on his desk were in a neat, precise pile, set at exact angles to the axis of the surface. In fact, he would not once refer to his notes. He always spoke from memory and with total assurance.

The clock showed the hour, the broadcast began. There was no introduction, no other person between the president and the people. I recall some of his words, but it was his integrity, strength and bravery that radiated out into the world.

"An insurrectionary power," he said, "has established itself in Algeria on the basis of a military *pronunciamento* . . . "

"This power has a facade—a quartet of retired generals—and it has a reality—a group of politicized, ambitious and frenzied officers. The competence which this quartet possesses is as limited as it is short term. But fanaticism deforms their perception and understanding of the nation and the world!"

Several times when he spoke he pounded the desk with a massive fist.

"In the name of France," he said, "I order that all means, I repeat, *all means,* be used to bar the route of these men until such time as they are overcome!"

President de Gaulle stared directly into the camera as he spoke. No one could doubt the strength of his feelings and his commitment.

"I forbid every Frenchman, and in the first place every soldier, to carry out any of their orders."

Once again he pounded the table.

He said that he was invoking the authority of Article 16 of the Constitution, which enabled the president, in time of grave crisis, to take exceptional measures.

"The fate of the usurpers cannot be other than that which the law in its rigour provides."

Then he said, with great power and profound emotion, *"Françaises, Français, aidez moi!"*—"Frenchwomen, Frenchmen, help me!"

It was over; the speech was finished. The television lights were turned off, the cameras stopped rolling, and the crew began quietly to dismantle the equipment.

Ministers rose and spoke quietly to the president, who nodded, but said little.

"We've done our part," Louise whispered to me. "Now it's up to the people of France."

CASUALTIES

We remained after the ministers and television crews were gone. I was anxious to question Roger and the others—where were Mai and Jacques? I tried to be patient.

"Monsieur le Président," Colonel Victoire said, "please instruct me what to do with Major Gerard and the security personnel we have in our custody."

"Have them incarcerated in the common prison," the president answered coldly. "They can be turned over to military authorities later. Please remain here yourself, with a detachment of loyal police."

"One moment, if you please," Roger said. "Our friends are holding approximately six hundred fifty men and their weapons in several locations."

The colonel spoke: "If I am given the locations of these traitors and their captors, I can have them removed to the large holding prison at Bercy."

"Excellent," Roger answered, "but you will need identification in order to persuade our friends to release these traitors to your custody."

"I think it would be best," Mother said, "if several of us accompany the police. Otherwise you might meet, shall we say, resistance."

"Very good," the colonel said. He marched out smartly, taking Major Gerard with him, accompanied by Mother, Paul, and Mohammed. They seemed very subdued, almost sad, to me.

Louise and I and Roger followed the president to his

apartment on the upper floor of the palace. Later, the colonel joined us.

Within minutes after the finish of the president's speech, vitally important messages came from Algeria, where half a million soldiers were stationed, and the generals had declared themselves in control. Unit after unit proclaimed its loyalty to the president.

The same pattern followed from mainland military units—men came spilling out of barracks onto parade grounds yelling, *"Vive de Gaulle!"*

In the streets of Paris, in front of the Élysée Palace, there were spontaneous demonstrations, with many cries of, *"Vive de Gaulle, Vive la France!"*

French television covered the streets and the parks, where hundreds of thousands of Frenchmen and Frenchwomen waved the Tricolor and cheered for the president.

Charles de Gaulle sat behind the table that had been returned to his quarters, listening and watching quietly. It was obvious to all of us that he was tremendously moved. The president's wife, Yvonne, sat in a chair next to him. From time to time she looked towards him with a smile on her lips.

The government switchboard was overwhelmed with calls, virtually all of them messages of support.

On television, the prime minister, Michel Debré, appealed to the people to go to the airports and prevent the possible landing of the parachutists. Later, the news channel showed views of Le Bourget with masses of people blocking the runways.

De Gaulle smiled briefly at the sight of the surging crowds flooding the airport, the security officers overwhelmed and unable to control them.

"You solved the paratrooper problem," the president said to us. "Frankly, except for you, I should never have imagined paratroopers coming up from holes in the ground rather than dropping out of the sky."

"May we hear from Roger?" I asked. "I would like to know what happened underground."

"Of course," the president said.

"All of our units received their pouches," Roger said. "We interpreted Willi's meassage to mean that each team should undertake its task as soon as it received its 'air mail.' We were all at the ready; almost everyone except your mother, Willi, had a weapon of some sort. Handguns they carried in their pockets, automatic weapons were of the type that disassemble, and they carried the parts wrapped in their coats or in sacks.

"The one assault that had to be coordinated was the one at the Nazi Bunker, which involved units led by Mohammed Almedienne and me. The pressure was great because we were among the last to receive our pouches. My group gathered at the unmarked exit; Mohammed's group gathered near the Denfert-Rochereau Metro station.

"We knew that the interior of the bunker wasn't large enough to hold more than a couple of dozen men, so we assumed that the DragonSlayers would string out along the tunnels, a hundred or more in each direction. At the agreed time, they would charge into the streets at several locations. We planned to enter from two directions, surprise them, and force a surrender.

"Mohammed and I estimated—very roughly—the length of tunnel it would take on each side of the bunker to hold one hundred plus men, and the distance and time each of our groups would take to block the DragonSlayers. We agreed upon 6:45 P.M. as the time to begin our operation. Our groups filtered through heavy traffic; with each passing minute, we grew more concerned about being able to strike simultaneously.

"As we thought, our enemies had set lookouts in the

tunnels. The guards were completely surprised by our approach—they had obviously not expected to be under attack. Each of our groups rushed the guards at virtually the same instant, and succeeded in taking them out."

I wondered what he meant by the phrase, "taking them out." Prior to that moment, I had almost envied the kids who were attacking the traitors underground, but I would never have been able to use a gun, a garrote or a knife unless under attack myself.

"Our groups hurried ahead," Roger said, "surprising the men lining the tunnel. Most were not holding their weapons, but had laid them aside, assuming they would be forewarned by the lookouts.

"A couple of men tried to grab their weapons, but we had little trouble subduing them. Mohammed's timing was almost identical to ours, and we met at the bunker tunnel. Several men and women were detailed to guard the surrendered DragonSlayers while the rest of us hurried to the bunker. I had brought my key along, but the metal door was partially open. We assumed the people inside had heard the commotion and were waiting to blast us.

"One of the Resistance people handed me a tear gas canister. I tossed it inside and shouldered the door shut. A fusillade of bullets struck the metal door from inside, but it was so heavily armored that the bullets didn't penetrate, although the sound of them splattering on the steel echoed hollowly in the tunnel.

"From inside, we heard lots of coughing, and some of the gas escaped around the tightly closed door. We started coughing a little, too. Unfortunately, none of us had brought gas masks. After a few minutes, I motioned our people to stand aside and slowly opened the door. People came rushing out, coughing, crying and moaning. Some of the gas came out too, but not enough to stop us from capturing the DragonSlayers.

"One of the people who stumbled out was Jacques. Through his coughing, Jacques managed to tell me that he and Mai were intercepted almost immediately by DragonSlayers and held in the Nazi Bunker.

"I asked him where Mai was. Suddenly a figure appeared in the doorway—a man in a paratrooper uniform, wearing a gas mask, carrying an automatic weapon in one hand and dragging Mai Pham with the other. He aimed his weapon directly at me, but Mai, despite her weakened condition, managed to slip her foot behind the man's leg and trip him, so that he spun, and the weapon fired erratically, above and behind him.

"I tore the weapon out of his hands and one of the Clandestin put a restraining hold on him. Mai had slipped to the floor and I reached for her. In that horrid moment, I saw blood pouring from the back of her neck. A bullet had passed through her head and she was unconscious. I picked her up and started to run towards the main tunnel. One of the Resistance people, a doctor, stopped me and checked her.

"He shook his head. 'C'est finis,' he said."

Roger was crying as he said these words.

"She's only eighteen years old," Louise protested.

For a minute, I totally rejected the idea. Mai was alive! Then, slowly, the horror, as Roger had called it, took hold in my mind. This lovely young woman, brave and clever, talented and generous—someone I had actually held in my arms, even if it was a Judo hold—this woman was dead. I could not help crying myself.

Madame de Gaulle came around the table and embraced us, one at a time, murmuring kind, sad words.

"Mes amis," the president said. "Je suis désolé. Je suis dévaste."

After a moment, he said, "Sometimes I believe that I have become immune to the deaths of soldiers in battle because that is what a general must learn, but when the fallen one is so young and courageous, I realize that I have deluded myself. I can never be hardened to such a loss. Yvonne and I pray that you will accept our profound sympathy and deepest regrets."

◆　◆　◆

The president arranged for my parents and me and Louise and Roger to spend the night at the Marigny, a palace across the street from the Élysée. We understood the president and his wife were deeply moved by the death of our friend and could not bear the thought of our being exposed to further danger of any sort. We were convoyed across the street by an escort suitable for a king. Our rooms were magnificent. The Marigny was a hotel in which distinguished foreign visitors often stayed, and we were being treated as important guests. I fell into bed, and although I did not fall asleep for hours, I was too exhausted to move.

It was not until morning that we learned that two other men were casualties of the conflict. One was an uncle of Jacques, who had been knifed by the DragonSlayers. He was recovering in a Paris hospital. The other was Nicolas Le Camus, who was shot trying to flee—he had been wearing a paratrooper's uniform. We had been told that Nicolas had communist sympathies, but, to everyone's surprise, he had allied himself with the DragonSlayers, who represented the extreme right. Nicolas would also recover.

"I didn't have a chance to tell you last night," Roger told us as we were served an elaborate breakfast. "We captured someone you know very well."

"Bersault!" I cried.

"No," Roger said. "Marc Vestien!"

I was so astonished my mouth fell open.

"He was not in the military," Mother said.

"But he was a supporter of Tony Bersault," Paul said.

"*Exactement!*" Roger said. "Although he wore a para-trooper uniform, I recognized him immediately."

"What about Tony?" I asked.

"So far nothing, but we haven't had reports from all of the Clandestin," Roger said.

"I took care of Raoul Larron," I said.

"Willi knocked him out," Louise said.

Roger was delighted. He shook my hand vigorously. I tried not to cringe—it still hurt badly from smacking Larron.

Everyone finally reported, but no one knew anything about Tony Bersault.

"We'll find him," I said, "and now we have a witness against him."

"Who is that?" Mother asked.

"Major Gerard," Louise said. "He told us that Bersault had recruited him when they both were in the air force in Algeria."

"What makes you think he will testify against Bersault?" Roger asked.

"I believe that Gerard was greatly shamed by the president last night," I said, "and as a result he may be willing to cooperate."

⋆   ⋆   ⋆

"I am sorry, William," the president said, "but granting your request has become impossible."

"I don't understand, *Monsieur le Président*," I said. "We're trying to track down one of your worst enemies."

"Last night," the president said, "Major Gerard was taken to the holding facility at Bercy. Because of his wounds he was placed in isolation in a hospital room, the door locked and a guard posted outside."

"He escaped?!" I almost exploded.

The president sighed. "A desperate kind of escape. This morning Major Gerard was found in his room, dead, his neck broken."

I was speechless. "How did anyone get past the guard?" Louise asked.

"No one did," the president said. "Colonel Victoire has informed me that Major Gerard hanged himself."

When I could use my voice, I said, "Last night I thought he was deeply ashamed of what he had done."

"Suicide," the president said, "is a cowardly act. It could never be regarded as atonement for his foul deeds."

✦   ✦   ✦

Jacques Rouen was permitted to visit us. When we met him in a sitting room of the Marigny, his face seemed puffy, his eyes very red. His arm was in a sling, and there were bandages over his left ear and his neck.

"We didn't know how badly you were wounded!" Louise exclaimed.

"My battle scars will heal," he said. "There is one wound that will not—the loss of Mai."

For a moment we were silent.

"Roger told us how she sacrificed herself to save him."

"That didn't surprise me," Jacques said. "She was a very generous person, with very little ego for one so young, beautiful and talented."

"There is one thing you may not know," Jacques said. "Although we were not formally engaged, Mai and I had planned to marry after I finished my degree at the Sorbonne."

I struggled not to show my surprise. Had I totally misunderstood the warmth she had shown me at the dojo and elsewhere? Did I misjudge her intentions the night I went to her apartment? The idea was humbling.

"We didn't know anything about your relationship," Louise said, putting out a hand to touch Jacques' arm.

"I'm so sorry," I said.

"Thank you," Jacques said. For a moment I thought he

was beginning to cry, but he gained control of himself and spoke again. "There was a private family service at the Buddhist funeral home near the Bois de Vincennes. Mai's family was kind enough to invite me."

I hadn't known that Mai was a Buddhist or that her family lived in Paris. I remembered a striking sculpture I had seen in her apartment, which I now realized was a highly-stylized Buddha.

"The night you practiced Judo with Mai in her apartment," Jacques said (*Bon Dieu!*—Good God!—I was thinking), "you probably noticed her unusual furniture and small sculptures. Mai designed and made all of those items herself, including the Buddha."

I gave Louise a smile that might have seemed brittle, but she wasn't paying attention to me; she was concentrating on Jacques. "We had no idea that she was so talented," Louise said.

Jacques seemed to sag momentarily, but then he visibly straightened. "Mai has been cremated," he said. "Her family are Mayahana Buddhists. Not all such believers utilize cremation, but that was the wish of her family. The urn carrying her ashes will be buried in a family plot in the Père Lachaise cemetery.

"Mai's mother was proud of her daughter's participation in the Clandestin. Of course she is deeply saddened by her daughter's death, but she well understands the spirit that motivated her.

"A service will be held at 3 P.M. tomorrow at the International Buddhist Temple in the Bois de Vincennes. Madame Pham has told me that friends of her daughter are welcome to attend. The family will wear black, other mourners will wear white, but that is not required of you. Afterwards, Madame Pham asked to meet with the young people briefly in the garden."

"We'll be there," I said.

"Certainly," Louise said. "Can we bring flowers?"

"Flowers are an important part of the Buddhist funeral," Jacques said, "but it would probably be best if you simply brought yourselves."

This time he gave in to his tears, not sobbing, just a gentle flow from his eyes down across his face. He wiped them away, while Louise put an arm over his shoulders. After a few minutes, he seemed to collect himself.

"Tell me about your flight over Paris and the struggle at the Élysée Palace," he said.

◆   ◆   ◆

Later that day, the president invited all of us to join him at the Élysée.

"Do you know why?" Louise asked.

"When I spoke to him about Major Gerard," I said, "he told me that wanted to honor us in some fashion. I told him our group would prefer remaining anonymous, but he was determined to acknowledge our efforts. I don't know precisely what he plans."

"We have only the clothing we wore when we came here," Mother said.

"I don't think he's preparing anything formal," I said.

We were escorted to the Salon des Ambassadeurs, a room distinguished by a magnificent fireplace, with a celebrated bronze and gold chariot of Phaeton on the mantel. Standing before the mantel was the president, in full uniform, flanked by two other officers wearing large quantities of braid and many rows of ribbons.

Louise gave me an unhappy look. The scene looked very formal to her.

"*Messieurs et Mesdames,*" the president began, "we are passing through one of the most difficult times in the history of our nation, and your contribution has been outstanding, courageous and deserving of high honor.

"I spoke privately to General William and told him that I wished to honor not only you, but the entire cadre of Clandestin, the former members of the Resistance, Doctor Guiscard, and everyone else associated with this remarkable enterprise.

"General William said to me that, while he and the others would appreciate any honor I would bestow upon them, he believed that a public ceremony would contravene the very meaning of the organizations and persons involved. He properly pointed out that the name of the young people's organization, Clandestin, refers to under-ground—in fact, secret—actions, and the success of the Resistance was based on its ability to operate surrepti-tiously. I could not disagree with this argument.

"I therefore said to General William that he must act as the representative of all who have participated in this noble venture. He protested, but I outranked him. I have con-cluded that I may bestow on General William a symbol entirely unique."

He nodded to one of the officers, who turned and took from the mantel a slim, blue velvet box.

"During and after the last war," the president said, "the United States of America bestowed upon me many signal honors. One of these was the Distinguished Service Cross. I have decided to confer on the young general my own medal, engraved as it is with my name. It is a very dear and prized possession of mine, and I bestow it with pride."

The president took the medal, hung on a circlet of red, white and blue ribbon, from within its velvet container. He lifted the ribbon over my head, and lowered it so that it circled behind my neck. Then he rested the medal on my chest, kissed me on both cheeks, and stepped back.

"You are a great soldier in the French tradition of honor

and courage under fire," the president said. "I salute you!"

And he did!

And I saluted him.

There was a brief moment of silence. Then the president smiled a grand and beatific smile from on high. The ceremony was over, the president and the officers marched out, and the rest of us embraced over and over again.

✦ ✦ ✦

Louise and I traveled together in a black government limousine, part of a small convoy of Citroens that was taking our group from the Marigny to funeral services for Mai Pham.

The Buddhist temple was in one of the great parks of Paris, the Bois de Vincennes, located southeast of Paris beyond the Boulevard Périphérique, the road that encircles the city. While most of the park is landscaped as an English garden—really a forest—it is best known for the zoological park, the zoo, one of the largest in Europe. There is also a horseracing hippodrome, plus botanical gardens, schools, a hospital, riding trails, etc., etc.

It is also the home of the *Centre Bouddhique,* including the International Buddhist Temple built in 1931 for a colonial exhibition, and since restored, including a new roof of 180,000 tiles, carved with an axe from a chestnut tree. The temple faces lovely Lake Daumesnil, of kidney-shaped design, complete with landscaped islands. The structure is long, low and gracefully arched and curved, sited to suit the lush greenery.

As we removed our shoes outside the entrance, we met many members of Clandestin and the Resistance. There were about one hundred fifty—most of those who had taken part in operation Raging Dragon.

The sanctuary was large, elegant in its austerity, built of rich, dark woods, exquisitely shaped and trimmed. On a raised platform, rose a great, gilded statue of the Buddha, about nine or ten meters high. Close to the altar was a small group dressed in black, which we assumed to be the family of Mai Pham.

After a few minutes, several tonsured monks in white robes appeared, carrying flowers, censers, and long sticks with what I took to be incense smoldering at the end.

The simple ceremony included various rituals marked by the graceful movements of the participants. I sensed the harmony between Mai Pham's Buddhist heritage and the Judo she practiced so well, a unique grace and formality echoing through both.

There were songs and chants recited in Vietnamese, interspersed with a few words of French. I thought I heard Mai's name a couple of times.

Afterwards, the family rose and walked out of the sanctuary. We followed them into a lovely garden area, replete with carved figures, stone lanterns and elegantly landscaped foliage.

The family was waiting, grouped around a lovely woman who so strongly resembled Mai that she was immediately recognizable as her mother. She was not crying and she held herself gracefully erect, but the lines in her face were more profound than the scorings of age; they marked the deeply etched pain of a mother. This woman had already lost her husband and daughter to war—both involving French colonies. Probably she had thought that when the family moved from Viet Nam to France she had left violence behind, and now her daughter had been lost to the same virulent disease.

Louise managed a graceful bow, to which Madame Pham and her family responded. Mai's mother put out her hand and took Louise's. Then she reached out to me with the other. She spoke excellent French, in a soft, melodic voice.

"You are Louise and William, the children of the Crouching Dragon," she said. "Your story is known to me because of my daughter, who admired you both. In our native land, the dragon is a sign of good health, prosperity and wisdom. I wish those things for you—and long life."

Even then her voice did not break, and a hint of a smile fluttered across her lips.

"We thank you, Madame Pham," Louise said. "Your daughter was a noble human being—a woman of great honor. We are proud to have known her and to have shared the most important events of our lives with her."

Madame Pham's gentle grip on our hands tightened briefly, then released. We moved away, bowing again to the family.

As we were leaving, Jacques came up to us and said, "The owner of the Raging Dragon has closed the bistro for this evening and is turning it over to us—food and drinks free."

I began to ask, "Are you certain—"

"—It is precisely what Mai would want," Jacques said firmly.

✦   ✦   ✦

At first, it was very quiet in the Raging Dragon. We spent a lot of time on introductions, because some of us had never met before. One man, who introduced himself as the uncle of Nina Forgére, one of the Clandestin, said to me, "I think it is remarkable that one hundred and fifty people, most of who didn't know each other, could work together to achieve so great a goal without extended planning and many arguments."

"It was necessary," I said. "I suppose that's why we were able to do it."

He clapped me on the back and went on his way. One person after another came up to congratulate me on the role I had played in thwarting the plot. I tried humility at first because I genuinely felt it, but after a while I simply smiled and thanked the people who spoke to me. I asked many of them if they knew anything about Tony Bersault, but no one had any information.

After a while, Mohammed said, "I think Mai would have ordered a glass of wine by now."

We laughed and that broke the tension.

I told Louise, "I only had one close friend, André, until our adventures at the Crouching Dragon. In a few months, I gained many friends, and now, I have many more."

"You're always surprised when you make friends aren't you, Willi?" Louise asked.

"Yes," I said. "That's true."

"You shouldn't be surprised, Willi. You earn good friends because you're one yourself—the very best kind of friend."

"The truth is, "I said, "that you're the best friend I've ever had—including André."

She kissed me thoroughly and a couple of people nearby cheered.

My parents were sitting quietly at the bar—my stepfather slowly drinking a beer and my mother sipping a glass of wine. I walked over and put one arm around each of them.

"Have I told you lately how proud I am of both of you?" I said.

They both hugged me—Paul's hug might have snapped a rib if he hadn't quickly released me.

The owner of the bistro, who had been watching television in his apartment above the Raging Dragon, came bursting into the bistro, shouting, "Generals Challe and Zeller have surrendered. They and most of the parachutist officers are in prison. The insurrection is over!"

A great roar went up in the bistro, and we became aware of the sounds of jubilation in the streets. The evening became more and more raucous as it went on. Finally, the 'Hôtel Marigny group' slipped away and returned to our temporary home for a good night's sleep.

AFTER THE
INSURRECTION

A few days after the surrender of the generals, the president "released" us from our luxurious stay at the Hôtel Marigny. My parents returned to Bonville, Louise to her aunt and uncle's apartment, Mohammed to his family, and Roger and I to his apartment.

Before we left, Louise, Roger and I had a brief meeting with the president. Colonel Victoire was present, but he wore a military uniform.

"Colonel Victoire is on authorized leave of absence from the police department," the president said. "Having proved his loyalty beyond any doubt, I have asked him, and he has agreed, to be in charge of my personal security staff. Certainly I could not ask him to make this sacrifice and reduce his rank, so he has been given the rank of colonel."

"It is no sacrifice, *Monsieur le Président*," the colonel said. "It is a privilege."

I asked, "Have you heard anything about the whereabouts of Tony Bersault?"

"We have been informed," the colonel said, "that he is presently out of the country, perhaps in the United States of America. However, this is only a rumor, and we have not been able to confirm it. We know that he resigned his commission and became employed by a new subsidiary of a major supplier of aircraft equipment, a company named Orion Systemes Aeronautique."

"The same initials, in different order, as the OAS!" I said. "Bersault told us, but I never connected it until this minute."

"Precisely," the colonel said. "Preliminary investigations have not revealed much about this company, although the principals in the parent corporation are known to have extreme right-wing sympathies."

Louise said, "Major Gerard told us that he and Bersault were DragonSlayers and members of the OAS, and that Tony had given the order to kill us."

"We can testify to that. Isn't our word enough to locate and arrest him?" I asked.

"We don't doubt you," the colonel said, "but the major is dead. We would require additional evidence before we could connect Bersault to the coup and prosecute him."

"Then Major Gerard removed our hope of confirmation when he killed himself," Roger said.

The colonel glanced at the president, before proceeding.

"We have reason to believe," the colonel said, "that Major Gerard did not commit suicide—that he was murdered."

"*Encroyable!*" I cried. "How could that happen?"

"We don't know," the colonel answered. "When we had a routine autopsy performed, we determined that the major had been injected with a soporific—a drug that put him to sleep. The marks on his hands that we originally assumed were from the rope, instead appear to be signs of a struggle. The major fought for his life. Someone—perhaps several people—subdued him, injected a drug, and then hanged him."

"Who had access to him?" Roger asked.

"It was a night of great confusion," the colonel said. "By the time the autopsy was completed, we found it impossible to find who might be responsible."

"Doesn't this prove how dangerous Bersault is?" I asked.

"There are many, many people who would have wanted the major dead," the colonel said, "including all of the DragonSlayers, the mutineers in Algeria, their supporters and co-conspirators in Paris and throughout France."

"It was Bersault or someone acting under his command," I said.

"Your instincts have proved thoroughly reliable," the president said.

"We will do our best," the colonel said "to insure that the investigation is pursued vigorously and the perpetrators found and punished."

There was nothing more to be said on the subject.

◆ ◆ ◆

When Louise and I, Mohammed, Jacques and the other members of Clandestin, returned to school, it was obvious that word of our exploits had preceded us—perhaps spread by our friends. None of that was surprising; it would have been inconceivable that the story could have remained concealed.

Unfortunately, the crisis wasn't over. There were still powerful elements, both civilian and military, who were unhappy with the prospective dissolution of the ties between France and Algeria.

"How long do you think this struggle will go on?" I asked Roger.

"Years," he said. "There is still vengeance and retaliation, violence and brutality. The OAS—the Secret Army Organization—remains active, and may in fact, become more desperate the closer Algeria gets to independence. Tens of thousands of settlers are disposing of their property and moving to the mainland."

"What about Tony Bersault?" I asked.

Roger shook his head. "As is often said in books and movies, I don't think we've heard the last of him."

◆ ◆ ◆

Mme Louvois knew all about our adventures and complimented us privately, but she still wanted us to complete our Paris project. She gave us a Michelin Green Guide of

Paris to follow, marking important places we hadn't yet seen and checking off a short list of major works at the Louvre.

We began our tour at the Cathedral of Notre Dame, almost within sight of the Raging Dragon, and the nearby Sainte-Chapelle, hidden in the hulking Conciergerie, with its historic law courts and prisons. Notre Dame is an eight-centuries-old symphony in stone, with noble stained glass windows, especially the dazzling rose window.

The Saint-Chapelle *is* stained glass, walls of it, nearly 618 square meters—6,672 square feet—so delicate the panels seem too fragile to stand, and yet they have survived for seven hundred years, and are the oldest original stained glass in Paris. Tens of thousands of tourists pass within a hundred meters of the entrance without ever knowing the Sainte-Chapelle exists.

Of course we visited the Louvre Museum, considered by many the world's greatest art museum (the French think it *is*, without question, the greatest).

"It would take us at least a week to really study this place," I said.

"Mme Louvois doesn't expect us to become experts," Louise said, "just get a taste of the wonders displayed here."

We wandered (rapidly) through the vast halls that housed the Greek, Egyptian and Roman antiquities, awed by the skill of the artists, astonished by the number and variety of the works—from mosaics to frescoes to statues and mummies, temples, columns and sarchopagi. We viewed Nike—the Winged Victory of Samothrace (great wings, no head), admired the lovely Venus de Milo (no arms, great face and body), and were amazed by the Egyptian Seated Scribe (intact) from 2500 B.C.

We saw the works of the Italian genius, Michelangelo, including his life-like marble statue, the Dying Slave. Mme Louvois's list included Medieval and Renaissance Italians who worked primarily in Florence from Giotto to Leonardo da Vinci—especially his Mona Lisa, which almost always has a crowd of tourists blocking the view.

Despite our best intentions, the galleries of Italian and Spanish greats became something of a blur. In the French galleries, we were moved by the works of David, Delacroix and Gericault, probably because we knew some of the history they portrayed.

In the Dutch gallery, Louise said, "I like the works by Vermeer as well as anything we've seen. I didn't realize you could actually paint light."

"How about Rembrandt?" I asked.

"True," Louise said,

"We'll have to come back from time to time," I said. "I'm enjoying this more than I expected."

There are dozens of museums in Paris, but we had no intention of running a museum marathon. To see the work of the impressionists, including Monet, Pissarro, Cezanne and Degas, even the works of Picasso, required trips to several locations. Paris continually adds and rebuilds museums of modern and contemporary art, and moves collections around.

We thoroughly enjoyed visiting the Rodin museum, a few steps from the Invalides, to view the work of France's great, late-nineteenth century sculptor. We had seen his sculptures, The Kiss and The Thinker, but the museum had a huge and varied collection.

Next we went to the lovely church of La Madeleine, styled like a Greek temple, and then up to Montmartre, the haunt of artists and writers. We viewed the city from the steps of the splendid Cathedral of Sacré-Coeur, with its glistening white domes and turrets.

"I think this is the perfect place to end our tour," I said.

"We haven't seen the Arch of Triumph, or strolled the

Great Boulevards," Louise said. "What about the Palais-Royal, the great exhibition palaces and the Pantheon?"

"I'm sorry, Mademoiselle, but the bus is leaving for Belgium."

"At least you can take me for a horseback ride."

Louise was referring to the lavishly carved and decorated carrousel near the foot of the Cathedral.

"Okay," I said. "But don't push any kids off the painted horses."

Parents and kids looked at us strangely, but we had a laughing good time.

We had saved the best for last—the films of Paris we hadn't yet seen. Our greatest favorite was the musical, *An American in Paris* (1951), with Gene Kelly and Leslie Caron. While the actual views of Paris were limited, the painted backdrops were marvelous and the Gershwin music was perfect. We enjoyed *Gigi* (1958), which also had excellent music, to go with wonderful views of the city and its turn of the century café society.

There were many others. We saw a couple of versions of *The Three Musketeers*, and also watched *The Razor's Edge* (1946), with Tyrone Power and Gene Tierney, *Cyrano de Bergerac* (1950), and *Moulin Rouge* (1951). Many of these films would be remade again and again in later years, but it was fun to watch the early ones.

We liked *Funny Face* (1957), with Audrey Hepburn and Fred Astaire, which had many Paris scenes, from the Eiffel Tower to the Flower Market, but we weren't moved by the film version of Ernest Hemingway's, *The Sun Also Rises*, released in the same year.

As I had hoped, Louise wrote our report, which Mme Louvois gave a high grade. It was very good—Louise was a terrific writer. I also think Madame Louvois liked us.

◆   ◆   ◆

A few days later, the telephone rang in Roger's apartment. Roger answered, and a minute later called out to me, "It's for you."

The phone was in the parlor, and I took the call there, standing. "*Allo, oui?*" I said.

The voice was hesitant, but clear. "Even in Bonville the word is out—you're a great hero and probably going to run for president when de Gaulle retires."

I gasped. "Can it be—is it really you?" I asked, reaching for a chair and sitting down, because I thought I might fall down.

"Yes, it's me all right. Don't you recognize your old friends? *I thought* you were getting too full of yourself."

"André!" I said, "André!" For a moment I had no further words.

"I know my own name," Andre said. "Is that all you've got to say for yourself?"

His voice sounded a little fragile, but he had his familiar sense of humor.

"Where are you, dear friend," I said. "How are you?"

"I came out of the coma suddenly about two weeks ago. Once they were sure I wasn't going to drop dead on them, they sent me home. I've been here about a week."

"Can you—are you—?"

"Don't pussyfoot around with me, Willi. Almost everything is in working order. I'm still a little slow getting around, but they say I'm going to get a lot better."

"That's wonderful, André. That's the best news I've heard in a long time."

"I've hardly heard any news, except you're supposed to be a giant among men. Tell me all about it, if you're still talking to farmers and other peasants."

✦   ✦   ✦

A couple of weeks later, Louise and I decided to go to Bonville to visit André and see what was happening at the

Crouching Dragon. We took a train from the Gare St-Lazare—an ancient steam engine pulling some weary cars over a tired, irritable roadbed. The seats were lacquered wicker, stiff and uncomfortable, while the windows were so dirty you might have thought we were traveling on a cloudy day, but the train was cheap and fairly fast.

Paul picked us at Caen in his beloved truck. As we approached Bonville, we saw the Dragon Tower rising before us, but a huge, orange-colored, metal construction crane partially blocked our view.

We stopped for a minute at my home, allowing me to embrace my mother and hug Chien. I hadn't seen him in months, and he leaped up so enthusiastically that he almost knocked me down. One of the sacrifices I had made in going to Paris had been to leave Chien behind. I was happy he didn't hold a grudge.

"I'd like to go to the castle now," I said. "Can Chien ride in the truck?"

Paul sighed. "Of course, but I don't want him riding in the bed and falling out. He'll have to sit in your lap."

"I don't think he'll mind," I said.

The drive to the Crouching Dragon was much easier than before. The new road had been built, running from what we called the Main Road, curving past Paul's shop and then in not-so-gentle turns right up to the main gate.

Paul patted my knee. "The president keeps his promises," he said, indicating the road, "but except for you it wouldn't have happened."

A number of vehicles were parked near the gate.

"At least they don't look like thieves or smugglers," Louise said.

We all laughed.

"I've seen enough of criminals and traitors to last me a lifetime," I said.

As we approached the gate, a man in a uniform held up his hand and said, "Please show me your passes."

"Passes?!" I said. The thought had never occurred to us.

"You know me," Paul said. "I've worked on vehicles here, and surely you know Louise Donnet and William Montreux—without them you wouldn't have this job!"

"I am sorry, Monsieur, but my orders are clear. No entry without a pass." He gave Chien a wary look.

I began to laugh. I said to Louise and Paul, "You see what government means? Even the three of us can't get in without a pass."

We laughed heartily, which made the guard frown and look uncomfortable.

"It's not your fault," Louise said.

"I will call the Director—Monsieur Bourgeois," the guard said, rather stiffly.

He dialed a phone mounted on the wall, and after a moment said, "*Monsieur le Directeur*, there are three people who wish to enter the castle. The young lady's name is Louise—"

"—Yes, sir! At once, *Monsieur le Directeur!*" He quickly hung up the telephone and said, "I am to bring you at once to the office of the Director."

"Not necessary," Paul said. "We know the way."

As we walked, Chien trotted along close to me, rubbing against my leg. Once inside the ward—the courtyard—we had a much better view of the Dragon Tower as the crane, swung away.

"The dragon has his jaw back!" Louise said.

"He looks like he has braces on his teeth!" I said.

"I think that's the framework holding the upper and lower jaw together until the concrete sets," Paul said.

"I'm keeping a close eye on it," someone said. "I certainly wouldn't want it to collapse again."

"Andre!" I yelled.

We had all been so focused on the Dragon Tower, we hadn't even noticed the tall table with a high bench set in the courtyard with André perched on it. He slipped to the ground and walked toward us, still limping, but moving quickly. I wanted to hug him, but he put out his hand. I understood; no hugging in front of all these workers. I shook his hand tentatively, worried about his condition.

"You can do better than that!" he said, and gave me a strong, firm handshake.

Louise didn't wait—she just hugged him.

"Notice anything?" André asked.

"No bandage," I said.

"There's a pretty long scar on my scalp, but my hair has grown back and you can hardly see it."

"That's wonderful," I said. "What's going on with the desk?"

"Jean Bourgeois came to see me," André said, "and when he learned I could get around fairly well, he gave me this job for after school."

"You're also going to school?" I said.

"Willi, I have a lot to catch up on," André said.

"Think of it as a long vacation," I said, feeling a little silly about joking that way. Andre just smiled.

"Odile is here today," he said. "Also the Chicken Soup Twins."

"Even Stephen?"

"Yes," André said. "At first everybody said he had been a traitor, but his brother Jules pleaded for him and the kids decided to forgive him."

"Denise worked here for a while," André said, "until they fired her. They say she was always flirting with the workmen, interrupting their work."

Denise had been the number one glamour girl of the

entire district, a sensational redhead with a truly remarkable figure. The night Louise and I had found her with Marc—well, that was another matter.

A familiar looking figure was approaching.

"Welcome," Victor Devereaux said, his balding, shiny head bobbing.

"We're very happy the dragon has his jaw back," Louise said.

"We're going to remove the supports today," Devereaux said. "Can you stay and watch?"

"Of course," I said. "May we go up in the tower?"

"Yes," the chief engineer said, "but first you must examine the Great Hall."

The last time we were inside the Great Hall there had been a lot of scaffolding and large panels of stone and glass laying on the earthen floor. We entered a totally different space. First of all, there was a wide-planked, wooden floor.

"Wait here," I told Chien.

"Don't worry," Devereaux said, "Chien may walk on the floor."

Chien gave a little yip and walked in—carefully.

"Why did you build a wooden floor?" Louise asked. "That isn't like the original."

"In fact," André said, "it is."

"That's right," Devereaux said. "When we examined the walls very closely we found—just below the level of the earth—the rotted remains of wood on all four sides."

"Now I remember," I said. "We cleaned a lot of debris out of the Great Hall, and some of it was wood. We never realized that it might have been flooring."

"It probably wasn't from the original," Victor said. "There hasn't been a true wooden floor in this space for over five hundred years. In most of the castles of this era, the floors were either earth or stone."

Louise asked, "Was there anything beneath the floor of the Great Hall?"

"Only some collapsed tunnels," André said, "filled in long ago."

"I'm glad to hear that," I said. "I would have felt like a fool if you had discovered an entire level of artifacts."

The floor was only the first surprise. Above us arched a completely restored ceiling, with the wood beams strengthened, and the entire area stained in natural tones.

"The windows are in!" Louise said.

They were all in place, a delicate tracery of stone in whorls and quatrefoils and *fleurs-de-lis.*

Glorious lambent panels of stained glass had been fitted into the frames—portraying scenes from the Norman dynasties. On this sunny day, outside light streamed through the brilliant colors and patterned the wooden floor in reds and greens and blues.

"You haven't said anything about the standards," André said, pointing to the wall opposite the windows, where a dozen flags of intricate design and flamboyant colors hung from long bronze poles set at right angles high on the wall. The designs included animals and plants and shields—but fortunately not the DragonSlayers.

"Our previous work seems pitiful," I said, "compared to all this. But I don't see the suits of armor."

Victor Devereaux hesitated for a moment. "They are being cleaned and repaired at a famous armory near Bayeux."

"Then what?" Louise asked.

"There is talk of moving the armor to the Musée de l'Armée in Les Invalides," Devereux said, "to add to their permanent collection."

"Never!" I said. "I've seen the collection in the museum and it's wonderful, but our agreement with the president requires that all of the armor found here be displayed here. Will I have to speak to the president again?"

"That might be wise," Devereaux said.

✦   ✦   ✦

It was easy to climb the steps in the tower, now that the debris from the explosion had been cleared and the damaged stone replaced.

Jean Bourgeois was using Roger's former apartment as an office. Inside was a modern steel desk for Jean, another for a secretary (who was busily typing away), drafting boards, files and busy corkboards.

"My friends!" Jean said, coming around the desk to greet us. "I'm sorry about the guard, but it's better to be safe."

We embraced.

"Considering what you've been through, you look very well," he said. "What do you think of our labors?"

"We're overwhelmed," Louise said. "Everything is so different, so wonderful."

'Is it really different?' Jean asked. He was frowning.

Andre said, "I don't think they mean it's not authentic."

"Have you seen Tony Bersault?" I asked.

"Not in several weeks," Jean said. "Before then came here occasionally—always angry, behaving as if the Crouching Dragon was property that had been stolen from him."

"He is the thief!" Louise said.

Devereaux asked, "Shall we go outside and watch them remove the supporting framework inside the Dragon's jaw?"

"I'd like to go up to the top of the tower and look inside," I said.

"May I suggest that you postpone that for a while?" Jean said. "The damaged walls have been repaired and the catwalks rebuilt, but we're still trying to find the right artists and technicians to restore Roger's great exhibit. There is a firm in Marseille that does similar work for motion picture companies—we're negotiating with them now."

✦   ✦   ✦

We all went outside to watch the workmen remove the braces on the dragon's teeth. As each section was removed, more of the dragon's angry jaws were revealed. When the last of the steel was gone, the Crouching Dragon looked like his old fearsome self again—his jaws ready to crunch and cripple any enemy.

We congratulated each other, said our goodbyes, and Paul drove us, first to Louise's house and then to our own. I had tried to be casual saying goodbye to Andre, but it wasn't easy. He had punched my arm, as young men sometimes do, and I said something silly and then we left.

"André's going to be fine," Louise said, as she got out of the truck at her home.

"I know," I said, "although he's still limping. What bothers me is that I don't know how much I'll be seeing of him in the future."

One of the momentous changes in the Montreux household was the addition of a telephone. Only a few other families, including the Donnets, had one, but Paul finally arranged with the telephone company to string the line necessary to reach our home, his garage, and a few other businesses nearby. It was considered a luxury and seldom used.

We had no more than entered the house than the telephone rang. All three of us were startled. A phone call was a major event. It turned out that this one was a turning point in our lives.

Paul answered. "One moment, please!" he said, and handed the receiver to me. "It is the president!" he whispered, eyes wide.

I took the receiver and a deep breath.

"It required the Sûreté to locate you, William," the

president said. "We didn't know you had abandoned Paris."

"Sorry, *Monsieur le Président.*"

The president said, "I have an important appointment for you and Mademoiselle Louise. We will expect you at the Élysée tomorrow by 9 in the morning. Dress well."

"We'll be there!" I said.

The telephone clicked. Our president wasn't a man to waste words.

"Louise and I have to be at the Élysée by 9 A.M. tomorrow," I told my parents.

"I'll drive you to Paris early in the morning," Paul said. "I'd rather not drive into the big city at night. We must leave by 5 A.M. to be certain of arriving on time."

"Thanks," I said. "I'd better call Louise. Do you know the Donnet's telephone number?"

"4622," Mother said, "but you need only ask the operator for the Donnets."

Louise answered the telephone, and I told her about the president's instructions and Paul's offer to drive us into Paris.

"What does 'Dress well' mean?" she said.

"Ask your mother."

"Okay," she said, and then hung up.

"I forgot something," I said. "My good blue suit is in Paris. We may have to leave even earlier."

"What about asking the chief engineer, Victor Devereaux?" Mother suggested. "He's about your size. Perhaps he'd lend you that nice blue suit he wore when he spoke to the townspeople in church."

"Is he staying here?" I asked.

"At M. Henri's inn—he's the favored guest."

The operator gave me the number and I called and made my request.

"Of course," Devereaux said, "I've never been to the Élysée, and now I'll at least be able to say my suit was there."

FORMALITIES

By morning, Paul's truck had been scrupulously cleaned, waxed and tuned for the occasion. Mother spread a blanket on the seat so we wouldn't get dirty. Victor's suit fit me pretty well—he was bigger in the chest, and the sleeves were a bit long—but it was still the most expensive clothing I had ever worn. He also gave me a white shirt, starched in the collar, and a burgundy-red tie.

I wore a pair of old shoes I had left at home. Fiercely polished, they didn't look bad. Mother also cut and combed my hair for me, slicking it in place with some kind of waxy stuff. Louise said it smelled like lavender and she liked it.

Louise had borrowed a pretty white dress from her mother, with an oval neckline that dipped rather low. I almost felt like blushing (not at how she looked but at my reaction), but Louise didn't seem in the least embarrassed and I had to admit it looked very good on her.

Louise's mother had styled her hair so that it sort of rolled under at her shoulders She said it was called a pageboy, but she didn't look like any boy I'd ever met. She had also borrowed her mother's patent leather black shoes with high heels. Thankfully, I had grown some in the past two years and I was still taller than she was—at least a few centimeters—even with heels.

When I saw how great Louise looked and how—formal?—maybe that's when I had my first clue how serious this journey was. Even then I had no idea what was coming.

✦   ✦   ✦

We left Bonville around 5 in the morning. Although it was still dark, Paul actually said I could drive the truck until we were very close to Paris, which was the greatest display of confidence he had ever shown me.

The traffic was heavier than we expected, but we still covered the two hundred and fifty kilometers in a little over three and one-half hours. As we entered the outskirts of Paris, Paul took over the driving. We passed through St. Germain en Laye, Nanterre, and Neiully, then through the Porte Maillot into the Avenue Charles de Gaulle which fed into the Avenue de la Grande Armée. Ahead was the Arc de Triomphe.

"It's too early to go to l'Élysée," Paul said. "You should arrive at precisely 9 A.M."

"Louise and I have visited many famous places in Paris," I said, "but we've never been to the top of the Arch of Triumph. Want to go?"

Paul nodded. "The problem will be finding a place to park."

"Maybe along the Champs-Élysées," Louise said.

The great stone arch rose before us, fifty meters high and almost as wide, at the center of the vast and circular Place de l'Étoile (later to be known as the Place Charles de Gaulle).

"They call it the Place of the Star," I said, reciting in my best tour guide voice, "because twelve boulevards radiate from it like the points on a star." We entered the grand paved circle with traffic pouring in from the dozen roads.

"Good Lord!" Louise said. "We'll be killed!"

Paul laughed, but it seemed like a racetrack with hundreds of vehicles rocketing along, all trying to cut each other off. You couldn't navigate along the outer edge because your progress was interrupted by one boulevard after another.

"Hold on," Paul said, "We'll see if the rule of the right

still works!" He bravely cut across traffic directly toward the center of the circle, dodging cars that seemed about to hit us, with horns blowing, brakes screeching. Then he cut across to the opposite side from the avenue we had entered, and into the Champs-Élysées.

"Victory!" he cried out, and maneuvered the truck into a parking space along the boulevard.

"I'm going to show you one of the best views of Paris," I said (importantly). "Follow me!"

"We'll be killed!" Louise said, repeating herself, believing we were going to cross against traffic to the arch. This from the woman who had landed an airplane in the Place de la Concorde.

"There's an underpass," I said knowingly, although in fact I hadn't known it until the very second I saw a sign that said "Underpass."

We raced through the narrow passage and came out in the middle of the Place. Under the arch was the Tomb of the Unknown Soldier and the Flame of Remembrance, relit every evening, dedicated to the millions of soldiers who had died in battle. A few wreaths lay beside the tomb.

There was an elevator to the upper platform marked "Closed for Repairs." I led the way towards the staircase, guarded by two uniformed soldiers.

"I'm sorry," one said, "but there's no admission until 9 A.M."

Paul drew himself up to his full height. "I, too, was a sergeant in the French Army," he said, "wounded at Dunkirk." (This was something I had never heard before). "I understand the meaning of rules and discipline, but I must inform you that this young gentleman and this young lady are meeting today with the President of the Republic."

Both soldiers laughed.

"Do you wish this gentleman to tell the president," Paul

said, "that you refused him admission to the *Arc de Triomphe*—in the *Place de Charles de Gaulle?*"

The soldiers were beginning to look uneasy.

"Telephone the Élysée Palace!" Paul said. "Ask if they are expecting Monsieur William Montreux and Mademoiselle Louise Donnet!"

A broad smile creased the sergeant's face. "You're the kids from the Crouching Dragon!" he said. "The ones who landed in the Place de la Concorde and battled the DragonSlayers!"

Louise and I nodded, not particularly modestly, and shook hands with both soldiers. They also shook hands with Paul, who was still eyeing them belligerently.

The sergeant pointed to the stairs with a flourish. "Please ascend!" he said, clicking his heels and saluting smartly.

Paul nodded and we followed him up the staircase.

"Does everyone in Paris know?" Louise asked.

"At least this time, it seemed to help," I said.

As we reached the platform, the morning sun was streaking the sky with banners of orange, red and yellow, intertwining like rippling scarves, dappling the city with kaleidoscopic patterns which blinked and flashed off windows, storefronts and vehicles. Paris was spread before and around us, the great boulevards radiating out like ripples in a pond, seeming to undulate in the changing light. The American writer, Ernest Hemingway, had said that if you had lived in Paris as a young man, you could always carry it with you—like a moveable feast.

The three of us were dazzled and momentarily speechless.

To the east, the Champs-Élysées, grandest boulevard of all, edged with chestnut trees and rimmed by gray, almost uniform buildings, rolled majestically to the Place de la Concorde.

Paul was leaning on the balustrade, taking in the city.

"The Eiffel Tower," he said, gesturing as if he had personally discovered the lacy steel structure that arched gracefully into the heavens, almost due south of our perch, past the eastwardly curve of the Seine. The river flashed blue and white in the sunlight, dividing the city into left and right banks before our eyes.

Beyond the Place de la Concorde rose the iron gates of the Tuileries, the walks and gardens leading to the open rectangular courtyard of the massive Louvre Museum.

"Have you been to the Louvre?" Paul asked.

"Yes," I said, "but only for a few hours—time to see the marble Nike, the Venus de Milo, Leonardo's Mona Lisa, some Italian Renaissance paintings, but not much more."

Louise smiled. "We'll go back and take our time."

"And have a picnic lunch by the pond in the garden of the Tuilieries," I said.

"This time," Louise said, "I'll know how to give you a good race with the little boats in the pond."

Paul was looking at the city with evident pride. "When I was here as a soldier," he said (another surprise), "the museums were closed. We climbed to the artists' section, Monmartre." He gestured northeast, toward the soaring, almost moorish spires that marked the Sacré-Coeur—the Sacred Heart Cathedral. "We stood on the steps of the church—a bunch of kids, not much older than you—on a morning like this, in the spring of 1940, before France fell. We were filled with patriotism and could not imagine that in a few weeks this magnificent city would be occupied by the Nazi army." His expression grew somber.

"You can see the Invalides," I said quickly, pointing slightly east of the Eiffel Tower to the golden dome, glittering in the sun. "Napoleon's tomb is there."

"Nearly as great a man as General de Gaulle," Paul said, with what was almost—I say, almost—a twinkle in his eye.

◆　◆　◆

Paul dropped us off before the palace, promising to find a parking space down the street and wait. Louise was smoothing her hair and I was straightening my tie.

"Your tie is perfect," Louise said.

"So's your hair," I responded.

The guard at the gate recognized us.

"The president is expecting you," he said.

We had barely climbed the few steps to the portico and reached the tall, glass doors, when they were opened by Colonel Victoire. At his direction, we seated ourselves on an upholstered bench in the Vestibule of Honor, the austere columned hall with limestone walls and a checkerboard floor paved with white and red marble, that we had seen before.

"Did you have any delays getting here?" the colonel asked.

"None," I said.

"Yesterday, the streets were lined with a million French people of all ages," the colonel said, "carrying French and American flags and cheering the President of the United States and his lovely wife." He stopped. "You didn't know the American president was here?"

It was embarrassing, but we had to admit it.

"I see," the colonel said. "There was a remarkable procession from Orly airport into the city: fifty black Citroens, escorted by the mounted, sabre-armed Garde-Republicaine. Voices were calling, 'Kenn-a-dee' and 'Zhackee.' The people haven't been this excited since the Allies entered Paris in 1943, led by General LeClerc and the Free French."

"I'm sorry we missed seeing them."

"Last night the President and Madame de Gaulle gave a state dinner in the Festival Hall for President Kennedy and his beautiful wife, Jacqueline—very formal with all the ladies in fashionable gowns and the men in black swallow-tailed tuxedos with white bow ties."

"I wish I had seen that," Louise said. "I don't suppose I could ask you what the ladies wore?"

"Ordinarily," the colonel replied, "I would not have been able to answer that question, but my fiancée gave me strict instructions to make careful note of the ladies' apparel." He smiled. "Naturally, I have relied on my trained powers of observation as an investigating officer to compile these data. I have yet not yet reported this vital information to her and I can use this opportunity to practice it on you."

"Excellent!" Louise said.

"Very well," the colonel began, glancing up as if the information were written high on the wall above our heads. "The lovely wife of the American president wore a slim, pink and white gown, made of—as the ladies of our staff told me—straw lace. It had a high, scalloped neck, cut low in back, with a narrow skirt that touched the floor. She wore a wrap—do you call it a stole?—of the same fabric, long white gloves on bare arms, and carried a glittering maillot purse."

The colonel gave Louise a brilliant smile, flashing his incredible white teeth. "How is that so far?" he asked.

"Perfect," Louise said.

"*Bien,*" the colonel said. "Madame Kennedy's lovely black hair curved low over her forehead with what I can only describe as wings at the side and a bun on top held by a pearl cornet, matched by long pearl earrings. I am sure this style has a name, but I do not know it.

"Madame Yvonne, the wife of President de Gaulle, wore a gray-blue, full-length gown without sleeves, and also with long white gloves. Her hair and jewelry were more, shall we say, conservative, but she looked quite beautiful."

This recital surprised me, but evidently pleased Louise—she was wide-eyed, a small smile at her lips.

"All of the ladies wore long gowns," the colonel continued, "many with bare necks and shoulders. The colors were
a rainbow, but not gaudy you understand. France is the very
soul of fashion and French women are the best-dressed in
the world. I must admit I was surprised when I learned that
Mrs. Kennedy's clothing was designed by a man named
Oleg Cassini, who, despite his name, is an American."

This was obviously a considerable concession for the
colonel to make.

"Are you interested in the men and their apparel?" the
colonel asked.

Louise immediately said, "Yes." My answer would not
necessarily have been the same.

"The American president seems very young," the
colonel said, "with a broad smile and a shock of dark hair,
rather tall. Our president has less hair (he is more than
twenty-five years older), but he is much taller and no one
can match him for imperious dignity."

Louise and I were nodding vigorously. Of course, no
one, not even the handsome, powerful United States president, could compare with our President Charles de Gaulle.

"All of the men wore formal dress, very elegant, but
since they were men, very similar in design—not at all as
individual as the women."

"Thank God," I said.

Louise laughed. The colonel smiled. He glanced at his
watch.

"It's time to speak to the president."

He led us up the steep, marble staircase to the private
apartments. The president sat at his favorite, elegant
table-desk, half-turned toward us, wearing a silk robe
over shirt and pants, reading glasses perched on his nose
as he wrote with long, powerful strokes on a document on
the desk before him. We were familiar with this scene,

having witnessed it on several occasions.

As we entered the room, I immediately noticed that the president seemed even more tense than when I had last seen him, his face more pale. The president's wife, Yvonne, stood by his desk. She smiled, but her expression was somewhat strained as well.

The colonel clicked his heels and saluted. The president rose to his full, awesome height, returned the salute and— smiled at us. He bowed to Louise, who did some form of curtsy, and took my hand in both of his huge hands. His grip was strong, but almost gentle.

"*Monsieur le Président,*" I said.

"*Mes amis,*" the president responded.

"Madame de Gaulle," Louise said for both of us, and she smiled again.

The president gestured to the two of us to sit in the gilt chairs opposite him, and Madame de Gaulle seated herself near him. The colonel remained standing, his feet apart, hands held behind his back.

"Yesterday at lunch," the president said, "and again at dinner, Yvonne and I conversed, most enjoyably, with the wife of the American president. Did you know her family name is Bouvier, that her grandparents were French, and that she speaks excellent French, herself? No? Well, it is true.

"I planned to have you meet the president and Madame Kennedy here today. I didn't tell you on the telephone because I did not want to alert anyone to their schedule.

"However, the crowds and the clamor over the Kennedys has been so great that their schedule was modi-fied. Fortunately, Yvonne has had an even better idea. Tonight we are having a State Dinner for the Kennedys in the Hall of Mirrors at Versailles and you are both invited."

Louise was looking from the president to her dress and back again.

"Quite right, Mademoiselle Louise," the president's wife said. "It will be a formal affair and you will need a gown to wear. Monsieur William must also wear formal dress."

I suppressed the desire to yell, "Oh, no!"

"I believe we can easily solve William's problem," Colonel Victoire said. "Among the staff of the Élysée and the Marigny are men of various sizes and shapes—one of them will surely have the full dress required for this event."

My expression must have been one of pleading.

"We must all make sacrifices for the nation," the colonel said solemnly.

"What about me?" Louise asked plaintively, looking at Madame de Gaulle.

"You are not my size, my dear," Yvonne de Gaulle said, "or I would gladly lend you something of mine. I have checked with the women from our staff and have been unable to solve the problem here.

"However, I have spoken to Madame Kennedy, and she has offered to help. We will arrange for you to be transported to the Quai d'Orsay, where the Americans are staying, and her staff will see that you are properly dressed."

"Madame de Gaulle," Louise said, rather breathlessly, "that sounds truly wonderful."

Madame de Gaulle waved a dismissive hand as she smiled.

"Enough of this," the president said. "I have heard that there is an American saying to the effect that 'Clothes make the man.' I assume this is a joke because in my experience the reverse is true." Fortunately, he was smiling.

"We will attempt to reschedule an appointment for you with the Americans for tomorrow," the president said, nodding to Colonel Victoire. "In any case, you will meet them, if only briefly, tonight."

25

REFLECTIONS

I looked in the mirror and blinked—and blinked again—but still couldn't believe what I saw. Colonel Victoire had located formal clothing that fit me perfectly—at least I thought it fit me perfectly because I knew nothing about how such finery should fit. The pants with their silk striping barely touched my shoe tops (the highly polished, narrow tipped shoes pinched a bit in the toes, but who was I to complain?), and the waist wasn't either large or small—which didn't matter because the pants were held up with white leather stays, another novelty for me.

Under a black swallow-tailed jacket, the tails of which brushed the back of my knees, I wore a white waistcoat over a heavily-starched, white shirt with a stand-up, wing-tip collar and a white bowtie, tied by a valet. My shirt sleeves extended beyond the sleeves of the jacket a few centimeters and were held together by silver cufflinks. I wore a starched, pointed handkerchief in my breast pocket.

The valet insisted on using a hard-tipped brush to flatten my blond hair, but that held for only a little while, and my tough hair kept slowly—I hoped imperceptibly—rising. I was virtually unrecognizable in the mirror.

Colonel Victoire, dressed exactly as I was, except for the rows of colorful ribbons on his chest, approved.

"Parfait!" he said. "Your beautiful young lady will fall in love with you all over again."

"But she isn't—"

"—Beautiful? Of course she is."

I had meant to say Louise wasn't in love with me, but the colonel was smiling. I think he knew what I had intended.

"Paul!" I blurted out.

"*Pardon?*" the colonel asked.

"Paul Montreux, my stepfather, is waiting for us outside. I completely forgot."

"I'll have him brought in."

"I don't think he'd like that; he isn't dressed for the Presidential Palace. I'll have to change and go look for him."

"No time for that," the colonel said.

Therefore, I marched out the doors of the Élysée Palace in full dress, accompanied by two guardsmen in splendid red and gold jackets and gold helmets, bearing swords. In this strange parade, my embarrassment was so acute that I found myself shrinking inside my clothing. I couldn't understand how the formal outfit could keep from collapsing with such a tiny person to support it.

Across the paving stones, out under the iron and gold gate and onto the Rue de Faurbourg St. Honore. Sure enough, just past the Place Beauvau, near the intersection of the Rue St. Honore and the Rue de Cirque, stood Paul, leaning against his truck.

At our approach he snapped to attention, bewildered but respectful. Obviously he had no idea who the young man in formal dress might be.

"Paul," I called out, and he nearly jumped out of his shoes. He bent forward, peering at me. Speechless.

"Paul," I said. "It's me, Willi."

I think he swayed a little.

"How are you?" I asked.

He nodded as if to say, "Okay."

"Louise and I are going with the president to the State Dinner at Versailles for President and Madame Kennedy. I'm sure we'll be all right. You can return to Bonville if you like."

He didn't move.

"Okay?" I asked.

He nodded, his eyes flickering from me to the guards and back again.

"Please tell Mother and Louise's parents and aunt and uncle that we're doing just fine."

A slight nod.

I held out my hand. Paul took it gingerly and we shook hands, me firmly, Paul a little weakly. He never spoke a word.

◆　◆　◆

At least fifty black French Citroen DS 19 sedans—the ones that looked like tilted oval flying saucers—were rolling toward Versailles, plus several Cadillacs carrying the American entourage. President de Gaulle, who had expressed admiration for an American Cadillac on that day almost two years ago when we had met him in the coastal town of Luc, had chosen this time to ride with his wife in a French-built vehicle. The American president's Cadillac was specially fitted to accommodate M. Kennedy, who suffered from chronic back problems.

I rode with Colonel Victoire in the car behind the president's Citroen and the security guard. Louise was in one of the American limousines; I later learned she was riding with the American president and his wife.

On this late spring day, the first of June, 1961, it was still light as we drove towards the great château, and the roads were lined with people waving French and American flags. Many were calling out some strange word I couldn't make out. Then I remembered what Colonel Victoire had told us about the crowds yelling "Zhackee," which was their pronunciation of the name of President Kennedy's wife.

We approached the Château of Versailles on the broad tree-lined Avenue de Paris, reaching the vast Place d'Armes,

CHÂTEAU & GARDEN (Partial)

1 – South Parterre
2 – Orangery and Lake
    of the Swiss Guards
3 – Water Parterre
•4 – Parterre of Latona
5 – South Quinounx
6 – Ballroom Grove
7 – Queen's Grove
8 – Fountain of Autumn
9 – King's Garden
10 – Fountain of Winter

11 – Chestnut-Grove
12 – Colonnade
13 – Green Carpet
•14 – Fountain of Apollo
•15 – Grand Canal
16 – Grove of the Domes
17 – Fountain of Enceladus
18 – Obelisk Fountain
19 – Fountain of Spring
20 – North Quincunx

21 – Star Grove
22 – Fountain of the blissful Ode
23 – Fountain of Summer
24 – Baths of Apollo
25 – North Parterre
26 – Pyramid Fountain
27 – Diana's Bathing Nymphs
28 – Water Avenue
•29 – Dragon Fountain
•30 – Fountain of Neptune

*Fountains & Ponds described in story

and then entering through the main gilt and black wrought - iron gate with the elaborate, gilt, royal seal overhead. The parade rolled onto the vast and uneven, brick-paved, interior courtyard, framed by the many-tiered baroque and classical façades of the château, extending for hundreds of meters. A grand, bronze equestrian statue of King Louis XIV stood in the very center. I was almost dizzied by images of brick and pale limestone, mansard roofs and chimney pots, arch after arch after arch—all three and four stories high, with dormers on the top floors of the mansarded sections. Visions of pilasters and columns, windows and balconies, hundred of statues. But it was not a jumble—rather, it was an orderly procession, as the courtyard narrowed in clearly defined sections, leading towards the columned château.

Around us spread a swirl of black vehicles, circling like great birds, disgorging men in black formalwear, women in cascades of gowns, soldiers and guards and aides, all resplendent in their varied uniforms—counterpointed by a dazzling troop on horseback. Somehow a pattern formed—a procession advancing. As if a chart had been laid on the great paving stones with a space plotted and marked for each vehicle, each horse, each person. People moved as if they had rehearsed this spectacle, flowing together, forming groups and cliques and segments and couples. Louise suddenly took my arm.

Dazzling smile; makeup subtle, but startling for me because I had never seen her wearing anything more than lipstick. Her hair upswept and held with a pin or clip or tiara—I didn't know what it was called. The fading light of the setting sun highlighting her lustrous hair, flickering off her green eyes, flashing on long, narrow earrings. She wore a pale-yellow, full-length dress, gathered at one shoulder ("in the Egyptian fashion," Madame Kennedy had told her), with a side drape. It was trimmed with embroidery and small stones ("brilliants"), with a slim silk ribbon and a bow of the same color at the waist. Long white gloves. A princess. This was a dream. A fairy tale. How had I won the princess?

I had to speak like a man, not a frog-throated boy. "Please take my arm, Princess, so that I may escort you to the ball."

What a smile! What a reward! Growing up might not be all bad.

"It is an honor, Prince William," Louise whispered, taking my arm.

I almost fell over backwards, I was trying so hard to stand tall.

The colonel was walking before us, a lovely young woman on his arm. Later we would learn that she was an aide to Madame Kennedy, Miss Everleigh. I would not remember her until we met again in Washington, D.C. Then she would wear a tailored suit and low heels, but this night at the Château of Versailles she wore a light-gray gown.

We were directed under the south arcade through an entrance on the ground floor. Instantly, we were transported back three hundred years into a spectacle of unparalleled grandeur. Each area was discreetly described to us by Colonel Victoire, Miss Everleigh smiling beside him.

"The Queen's Staircase," he said.

It was a dazzling sight—the steps wide, the balustrades of veined marbles in harmonious shades of green, brown, gray and black. The black marble railing was broad, smoothly fitted, velvety to the touch. The staircase was open in design, the ceiling arching about ten meters above us. Set into the walls were remarkable paintings that continued the arches and columns in perspectives so realistic they seemed to go on forever.

Gold had been applied with lavish hands: gilded metal reliefs of sphinxes and men and grand vases above the entrances on the upper floor, and gilded panels set into the tall white doors; gilded capitals topped marble columns and gilded cornices edged the ceiling.

We passed through the King's Guardroom, a confection of white and gold and marble and crystal, and then into the King's First Antechamber. On this level, all of the floors were wooden parquet in the famous Versailles diamond pattern.

"In the time of Louis XIV," the colonel said, "the king ate his meals here, his back to the fireplace, sometimes alone, sometimes with others. Occasionally, twenty-four violins played a concert during supper. On certain days he received petitions from the common people in this room."

I tried to imagine the king, gilt and brocaded, white-stockinged and black-buckled, with a huge curling wig falling to his shoulders and beyond. But I could not construct his face.

We entered another antechamber, called the "Bull's Eye Room," where courtiers waited before it was time for them to meet the king. It was even more elaborately decorated than the first antechamber, with tall windows that opened to the marble entrance courtyard and a great oval window high in the room—called the Bull's Eye—that shared light with the next, and most important, room of the royal suite.

"This is the King's Bedchamber," said Colonel Victoire. "The king met his courtiers here every day."

The walls were covered with panels of fabric, draped, brocaded, gilt, separated by Corinthian-capped pilasters and mirrors with bas-relief putti—cherubs—above. Oval cutouts with paintings were surrounded by carved figures. An arching cove over the bed was surmounted by a carved figure of the king and more putti, plus horn-blowing angels, everything encrusted with gold.

A low, glittering balustrade before the king's bed was elaborately carved with bulbous posts and an ornate railing. The bed was half-hidden by a canopy and tapestries, woven of silk, with gold-and-silver-embroidered red brocade. We had a brief vision of gilt chairs, upholstered with the same red, silver and gold pattern, and of vases with white feathers above the canopy at each of the four corners of the bed. Paintings in gilt frames rose above the carved cove that surrounded the room. A chandelier with huge, faceted petals of glass glittered in reflected light.

A moment later we were in the Council Chamber, with the same parquet floor, the walls white but framed and ornamented in gold, a graceful, purple marble fireplace with a mirror above, great vases, busts of heroes, two more chandeliers and gold-brocaded chairs and cloths. It seemed almost spartan compared to the King's bedchamber.

Here we were received by the presidents of France and the United States and their elegant wives and many functionaries of undetermined rank and title. I sort of bowed and Louise curtsied. President de Gaulle nodded and whispered something to Madame Kennedy, who smiled at us as if we were really important, and not just a couple of lost children, floating through a fantasy.

Colonel Victoire had warned me not to bow to the American president and his wife, but I couldn't help myself, and Louise curtsied again, regardless of the rules. Jacqueline Kennedy wore a sweeping pale-blue, off-the-shoulder gown, with a diamond necklace around her lovely throat and pendant earrings and a diamond tiara in her hair.

Her smile—everything about her—dazzled me. I thought my mother was very pretty, with her blonde hair, blue eyes and slim figure, and Louise was the best looking girl I'd ever met, but Jacqueline Bouvier Kennedy was simply the most beautiful woman in the world. I wouldn't think of going into details about the figure of the wife of the president of the United States, except to say she was slim and not unusually tall.

"You must be William and Louise," she said in perfect French, speaking in a voice that was a bit wispy and higher than I expected, but her deep brown eyes were so compelling

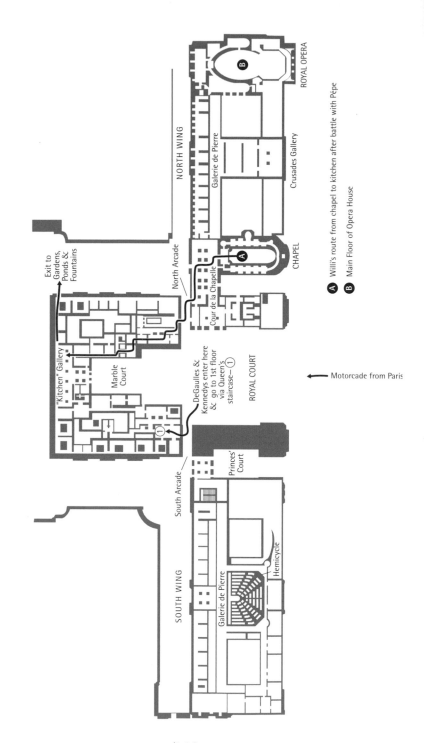

NORTH WING

Galerie de Pierre

Crusades Gallery

ROYAL OPERA

Exit to
Gardens,
Ponds &
Fountains

North Arcade

Cour de la Chapelle

CHAPEL

"Kitchen" Gallery

Marble
Court

DeGaulles &
Kennedys enter here
& go to 1st floor
via Queen's
staircase—①

ROYAL COURT

Motorcade from Paris

South Arcade

Princes'
Court

SOUTH WING

Galerie de Pierre

Hemicycle

Ⓐ Willi's route from chapel to kitchen after battle with Pèpe

Ⓑ Main Floor of Opera House

CHÂTEAU OF VERSAILLES

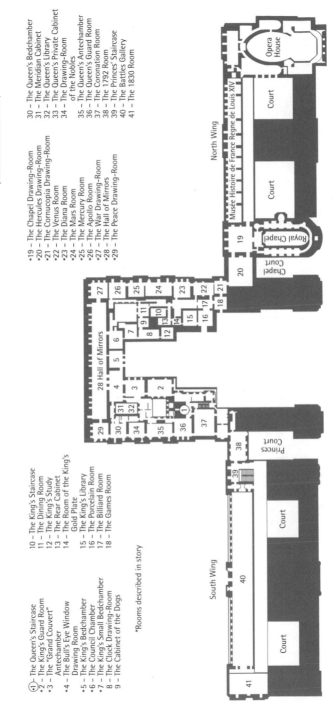

THE FIRST FLOOR LAYOUT
(Floor above Ground Floor)

①- The Queen's Staircase
*2 - The King's Guard Room
*3 - The "Grand Couvert"
    Antechamber
4 - The Bull's Eye Window
    Drawing Room
*5 - The King's Bedchamber
*6 - The Council Chamber
*7 - The King's Small Bedchamber
8 - The Clock Drawing-Room
9 - The Cabinet of the Dogs

10 - The King's Staircase
11 - The Dining Room
12 - The King's Study
13 - The Rear Cabinet
14 - The Room of the King's
    Gold Plate
15 - The King's Library
16 - The Porcelain Room
17 - The Billiard Room
18 - The Games Room

•19 - The Chapel Drawing-Room
•20 - The Hercules Drawing-Room
•21 - The Cornucopia Drawing-Room
•22 - The Venus Room
•23 - The Diana Room
•24 - The Mars Room
•25 - The Mercury Room
•26 - The Apollo Room
•27 - The War Drawing-Room
•28 - The Hall of Mirrors
•29 - The Peace Drawing-Room

30 - The Queen's Bedchamber
31 - The Meridian Cabinet
32 - The Queen's Library
33 - The Queen's Private Cabinet
34 - The Drawing-Room
    of the Nobles
35 - The Queen's Antechamber
36 - The Queen's Guard Room
37 - The Coronation Room
38 - The 1792 Room
39 - The Princes' Staircase
40 - The Battles Gallery
41 - The 1830 Room

*Rooms described in story

Hall of Mirrors

Musée Histoire de France Regne de Louis XIV

North Wing

South Wing

Opera House

Royal Chapel

Chapel Court

Princes Court

Court

• 343 •

and her smile so glorious that every word seemed lyrical and special to me.

"Yes, Madame Kennedy," was all I could think of saying.

"I'm looking forward to speaking to the two of you," she added.

I nodded, smiled, and moved slowly on. Then I was shaking hands with the American president, who looked much too young, with his great shock of dark hair, grinning the famous wide-toothed grin that we recognized from newsreels.

"President and Madame de Gaulle spoke very highly of you," he said in a clear but regional dialect, "but they didn't tell me you were so good-looking." While his glance took in both of us, I was certain he was talking to Louise. She smiled serenely, and once again I realized that although we were the same age, she was much more mature than I.

We murmured our thanks and continued along the line, not knowing who the people were, sometimes received with smiles (the Americans), sometimes ignored (the French), but too much in a daze to understand much of anything.

Suddenly we were in the *Galerie des Glaces,* the Hall of Mirrors. The rooms we had seen before were mere appetizers. This great chamber was seventy meters—more than two hundred feet—long, with smaller square rooms, the Drawing-Rooms of Peace and War added to either end. The floor was the Versailles parquet, while the great carved and painted ceilings arched across a gallery more than a dozen meters—thirty-odd feet—wide. Along the inner wall, paneled mirrors with arching tops five meters high followed one after another after another. They were framed with many-hued marble pilasters, topped with gilt capitals and garlands of gold, then bands of white and gold, and above that, a long carved and gilt array of figures and shields, helmets and panels.

The arching ceiling, more than eight meters high at the

pinnacle, was divided into panels by strips of carved gold. The panels were painted by Charles Le Brun and assistants with scenes from mythology and events from the reign of Louis XIV, all in cunning perspective.

Opposite the mirrors, seventeen (I counted them), huge windows were set in deep niches, covered with now familiar patterns of marble and gilt, looking out on gardens that stretched to the horizon, still glowing in the setting sun. The windows were separated by eight marble and porphyry busts of Roman emperors and eight marble statues. Ten pairs of chandeliers of silvered bronze with dozens of tall, candle-shaped fixtures topped with electric bulbs where once real candles had flickered, now flared and sang from the ceiling.

Spaced along both the mirrored and the windowed walls were a couple of dozen individually carved and draped, gilt figures of women, standing with one knee bent, leaning forward from toes to waist, but arching their upper bodies. They carried gilt torches, whose glow was provided by electric lights, shimmering in a flutter of carved glass leaves. Each of these wonders was twice as tall as a man.

The hall was filled with tables, glistening with brocaded cloths and great heaps of silverware and glass. Sunlight still slanted through the windows, joining with millions of refractions of electric light glistening from mirrors and torchieres and chandeliers, to bathe the entire scene in a warm and lustrous glow.

At first, all I saw was glitter and gold and fragments of marble, faces of stone, golden angels, fluttering lights. Visions surrounded me, as if I were suspended in a huge mirrored vessel with images flickering everywhere. I was so dizzied that I walked cautiously, afraid of a misstep.

I did bump into a waiter, carrying a tray of something or other. I turned to apologize, but he didn't seem to hear me.

Louise whispered, "He should have slowed down and

watched where he was going."

Louise is right, I thought. *That guy is moving much too fast for this kind of crowd.*

But that was forgotten as we were seated, about a hundred kilometers from the long main table, where the two presidents and their wives and ambassadors and ministers and consuls and cabinet secretaries sat. I was happy to be far away, able to see a lot, but not required to do much.

Miss Everleigh, the American lady, leaned across our table to speak to Louise.

"Mrs. Kennedy's gown is by Givenchy."

Louise nodded, knowingly.

When the others were distracted, I asked Louise in a whisper, "What is a 'zheevonchee?'"

She couldn't help a brief, strangled laugh before she spelled the name for me. "It's a man," she said, "not a thing—one of France's great fashion designers."

She turned to Miss Everleigh and said, "I understand that except for tonight, almost everything Madame Kennedy wears has been designed by Oleg Cassini, the American designer."

Miss Everleigh smiled. "Yes, he created a special wardrobe just for this trip." And she began an enthusiastic description of Madame Kennedy's wardrobe to Louise.

Colonel Victoire and I looked at each other.

Soon the serving of food began. So many courses, so many wines. I had little idea of what I was eating, although it all tasted incredibly good. I saw more different wines in one evening than I had seen in my whole life. I took a sip of each, finished none. Louise did the same.

The polished mirrors and marbles, the wooden floor, reverberated with the sounds of conversation, glass and dishware, the footfalls of servers and guests.

I saw someone I recognized: M. Noir, the agent of the Sûreté. He was dressed as a waiter—surprising because he was a director. When I caught his eye, he did not smile. I leaned over and said to Louise, "Did you see—?"

"—I thought I knew him," she said. "He seems to be very busy, but he never carries any trays. Now I understand why."

"I wonder," I said.

Waiters and other serving personnel were everywhere, many of them flowing through the entrance to the Drawing-Room of Peace. There was also a great deal of activity behind the main table, through the doorway that led back to the Council of State Salon.

I was beginning to feel on edge; perhaps even the few sips of wine were too much for me. Probably the starched shirt I was wearing and the heavy duck-tailed formal had something to do with it. Also, the shoes the colonel had found for me didn't really fit; they were beginning to pinch, but there was nothing to be done about that.

A face blurred past—familiar, but not M. Noir's. This man was also wearing a server's uniform. *I know this person,* I thought, *except something about him is different.*

Colonel Victoire had noticed my reaction. "Is something wrong?" he asked.

"I'm sorry," I said. "I thought I saw a man I knew, but now I'm not so sure."

The colonel's expression said, *"Think harder! It may be important."*

"The hair!" I said aloud, almost involuntarily. "The man I saw just now has very short blonde hair and a dark mustache. The man I'm thinking about has long, pepper-and-salt hair—a very large head of hair—Bersault, Tony Bersault!"

The Colonel immediately rose to his feet, apologizing to Miss Everleigh.

"Come with me," he said to me.

Louise and I followed him. Miss Everleigh would have to sit alone.

Colonel Victoire drew me aside and asked, "How was he dressed?"

"Like the other service people."

"Where did you see him?" he asked.

"Going into and out of the Council of State Room. There was another guy, too. He bumped into me earlier and I just saw Tony talk to him."

"Describe him."

"Your height, but more slender. Swarthy complexion, a crooked nose like a fighter's and a weak chin. Gray hair, but not as old as his hair."

The colonel whispered to a waiter, who quickly moved away, and spoke to another waiter, who didn't even nod.

"Thanks," the colonel said. "You can go back to the table now."

"Are you kidding?" I said, perhaps a little rudely. "Those guys are after us, too."

We followed the colonel into the Council of State Room. Waiters were passing up and back, and several men and women in anonymous dark clothes were standing off to one side. The colonel gave them the descriptions of the two men, and they immediately scattered.

"I must inform the president," he said. "Wait here."

He hurried back into the Hall of Mirrors. People kept hurrying past us on their way to the food preparation areas.

"So Tony cut his hair and dyed it blonde," Louise said. "It was great that you recognized him."

"You would, too," I said. "I was just lucky he turned to face me—if he'd kept on walking I would have missed him."

A couple of minutes passed.

"We're wasting valuable time," I said. "Let's see where the waiters go."

We followed two waiters with empty trays, who immediately exited the Council Chamber, hurried through a couple of rooms and descended a staircase.

"The main kitchen must be on the ground floor below the Hall of Mirrors," Louise said. "They carry food and dishes up and down those stairs."

As I was trying to decide what to do, the man with the crooked nose slipped past me, head averted, but I recognized him.

"Wait a minute!" I said.

I yelled to Louise, "Tell the colonel I'm following that guy."

She spun around and headed back to the Hall of Mirrors. I was walking fast, trying to catch up with the man with the crooked nose. Swarms of serving people blocked my passage and I had to push through, annoying a few, who glared or cursed me under their breaths. I didn't stop to apologize.

The guy I now thought of as "the boxer" because of his broken nose, moved as if he was going to go down the steps, but then took off in another direction. I followed, slipping through one lavishly decorated room after another. Signs told me I was hurrying through the Diana Drawing Room, the Venus Room, the Cornucopia Drawing Room.

I felt constricted in my fancy clothing, and I started stripping off my long black, swallow-tailed jacket, bumping into people as I flung out my arms, astonishing others as I threw the jacket aside.

Then we were past the crowd of workers, leaving only the boxer and me. He began to run.

"Hold on!" I yelled. "I want to talk to you!"

We were in the Hercules Drawing Room, a vast space, nearly twenty meters long and fifteen wide. Still running hard, I tore off my white waistcoat, which released my chest. Stumbling, I kicked off the shoes. But I still wore long, fancy silk stockings, and I was slipping and sliding on the parquet. I pulled them off so I could run on my bare feet. I must have been a sight, lunging and jumping and dancing and spinning as I removed shoes and stockings—slipping, sliding and staggering along.

About this time I began to think, *What do I do when I catch this guy?* There wasn't time to puzzle that out. I followed him into the large drawing room in front of the Chapel. Then the boxer hurried through a set of very tall open doors and onto the gallery of the chapel itself.

The chapel was so lovely, I had to fight distraction: marble floors in geometric patterns; small chapels in arched arcades below; galleries above with tall columns and a great, gilt organ; a curved apse at the far end; an amazing gilt altar set on oval marble steps; a magnificent gilt Gloria, rays of light, angels above and below, great candlesticks as tall as a man.

I didn't stop running. I was only a few strides behind the boxer, but gaining very slowly. I suddenly realized that I was making a mistake. He was going to circle the gallery and lead me back out through the very doors through which we had entered. I spun on my heel and ran back the way I had come, forcing myself to accelerate until we were running parallel to each other on opposite sides of the gallery. I was a couple of steps behind because I had lost time following him around.

My feet were getting very sore from running on hard floors, but I pushed myself and ran even faster. If he escaped from the chapel, I wasn't sure that, without shoes, I would be able to continue chasing him.

Where were all the soldiers, guards and police? Where was the colonel? I struggled to lengthen my strides, grimacing every time I hit the floor.

Although we were running step-for-step, aiming for the exit, I wasn't going fast enough to cut him off. I launched myself at him in a desperate attempt to catch up. At that instant I saw that he held a knife in his hand. I twisted to avoid the knife, but managed to strike his other shoulder, and we crashed to the floor. The impact knocked the knife from his hand, and we both scrambled after it. He was closer, but I kicked him in the butt and sent him lurching to the floor. I fell on top of him, trying to grapple him into submission. We were rolling on the floor and he was trying to break free.

He pulled loose for a second and started to stand up. I punched him square in the middle of his chest, and he staggered back against the balustrade, twenty feet above the main floor of the chapel. He came off the balustrade swinging and hit me in the face. I was trying to grab his arm, but he was struggling so violently, I couldn't control him. He pulled back and braced against the railing, then shoved off and started to kick me. I ducked under his foot, drove my shoulder under his leg, and lifted him partially off the floor.

He slipped and staggered sidewise on one foot, wildly flailing his arms, while I continued lifting so I could throw him.

"Let go!" he screamed—the first words he had said.

But I didn't ease up. Then I realized he had pulled a small sap from his pocket—one of those things you smack people with—and I gave another shove that pushed him up onto the balustrade.

As he tried to twist and get away from me, he lost his grip on the railing and fell over with a scream. The scream didn't end until I heard the sickening smash of his body against the floor of the chapel below.

He was spread-eagled on the floor, blood on his head, motionless. There was a spiral staircase in a corner of the gallery and I hurried down, two and three steps at a time.

No, I was thinking, *Don't! Please don't.* I couldn't even think the word; I meant, *Don't die.*

He was lying on his back, his eyes closed, but he was breathing—fast and shallow breaths. Blood was seeping from his ears, from the corners of his mouth, from a wound on the side of his head. As I leaned close, I saw him head-on for the first time.

"Pêpe!" I said. "I'll get help!"

He gurgled and whispered something. I dropped to the floor and listened. There was twisted, bloody grin on his face. His voice was hoarse.

"Too late," he whispered, and a word that sounded like "kitchen." Then he was silent.

I ran out of the chapel on the ground floor, yelling, "*Au secours!*—Help!" Again and again. Suddenly, from under the entry arcade, two policemen and a squad of soldiers came racing towards me.

"A man!" I yelled, "In the chapel—badly hurt—hardly breathing."

One of the policemen began to ask me questions.

"No time!" They all turned towards the chapel.

"Wait! Some of you come with me. There's a plot against the president—we must go to the kitchen at once!"

They stared at me, with my jacket and waistcoat gone, my tie untied, my hair a mess, and bare feet, but I wasn't going to wait for them to figure things out. I started running backwards, yelling, "My name is William Montreux. I'm the guest of both the American and French presidents. Colonel Victoire, the army and the Sûreté are searching the building for terrorists. Do you want to stare at my bare feet or save your president?!"

I guess I sounded convincing, because the sergeant yelled at his squad to follow me, and the two policemen ran to the chapel. That let me turn and run forwards.

"We're going to the gallery under the Hall of Mirrors," I yelled.

"We should evacuate the guests!" The sergeant cried.

"Find Colonel Victoire!" I said. "Ask him what to do."

The sergeant sent a soldier racing up the stairs.

We were beginning to run into serving people, soldiers and guards. They would have stopped me, except for the sergeant yelling at them to follow us.

"Who was the man in the chapel?" the sergeant asked, puffing along beside me.

"His name is Pêpe. He's supposed to be in jail for bombing the Crouching Dragon in Normandy," I said. "His hair is bleached and his nose is broken, but I finally recognized him."

The crowd of servers became even thicker as we approached the ground level gallery used as a kitchen. The smells of food were strong and the air was very warm.

"What will we find?" The sergeant asked.

"Not sure," I huffed. The memory that drove me was the time Mayor Bersault had sent Pêpe to set explosives in the wall of the Crouching Dragon. "Maybe a bomb," I said.

The sergeant yelled to soldiers in the corridor. "Bomb squad!"

Several raced off, the rest followed us.

We entered the gallery below the Hall of Mirrors. Despite the noise we made, chefs and serving people continued working. These were Frenchmen preparing food. What could be more important?

"Block off both ends of the room!" the sergeant ordered. "Don't let anybody in or out!"

The soldiers cordoned off the area. Waiters trying to get in or out were complaining. A few men in cooking clothing were trying leave through the exit at the far end of the room, but the soldiers stopped them. Other soldiers were spreading out through the gallery, searching—they didn't know for what.

I was walking barefoot through water standing on the floor, some of it quite hot, and involuntarily I danced a little, making a few serving people laugh.

"Silence!" the sergeant roared. Then to me, a fierce whisper, "Do you know what you're doing?"

Several men dressed in bright yellow jumpsuits and yellow hardhats entered the gallery from the far end: the bomb squad. The sergeant, responding to a signal from one of them, called out, "Everyone, out of this hall, quickly!"

Many began to protest. "We are cooking for the president," "Have you gone mad?" and the like. The soldiers were herding them towards the exits.

I was staring about, searching for a clue. There was a small, gray-haired man lurking near the exit. I grabbed him and pulled off his white chef's hat.

"Joseph!" I said. "What are you doing here?"

"Who is he?" the sergeant asked me.

Joseph looked very agitated, turning his back towards the gallery. "I don't know who you are," he muttered. "I'm feeling ill and I must get out of here, *now*!"

The leader of the bomb squad, a flinty-eyed man who was all jaw, suddenly stood beside us.

"You're not leaving," he said to Joseph. "You're going back in!" And he began dragging him towards the center of the room.

"No! No!" Joseph cried out as the squad leader shoved him along.

"There!" Joseph squealed, pointing to a haphazard pile of white boxes, marked with names like "flour" and "sugar." I estimated they were directly underneath the middle of the main table, where President and Madame de Gaulle and President and Madame Kennedy were sitting. Louise was probably somewhere near there, too. I wanted to go upstairs, but the sergeant wouldn't let me leave.

"Not yet," he said.

The bomb squad leader signaled to the soldiers at both ends of the hall, and they began herding everyone out of the kitchen area again—everyone except his squad and Joseph—Joseph Manet.

"Ten minutes," Joseph said, in a quavery voice. "Not more than ten minutes!" He was shivering as he spoke.

I checked my watch, but my heart was racing twice as fast. The soldiers were pushing me out of the room, along with the others. I had a glimpse of the bomb squad approaching the white boxes, but then we were in the next room and the next, and seconds later we were outside, in the vast gardens of the palace. They hurried us between fountains and basins, flower beds and hedges, onto the long mall known as the *Tapis Vert*, the green carpet.

A number of ornate lighting standards lined the walks, but the illumination was slight, except at the fountains and ponds, which were brightly spotlighted. Rows of fresh-smelling red, white and yellow flowers lined the walks. It was strange to observe this serene and peaceful scene—the sweet-smelling vegetation, timeless statuary, splashing water—knowing that an explosion might occur at any moment, destroying the great palace and killing hundreds of innocent people.

I stopped in my tracks. "Why aren't they evacuating the Hall of Mirrors?!" I asked.

There was no answer, so I turned and began to push through the crowd of people who had been evacuated from the gallery. I had only moved a few steps when one of the officers grabbed me.

"Where are you going?" he asked.

"I have to warn the people in the Hall of Mirrors."

"Nobody goes back into the building until the bomb squad is finished!" he said. His hand moved to the automatic at his waist.

"The presidents and their wives are in there!" I said. "Don't you care?"

"Calm down," the officer whispered.

I was furious, but I didn't dare challenge him.

We were more than one hundred meters away from the palace. Many spotlights washed the walls, which looked ageless and sturdy. Much of the palace had been built three hundred years earlier, and had survived wars and revolution. Would it suddenly explode into millions of fragments?

The officer with the gun tried to distract me. I vaguely heard his words.

"Look," he said. "The Apollo Fountain." He pointed to the large, almost quatrefoil-shaped basin where great bronze horses were rising through the water, pulling the chariot of Apollo in which rode the Sun God himself—the god to whom Louis XIV had been compared—*Le Roi de Soleil*—the Sun King. Other figures rose from the waters, including sea creatures and humans (or gods?) blowing horns.

Water rose into the air from dozens of jets in rhythm with music. An orchestra was playing in the garden, blending with the cascades and fountains.

"Why are they playing now?" I asked, "when there is so much danger?"

"It's better," the officer said, "if the musicians follow their pre-arranged program."

"Maybe," I said, "if they play loud enough, it will cover the sound of any explosion."

The officer seemed to shudder.

The fountain between us and the palace was suddenly flooded with light—a many-tiered invention, with gilt creatures gesturing toward a stone sculpture at the highest level.

"Latona," the officer said, "the mother of Apollo." He seemed pleased to share this information with me. I checked my watch, certain ten minutes had passed. I couldn't believe he was describing fountains while so many lives were at risk, and I was trying to come up with a way to escape.

"The Finale," he said, "is the display at the Dragon Fountain."

"There is a Dragon Fountain?!" I asked.

"Yes, in front of the Neptune Basin. All the other fountains must be turned off to serve it—the jets of the Dragon Fountain reach over forty meters into the air."

"Where?" I asked, and when he pointed to an area almost due east of the palace, I pulled away from him and began to run.

"Wait!" he called out. "The bomb squad!" He didn't shoot me.

I ran along narrow walks that pierced many arbors, crossing *allées*, following an angle where there were no workers or soldiers to intercept me. Everyone else was trying to stay away from the château, and I was running towards it, but the fact that there was a Dragon Fountain strengthened my resolve.

As I ran closer to the château, I saw two men dressed in bomb-squad-yellow running from an exit at ground level. If I judged right, they were headed towards the Dragon Fountain or the Neptune Basin to drown the explosives. If the bomb exploded before they reached the water, it might still do tremendous damage.

The spotlights flared on at the Dragon Fountain, highlighting the strange creatures that peopled its waters. Spouts of water rose high into the air, and the orchestra played loudly.

I dodged one soldier, then a couple of others. It seemed like I was playing a game, a kind of football, on a dangerous field. I hurdled low hedges, stumbling and regaining my balance as I closed with the bomb squad. They seemed completely unaware of me.

"The Neptune Basin," one of them called out. "It's deeper!"

I was now only a few steps away, but they still hadn't seen me, nor could they hear me with the music playing and their own feet rapidly striking the gravel path. They had begun to circle the round basin of the Dragon Fountain when one of them tripped. He lost his grip on the carton containing the bomb, which made the other man stagger and lose control of his end of the container, which began to fall to the pathway. I raced up, grabbed the end of the carton, and, with all my remaining strength, flung the whole thing into the Dragon Fountain. The carton splashed in the water as we threw ourselves down on the ground below the rim.

Spumes were still rising placidly into the sky, but the orchestra had stopped playing. There was silence, except for the pleasant sounds of splashing water.

I cringed as low as I could, wishing I could burrow into the ground.

Seconds passed. A minute. Still nothing. Another minute.

The bomb squad guys and I couldn't resist. We slowly raised our heads above the rim of the fountain. The carton holding the bomb had lodged itself in the jaws of one of the dragons, which seemed to be chewing on a corner, while the other end dipped into the water. As we watched, frozen, the carton slipped out of the dragon's teeth and slid into the water, sinking slowly to the bottom while bubbles rose from it.

After an eternity, the orchestra resumed playing.

26 IN CONCERT

Colonel Victoire, Louise and I, and the leader of the bomb squad stood together in the shadows behind one of the oval grilles that guarded the enclosed boxes at the highest level of the Royal Opera House. The audience section of the chamber was elliptical near the entrance, with four tiers of boxes. It was pinched a bit at the center, then flared slightly towards the grandly draped and curtained proscenium stage with its great gold shield and flaring rays of the Sun King above. Fluted Corinthian columns soared to a gilded cornice, and above it a series of oval-screened openings were inset in the next arching level. The screens allowed discreet viewing of the theatre (we were behind one), and then, above everything rose the elaborately-muraled ceiling. All of the construction was of wood, gilded, glazed, painted.

The presidents and their wives sat in the King's Box at the center of the main balcony, under a half-cupola ceiling. A private grille had once protected the King's party from prying eyes. In later, more democratic times, the grille had been removed and the box was open.

The entire interior of the opera house was a masterpiece of trompe l'oeil—a kind of visual deception where objects that are actually flat appear three-dimensional, and scenes seem to flow into the distance, but are actually painted on the walls. Even the marble panels and grilles were painted; you wanted to touch them to see if they were real.

The large stage was perhaps the best example of this art,

appearing to repeat the ellipse at the opposite end of the theatre, but the columns and arches were painted on the wall behind the proscenium. The major three-dimensional objects were the great royal arms centered above the stage and the ring of chandeliers and lumieres that lighted the theatre—most of it.

Some seven hundred people were in attendance. The music of Tchaikovsky's Black Swan duet filled the acoustically-perfect theatre, and the dancers on the stage moved in flawless harmony. At least that's what Louise told me later; I wasn't really watching the performance.

Colonel Victoire had already praised and thanked me, and Louise looked so proud of me that I almost blushed. The captain of the bomb squad, a tightly wound man who was all iron chin and cheekbones, congratulated me, too, but at the same time implied that it was my fault that a soldier—namely, him—had tripped and lost his grip on the bomb. The colonel gave him an incredulous look, mumbled something about ingratitude, and the captain quickly changed his tune.

"What happened to you?" I whispered to Louise.

"After I told Colonel Victoire where you were going," Louise said, "he spoke privately to the president, and they arranged to send the guests to the Opera House early and serve dessert there instead of in the Hall of Mirrors."

"You mean when we were disarming the bomb, everybody was already out of the building?" I asked.

"Willi," Louise said, "the château wasn't empty and nobody knew when a bomb might explode, if there was one. Except for you, everyone would still have been sitting in the Hall of Mirrors when the bomb exploded. You prevented a terrible tragedy. "

The presidents had been informed of everything and the vigilance of the guards had been redoubled. To deflect a potential international crisis, the kitchen and serving people were told that the bomb threat was a hoax, and the box we had drowned actually contained spices.

"What about Tony Bersault?" I asked Colonel Victoire.

"If he was here," the colonel said, "we haven't found him."

"He was here," I said firmly. "His hair was clipped short and dyed blonde and he had a new mustache, but it was him."

"The grounds here are vast, and it would have been relatively easy for him to escape."

"What about Pêpe?"

"Pêpe?" the colonel asked.

"The man I fought with in the Royal Chapel. The Sûreté arrested him at the Crouching Dragon, after he placed a bomb in the wall."

"When the police entered the chapel, there was no one there. They found traces of blood, but no body."

"I tell you, he was almost dead. He uttered a word that sounded like 'kitchen.' Otherwise, I wouldn't have known where to go. I thought it was like the confession of a dying man, and I believed him."

The colonel shrugged his shoulders. "Either he was in better condition than you thought, or someone helped him—or perhaps carried his body away."

"In the first place," I said, "he's supposed to be in prison, but instead he was here. Larron was supposed to be in prison, but some judge let him out on bail. We caught him again, but who's to say he won't be freed again? If you're connected with the Bersaults, the laws don't seem to mean much."

The colonel was silent.

"This is all so confusing," I said. "Joseph Manet also surprised me. When Louise and I secretly overheard him talking to Pêpe and Mayor Bersault at Bersault's estate in Normandy, Manet walked away in anger, saying that Bersault was so dishonest he could no longer work for him."

"Manet told the Sûreté," the colonel said, "that his children live in Algeria, and Bersault's people threatened their lives if he didn't help them. Manet also implicated one of the chefs working tonight—a former military cook who is a supporter of the Algerian Secret Army, the OAS. This man was able to get Manet a job in the kitchen."

"Manet was a horse trainer!" I said.

"There was one other thing," the colonel said. "Police found this lying on the floor of the chapel."

He handed me a black and white shield: the mark of the DragonSlayers.

I almost put my fist through the gilt screen in front of me.

Colonel Victoire seemed abashed. "We will have to do a better job investigating all personnel who have access to the president.

"A chef!" he said, as if, for a Frenchman, it was inconceivable that a chef would plot against his own country.

"We couldn't connect Bersault to the thieves who damaged the castle," I said, "We didn't catch him when the DragonSlayers attempted a coup against President De Gaulle. Now, he came within a few minutes of blowing up the presidents of France and the United States. I won't feel good until we put that man away for good—one way or another!"

◆　　◆　　◆

I smoldered during the rest of the performance. Louise placed a calming hand on mine, and I tried to smile, but I couldn't quite do it. I'm sure the music was wonderful—the audience cheered and there were several curtain calls.

After the ballet, the guests were escorted outside to see a repeat of the Water Spectacle we had watched during our "adventure."

The presidents, their wives, and their closest aides, waited in their box. Colonel Victoire led Louise and me and the bomb squad leader to them.

President de Gaulle gripped my hand in both of his. "I told the president and Madame Kennedy that you were very brave young people. You have proved that I was understating your courage. On behalf of France, we thank you." He released my hand, kissed Louise's hand and shook the hand of the leader of the bomb squad.

Madame de Gaulle embraced Louise and me and whispered her thanks.

President Kennedy said, "You are indeed remarkable young people. We, too, are astounded by your courage and extend our gratitude to you. Perhaps, young man, we should appoint you head of our Central Intelligence Agency."

Everyone laughed, and Madame Kennedy embraced both of us. "The CIA can't have you," she said. "I need you, myself. Will you please come to the American embassy tomorrow morning?"

Pleased, if perplexed, we looked to the President of France.

"Prior to World War II," de Gaulle said, "the United States helped sustain England and, eventually, all of free Europe against the Nazis, by a program called 'Lend-Lease.' We will lend you these young people—briefly—but we won't lease them."

27 AMBASSADORS

We spent the night at Élysée Palace at the insistence of the president and Madame de Gaulle.

"For the time being, I would prefer that you remain at the palace," the president said. "With the help of the estimable Colonel Victoire, we can keep a closer eye on you. I am hopeful that in time, the great split in the French people will be healed and virtually all will accept the independence of Algeria with equanimity."

"For how long will we remain here, *Monsieur le Président*?" I asked.

"I prefer not to make long term plans. We'll review the situation every few days."

"I'm sorry to bring up a small problem," Louise said. "We have only the clothes on our backs—and mine belong to Madame Kennedy."

"I'm certain," the president said, "that we can help you solve that problem."

"Do you know, *Monsieur le Président*," I asked, "what the purpose is of our visit to the embassy tomorrow?"

"I think it would be best," he answered, "if Madame Kennedy told you, herself."

◆　◆　◆

My room in the palace was so elegant that I was afraid to touch anything. Someone had turned down the bed, revealing sheets, pillows and a coverlet that seemed too valuable to use for sleeping. I wondered if I should sleep on the rug to avoid damaging anything.

A valet soon arrived with some of my own clothing—including my best blue suit—from Roger's apartment. The valet, who smiled but said almost nothing, also provided me with light-blue, silk pajamas with the French *fleur-de-lis* embroidered in white on the pocket, a velvet robe of dark-blue, corded in the lighter blue of the pajamas, and dark-blue leather slippers.

I thought of sleeping naked to avoid wrinkling the clothing, but finally couldn't resist trying everything on. It was wonderful to feel such richness against my skin, and slipping in between the luxurious sheets was another unexpected pleasure. *Maybe,* I thought, *it wasn't such a bad deal to be the President of France.* Then I remembered the dozens of attempts that had been made on de Gaulle's life, and I decided that being a good aeronautical engineer—even flying new and untested aircraft—might be a much safer profession.

◆　　◆　　◆

The Americans provided a black Cadillac limousine to deliver us to their embassy. It was almost identical to the Cadillac that had coughed to a stop in the town of Luc on the Normandy coast on the 6th of June, 1959, which my stepfather, Paul, had repaired in less than a minute—after I had "rescued" him from a bistro. We were driven in this elegant machine a few hundred meters to the American embassy (*L'Ambassade de l'États Unis de Amérique*), a dignified building with an entrance on the Rue Gabriel, just a few steps away from the Place de La Concorde. A crisp American flag mounted on a flag pole snapped in the breeze on a clear, sunlit second day of June, 1961, a smiling day that gave no hint of the previous night's dangers.

The building was well, but discreetly, guarded by Americans within, and French police and soldiers outside—surely the foiled bomb attempt had caused increased security arrangements. Nevertheless, the American officials greeted us warmly.

Louise wore a simple, dark brown dress with a high neck supplied by a member of the Élysée staff. Of course she looked sensational. Louise had brought with her the gown and accessories Madame Kennedy had provided for the great evening; when she handed everything over to a smiling young woman as we entered the embassy, I thought I saw a wistful smile on her face.

As we waited, I noticed a pile of cartons, piled neatly against a wall. They were all banded in a white tape which bore a continuous series of circles with symbols inside them. When I cocked my head to the side, I realized that the markings were in the form of a winged dragon sitting on a globe that seemed to represent the world. There was text inside, and by squinting I read the words, "Flying Dragons."

Of course, that reminded me of my cap, and the airplane I had seen landing at Le Bourget, which had borne the same symbol I now saw on the tape.

I was curious, so I asked the pretty young receptionist, "Can you please tell me what the symbols on the tape mean?"

She smiled and said, "The contents are personal, but I don't mind telling you that they belong to Mrs. Kennedy, and they were shipped to Paris on an American freight carrier named 'Flying Dragons Airlines.'"

"Thank you," I said, happy to have another clue.

In a few minutes we were led to a large sitting room. Along the way we learned that the embassy furniture was French and tasteful, and that virtually all of the paintings portrayed famous Americans, including George Washington, Abraham Lincoln, Franklin Roosevelt, Dwight Eisenhower and President Kennedy, whose youthfulness continued to astonish us.

In the sitting room was a painting of such mysterious

abstraction that I couldn't decipher it—I couldn't even read the name signed in the corner. There was obviously a lot I didn't know about American culture—or French culture for that matter.

Coffee arrived almost immediately, together with plates of rolls and little cakes that smelled so good I was certain they had been baked that morning. I didn't dare use cream or sugar in my coffee—I was afraid I would spill something.

In a minute or two, the door opened, and a smiling Jacqueline Kennedy walked in. We rose and exchanged greetings. As I said before, she was the most beautiful human being I had ever seen. The suit she wore (putty-gray, according to Louise), fit her just so, and it was simple enough that even I could appreciate it. It's amazing how elegant something simple can be, when many people seem to think you need curlicues and furbelows and all kinds of complicated stuff to look classy.

Her chestnut hair was lustrous and framed her face. Although her chin was pert and the line of her throat classic, her face was more broad than heart-shaped. Her cheeks were round, but not especially prominent, and her nose was neat and straight, a little broad at the nostrils, but that suited the rest of her face. Her skin was flawless, delicately peach in tone.

Madame Kennedy's eyes captured me again—deep brown, wide-set and flashing with radiance and charm. She focused those eyes on you when she spoke—or when you spoke to her—and then there was nobody else in the world. Her voice, as I had noticed the previous evening, was smaller than I expected, but her eyes were so compelling and her smile so dazzling, every word seemed musical.

"Good morning," she said in French. "I hope you had a pleasant night, despite the events of yesterday."

"Yes," Louise said, smiling her own glorious smile. "The accomodations at the Élysée Palace are quite acceptable."

Madame Kennedy laughed, a tinkling laugh that set those wonderful eyes sparkling again.

"We have been staying in a lovely apartment at Quai D'Orsay," she said, "which has been furnished in a style only the French can achieve."

Mrs. Kennedy's French was very good. She enunciated carefully and could express herself easily and accurately. Her accent wasn't bad either. Perhaps a little flat—American sounding—but we had no difficulty understanding her.

"I must state again our gratitude—the heartfelt appreciation of the president and myself and all of our staff—for your noble efforts."

"It was our privilege to be of service," I said, thinking that was a little stiff and might have sounded arrogant, but Madame Kennedy smiled again.

"President de Gaulle and Madame de Gaulle had told us of their high regard for you, even before your latest, remarkable exploits. I had suggested that we might invite you to be our guests in the United States for two weeks, to meet some fine young Americans, and visit the wonderful sights of Washington, D.C. and surrounding areas."

(My heart was racing. Would two weeks be long enough for me to find my real father—Alan Stevens?)

"However," Madame Kennedy continued, "after last night, Jack and I" (only Americans would use such casual phrasing), "had another idea. I have spoken to President and Madame de Gaulle about our intention to begin extensive restoration of our own presidential residence. We're planning to use a famous and highly respected French designer, Stephane Boudin, to assist in this work. As you know, the District of Columbia owes its overall design to a Frenchman, Pierre L'Enfant, who worked with President George Washington to lay out our capital city, a plan based on Versailles."

"In fact," Louise said, speaking for the first time, "I don't believe either of us knew that."

I nodded in agreement.

Madame Kennedy smiled. "I'm pleased you don't pretend to have knowledge you do not possess. That will help save us from making foolish, egotistical errors."

We both noticed the "us."

"Jack and I have been thinking of inviting young people from other countries to spend a year as aides in the White House, sending our own young people to such countries as a form of cultural exchange. The idea is to give all participants knowledge of another country and its political system and, ideally, to help the cause of peace and international understanding. Last night, I suggested to Madame de Gaulle that the two of you would be absolutely perfect for this program."

She waited for a moment, perhaps aware that we had stopped breathing.

"Are you interested in participating?" she asked.

"We would be thrilled," Louise said, promptly and strongly, speaking for both of us.

I nodded several times. A year in the United States—how many times had I dreamed of searching the country for my father?

"Very good," Madame Kennedy said. "Are you certain this will be acceptable to your families? We will, of course, pay all travel and living expenses, including school tuition, and a small stipend for other expenses."

"That's wonderful," I blurted out. 'I know my parents will agree."

"Mine, too," Louise said. "They'll be thrilled."

"Good," Madame Kennedy said. "We would like you to begin this fall when the school year begins, if that is satisfactory."

We both nodded. I wanted to jump in the air and cheer and hug Louise, but of course that wouldn't have been appropriate.

"I understand you both speak English," Madame Kennedy said in English.

"We can read pretty well," I answered in English, "and understand what is said, unless it is too complicated. As for our speech, you now have a sample."

This wonderful lady smiled again. "You will be fine— Americans love to hear their language spoken with a French accent."

"Is that true for young women, too?" Louise asked.

"*Absolument!*" Madame Kennedy responded. "However, I would like to make a suggestion. We sponsor in Paris a so-called immersion program, used for diplomats and others who must learn a new language very quickly. I think this program will be helpful for both of you."

"That sounds very good," Louise said.

"Even though we'll be working at the White House, you expect us to go to school?" I asked.

Madame Kennedy looked at me with unblinking eyes.

"Of course, we want to attend school in America," I added hurriedly.

She laughed gently. "There are many fine college preparatory schools in Washington, and if your studies have already prepared you for college, we can arrange entrance on a student exchange program for you to attend either George Washington or Georgetown University."

Louise was delighted. "I've heard of them. Both universities have fine reputation. I'd be honored to attend either one."

"I'd prefer George Washington University," I said, "because it has a school of engineering, which is my chosen career, and Georgetown doesn't."

Both ladies seemed surprised.

"I've always hoped to go to America," I said, "and I looked up engineering schools in the library at the Sorbonne."

Louise said, "I spoke to our friend, Mohammed Almedienne. His father, who is highly placed in the French Foreign Ministry, is being re-assigned to the United States. Mohammed is planning to attend the Georgetown School of Foreign Service. I believe I may choose a diplomatic career, so Georgetown would be perfect for me."

"It would be best," said Mrs. Kennedy, "if you both attended the same college. That would make it easier . . . for all of us. Please discuss this together and advise us of your decision."

"Of course, Madame Kennedy," Louise said. "But I must ask you a question: "How can we help in refurnishing your presidential residence? We know nothing of design."

"You're French," Madame Kennedy said. "The French have an innate sense of design and fashion."

Her smile was whimsical, but I wasn't buying it. Still, I didn't know how to say anything without being rude.

"We thank you for your confidence," I said. "May I make one suggestion, please?"

She smiled.

"Our mentor is a fine scholar named Roger Guiscard, who presently teaches Archeology and Ancient History at the Sorbonne. He was a brave member of the Resistance and he made a gift to France of the castle known as the Crouching Dragon. President de Gaulle may have told you about it. Doctor Guiscard also helped us intercept the people who were attempting a coup against the government in April. Perhaps you could arrange an appointment for him at an American university. He would be a credit to any faculty."

"We don't have any control over our universities, which are completely independent of the government, "Madame Kennedy said.

"That's what President de Gaulle told me about Professor Guiscard two years ago, but, with the president's encouragement, the Sorbonne managed to find a place for him."

Madame Kennedy smiled again. "We'll see what we can do."

"We understand you're leaving on an important trip to Vienna," Louise said, "to meet the leader of the Soviet Union. For the sake of all of us, we wish you good fortune."

"Thank you—I'll tell Jack what you said. I'm looking forward to seeing you again when you reach America in the fall. We'll be in touch about all the necessary arrangements."

With that she rose, and we stood up, too, and shook hands—except that on impulse, I bowed over her hand and kissed it.

Madame Kennedy smiled. "That will go a long way in America," she said. "Oh, and by the way, Louise, I'd like to make you a gift of the clothing you wore at the State Dinner. Will you accept it?"

"Do women kiss other women's hands?" Louise asked, absolutely glowing.

◆　◆　◆

We hardly spoke until we had been transported back to the Élysée Palace in the American limousine. Once we were inside the grand vestibule, and despite the presence of the guards, we grabbed each other and hugged and hugged and hugged and hugged.

"Ahem," said Colonel Victoire, who had come into the hall unnoticed as we were embracing.

We sprang apart.

"We're going to America!" Louise cried out.

"Yes," I said. "We're going to America, and I'm finally going to find my father!"

Historical Timeline

HISTORICAL TIMELINE—
ACTUAL EVENTS IN *THE RAGING DRAGON* 1944-1961

1944–PRESENT	Over 120 former colonies (primarily in Africa and Asia) become independent nations
1954-62	Guerrilla, then civil war in Algeria; eventual independence; 500,000 French troops in Algeria
1954	France defeated in Indo-China; country split into North and South Viet Nam
10/54	Algerian Nationalists Announce Rebellion
05/58	France close to civil war; army plans operation "resurrection"—Paratroopers to surround Paris and place Charles de Gaulle in power
06/01/58	National Assembly votes de Gaulle into power
06/04/58	De Gaulle speaks to huge crowd of settlers in Algiers: "I have understood you"
09/28/58	People approve new constitution; de Gaulle given vast powers
10/58	FLN – National Liberation Front refuses de Gaulle peace offers
11/58	First Berlin crisis; Soviet Chairman Khruschev threatens strong action if USSR doesn't get its way; U.S., France, Britain stand firm
12/21/58	De Gaulle elected first president of Fifth Republic by huge majority
1/08/59	De Gaulle inaugurated as president of France
1/59	Fidel Castro becomes leader of Cuba
Spring-Summer 1959	General Challe unleashes brutal war in Algeria; 1,000,000 Algerians in camps; war is military success, political failure
9/16/59	De Gaulle announces "self-determination" for Algeria
9/59	Extremist White settlers form FNF—Front National Français; violence accelerates
1/18/60	Gen. Massu, leader of French Army in Algeria, states they will not obey de Gaulle's orders
1/60	De Gaulle fires Massu and other officers; "Barricades week"— battle between FNF and students versus gendarmes

01/29/60	De Gaulle on TV: "Algerians shall have their own destiny—no concessions to would-be usurpers (FNF)" Ordinary soldiers declare their loyalty over heads of their officers
5/60	US surveillance plane U-2 crashes in Russia; Khruschev walks out on summit meeting—world fears nuclear crisis
9/60	Talks with FLN fail; Anti-war manifesto by French intellectuals; street demonstrations including unions and students
	Khruschev pounds shoe on desk at UN
11/4/60	De Gaulle announces an "Algerian Algeria."
11/09/60	John F. Kennedy elected president of US
12/09/60	De Gaulle in Algiers to speak for independence— 4 attempts on his life

1/08/01	Decisive vote for de Gaulle and independence for Algeria
1/61	Disaffected white settlers form OAS – Algerian Secret Army
4/14/61	Russian Yuri Gagarin is first human being in space
4/17/61	"Bay of Pigs" failed invasion of Cuba by anti-Castro Cubans supported by US
4/22/61	Army announces it is in control of Algeria—mainland invasion by paratroopers expected; de Gaulle declares emergency
4/23/61	De Gaulle in uniform addresses nation on TV: "Frenchwomen, Frenchmen, help me!" Immediate support of people and troops
4/27/61	Coup leaders surrender
5/05/61	Alan Shepard is first American in space
5/31/61	President and Mrs. Kennedy arrive in Paris— streets lined with admirers
06/01/61	State Dinner for Kennedys in Hall of Mirrors at Versailles Château

LEN LAMENSDORF

A multi-published author with several novels, a feature film and full length plays to his credit, Len Lamensdorf draws on his extensive travel experience to create realistic settings for his works. His recent novel, *Gino, the Countess & Chagall,* won 3 national awards, and was called by reviewers, "A gorgeous travelogue and art history saga," and "A great traveling companion."

In Book 1, *The Crouching Dragon,* winner of the prestigious Benjamin Franklin Fiction Award, Lamensdorf transported his readers to post World War II French Normandy, and in Book 2, *The Raging Dragon,* he provides a virtual guidebook to Paris, including maps of the city, the Château of Versailles and the underground *Metro*—plus drawings and diagrams of aircraft.

Book 3, *The Flying Dragon,* with its wonderful tours and maps of Washington, D.C., and drawings of aircraft in the exhibits of the National Air & Space Museum, will soon follow.

METRO MAP OF PARIS

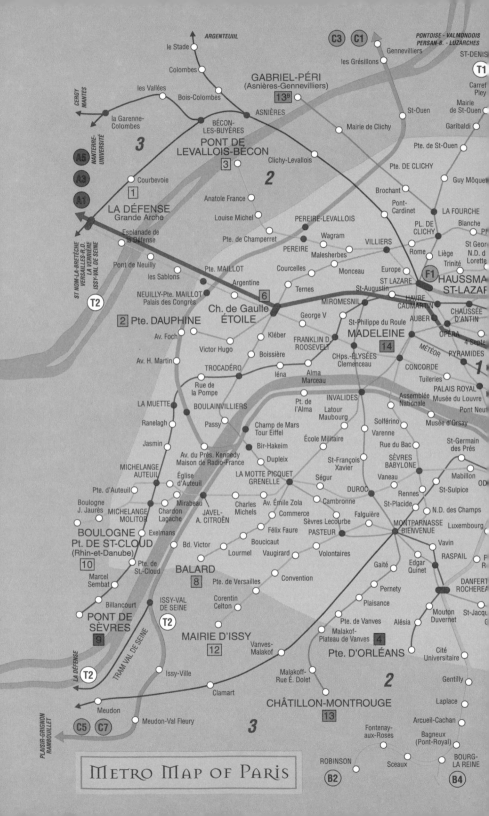

METRO MAP OF PARIS